THE ARSENAL OF DECEIT

THE
ARSENAL
OF DECEIT

A NOVEL

DONALD LEVIN

Poison Toe Press

For Lonnie,
with appreciation,
Donald Levin
11/19/23

This is a work of fiction. All of the characters, establishments, events, locales, groups, dialogs, and organizations portrayed in this novel are either products of the author's imagination or are used fictitiously and are not construed as real. Any similarity to real persons, living or dead, is coincidental and not intended by the author.

ISBN: 978-0-9972941-9-4

Cover design: Joe Montgomery

Author photo: Bruce Harkness

First edition published 2023

Printed in the United States of America

For Sue

"We must be the great arsenal of democracy."
—Franklin D. Roosevelt, December 29, 1940

"Sometimes the things we think are lost are only hidden, waiting to be rediscovered."
—Anthony Doerr

"We burn this city every day."
–Philip Levine

THE ARSENAL OF DECEIT

1

EVA SZABÓ

[Monday, March 31, 1941]

One after another they come, limping in or carried, as regular as the cars turned out by the great American industrial giant. Eva Szabó registers them in the order they arrive:

The operator who smashed his hand in the Foundry Machine Shop.

The electrician from the Motor Building who collapsed after a twelve-hour shift.

Two men who were hit by debris from an explosion in Blast Furnace C. Several others with burns from the blast.

The carpenter who fell off a scaffold in the Administration Building.

The man brought in when a swinging crane caught him in the back near the Sand Storage area.

And now, the latest case, the man who hops in, his right foot wrapped in a bloody apron. Another man props him up.

"What happened?" Eva asks him.

The guy with the bad foot can't speak; he's dazed, like he's in shock.

The other guy says, "A sheet of glass fell on his foot."

Nadine Denton pushes a wheelchair behind the injured man. "You," she says, tapping his shoulder, "sit."

He falls into the chair.

Nadine says, "See this young lady?" She points at Eva. "She'll check you in. Then we'll see what's what."

Eva records the date (March 31, 1941), the worker's name (Chester Kowalski), his department (Glass Plant), badge number, description of the injury, and how it happened.

Nadine wheels him back to an examination room. "You can get back to work," she lobs over her shoulder at the injured man's helper.

Who tosses a wink at Eva and leaves.

Before the next injured worker comes in, the phone rings.

"After you get that," Nadine calls, "find one of the Marys to give me a hand."

"Will do."

Nadine Denton, the head nurse. Two other nurses are both named Mary. Nadine calls them One and Two. Nadine's not the most pleasant cupcake, but she's tough and she knows what she's doing.

Eva is the receptionist of the Ford Rouge Assembly plant hospital's First Aide Clinic. She's new, barely three weeks in. The plant has its own on-site hospital to care for the injuries plant workers sustain. It's convenient for non-severe injuries so a worker can return to the job and complete the shift.

On the phone is a secretary from the Administration Building. One of the other secretaries fainted. They want a nurse to come over and check her out.

Eva looks for the Marys but they're both tied up with patients.

She goes to tell Nadine about the phone call. Nadine and a doctor are working on the man from the glass plant. Nadine has cut his boot and sock off. The foot's a bloody mess.

"We can't spare nobody," she says.

"I can do it," Eva says.

Nadine looks at Eva like, *You?!*

"You have your hands full here," Eva says. "The desk is quiet. I'll run over, see how she's doing. If it looks serious, I'll come back and get you."

Nadine mulls it over.

"Suppose it's not a good idea to keep the bosses waiting," she decides.

"I think so, too."

"Fine. But make it snappy. She's probably pregnant and missed her breakfast. Just needs to lie down for a while."

"Got it."

"Before you go, call a meat wagon for this guy. We can't do nothing for him here. Foot's like ground chuck. He needs to go downtown."

Whoever needs more medical attention than the plant hospital can provide goes to Sidney Sunby Memorial Hospital in River Rouge, or, if they are really bad, like this guy, downtown to Henry Ford Hospital or Receiving Hospital.

The Administration Building occupies the periphery of the sprawling plant, off Schaefer Road in Dearborn. Eva sets off across the site.

She buttons her winter coat against the slight drizzle even though it's a balmy day.

A balmy day in hell, that is.

She loves to be out of the hospital, but all around her is unbearable noise: machines throbbing, presses pounding, whistles screeching, men shouting to be heard over the din. The ground itself shakes.

Worse is the smell. The air reeks of sulphurous smoke, burning rubber, scorched metal, gasoline fumes. The foul taste on Eva's tongue is as awful as the racket inside her head.

How do they stand it, the men who work here?

How will *she* stand it while she's here?

She goes inside the broad, four-story Administration Building. It houses purchasing, sales, advertising, and accounting, as well as the office suites for Henry Ford, Harry Bennett, and other executives. A guard directs Eva to the Service Department in the basement, where the woman fainted.

Nadine was right. The young woman is pregnant. She upchucked her breakfast this morning and hasn't eaten anything since. She fainted from hunger.

Eva wets a towel and dabs it on the woman's cheeks and forehead, and sits with her in the Ladies' lounge while another secretary brings her a blueberry muffin.

"Thank you," the woman says.

"Sure. What's your name?"

"Gloria."

"I'm Eva."

"Pleased to meet you."

Eva sits with her for a while longer, then, when Gloria says she feels better, Eva walks her back to her desk.

She looks around for Harry Bennett, the head of the Service Department. Despite its name, the Service Department is Henry Ford's security force—his goon squad manned by thugs and ex-cons. They're the ones responsible for the anti-union violence in Ford's plants around the country. Eva's seen pictures of Bennett in the papers, a cocky little rooster with a bowtie. People say he's the one who runs the place, not Ford.

She'd like to see him in the flesh.

Unfortunately, he's nowhere around.

On the way back to the hospital, Eva sees a knot of men outside the Fabricating Shop. She lingers to listen to what they are saying. Loitering anywhere is prohibited on the grounds of the plant— Henry Ford and Harry Bennett don't want any union talk—so small groups, like these guys, form conspiratorially and disperse quickly in out-of-the-way places, around the corners of buildings.

They talk in low voices about the dozen work stoppages over the past month. About the possibility of a strike.

About the violence Harry Bennett's thugs continue to rain on the workforce when they talk about the union, the United Auto Workers-Congress of Industrial Organizations, the UAW-CIO.

One of the men turns, sees Eva.

She hurries away before he can say anything.

The men scatter.

In the hospital on the second floor inside B Building, the emergency clinic is backed up. A line of workers stands on the steps leading to the second floor.

Nadine will not be happy.

Inside she runs back and forth between the examining rooms and the desk.

As Eva knew she would, Nadine blasts her—"What the hell took you so long?"—and doesn't wait for a reply before she orders Eva back to the reception desk.

To anyone else, especially a new hire, Nadine's tone might be upsetting. But her irritation rolls off Eva's back.

In truth, Eva is not here just to work at the medical facility.

She's here for a different reason.

Which she's keeping to herself.

She settles back behind the desk. The next patient stumbles forward and Eva starts his intake. He has burns on his arms from an explosion in the Auto Frame Painting and Drying Oven.

2

CLARENCE BROWN

[Monday, March 31, 1941]

He hears the man's cries for mercy all the way outside.

"Oh, Jesus! Oh, Jesus!"

Parkside Hospital, formerly Dunbar Memorial Hospital, established when Negro doctors and nurses were barred from the white hospitals in town. A nurse points him toward a room at the end of the narrow hall.

Clarence Brown doesn't need directions; he could just follow the voice of the man calling for Jesus.

Two doctors and a nurse are working on him. Clarence recognizes the physicians. Dr. John Jemison and Dr. W. Harold Johnson. Jemison works at Parkside; he's been treating Clarence's wife Bessie. Johnson founded another colored hospital in Detroit, Trinity Hospital. Jemison must have called him in to help.

Because the man on the table surely needs it. He is squirming in agony. Both doctors are trying to keep him from thrashing around. The nurse has cut his workman's clothes off him. He looks like his right side has been dipped in acid. From his face down to his waist, his skin seems raw, puckered and red. A caustic odor rises from his burned flesh.

"Help me, Jesus!" he cries.

The doctors are trying to bathe the man's tortured skin in what smells like vinegar. He's not making it easy for them. As soon as a cloth touches his skin, he howls.

Clarence feels a hand on his arm.

The head nurse, a stout Negro woman in white with a nurse's cap like wings sprouting from the back of her head.

She beckons him away.

He follows her back to the nurse's station, in a room near the front of the building.

Clarence says, "Are you the one called the police?"

"I am," the nurse says.

"Detective Clarence Brown." He shows his Detroit Police Department badge. "What happened?"

"Poor man got a pan of boiling lye thrown in his face."

"Did he say who did it?"

"You're not going to believe this."

Clarence says, "Oh, I've seen so much on this job, there isn't a lot I wouldn't believe."

Black Bottom. His patch.

One of the few areas in the city of Detroit where Negroes are allowed to live.

Also one of the poorest and most run-down.

He searches for Ida James. She lives in a rooming house on Beaubien near Gratiot, the northern boundary of Black Bottom. Top floor. According to the nurse, Ida is the common-law wife of Bobby Henderson, the man writhing in pain back at Parkside Hospital.

Clarence calls in to request a patrol officer meet him at the house.

He waits a few minutes; when nobody shows, he decides to go up.

The building's front door hangs open. Clarence trudges up the stairs through the perfume of old wood.

Near the upper landing he sees dark stains on the wooden stairs. Smells the acrid stench of lye.

Clarence bangs on Ida James's door. No answer. He turns the doorknob and the door opens. He draws one of the two pearl-handled .45s he wears in holsters on his gun belt and steps inside.

It's one large room, a kitchen-dining room with a table, two chairs, and a flat-top stove. No other furniture. Peeling paint on the walls. 1941 calendar from The Detroit Bank showing the head of an

Indian brave, nailed above the table. An artificial rose in a vase under it, maybe Ida's sad attempt to make the place brighter.

"Hello?" he calls. "Miss James?"

No response.

"Anybody home?"

He approaches a door to the rear of the apartment.

He goes to turn the handle when the door flies open and a woman bursts out screaming. "Get out my house! Get out my house!"

Before he can sidestep her, she pummels his chest with her fists.

The metal plates he wears as home-made armor hurt her more than she hurts him.

She rears back to strike him again but the big man grabs her arm. Twists it to turn her around.

Clarence holsters his weapon.

"You get out my house!"

"Calm down, Miss James," he says. He holds her until she stops struggling. "Look here. Did you throw a pot of lye at your husband?"

"I did. And I'd do it again."

"Why would you do that?"

"He smack me in the face. You see these?" She turns her cheek toward Clarence. Bruises swell the side of her face. "I'm sick of him smacking me around. He won't do that again, believe you me."

No, Clarence thinks, I don't expect he will.

"I'm going to have to arrest you for doing that," he says.

"You do what you have to. You just make sure you arrest him, too."

She lets him cuff her hands behind her back.

He walks her out of the apartment and helps her down the stairs.

Before he gets out to the front porch, a man inside the house stops Clarence. Says, "Mr. Clarence?"

Clarence nods. The man is light skinned and bald.

"There's something down the basement you need to see."

"What?"

"Come with me," the man says, "I'll show you. Around the back and down the steps."

The harness bull has arrived. Clarence hands Ida over to him, says, "Put her in your squad car. Stay with her for a minute."

Clarence follows the man through to the back of the house. A stairway leads down to the basement.

No light. Dark, dank, cold. Clarence feels his way down. At the bottom of the landing, the man stops. Points to a small bundle wrapped in a blanket. Tiny.

A dog or a cat, maybe?

Clarence says, "What's this?"

"Look for yourself."

In faint light from a dirty basement window, the only other things Clarence sees are outlines of the usual basement junk: broken furniture, suitcases, bicycle frames, all hazy with dust and cobwebs.

Clarence picks up the small bundle and carries it up the stairs. It's light, maybe five pounds.

The man follows him.

Clarence lays the bundle down gently on the floor in the back landing where the light is better. The blanket is woolen, soiled from the basement but thick with a smart satin edge.

He unwraps it.

Inside is an infant.

A tiny boy, no bigger than a minute. Newborn, even.

Dead.

But there's another problem:

This child left in a tenement in Black Bottom is white.

Clarence says, "How long has this child been here?"

"One of my kids found him this morning."

"And you're just now telling somebody about it?"

The man bristles. "Didn't know who else to tell. You the only police anybody trusts around here."

Clarence sighs. That's hard to argue with.

He backs off, says, "Appreciate you telling me. I'll take it from here."

He calls it in to Lieutenant John Hays, the supervisor of the segregated squad of Negro detectives formed to work on Negro cases. Clarence works this detail.

Hays isn't available. Instead, he gets through to Lieutenant William Wilson, Hays's second-in-command, like Hays a Negro a few years older than Clarence.

Wilson says, "Stay with the body. I'll send a wagon for the

remains. Who else knows?"

"Just a guy who lives in the building. He showed me the baby. I got a uniform here with me, but I haven't said anything to him."

"Don't tell him nothing. In fact, get rid of him. You stay there and wait for the wagon."

Clarence says, "You're not going to send a forensics team?"

"Don't worry about what I'm going to do," Wilson snaps. "Just do what I tell you. Watch for the wagon."

Wilson disconnects.

Clarence stands at the callbox. He doesn't like how this is starting. Why isn't Wilson sending a forensic team to start finding out what happened?

He walks back to the patrolman. Tells him to take Ida James back to the station house for booking.

"What did you find down there?" the bluesuit asks him.

"Wasn't good. We'll talk later."

Clarence expects a coroner's van. In twenty minutes, an unmarked car shows up. Clarence knows the driver: a white detective named Roger Clendening.

Clarence waves him over.

Clendening parks, walks over to the porch. Looks at the little bundle on the floor. "That it?"

It.

Clarence says, "What are you going to do with him?"

"Nothing you need to worry about."

Clarence swallows his annoyance.

It's what you do. Clarence has been on the force since 1927. He's still expected to know his place. It's a game you play, with rules. You know the rules, you get along. Or you don't.

Clendening scoops up the baby in the blanket. He covers the bundle with his big overcoat and hustles to his unit.

The man from the house who showed him the baby comes out onto the porch.

Clarence says, "What's your name?"

"Sonny McGhee."

"Sonny, any idea who the child belongs to?"

"Nobody living here, that's for sure," Sonny says. "I know

everybody in the building. That baby ain't nobody's. White baby don't live here for sure. What y'all going to do about it?"

Clarence shakes his head.

He means, *I don't know what this world is coming to.* But Sonny takes it another way.

"Just what I thought," he spits. "Nothing. You might be colored like us, but inside you just another white man trying to keep us down."

"Hey now," Clarence says, "you know you don't believe that."

"Don't be telling me what I believe." Sonny starts back into the house.

He stops and turns toward Clarence. "Tell you something else for free. White man keeping us in this shithole place—that seem right to you?" He kicks the doorframe. It rattles. "Wouldn't nobody live here, he had a choice. But poor colored people can't live nowhere else."

Like it's Clarence's fault.

Before Clarence can reply, Sonny says, "You come back and let me know when the colored man got a decent place to live in this town."

He goes inside the house.

Clarence knows he's right.

Right is right.

It's 1941, and they still keep us penned here. There are only three other neighborhoods around Detroit where Negroes are allowed to live. People with means can live in the middle-class neighborhoods of Conant Gardens, at Eight Mile and Wyoming in northwest Detroit, and at Grand River and Tireman on the west side. But restrictive covenants in neighborhoods across the city limit where else Negroes can live.

Clarence watches Clendening rolling away down the street. He turns off Beaubien onto Gratiot.

Clarence keeps his eye on the car until it disappears.

He has a bad feeling this might be the last time anybody sees that child's body.

3

DENNY RANKIN

[Monday, March 31, 1941]

"Rankin—my office."

Sitting at his desk, Denny Rankin doesn't move. He's bent over a case file. Two bandits stole ice worth $100,000 from Traub Bros. & Co. Jewelry on Washington Boulevard. He's working it.

Captain Dietrich throws him the hairy eyeball all the way across the squad room. Says, "Today would be nice."

Denny closes the file and follows Dietrich into the captain's office. "You're up," the captain says. He is a tall man in a rumpled suit smelling of cigars. "I need you on a home burglary."

"Where's Phil?" Denny looks out at the squad room. Phil Wheaton was just around . . . where did he go? "I thought he's up next."

"Yeah, he had to leave. Personal emergency."

"What happened?"

"His daughter's missing. He had to get home."

"The thing is, boss," Denny says, "I'm in the middle of the Traub case. I'm trying to arrange a witness trip to White Pigeon. State troopers caught a pair looking good for the heist."

"As of now, this takes priority."

Denny demurs.

"Hey, cheer up," Dietrich says, "I'm giving you a priority case.

You should be happy."

"Yeah," Denny mumbles as he walks away. He told the Traub brothers he's closing in on the thieves who broke into their jewelry store; now that's on hold. "I'm thrilled to death."

At the scene, Denny sees why this case jumps the line. The house is one of the Tudor mansions in Palmer Woods. A swank section of the city. Huge houses, curving streets, lush lawns.

Money doesn't just talk in Detroit, it screams at the top of its lungs.

Out front are two squad cars. A black Ford town car in the drive-way. The forensics men in their truck wait for the go-ahead to get to work inside.

The drizzle from earlier has stopped. A trio of uniforms stand talking on the front walk. They give Denny the fisheye. One of them pushes Denny backwards with his billy club.

Another cop says, "Nix. He's a dick."

Denny flashes his buzzer. Says, "Rankin, Robbery. What's going on?"

The bluesuit who spoke up consults his daybook. "Owner's name is Mueller. House was broken into this morning. Eight large in cash plus his wife's jewelry—all missing."

"Anybody hurt?"

"Nah. Just the dough and trinkets."

Denny goes up to the front door and examines the lock. Seems intact. He goes around the outside of the house. The side door also seems intact.

A screened-in porch takes up the back of the house.

Here we go: the screening has been cut. Two of the rectangular panes of leaded glass in the metal casement windows in the back of the house have been smashed. Two windows hang open.

Denny peeks in. The windows open into the kitchen. The thief cut the screen, smashed the windows, unhooked them, and crawled in-side. Whoever did it would have to be small. Possibly a woman?

A figure looms into view inside the house. Says, "Who are you?"

A tall but stooped man, dressed in a business suit. Face puckered as if he just ate a bad oyster.

Denny identifies himself.

"What are you doing out there?" the man says.

"This looks like where the burglar made entry."

"Gee," the man says with heavy sarcasm, "I guess you really are a detective. Want to come inside, Sherlock? See what other obvious clues you can deduce?"

Denny glares at him but swallows his irritation.

Jesus, people can be annoying.

He finds the back door and goes inside. Up close, the man is in his fifties, balding, with a gray fringe of hair. Round glasses. Creases in his long, vinegary face.

"And you are?" Denny asks.

"Dr. Prentiss Mueller. I own this house. Where's Detective Wheaton?"

"He had a personal emergency. I'm here in his place."

"I specifically asked for him."

"You got me instead."

Mueller frowns.

"Where were you when this happened?" Denny asks.

"At work. My wife was at a breakfast meeting with one of her clubs. My housekeeper had the morning off. She discovered the break-in when she got in, around eleven. She called me, and I told her to phone for the police. Naturally, I came right home."

"Any idea who might have done this?"

"I'd say finding that out is your job."

Except for shards of glass in the kitchen, the house looks to be undisturbed. Plush carpets. Flocked wallpaper. Overlarge, plush furniture, designed to impress. Grand piano in the living room.

A slender woman in a mauve suit perches at the edge of a massive sofa. She sits stiff-backed with her hands folded in her lap as if waiting for a concert to begin.

"I understand money was taken," Denny says.

Mueller crooks a finger. Denny follows him through the house. "My wife," Mueller says, offhandedly, when they pass the woman on the sofa.

Denny nods. "Ma'am."

She ignores him. As warm as her husband.

Mueller leads Denny up the stairs to the second floor.

"My study," Mueller says. Shelves of chemistry books. Cupboards and drawers on a bureau are open, the contents upended. A desk with drawers pried open and askew. "Here's where the money was taken. Eight thousand cash."

"Who knew it was here?"

"No one."

"Not even your family?"

"No one."

"Who else is in your family besides your wife?"

"My son, Heinz. And my daughter, Wanda."

"Were they home?"

"I said they don't know about the money, didn't I, Sherlock?"

"I'm asking if they were around, sir. I'd like to speak with them."

"They're not here."

Mueller articulates his words carefully for the dense detective.

Denny goes into the hall. Four other doors off the hallway upstairs. Two are closed. One is the bathroom. Denny peers inside the other. The master bedroom, with drawers pulled out and contents—women's slips, bras, and panties—strewn about. An empty jewelry box lies on its side on a makeup table.

Denny says, "I'll need a list of what's missing."

Behind him, Mueller says, "I'll get you one. Besides the cash, my wife's rings, bracelets, necklaces. All irreplaceable."

Denny knows the drill: he'll get the list out to the Pawnshop Bureau, but they'll tell him not to hold his breath.

Two doors lead to walk-in closets. One contains men's clothes—suits and ties—the other women's clothes. A few hanging bags bear the label, Richland Furs. He touches the bags; they're full.

"What about the other rooms?" Denny asks.

"Don't worry about those. They're locked and undisturbed."

Both rooms have a padlock on a hasp keeping them locked.

From the outside. An odd feature of a home.

Denny says, "You already checked inside?"

"I already checked," Mueller says. Testier than ever now.

"These are your children's rooms?"

Mueller gives a dramatic sigh. "Yes."

Denny says, "What about the basement?"

"I keep the door to the basement locked. I checked. Nothing was taken down there."

Lot of locked rooms in this house, Denny thinks.

He says, "I'm going to bring in the forensics team. They can start looking for fingerprints."

"Is this really necessary?"

Denny takes a long look at Mueller.

"There are many visitors to my house," Mueller says. "It stands to reason you'll find a variety of prints here. Fair warning."

"Maybe so. Unless all your visitors rifle through your wife's jewelry box, we'll get an idea just who was up here."

Mueller narrows his eyes at Denny. "When did you say Detective Wheaton will be available?"

"I didn't."

Mueller scowls, says, "I may have to make a few phone calls. I know important people at City Hall. I want him in charge of this."

"Knock yourself out, sir."

Denny waves in the forensic technicians. Tells them where to focus in the house. They go about their work and he goes into the living room, where Mueller's wife still sits straight-backed. He feels waves of hot rage radiating off her.

Denny says, "I'm Detective Rankin. Sorry this happened."

Her gaze is, if possible, even more dismissive than her husband's as her head swivels the tiniest bit in Denny's direction. She does not deign to respond.

"I understand you lost jewelry?" Denny says.

A barely perceptible nod.

"Anything else you can think of? I notice you have furs in your closet. Are any of them missing?"

"Common criminals don't steal furs," she says. German accent. Still doesn't look at him.

And thank you for telling me my business, Denny thinks.

Mueller comes downstairs. "Frieda," he says, "this man bothering you?"

She raises a lazy hand of unconcern; Denny is much too far beneath her notice to bother with.

On the coffee table in front of her, a newspaper's orange masthead catches Denny's eye. Spread out are a half-dozen issues of incendiary radio priest Father Coughlin's paper, *Social Justice*.

The lab guys and the print team start their work. One of the bluesuits calls Denny outside. "Radio call for you."

On the squawk box in the car is Dwight Dietrich. "What's up?"

That was fast. Mueller must have made good on his threat to "make a few phone calls."

"Just getting the forensic team started. Guy says he lost a load of cash and jewelry."

"He's got powerful friends," Dietrich says. "He's a big shot at Ford's. He called his friends and they just called me. You already pissed him off. You need to tread lightly on this one, Denny."

"Doing my job, sir."

"Yeah, well, work it like you've never worked it before—you know, do a *good* job. Close it fast."

"Yes sir."

"Between you and me, you close this pronto, there's an inspector's spot opening in the Twelfth. I can make sure you get preference."

The Twelfth. The one taking in Palmer Park and his own house.

Or the house he used to live in, he corrects himself.

"I'd appreciate it, sir."

Denny calls for more bluesuits. Three cars show up. Five men. He sets them on a house-to-house to find anybody who might have seen a stranger go in or out of the Mueller house that morning.

They come up empty-handed. Nobody saw anything.

4

EVA SZABÓ

[Monday, March 31, 1941]

The rest of the day flies by.

Two men come in with fingers lost through inattention or mechanical malfunction, one man's digits wrapped in greasy rags, the other's not able to be salvaged.

Other men come with back pains from lifting heavy sheet metal. Repetitive injuries, strains to arms and legs and shoulders from performing the same mechanical motions for hours on end.

Toward the end of the day, two brothers come in. Their injuries don't look mechanical; they are bloody and bruised, as though they've been savagely beaten. They refused to say who did it, or why.

Eva tries to get it out of them. They stay mum.

Nadine doesn't treat them because she claims they don't have work-related injuries. Eva copies their names on a sheet of paper she hides in her pocketbook.

By then the flow of men has eased and Nadine and Eva have the chance to sit. Nadine greases her hands with liniment and the room fills with camphor. She keeps a bottle of Sloan's Liniment on her desk and during the day she slathers the stuff over her hands. Her finger joints are swollen and misshapen.

She lights a cigarette and the harsh tobacco smoke battles the camphor.

Eva finally gets a chance to tell Nadine about the pregnant woman in the administration building. She asks Nadine where she learned to be a nurse, and Nadine tells Eva she was in the nursing corps in the Great War.

"I saw some things," Nadine says.

Eva waits for her to elaborate. She wants to hear about the blood, battles, and bodies Nadine saw overseas so Eva can get some insight into the head nurse.

Nadine says nothing more.

She gets a thousand-yard stare and Eva leaves her to her memories.

Her shift over, Eva lets the throngs from the factory sweep her out to Miller Road. She walks down to Dix Street. Stops at the corner.

A friend, Magda Kozma, had invited her to Kovac's Beer Garden in Delray, the neighborhood in southwest Detroit where Eva lives. "George's going to pop the question tonight," Magda said; she's been hinting for weeks to her boyfriend that she wants to get married, and it looks like tonight's the night for the proposal.

Eva told her she might make it later. First she wants to stop in at the Rouge Tavern, a bar and grill a half-mile south of the plant. It is one of a dozen bars lining Dix, before- or after-shift stopovers for the workers.

She tried another one two weeks ago, the Dix Bar and Grill. It was as unexciting as its name. Filled with men too exhausted to do anything but slump over their beers before dragging themselves home. They had only enough strength to glance at her when she walked in before returning to their drinks and their troubles. It was a bust for information-gathering.

The Rouge Tavern, on the other hand, is jumping.

Glenn Miller plays on the jukebox. "Moonlight Serenade." A younger set than the Dix crowds the joint. The men here may be tired from their impossible days, but they still have pep. A few women are here, too, scattered throughout the room, heads thrown back in laughter, the centers of attention for groups of men at the tables.

A stool opens at the long bar and Eva takes it. She gets the bartender's eye and orders a whiskey neat. The barkeep gives her a funny look but serves it up for her. Canadian Club, from across the river in Windsor.

The bartender keeps an eye on her. Well, a woman alone . . . who knows what he thinks she's here for. Especially since she's not as grimy as the ones who work on the factory floors.

She takes a sip of the drink, feels the burn go all the way down to her toes and then back up to her face. She's not a souse—her stepmother doesn't allow booze in the house—so she needs to be careful with her alcohol intake.

She swivels her stool to look out over the bar. The laughter and shouts of men compete with the music.

One guy catches her eye. He sits at a table with three other men. Their heads are together in deep conversation.

He happens to look up. He nods at her, raises his beer in greeting.

Five minutes later he slides onto the stool next to her at the bar.

"Hiya," he says.

She says, "Hey."

"Never saw you here before."

"First time."

"I'm Anton Luedke."

"Eva Szabó."

"Pleased to meet you." He wipes his hand on his pants and holds it out.

"Likewise."

They shake. His hand is hard as a brick.

"You here by yourself? Come over and join me and my buddies."

"I wouldn't want to intrude."

He waves it away. "Just chewing the fat. Come on. Meet the guys."

She follows him back to his table with her drink. He introduces Kevin McNamara. Eddy Singleton. Frank Ennis. She makes a special effort to remember their names.

All are scruffy and suspicious of her. None of them stand or offer to shake her hand. None seem particularly happy to see her there.

Anton takes an empty chair from the next table and holds it out for her.

"Eva's first time here," Anton says.

"Where do you guys work?" she asks.

"I work in the Glass Plant," Anton says. "Eddy and Kevin are in Motor Assembly. Frank's in the Foundry."

"What about you?" Anton asks. "Ain't many women at Ford's."

"I'm the receptionist in the First Aide Clinic," she says. "I've only been there three weeks."

Anton says, "I heard one of our guys was over there today. Dropped a sheet of glass on his foot. Dumb ass. Pardon my French."

The four men shake their heads in sympathy. The Rouge is a dangerous place to work. Henry Ford is famous for not caring about safety in his factories. He's said he thinks it's up to the workers to be more careful on the job; then they wouldn't have so many accidents. To him they're as replaceable as tires on the cars; if one goes bad, you throw it out and get another one just like it.

She decides to toss out a baited line.

"So," she says, "I've been hearing a lot of talk about unions. Any of you guys in the union?"

They throw each other a quick glance. They get tense, clam up.

She hopes the question wasn't a mistake.

"Why you want to know?" Anton asks.

"No reason," Eva says. "I hear a lot of talk about it in the clinic. Wondering where you guys stand on it."

"You ain't no spy, are you?" Frank asks.

"Me? No!"

Frank says, "You sure?" The menace in his voice makes her antsy. He wears a gold UAW pin on the pocket of his work shirt.

He sees her looking at his pin. He says, "Wasn't so long ago you could get fired just for wearing this."

Anton says, "The union's pressing hard to get recognized. And Old Man Ford, he hates it. He'll never give in."

Frank says, "He'll give in."

Eva adds bait to the line.

"Personally," she says, "I hate 'em, unions. No offense," she quickly says to Frank, who looks like she just spit in his beer. "My old man got beat up by a couple of union guys about ten years ago," she continues. "Poor guy never did get back on his feet. So no, don't talk to me about unions."

"You ain't a spy, and you hate the unions," Frank says, "why you so interested in them?"

Time to backtrack.

"No, I'm new. Just trying to get the lay of the land. The guys who come into the hospital, I hear a lot of them talking about the union.

That's all."

Frank says. "I don't trust you."

"Hey now," Anton says.

Frank takes his beer and walks away.

"Don't mind him," Anton says. "He's pro-union all the way."

"Yeah, no problem." She presses. "I hear there's a lot of Communists in the unions, that's all. Lots of Jews, too."

"Jews," Kevin spits out. "The sooner we get rid of them, the better."

The men all agree on that.

She looks to Anton. He gives her a nod, like he's reconsidering her.

She interprets that to mean she's on the right track after all. She's made an opening with them.

Eddy says, "I gotta get going."

"Yeah," Kevin says, "I better head out, too." He turns to Anton. "You coming?"

Anton tells Eva, "They're my ride. I better get moving."

Eva says, "Nice to meet you all."

The other three nod stonily and leave. Anton says, "You gonna be okay here by yourself?"

"Yeah, good. I'm going to get home myself soon. I'll just finish my drink and I'll be fine."

"See you again."

She watches them make their way through the crowd and smoky haze to the front door.

Suddenly she can't wait to get out of this place. She hopes she hasn't pushed them too hard with her union talk. She knows it's just a pose, but she made herself uncomfortable with it.

She knows she was supposed to go slow, but it's taken so long to make contact with any of them.

And she never was known for her patience.

5

CLARENCE BROWN

[Monday, March 31, 1941]

The Hunt Street precinct house. Monaghan, the duty sergeant, glares at him.

Clarence returns the look.

If he had a nickel for every one of those he's gotten from other coppers since he started as a patrolman, he could retire to a tropical island by now.

You either roll with it or punch back. Most of the time Clarence rolls with it.

He goes up to his desk in the station's second floor Detective Bureau. There are more colored detectives and patrolmen than there used to be in the Detroit Police Department, so he isn't the only one in the station anymore. Four others are assigned to this station because it's the closest one to Black Bottom and Paradise Valley; the segregated squad is based here. They are still not welcomed or appreciated by the white officers.

He rolls an incident report form into his aged Remington and starts two-finger-typing his report.

He writes up only his encounter with Ida James and Bobby Henderson. Wilson, his junior lieutenant, told him not to tell anyone about the baby.

Clarence knows something's wrong whichever way he looks at

it. But Wilson can rain a world of hell down on his head if Clarence defies him. Wilson has told him many times before: go along to get along. It's not in Clarence's nature, but he tries. He tries.

He finishes his report on Ida James and leaves it with the Bureau secretary for processing.

He goes back to his typewriter. He looks around to see if anyone's watching. Satisfied no one is, on a new sheet he types up notes about his discovery of the baby's body. Where, how, when, what he saw, what Wilson told him to do and not to do.

If this comes back to bite anyone in the ass, Clarence knows it'll be him. He wants it down on paper just in case.

He folds up the sheet of notes and sticks it in an envelope at the back of the bottom drawer of his desk.

Where ever you are, little man, I'm not going to forget you, he promises the infant in the smart wool blanket.

6

DENNY RANKIN

[Monday, March 31, 1941]

He spends the rest of the day on the phone.
Denny calls the lab to say he's waiting for the forensic results from the Mueller house. They're not ready yet.

He calls Captain Dwight Dietrich to let him know what he's found and where the investigation stands. Dietrich already grumbles about it.

He calls Phil Wheaton, hoping to find out news about Phil's daughter. He calls Phil's home a half-dozen times, but never gets through; the line is always busy.

He calls the Pawnshop Bureau to let them know about the stolen jewelry. He tells them he's sending over the list Mueller gave him. They tell him not to hold his breath.

The list includes three diamond rings, an opal set in gold on a necklace, half a dozen ruby and silver necklaces, five gold bracelets, and an emerald anklet.

Gold, gems, silver. Like the contents of a pirate's treasure chest.

He calls the Rouge plant to find out where Mueller works. He hopes this will clue him in on why Dietrich is involved.

To his surprise, Denny learns Prentiss Mueller isn't one of the top managers. He's a chemist working on extruded plastic coatings for automobile trims. He's not even the top guy in the Chemistry Department, though he is the head of a research team.

He lives in a pretty fancy house for a low-level guy. Where's his money come from? Maybe he's independently wealthy. Or his wife is. It might explain her attitude.

Denny still doesn't know why Mueller gets the full-on treatment from the department. What else here doesn't Denny know about?

He works steadily. The graft trial is on pause today but it sits in the back of his mind.

He checks the files to see if there have been any other break-ins in the Muellers' Palmer Woods neighborhood recently. Maybe this was part of a pattern.

He finds reports of three break-ins going back four months. The bums who pulled two of the jobs are in Jackson State Prison; he makes a note to track down the third guy.

Late in the day, Denny gets a visit from the head of the fingerprinting team. As Mueller predicted, they picked up dozens of fingerprints from the house: mostly partials and smudges. It will take a while to identify the ones they are able to; others they may never know.

"What about the jewelry box?" Denny asks.

"Lots of prints and smears on that, too," the tech tells him. "Take a while to work through it all. We got the parents' prints last night, but without the kids' prints, we're whistling in the dark."

So the first task is getting the kids' prints for elimination.

He tries Phil Wheaton one more time. Still busy.

Phil's cop sled is missing from the driveway at his home in Redford.

Denny rings the doorbell. It's a small brick bungalow, neat and tidy. Just the three of them live here: Phil, his wife Lena, and their daughter Charlotte.

Lena comes to the door. Her auburn hair's tied back. She has dark circles under her hazel eyes. The light of hope she brings disappears when she sees who's standing there.

She opens the door for him to come inside. He wraps her in a hug. He feels her trembling, a constant vibration from the fear inside her.

"How you doing, hon?" Denny asks.

He steps back. She shakes her head. "I can't stand this."

"Still no news?"

"No. Come in. Want coffee?"

She leads him into the kitchen. Another woman sits at the table. She looks as ragged as Lena.

"Denny," Lena says, "this is my sister-in-law, Esther. Esther, Denny works with Phil."

Denny nods. Esther extends a hand for him to shake. Cold and smooth, like stone.

Denny says, "Nobody's heard from Phil since this morning. Just wanted to check to see what's going on."

"He's out," Lena says. She sits beside Esther, who puts an arm around her. "He's trying to find Charlotte."

"You haven't heard from her?" Denny asks.

"Not a word," Lena says.

"Since when?"

"Since two days ago."

"Did Phil file a missing person?"

"No. He said he didn't want to get the police involved so soon."

So soon?

Not getting the police involved seems like an odd choice for a police detective whose child is missing.

Denny stands there for another few moments. Once at a Christmas party at the station, things got loud and Lena got drunk and sidled up to Denny in a corner. Rubbed against him. Leaned in to kiss him full on the lips. Denny smelled her flowery-perfumed makeup and tasted her gluey lipstick. Then she walked away like nothing ever happened and she never mentioned it again.

Now he says to her, "Anything I can do?"

"Help Phil find my daughter."

"I will. Keep me posted if you hear anything."

"Thanks, Denny." She walks him to the door. Gives him her cheek to kiss.

Back in his car, Denny sits and ponders. Would Phil know where to look for his daughter? She was sixteen. Would Phil know her friends? Where she liked to go?

Phil wouldn't, Denny decided. But he knew where Phil himself would go if he wanted time to think.

Or keep himself from thinking, as the case may be.

7

EVA SZABÓ

[Monday, March 31, 1941]

She lives in Delray, within a long walk of the Rouge complex. It's a brick house on South Street, down the block from the Holy Cross Hungarian Church.

She's a longer way from where she started, she considers as she walks home.

She was born in Budapest in 1916. Her mother Anna was killed in the White Terror in Hungary in 1919, when suspected Communists (including many Jews like her mother) were rounded up, imprisoned and slaughtered.

After that, her father Lazlo knew they would never be safe in Europe. He brought Eva to America.

Eva has a younger stepbrother, Josef, who came bundled with her father's second marriage, to Ágnes. Also from Hungary, Ágnes came over with her late first husband years earlier than Eva and Lazlo.

Lazlo died two years ago. Shortly afterwards, Josef moved out. He stops by every few weeks to say hello to his mother, who misses him terribly. Eva lives alone with Ágnes.

It's hard. She'd always been closer to her father than Ágnes. The year after her father died, Ágnes had a stroke that paralyzed the right side of her body. So far she's been able to take care of herself, and Eva has felt okay leaving her alone during the day.

Lately, though, she's noticed Ágnes seems to be slowing down, having more trouble finding words and being crankier than ever. She's also developed an old lady smell; she doesn't keep herself as clean as she should.

As she approaches the house, Eva sees a figure waiting for her on the front steps in the pool of light from over the porch. She sees the flare of a cigarette, the drift of smoke. The shadow of the smoke drifts on the ground at his feet.

Her heart sinks.

He turns to watch her approach. "Hey," he says.

She sits beside him on the steps. "Hey."

He makes a face. "You smell like booze," he says. "You been drinking." A statement, not a question.

Here we go, she thinks.

"I had a drink with a few co-workers from the plant."

Vincent Németh scoffs. "The plant."

He takes a long drag on his smoke. "I thought we were supposed to meet up at Kovac's." Kovac's, their neighborhood bar, West Jefferson and the corner of Post Street in Delray. "Didn't know you had other plans."

"It was a last-minute thing. By the time it broke up, I was just too tired. I came home instead."

"Jesus. The plant, the plant . . . that's all you talk about anymore."

"It's my job."

"Well, you missed Kovac's. George popped the question. Got down on one knee and everything. She pretended like it was a surprise."

"Sorry I missed it," Eva says, more to mollify Vincent than because she actually is sorry. Marriage occupies the number one place on her girlfriends' minds. Not on hers.

"Magda said maybe we're next," Vincent says.

"You and me?"

"Yeah."

A dozen ways to say *that's never going to happen* run through Eva's mind. When she doesn't reply, Vincent says, "How much longer are you going to go on with this plant thing?"

"I have to work. My mother can't, so it's down to me. I didn't work, we'd starve. We'd have no place to live—."

"I gave you a solution."

His solution: a proposal of marriage.

She says, "I'm not ready for your solution."

Never mind the fact that I don't love you, she thinks.

Or will never be ready.

She knows better than to say it now, when he's annoyed.

"*I'm* ready," he says. "My old man's teaching me to cut hair. I'm going to take over his shop when he retires."

His father owns Albert Németh Barber Shop on West Jefferson in Delray.

This is too much for Eva to deal with. She stands. "I have to go inside."

He stands, too. "Can I come in for a little while?"

"Not tonight, okay? I still have to get Ágnes ready for bed. And I'm beat."

"Yeah, right. From working at the *plant*."

He spits a flake of tobacco off his tongue. Flicks the butt into the street.

Eva watches it arc and bounce in a flash of sparks.

Vincent says, "I can take a hint. I'll see you later."

He takes off into the night.

Good, she thinks; go. You can take a *hint*? I told you flat out no. That's a *hint*?

Inside, Ágnes sits at the dining room table with an empty cup.

Her stepmother says, "*Elkéstél.*"

Translation: You're late.

Another country heard from.

Eva says, "I met friends after work."

Ágnes once spoke perfect English; lately she refuses to say anything except in Hungarian, an aftereffect of her stroke. Eva speaks Hungarian, too, but prefers English.

A small show of resistance to her stepmother's dominion over her life.

"Did you have dinner?" Eva asks.

Ágnes waves the question away.

Eva doesn't feel like probing what that means. She leads the older woman up the stairs to bed. Ágnes needs a bath, but Eva is too tired to give her one tonight.

But she's not too tired to write out her notes from her shift today. She knows if she skips a day, she will never catch up.

She retrieves her notebook from the drawer in her bedside

nightstand. Atop the nightstand sits a small menorah, one of the few personal items she took with them when they fled Hungary. It belonged to Eva's grandmother, Lazlo's mother Sarah. Eva has never used the menorah during Hanukkah; she and her father never celebrated even though they are Jewish.

Well, she is. After they arrived in America, her father turned away from his religion entirely. Frightened by the treatment he saw Jews receiving in Europe, and disgusted by what people said about Jews in his adopted city, he sent both Eva and her stepbrother to school at Holy Cross Hungarian Catholic church after he married Ágnes, who is Catholic.

Eva complained so much about the terrible things the nuns said about Jews—Christ killers! Cheats! Money-grubbers!—that he relented and sent her to the public school, Nordstrum Intermediate in Delray.

The other memento she keeps from the old days is a chai on a pendant she wears around her neck. Composed of the Hebrew letters meaning "alive," the chai was a present from her mother when Eva was an infant. She always wears it—but she's always careful to keep it hidden from sight.

She once read a line in a library book—"I imagined that I bore my chalice safely through a throng of foes"—and that's how she thinks of her Jewishness . . . she bears it like a secret through throngs of foes on the streets of Delray, Dearborn, and Detroit.

She takes her notebook downstairs to the kitchen table. Eva shows up at the plant every day, but that's not her primary job; she works for Elizabeth Waters, a private investigator. Eva reports to Elizabeth every few days; Elizabeth recommended Eva keep a daily journal to prepare herself for those reports.

Tonight Eva lists the kinds of injuries she saw, including the pair of brothers who were beaten and sent away by Nadine without treatment. She mentions her drink at the Rouge Tavern. She mentions Frank, the pro-union Foundry worker. She should get to know him better.

When she finishes writing, she shuts the lights off, locks the front door, checks the side door, and goes upstairs to fall into bed.

She's no stranger to hard work—she held down two jobs before starting at the Rouge—but she feels a particular kind of stressful exhaustion in her situation at the clinic. She wouldn't have thought keeping up a front, pretending to be a different person, would be this hard.

Telling lies about her father in the bar tonight was especially hard. Despite what she told the men, her father was devoted to the union. He worked at the Rouge plant until he was laid off during the Depression.

Then he took part in the Ford Hunger March in 1932 and got a whack on the head from a Dearborn policeman's billy club. It not only gave him a concussion but took him permanently out of the workforce with recurring headaches and dizziness. He couldn't work; he had days he couldn't stand because his balance was so bad.

That was how she met Elizabeth.

Without her father working, the family was hurting for money. To bring in cash, Ágnes became a seamstress (which Eva found funny since their family name means "tailor" in Hungarian). Eva dropped out of high school at sixteen to work as a cashier at Szalacsi Groceries on West Jefferson to supplement the family's income.

It still wasn't enough to let them squeak by each month.

Eva found a second job, selling candy on the confectionary counter at the Delray Theatre near her house. She was working there the night Elizabeth Waters came to see her. She said she represented a lawyer named Maurice Sugar, who wanted her parents' permission to go after Henry Ford for money to cover her father's expenses for the medical care he needed after the Hunger March.

"I tried talking to your parents," Elizabeth said, "but I didn't think I was getting through to them. They told me to talk to you."

"No," Eva said, "Papa doesn't understand as well as he used to."

She couldn't take her eyes off Elizabeth. How well the woman carried herself! She had such presence. Such confidence. Eva was not used to seeing women like Elizabeth; she was used to the *feleségek* she saw around Delray, frumpy women with thick, tree-trunk legs and faces like boiled potatoes.

Elizabeth was tall, slender, blonde, dressed like a private eye in the movies, in a trench coat cinched around the waist and a fedora tipped over one eye.

For her part, Elizabeth kept looking at Eva, too, standing there in her candy girl smock with Delray Theatre printed on it. Eva couldn't imagine how she looked in Elizabeth's eyes.

"You're bringing in all the money now in your family?" Elizabeth asked.

"My stepmother does sewing for people, and that brings in a little. But I work two jobs. I'm thinking about getting a third one."

"What's your other job?"

Eva told her about the grocery store.

"You're pretty energetic," Elizabeth said.

"Not a matter of energy when you don't have a choice."

In the end, Maurice Sugar couldn't get any money for them. Henry Ford said it was the Jewish Communists who provoked the attack, and wouldn't pay out a dime for anyone hurt in the protest.

When Elizabeth came with the bad news, she told Eva she liked her and wanted to help the family. Elizabeth asked Eva if she would like to learn how to become an investigator, and Eva said yes.

Elizabeth told Eva she used to work for Maurice Sugar. When she went out on her own as a private eye, Maurice helped her establish her office. Waters & Associates, Confidential Investigations.

Elizabeth still does the lion's share of her work for Maurice Sugar, but she also takes on clients here and there as she has the time. Much of the outside work consists of following cheating spouses; she hated to take it on, but like Eva she needed to make ends meet.

Elizabeth and Eva agreed on a try-out: Eva would follow a cheating man and see what kinds of photos she could take.

Fortunately, Eva had no problem with cheating spouses.

She performed perfectly, even getting a shot of the man and woman together in bed taken between the inside drapes of the hotel where they met once a week. They were on the second floor, but it was no obstacle to Eva; she asked a nearby electrical worker if she could borrow his ladder and flirted with him until he said yes.

Impressed at her initiative, Elizabeth sent more work her way over the next few years—cheating spouses, witness interviews, accident investigations—and told Eva she would bring her on permanently as the agency's finances improved. This finally happened two years ago; Eva quit the grocery store and theatre and began working for Elizabeth full-time, answering phones, doing surveillance, and learning the business of investigation.

In her current assignment, Elizabeth arranged for Eva to join the Ford Assembly plant hospital as a clerk. As Elizabeth explained to her, the National Labor Relations Act prohibited the kinds of anti-union activities Ford's man Harry Bennett had his Service

Department thugs engage in, like beating and flogging union organizers and spying throughout the plant. Eva's assignment would be to observe and report on anti-union activity to Elizabeth, who would then report it to Maurice Sugar. He, in turn, would report it to the National Labor Relations Board.

She places her notebook back in the nightstand drawer and takes a book from it. She always has to read before she goes to bed; it's a habit her father helped her develop when she was little and he'd read to her every night.

Tonight she is reading *Native Son*, published last year. She borrowed it from the library.

She gets to the part where Bigger Thomas gets ready to suffocate Mary—Eva knows it's coming—and she has to put the book down. There's already too much violence against women in real life; she can't deal with it happening in fiction, too. At least not tonight.

Before sleep takes her, her thoughts turn to Vincent.

Perhaps making the connection between Vincent and violence is not accidental, she thinks; it's worth remembering; Vincent always seems to be tightly wound, and part of her always fears him exploding into violence. He's friends with her stepbrother Josef. Vincent hates her working at the Rouge and reminds her every chance he gets. He doesn't know what her real job is, and that's how she wants to keep it.

She went out with him a few times, and she likes him okay. They've never talked about her being his girlfriend; in fact, she's told him she's not. He seems to have assumed she is anyway, with all the rights that go along with it. They need to have a talk about it.

But not tonight. She gladly puts it out of her mind.

Like Scarlett O'Hara, she'll think about it tomorrow.

8

CLARENCE BROWN

[Monday, March 31, 1941]

Bessie sits with her foot up on the hassock in their living room when he gets home. Her cane rests beside her. Blood has soaked through the bandage on her left ankle.

Clarence hangs his overcoat in the closet. He takes off his gun belt with the two pearl-handled revolvers and hangs it on the peg by the front door where he can get at it fast if he needs to. Hangs his suitcoat in the front closet. He eases his home-made bullet-proof vest over his head.

His armor. Two metal plates connected by two leather straps. He cobbled them together when he first made detective; he figured—correctly, as it turned out—a Negro detective in Detroit would need all the protection he could get.

He leans the plates against the wall.

"Hey baby," he says. Kisses his wife on her clammy forehead. He puts the back of his hand against her cheek to feel for her temperature. The doctor told him to watch out for fever.

Her skin is cool.

"What kind of day was it?" Clarence asks.

"Same old same old."

She makes to get up but he touches her shoulder to keep her down. "Stay there. I want to change the bandage before you do anything."

"Miss Maxine changed it this morning."

"It needs changed again. Soaked through with the infection. You can't feel it?"

"Feels the same as always."

"You rest there for another minute while I clean you up."

In the kitchen he fills a deep pot with hot water. As it fills, he smells a pie. Guesses it's a berry pie.

He opens the door to the oven. Sure enough, there's a raspberry pie on the wire rack.

He checks the icebox. A nice big bowl of stew. Both pie and stew are from Miss Maxine, a member of Bessie's sisterhood at the Second Baptist Church. The women alternate days to come over and watch her and help her out.

Clarence has run out of words to thank them.

Bessie hasn't been able to do much since the middle of last year. She used to work at Harper Hospital, cleaning patient rooms. One day she slipped on a wet floor and broke a bone in her leg and several bones in her foot. Dr. Jemison at Parkside Hospital put a cast on her, but when he cut the cast off, he discovered a deep pressure sore on Bessie's ankle from rubbing against the cast.

When the wound got infected, Dr. Jemison did more tests and told her she had diabetes, and that's why her ankle wasn't getting better. He told her to change her diet and cut out all the sugars.

(Clarence must remember to tell Miss Maxine that Bessie isn't supposed to have sugary desserts anymore.)

Dr. Jemison also said Bessie needs to continue to stay off the leg. He treated her with penicillin. The sore was improving, but slowly.

Bessie took to her bed or, if she felt up to it, the couch in their living room. Members of her sisterhood at the Second Baptist Church came and helped her out as much as they could, cleaning the house and cooking dinners and doing her laundry. Dr. Jemison got her a wheelchair, and with Clarence's help she can get to church on Sundays.

Clarence built a ramp for the wheelchair from the sidewalk to the porch. Except for church, Bessie doesn't seem to want to go anyplace anymore.

Worried to distraction, Clarence has taken as much time off as he's been able to, but he's docked for every hour away from the job. And with Bessie not working, he can't take too much more time off.

Now he pulls a stool over and, gently and slowly, unwraps her ankle so he can clean it the way Dr. Jemison taught him, dabbing with a soft cloth and soap and water.

He concentrates on ministering to her ankle without causing too much pain.

After he warms up the stew Miss Maxine left for them, he helps Bessie back into the living room. For a while they sit as they always do at night— the radio playing, Bessie reading the *Detroit Tribune* or the *Free Press* or one of the history books she always has going from the library, Clarence himself working on the baseball league he sponsors for the Black Bottom boys. The boys decided they wanted to call the league the Clarence Brown League, which he loves. His main team call themselves the Brown Athletic Club Nine (BAC 9 for short).

After the first of the year, he starts working out the schedules for tryouts (they will start in April or May, as soon as the uncertain Detroit weather allows) and games for the teams. Once every summer he arranges for a game to be played at Briggs Stadium, where the Detroit Tigers play. The kids love it.

When she gets tired, he helps Bessie into their bedroom and into bed. He has made a frame out of a cardboard box. It fits over her foot to keep the covers off her ankle and help her sleep.

He turns the light out. Kisses her goodnight. Goes out to the living room.

He stands gazing sadly around the room, thinking the empty room represents the emptiness in their lives since she fell.

He hears a noise from the basement.

He grabs one of the pearl-handled .45s from the holster hanging by the door.

Goes through the dining room to the kitchen. A door leads off the kitchen to the back hall and the basement.

Stairs also go up to the second floor, where one of Bessie's coworkers lives with her children. Clarence has forbidden all the kids from his basement unless they are specifically invited.

He hears a noise again.

This time he pegs it: the *clock-clock, clock-clock* of a ping-pong ball on the table down there.

He creeps down the stairs, gun at the ready. The door to the basement is shut but Clarence sees a light under it. He hears movement behind it. An intruder.

He throws the door open and holds up the gun.

A kid freezes beside the ping-pong table.

A ping-pong ball bounces crazily across the floor.

Clarence knows the kid.

Malone Coleman. He used to catch for the Eight Mile Road Eagles, a rival team to the BAC 9. He was here a few times for Clarence's Saturday afternoon parties with the other kids from the neighborhood.

The ping-pong table is folded in half; Malone hits a ping-pong ball against the upper half of the table, playing against himself.

Clarence sticks the gun in his belt. "Malone? What are you doing here?"

"Mr. Clarence. I didn't think you could hear me."

"You didn't think I could hear you play ping-pong in my basement at nine o'clock at night?"

Malone doesn't say anything.

Clarence gives him the eye. He's a big kid, must be seventeen or eighteen by now. Clarence remembers watching him on the ball field, thinking how Malone was physically quick but mentally slow. Not retarded, exactly, but not as quick on the uptake as the other kids.

He was quick to anger either out of frustration or the feeling he was being mocked for being slow.

Since the last time Clarence saw him, he's grown into a man. His voice has deepened, he's filled out—he used to be skinny as a broomstick but now he's thick around the chest with long legs—and he's working on a wispy mustache.

He's also lost the dullness in his eyes that made people believe he was slow. It's been replaced by what strikes Clarence as a wary sadness.

"Come over here," Clarence says finally. Waves him close. He reaches out to shake Malone's hand.

He guides Malone into a corner where two cases of Coke are stacked. Clarence takes a bottle, pops it open with a church key on a string, and gives it to Malone.

He pops one open for himself. Says, "Sit down."

Malone obeys.

Clarence clinks bottle necks. Takes a sip. Malone follows him.

"Now," Clarence says, "why don't you tell me what you're doing in my house."

"I snuck in," Malone admits.

"When?"

"Today. Before."

"Nobody saw you?"

"No."

"No what?"

"No sir."

Clarence considers the young man in front of him. The kid has a fresh bruise on the side of his face.

"You been down here all day?"

"Yes sir."

"Doing what?"

"Sitting."

Clarence watches him, waiting for more.

"Once it got dark out and I didn't hear you all moving around upstairs, I thought I'd play ping-pong."

"You didn't go to school today?"

"I'm done with school, Mr. Clarence. I quit."

"What do you do instead?"

Malone shrugs.

"Where do you stay?"

"Over there on Mullet."

"Who with?"

Malone says nothing. He takes another swig of Coke. Stifles a small burp.

Clarence asks, "Who you stay with? Your mama? Your daddy?"

"Daddy gone," Malone says. "Only ever been me and mama and the babies. And my auntie. She stay with us, too. And my mama's boyfriend," he adds as what seems like a bitter afterthought.

"Don't you think your mama's going to worry, you're not home?"

"My mama don't care where I am. She gone most of the time. Don't see her for days on end. And when she do show up, like last night, she always drunk. My auntie, she take care of us."

"She treat you good?"

"Yes sir. But Mama, she beat me when she home."

"That how you got that bruise?"

"Yes sir. I go home, she gonna beat me again."

"She beat the little ones, too?"

"No sir. Just me."

Malone looks like he's going to say more, but he swallows it.

Clarence watches him for a few moments. He has heard his share of lies, and trusts his ability to spot a liar. He believes this boy. "You have someplace to stay?"

"No sir."

"What were you planning to do tonight?"

Malone shrugs.

"You think you were going to stay here?"

Another shrug. "I guess."

Clarence takes a swig of his pop. Asks, "What's your auntie's name?"

"Mary Coleman."

"She got a telephone?"

"Yes sir."

"Make you a deal," Clarence says. "You can stay here tonight. But first we have to tell your auntie where you are. She's probably worried about you."

Malone is silent. Downcast. "I'm not going back home long as my mama's there."

Clarence considers the young man. "I'll talk to your auntie about you staying here for a while."

Malone brightens at once.

"But you can't sneak in anymore."

"Yes sir," Malone says. "Thank you, Mr. Clarence."

"And after we call her," Clarence says with a big hand on Malone's meaty shoulder, "I'll open the table up all the way and hand you your raggedy ass in ping-pong."

9

DENNY RANKIN

[Monday, March 31, 1941]

Nancy Whiskey Pub in Corktown. One of the oldest bars in the city. Since the early years of the century, cops have come here after their shifts to get soused and complain. Today it's still a home away from home for lots of coppers, including, right now, Phil Wheaton.

The joint is empty except for a handful of drunk ex-cops sunk in their misery in the room's beery fug. Denny spots Phil sitting by himself at the far corner of the long bar, hunched over a shot glass.

Denny slides onto a stool beside him. Phil lifts his head, ready in a second for a fight. Phil's already in his cups.

So much for looking for his daughter.

When Phil sees the intruder's Denny, he relaxes. Sighs. Turns back to coddle his hooch. "Lena send you?" he asks.

"No. She thinks you're out looking for Charlotte."

"I was. Until I realized I dunno where to look. No idea, Denny. I don't know nothing about my own daughter. Can you beat that?"

The bartender comes over. Denny points to whatever Phil is drinking. The bartender sets him up and sidles away.

Denny lifts the glass. "To finding her, safe and sound."

Phil clinks Denny's glass. "From your mouth to God's ear." Phil tosses back what's left and signals for another.

A tear creeps down his face. "I can't do this by myself."

Denny puts a hand on his arm. "You don't have to. Whatever you need, I'm here, pal."

"I can't look for Charlotte and do my job and take care of Lena."

And drink yourself to death, Denny thinks; don't forget that part.

"No worries," Denny says. "You need me, I'm on the case."

Phil wipes his cheek with the back of his hand.

"Does Charlotte have a boyfriend?" Denny asks.

"I dunno."

"Maybe Lena knows?"

"Lena dunno either. Trust me."

Phil taps his glass on the bar. The barkeep comes back and refills it. He gives Denny a look—*You gonna do something about this guy or am I?*

Denny nods—got it—and the barkeep goes back to wiping glasses at the other end of the bar.

Denny says, "Lena told me you don't want to file a missing person on her?"

"You really think it'll make a difference?"

"Put her on the radar, yeah. One more thing to try."

Phil sighs again. "I'll wait," he says. He doesn't explain.

Phil knocks his drink back.

He stares into the bottom of his empty glass.

He starts to cry. Sloppy, drunken sobs.

The station house is quiet at this late hour. The few dicks on night duty slump over their desks, tapping pencils, doodling on their blotters, staring out the window.

The graft trials were supposed to continue today. The first trials coming out of Circuit Judge Homer S. Ferguson's one-man grand jury indictments from 1939. Judge Ferguson's grand jury uncovered a widespread conspiracy in the Wayne County Sheriff's Department and the Detroit Police Department. His investigation focused on Wayne County Prosecutor Duncan C. McCrea. In 1935, McCrea hired his friend Harry Colburn to be his chief investigator. Colburn was a tailor with no experience as an investigator, but he and McCrea were friendly.

McCrea approached Colburn with a plan to skim money from local slot machines, card games, policy bookmakers, and disorderly houses. But Colburn was at sea because he also had no experience in running this kind of operation.

So Colburn hired *his* friend Sam Block as a bagmen collecting money for McCrea. And Sam Block took along *his* boyhood friend, newly-minted Detroit Police Detective Denny Rankin, for protection.

Block skimmed a little off the take to pay Denny each time. Denny figured everyone was wetting his beak back then; why shouldn't he?

Denny hasn't been indicted in Ferguson's grand jury investigations because Block kept his name out of it.

Up until now. Each time the phone rings, Denny expects it to be special prosecutor Chester O'Hara's office, wanting him to come in for an interview.

Instead, on trial are McCrea, former Wayne County Sheriff Thomas Wilcox, former Undersheriff Bernard McGrath, former Detroit mayor Richard Reading, and more than thirty others from the Wayne County prosecutor, the sheriff, and the Detroit police.

Everybody's hoping all the shoes have already dropped. Denny knows they haven't.

Once the trial got under way on January 7th, Denny didn't believe he would stay anonymous for long. He was afraid it would be just a matter of time before his name surfaced. And then he would be well and truly fucked.

Now he asks one of the other detectives, "Hear anything about the trial?"

"Yeah," says Edward Buntzen. The other cops call him Burner Buntzen. They had to explain the nickname to him; he's still not clear about it. "I heard Colburn just changed his plea."

"No shit?"

"Yeah. He pled guilty. He's gonna testify against McCrea."

Earlier, McGrath changed his plea and testified against his boss, former Sheriff Wilcox. Now Colburn's doing the same to McCrea.

The big question in Denny's mind is: what does it mean for me?

He looks around in wastepaper baskets until he finds the late edition of the *Detroit Times*. The headline screams:

COLBURN GUILTY!
Changes Graft Plea

That'll shake things up alright. The trial's on hold while the lawyers sort it all out.

Denny reads through the article. He doesn't see his name.

The other articles on the page are all about the war:

5 Warships Sunk, Italians Admit
RAF Bombing Raids Make Belgians Joyous
2 Ships Scuttled by Axis Crews

The isolationists are squawking, but Denny doesn't see any way to keep the U.S. out of the European war.

He scans the rest of the paper, but sees no other news about the trial. Especially no mention of a detective sergeant named Rankin.

He folds the paper back up and tosses it in the trash basket. Sits back. Lights up a smoke. Takes a swig of hooch from the flask in his jacket.

He's putting off going back to his room at the Wolverine Hotel on Elizabeth Street downtown. Well, who wouldn't? When his wife Hazel threw him out of their house, he first moved into the downtown YMCA. It felt too much like being in jail: a single bed in a tiny, cell-like room. He moved to the Wolverine. It's a little bigger and cleaner than the Y. Not a bad flop for eight bucks a week.

On the evening before the graft indictments were handed down, thinking he would inevitably be named, Denny came clean to Hazel about his role.

Yes, he accompanied Sam Block when Sam acted as bag man.

Yes, he provided protection for Sam.

Yes, after a night's haul, Sam would give him a cut of the collection for his trouble.

Yes, they kept that up for a few years.

No, Sam Block didn't name Denny when Sam was arrested. He didn't name him for reasons Denny doesn't understand, but Denny wasn't going to argue.

He told Hazel because he needed to get it all off his chest. And so it wouldn't be a surprise if the grand jury came calling.

She told him to pack his things and get out of their house.

Nothing says "For better or worse" more than giving your husband the broom at the first sign of trouble.

Hazel won't let him see her two girls, either. Her two children by her first marriage. She says Denny's a bad influence on them.

As for the girls, they aren't wild about him anyway. When he first moved out, he made a big deal about wanting to see them, and Hazel let him take them to the movies a few times. Then they started refusing to see him, and he stopped asking.

If his life isn't ruined, it's making a good imitation of it until real ruin rains down on him.

He stubs out his smoke.

Time to go.

He stands. One foot in front of the other, he tells himself. Moving isn't the same as progress, but for now he'll settle for moving.

It could be mistaken for progress if you look at it askew, head sideways, and sort of squint at it.

10

EVA SZABÓ

[Tuesday, April 1, 1941]

W hen she goes to wake her stepmother in the morning, Eva
discovers Ágnes has fouled her bed during the night. Eva
has to clean the shit from Ágnes's withered body, then
bathe her, then change the bedclothes.

By the time she gets the older woman into a clean outfit and
makes her breakfast, Eva has to run for the streetcar if she's going to
get to her job on time.

It's an overcast day, chilly now but expected to reach the upper
40s later. The street car is packed with Ford workers. Usually dull-
eyed and sleepy before facing the hell of the day's first shift, today
they seem invigorated and chatty.

What's going on?

She feels eyes on her. She looks around. She sees him, squeezed
in down at the front of the car. The man stares at her, without even
an effort to turn his eyes away when she spots him.

Frank, one of Anton's pals. The union guy.

Watching her. Doesn't seem too happy about what he's seeing.

Now he's making his way toward her.

He angles in beside her in the jostling car. Says, "Alright, who are
you really?"

The night before at the bar she didn't notice he talks out of the
side of his mouth. Like a gangster.

"I told you last night," she says, "my name—"

"I don't care about your name. I mean what's with all the talk about the union?"

"No," she says, "I told you, I just want to know what's what."

"Why shouldn't I believe you're a spy for the company?"

He glares at her with dark blue eyes under shaggy brows.

I would love to take a risk with him, she thinks. Maybe open up to him, tell him she was only making it up about being against the union, she's for the union a hundred percent, her dad was a union guy, he was in the Hunger March in '32, the cops hurt him bad . . .

But she doesn't.

She reminds herself she doesn't know him. He could be anybody. He could be a company spy pretending he's for the union—she's heard about such things.

"All I can tell you is," she finally says, "I'm not a company spy."

Then she goes on the attack. "Are you?"

"Me? Hell, no." Insulted she even should ask. "I'm for the working man."

"Then we see eye-to-eye."

"If that's true," he says, his voice softening, "you better be careful who you talk to. Say too much to the wrong people and you'll be sorry."

He turns away from her. "Today's a big day," he says. "*Big* day."

As the tram approaches the plant, everyone in the car is looking at what's going on outside.

Frank's right, whatever's happening here is big.

Car horns blaring. Men shouting.

A barricade blocks the road by the plant.

It's like a carnival where the streetcar lets them off. Cars are parked fender-to-fender in front of entrances to all the gates. Four lines of men walk around the perimeter of the plant. She sees a scattering of picket signs.

They are picketing the Ford Rouge plant. There must be hundreds of men walking the picket lines.

Eva presses as close as she can to Gate #4 on Miller Road, where she usually enters.

A dozen Dearborn cops in long coats and puttees with high boots swing their billy clubs and block the entrance. They look like they are dying to go after the men. These are the brutes who beat her father senseless.

As she watches, one cop takes after a striking worker. The worker fights back and a group of other strikers surround the cop. Only other coppers muscling their own guy away keep him from being set on by the strikers. She worries this will turn into another massacre like the one in 1932.

"What's going on?" she asks a guy next to her. He doesn't look like a plant worker; he's thin, well-dressed, a little older than she is. Dark wavy hair. Nice looking. He holds a camera with a long, complicated lens. A camera bag hangs from his shoulder.

"It's a walk-out," he yells over the din of the men around them.

"What happened?"

"Eight men were fired overnight from the Rolling Mill. The other guys on the floor walked out. The protest spread from building to building."

A sound truck circles the plant, calling out the men to strike.

"Is everybody out?" she asks.

"Most of them. I hear there's a group of about a thousand Negroes still inside. They say they're not coming out. Too loyal to Ford."

The Negro workers who came to the plant hospital told her they distrust the unions because the rank and file don't want to let them in. Plus, Henry Ford was good to them. Ford was the first auto maker to hire Negro workers—even if he put them in the most dangerous jobs.

Eva says, "Are you a reporter?"

The man with the camera says, "Free-lance photographer. Hal."

"Eva."

They shake hands.

"Eva, this is amazing. It's historic! I want to get as many photos as I can."

A tussle breaks out down the picket line as more men form lines of strikers around the plant. Hal turns to her, says, "Gotta catch this. Stay safe!"

"You, too."

He's off, taking in the action through his camera viewfinder.

Eva doesn't have her notebook with her. She takes out a pencil and a folded sheet of paper. She starts making notes.

He's right; they're present at history in the making.

She looks around. She walks by the strikers, several rows deep and high-spirited.

And what is she supposed to do?

She won't cross the picket line. She feels like jumping in and grabbing a sign and walking in solidarity with the men. Solidarity with her father.

The mood is festive. The men have been waiting for this—a reason to strike, to push things as far as they will go until Ford will have no choice but to negotiate.

"There you are!"

Nadine, camphor smell and all. She yells into Eva's ear. "We have to go inside."

"No! I'm not going to cross the picket line."

"I don't want to, either," Nadine shouts, "but we have to."

She holds up two cards. "We got passes from the union to get through the line. We're necessary workers. The union made a deal for necessary workers to go in."

"Why am I necessary? I'm just a secretary."

"No, you work at the plant hospital. We have to stay open for the maintenance men."

"What maintenance men?"

"The union's letting maintenance men stay and keep the fires up in the foundry and the mills. If they're on the job, we have to be. Plus there are still men who haven't walked out. Come on."

Nadine drags Eva through the squad of Dearborn police who are protecting the entrance to the gate.

"But I don't want to," Eva protests as Nadine pulls her inside the gate and across to the building where they work.

The men on the picket line jeer at them.

Eva wonders what her father would say if he saw her now.

11

CLARENCE BROWN

[Tuesday, April 1, 1941]

The call comes through on his radio car: "Shooting at the Rexall on Hastings."

Clarence knows the pharmacist, an older Jewish man named Sol Weintraub. He's owned the store for years, since back when Black Bottom was a predominantly Jewish neighborhood. He has a reputation in this community for fairness. He treats his customers with respect.

Clarence has had dealings with him in the past; once ten or so years back a guy was stealing cough syrup with codeine from Weintraub and the other druggists in Paradise Valley.

It turned out the thief was stealing cough syrup for his son who had pneumonia. "If he had just told me," Sol said back then, "I would have given it to him for free."

Clarence finds a chaotic scene outside the Rexall. A group of lookie-loos has gathered outside to see what's happening. One older woman spots Clarence, says, "Mr. Clarence, what's going on?"

"I'm about to find out."

Inside the store, Sol is lying on the floor, his back against a counter. He has been shot through the foot and grimaces in pain. His clerk, Selma, bleeds from a cut on her forehead.

A neighborhood boy who works at the store stands off to the side, eyes wide in fear.

"Did you call an ambulance?" Clarence asks Selma. She is too upset to answer. Clarence points to the boy. "You," he says, "call an ambulance. Right now." Clarence looks at Sol's foot. It's soaked in blood. "Then get me a clean towel," he tells the boy.

The boy jumps to the phone behind the front counter.

Clarence kneels beside the pharmacist. "Sol," he says, putting a hand on the man's shoulder, "you're going to be all right."

Weintraub nods. He pats Clarence's arm. Sol's round bald head and white mustache are damp with sweat.

Clarence says, "The boy's calling for an ambulance. What happened?"

"He came in waving his gun around. Then he hit Selma over the head and came right behind the counter. Said he wanted all the money in the till."

"Sol, you could have been killed!" Selma cries.

The stock boy comes over with a towel. "Thank you," Sol says.

Clarence gently wraps Sol's foot. Says, "This'll do until the ambulance gets here. Are you comfortable?"

"I make a good living," Sol jokes.

"A regular comedian," Selma says.

Sol came to America from Germany after the Great War. Not much scares him.

Sol sighs, says, "Listen, I told the punk I'm not giving up my money for any *putz* with a gun. Then I pushed him away from the pharmacy counter. Then he shot me and ran off."

"That was a pretty dumb thing to do," Clarence says.

"You think I'm gonna let a punk like him push me around?"

"Did you know him?" Clarence asks.

"Of course," Sol says. "He comes in every week. Tries to cadge money off me."

"Who was it?"

"Darron Cummings. Goddamn rat bastard."

Darron Cummings had a long history with the police as a juvenile. Clarence tried many times to get him involved with his baseball league, but Darron had no use for it. Now over eighteen, he's started getting into serious trouble.

Clarence waits for the ambulance, then takes off after Darron.

The young man lives on St. Antoine. Clarence has picked him up there at least a half dozen times. Shoplifting, robbery, assault . . . the crimes increasing in violence as Darron has grown older.

Darron stands by the steps outside his house, a rickety wooden two-family. Clarence smells the skunky odor of reefer as he walks up to Darron's porch.

Darron says, "Hey, Mr. Clarence. What's shaking?" Cocky, arrogant smile on his face. The shitbird doesn't even feel the need to lie low.

"We need to talk."

"Sure thing, Mr. Clarence. Always willing to help the police."

Just as Clarence knows Darron, Darron knows Clarence. He knows Clarence is a big, aging, out of shape man who no longer chases down the villains.

So Darron snuffs out the reefer on the wooden steps of the porch. He pockets it and with a grin takes off running down St. Antoine.

Clarence watches him go. Hears his laughter in the wind. No way will the big clumsy man catch the young thief. I'll get you sooner or later, Clarence silently promises the running man.

Clarence gets back in his car. On the way to Darron's, he passed the house where he found the dead infant. 975 Beaubien.

He heads there now.

Clarence parks outside the building. He never did reach everyone in his canvas the other day. He gets out of the car, straightens the metal plates under his coat, and trudges up the front stairs. He climbs to the top floor and works his way down.

This time he gets to speak with people who weren't there when he found the baby. But—no surprise—nobody saw anything. He doesn't tell them the baby was white, but asks: any young people live here? (Just people's little kids.) Any women been pregnant lately? (No.) Anybody heard a baby crying? (Nobody knows for sure . . . suddenly everyone in the building is deaf and blind.)

Clarence is used to being stonewalled, but not usually to such an extent as this. People in Black Bottom and Paradise Valley know him. They know he's one of them, even though he's a police detective. They know they can always rely on him to break down—or at least mitigate—the long-standing barrier between Detroit police and the Negro community.

While people may make a show of resisting his questions, usually a witness will come forward with the information he needs because they trust he's on their side. Unlike the rest of the force.

But not now. The residents of this building claim they saw, heard, and know nothing about the existence of a dead baby in their midst.

Clarence begins a canvas of the buildings nearby. He has little hope of learning anything.

Again he is surprised.

In the tenement across the street, one of the residents says she was getting ready to leave for work on Friday when she saw a white man go around the back of 975.

He may, or may not, have been carrying a little bundle; she couldn't be sure.

"Usually don't see no white men around here, unless it's the police or workmen. He didn't look like either one to me."

"What did he look like?"

"I only knew he was white because I saw his face when he was coming out," the woman says. "I was leaving when I saw him going in. I realized I forgot my lunch, so I went back upstairs to fetch it and when I came outside there he was, coming out from around the back of the building."

"Did he have the little bundle with him when he came out?"

"No sir, Mr. Clarence. He didn't have nothing. I'm sure of it."

"You were going to tell me what he looked like," Clarence prompts.

"He was tall. And had a hat on."

"What kind of hat?"

"A fedora, like you wear. He also had a big grey coat on. Look like it was too warm for the season."

"Which direction did he come from?"

She points up Beaubien. North. "Came from there, went back the same way."

"Would you recognize him if you saw him again?"

She purses her lips. "I was in a hurry . . . probably not."

"That's fine." Clarence gives her his business card. "Call me if you think of anything else?"

"I surely will, Mr. Clarence."

"I appreciate it. Just one more question. Did it look like he knew where he was going?"

"Not sure what you mean."

"What I mean is, did it look like he was headed straight for that building across the street? Or did it seem like he just decided to go inside any random building?"

"I wasn't studying the man. It's just luck I happened to see him at all."

Clarence thanks her, and continues with his canvas.

Nobody else he talks to saw, heard, or knows anything.

Nobody remembers seeing a man going into 975 carrying a little bundle that could have been a baby.

12

DENNY RANKIN

[Tuesday, April 1, 1941]

He double-parks his unmarked down the block from the Fox Theatre. It's as close as he can get; an ambulance and a half-dozen police units block traffic.

The scene is at Woodward Avenue and Vernor Street in downtown Detroit.

A half-dozen harness bulls huddle around a figure on his back on the cold sidewalk. Two ambulance attendants tend to the injury on the right side of his chest. The guy's sucking air like crazy.

Denny looks to one of the attendants. "What's going on?"

"We got to get this jamoke to the hospital," the attendant says. His name, *Wally*, is embroidered on his jacket. "He's fading fast. They told me to wait for you." Wally points his chin at the coppers.

"All right," Denny says, "I'm here. Get going."

The two attendants roll a gurney next to the man on the ground and lift him onto it.

Denny turns to the cops. "What happened?"

One cop says, "Guy in the squad car over there? Goes nuts, starts shooting at civilians. This poor sap was in the wrong place at the wrong time and caught one."

"Why am I here? Dispatch said this was a robbery."

Denny is a detective in the Robbery Division. Nothing here says robbery. Dietrich will be pissed enough he's here and not giving all his time to the Mueller break-in. But nobody else was around when the call came through.

"Must have got it jumbled," the cop says. "This ain't no robbery."

Denny turns toward the squad car where the shooter sits. "Anybody know him?"

The bluesuits stamp their feet. Nobody looks at Denny. A cold wind sweeping off the river all the way up from the foot of Woodward makes him shiver.

"Somebody tell me something, for Chrissake."

"He's one of us," one of the cops says.

"A copper?"

They all nod.

"Name's Ostrowski," the cop says. "Patrolman. Works the Fifth."

Denny doesn't know the name. But the Fifth Precinct station, McClellan and Amity Streets, is way the hell on the east side.

"What was he doing over here?" Denny asks.

Nobody has an answer.

"Anybody else hit?" Denny asks.

They shake their heads. "Good thing he was a lousy shot," one of the others says.

This gets a nervous laugh out of them.

Knuckleheads.

Denny heads for the call box on the corner. Gets through to Homicide. He tells them about the mixup. They tell him they came up short today, nobody's available. Asks if he can take it this one time as long as he's there. One of the Homicide dicks'll take it over soon as he's free.

Denny says sure.

He makes for the car where Ostrowski sits. He hopes one of these morons at least had the bright idea to take his gun away.

Denny nods to the bluesuit babysitting Ostrowski. Asks, "You get his weapon?"

The cop shakes his head.

"Did anybody?"

The cop shrugs.

Denny thinks: Jesus, Mary, and Joseph.

He leans into the car. The strong smell of booze mixes with Ostrowski's BO. Sure enough, he's a copper; he's sitting in the squad car in full uniform.

"Hey," Denny says.

Ostrowski looks up. His eyes are red, unfocused, drunken.

A true credit to the uniform.

"I'm Detective Sergeant Denny Rankin," Denny says. "They tell me you shot a civilian."

Ostrowski says nothing.

The copper behind him says, "He shot at several civilians. Missed them all, except for the guy he plugged."

He really is a lousy shot, Denny thinks.

A good lesson about shooting while drunk.

"Where's your service weapon, Officer Ostrowski?"

Ostrowski pulls it out of its holster. Hands it up to Denny.

Denny gives it to the babysitter cop. Says, "Find an evidence bag for this, will you?"

Denny turns to Ostrowski. "Can you tell me why you did this?"

Ostrowski puts his head in his hands and begins to weep.

Won't get anything more out of him now. Not until he sobers up.

Denny straightens. Slams the car door closed.

The cop comes back with Ostrowski's gun in an evidence bag. Denny takes it, writes "Ostrowski shooting, 12:17 p.m., 4/1/41" on the flap.

"Way I heard it," the cop says, "he came out of the Woodmont and just started shooting at people at random."

The Woodmont Bar and Grill, a few blocks south on Woodward. Across from the State Theatre.

"He said he was drinking there," the cop adds.

"He was drinking in a bar during the day? In uniform?"

"That's what he said."

Denny sighs. "All right," he says, "take him in. Throw him in a cell and let him sober up."

"We going to charge him?"

"No, we're going to give him a medal for being so brave and honest. Of course we're going to fucking charge him."

"Jesus, just asking," the bluesuit mumbles.

Back across the street, the victim is gone from the sidewalk. I didn't even get his name, Rankin thinks. Turns to one of the cops who's still there. "What's the guy's name, the vic?"

"Edgar Vanarian," the bluesuit says.

"Any witnesses?"

"Yessir. We interviewed them."

"What's their story?"

The cop tells him. The stories line up with what the other cops said.

Denny says, "Did it seem like Ostrowski knew Vanarian?"

"Don't seem like it. Guy's a dishwasher in here." He throws a thumb over his shoulder at the diner they're standing in front of. The Mayflower Café.

"Who took the report?"

"Me," the cop says.

Sullivan on his name badge.

"Get it to me before you clock out tonight, yeah?"

"Yessir."

Sullivan gets in his squad car to travel back to the precinct house.

Denny stays and examines the scene. There are chips in the brick of the walls around where Edgar Vanarian fell. Likely from Ostrowski's shots. One of the window panes in the diner has a piece of cardboard taped over it.

The joint's dark inside. The front door's locked. According to the hours on the door, they should be open. They must have closed up after this all happened.

Denny looks over the scene for a few minutes longer, then walks across Woodward and down to the Woodmont. It's an art moderne building on the corner of Woodward and Montcalm. Enameled beige steel panels on the outside wall. A red door at the bottom of a round tower.

Across Woodward, the State Theatre attraction board advertises *Love Thy Neighbor* with Jack Benny and Fred Allen, and *Texas Rangers Ride Again* with John Howard and Ellen Drew.

Inside the Woodmont is smoky and dark. The barkeep gives him the fisheye. Denny flashes his buzzer. Asks, "Was a uniformed cop in here a little while ago?"

The barkeep's no mental giant. Denny can see his dull eyes trying to figure out what's the right answer. Whether Denny wants the cop to be in here, or doesn't want the cop in here.

"This isn't a test, pal," Denny says. "Yes or no. Was he in here?"

"What did he do?"

"The nuns teach you never answer a question with a question?"

"Cops're in here most days."

"Yeah," Denny says, testy now, "I'm talking about today. Little while ago. Keep up, will you?"

The barkeep takes a swipe at the bar with a dirty towel, like he's thinking about it. It's an effort.

"Big guy," Denny prompts, "in uniform, whiffle cut hairdo?"

"Yeah, he was in."

"How long was he here?"

"Came in to drink his breakfast and then stayed, knocking 'em back. Sitting over by the window. Left about an hour ago."

"Pretty plastered when he left, was he?"

"Couldn't walk a straight line."

"How'd he seem? He look angry, upset about anything?"

"Upset? Oh brother," the barkeep says, "he looked like the world just took a shit on his pet rabbit."

"He leave by himself?"

"Yep. One minute he was there, next he jumped up and ran out. Would have been nice if he'd paid his bill. Probably thought it was all on the arm, just like everything else is with you guys."

When he gets back to the station house, Denny finds Sullivan's arrest report on Ostrowski.

Sullivan's idea of the English language makes the going rough, but he puzzles through it.

The report makes it seem like the shooting was entirely random.

As near as Denny can make out, nothing looks any different from what it seems: the drunken misadventure of a policeman who's a disaster in uniform and who will soon be an ex-copper.

Denny has Ostrowski brought up from Holding and put in a sweat box. Denny examines him from the observation room. Ostrowski sits the same way he did in the squad car, with his head down.

He picks his head up when Denny enters the box. Denny sits across from him. The drunk's bleary eyes gaze back at him.

"Remember me?" Denny says. "Detective Sergeant Rankin?"

Ostrowski nods.

"Thaddeus," Denny says. "What do your friends call you?"

"Ted."

"Okay, Ted. You're here because you shot a man named Edgar

Vanarian. Do you know him?"

"No."

"Want to tell me why you shot him?"

"I dunno."

"You remember going to the Woodmont Bar?"

"Yeah."

"Remember getting shit-faced? While on duty?"

"Yeah."

"Remember coming out and shooting up the street?"

Ted lowers his head. Nods.

"But you don't remember why."

"I guess I was drunk."

"You're an officer of the law, Ted. Not only are you not supposed to be drunk on duty in the middle of the day, but you're supposed to protect the citizens, not shoot at them. Sort of a basic difference in approach."

Ted says nothing.

"Help me here, okay? I'm trying to understand why you shot up the street."

"I was angry, I guess."

"Angry about what? You have a fight with somebody?"

Ted doesn't reply.

"Nothing else to say?" Denny asks.

Ted says nothing.

"Alright. You know the drill," Denny says. "You'll spend the night in the cells and be arraigned in the morning. Anybody you want me to call? Wife, maybe? Friend on the force?"

The unhappy man murmurs, "No."

Denny leaves him with, "Better hope the guy you shot doesn't die."

Ted stays mum.

13

EVA SZABÓ

[Tuesday, April 1, 1941]

The day turns eerily quiet in the hospital. A madhouse rages outside the gates: lines of strikers picketing, cars in the street five and six deep, Dearborn cops milling around all the gates, reporters prowling, seeing what they can dig up.

At the hospital, the radio news plays all day. Harry Bennett comes on and says 7,000-8,000 men have launched a sit-down strike led by Communist terrorists trying to sabotage the nation's defense program.

Union leaders are also interviewed and say Bennett's lying. There are no sit-down strikes anywhere in the plant (sit-down strikes are prohibited by the Supreme Court), and hardly any defense work is currently done at the Ford Rouge Plant.

A few maintenance men come in with burns from the fires they are supposed to keep up. Several Negroes come in with injuries from fights with strikers. They're the only workers who have not walked out. Nadine hates to deal with them and gives them as little attention as she can get away with. Eva, on the other hand, is happy to talk with them. She asks why they're still working.

They tell her they don't trust unions. Their pastors tell them Henry Ford is the only chance they'll have for a fair shake, so they need to stay loyal to him. Eva can tell the men are not totally committed to either the union or to Henry Ford. They're in a tough place.

In the lulls during the day, she looks in the files for the two beaten men who came in yesterday. She took their names and work stations, but she wants their addresses.

Jack and William Fisk. They share an address, on Michigan Avenue in Dearborn.

Nadine turned them away for not having job-related injuries. Eva wants to find out if their injuries are related to anti-union activity.

At the end of her shift, Eva makes her way through the strikers and walks out to Wyoming. Takes the streetcar up to Michigan. She transfers to the Michigan Avenue bus line. Walks up to find the men's address.

It's a rooming house near Oakman Street. They live behind a rail line that shuttles materials into the plant.

The downstairs door to the old frame building is unlocked. She steps inside and meets the stomach-turning odor of old cabbage. There are no names on the mailboxes in the foyer, just apartment numbers.

She finds them in the rear of the third floor. She recognizes the one who opens the door. She can't remember which he is, Jack or William.

She introduces herself, says, "I saw you yesterday at the hospital at the plant."

The man's injuries have bloomed yellow and purple. His split lip is swollen and crusted over.

He nods.

"Are you Jack Fisk?" she asks.

"Billy."

"Oh, Billy, sorry. Remember me from the hospital?"

He shakes his head.

"I checked you in."

He shrugs.

"How are you feeling?"

Billy stares at her. His look says *How do you think I feel?*

She says, "Can I come in and talk to you for a few minutes?"

"What about?"

"I just want to ask you about what happened."

"I told the other nurse what happened." Nadine, he means. "Me and my brother, we had an argument with these guys. They beat the crap out of us."

"I just want to ask you about it, if you have a minute."

"What else can I say? I got nothin' more to tell you."

Billy closes the door in her face.

She sticks her foot in the opening. Says, "Will Jack talk to me?"

He kicks her foot out of the doorway and closes the door. She waits, hoping he will ask Jack. She waits for another minute. She hears voices, can't distinguish words.

She gives up, starts back downstairs.

The door opens.

"You want to know what happened?" says the other man. This must be Jack. If anything, he got the worst of it. His arm is wrapped in a cast and hangs in a sling around his neck. Gauze packs his nose. He lost his two front teeth.

"I do," she says.

"What for?"

"If we know what happened," she says, climbing back up the stairs, "maybe we can prevent it next time."

Jack snorts. "You believe that, I got a bridge in New York to sell you."

Still, he opens the door wider. "Come in."

The apartment is small and spotless, neater than she would have expected from two male auto workers. One big room: living room, dining room, kitchen. Doors leading off from the kitchen: their bedrooms, maybe the toilet.

Sparse furnishings: a sofa, two easy chairs, a dining room table and four bridge chairs, a radio on a small stand beside the sofa.

Jack drops onto an easy chair with a grunt. "Want anything?" he asks. "Billy's just making coffee."

"I wouldn't mind a cup," Eva says.

To Billy in the kitchen, Jack says, "Hey. Bring the lady a cup, too." Jack's voice is deep and full, like a trombone.

Billy throws her the malocchio but gets another cup out of a cupboard.

In a few minutes Billy limps back with two cups.

"You guys doing okay?" she asks.

"Do we look okay?" Billy sneers.

"No," she admits.

Billy looms.

"Just going to stand there and look ugly?" Jack says.

Billy scowls. He takes the hint, turns and goes through one of the doors off the kitchen. Slams it behind him. The sound echoes off the plaster walls like the crack of a gunshot.

Jack holds his cup awkwardly, with his good hand. He blows across the mouth, takes a noisy slurp. "He's a hothead from way back. Look," he says, "I know you're not here to find out about us. What do you want?"

She lowers her voice. "I want to know who did this to you."

"What's it to you?"

"I know there are anti-union thugs in the plant," she says. "Was it them?"

"Kiddo," Jack says, "what makes you think I'd tell you?"

She looks at Jack more closely. At first when he came into the hospital at the plant, she thought he was close to her age. As she examines him, she sees he's older, maybe in his forties, with his grizzled, bruised face.

"You can trust me," she says.

"Yeah? You know what I think? I think you're one of those company spies."

His certainty shakes her.

He's right—she is a spy, though not for the side he thinks.

He takes another slurp of coffee. She takes one, too, but quieter. The coffee tastes awful. Bitter and strong. It leaves an oily aftertaste. She sets the cup down on the table between them.

"I hate to disappoint you," Jack says, "but it wasn't company spies who did this."

"Who was it?"

"You ever gambled?"

"No."

"I do. A lot. Know where I do most of my gambling?" She shakes her head. He says, "The plant."

"The Rouge? During working hours?"

"Why's that so hard to believe?"

She finds it impossible to believe the men have time to gamble when they aren't even supposed to talk to each other. Ford laid down the law through his henchman Harry Bennett. They don't want the workers plotting with each other about a union on company time.

But they have time for gambling?

"You don't know because you're not on the factory floor," Jack says. "There's a huge gambling racket there. Huge."

"What kind of gambling? How can you play dice and cards during working hours?"

"Nah. There's people throughout the plant who take bets on horseraces, baseball games, football games, hockey games, the numbers, policy handbooks . . . you name it. If you come up short with any of these mugs, you pay the piper."

He holds up his arm. "Me and Billy, we owed this guy a lot of dough."

"Who runs it?"

"The Sicilians. You know the Sicilian mob in town? Joe Zerilli? Sam Lucido? Ever hear either of those names?"

"No."

"Oh toots. You live such a sheltered life."

"Does Ford know about this?"

"Know about it? He's *in* on it. Those guys, Zerilli and Lucido? Ford hobnobs with them. They got his permission to do it. Day to day, Harry Bennett runs things. You heard of him, at least?"

"Sure."

"He gets a cut of every dollar suckers like us bet."

"Are you serious?"

"As a heart attack. Nothing happens in there unless Harry Bennett knows about it and gives it his okay. Especially if it lines his pockets. He's a regular Jew that way. Tell you another thing," he says, getting warmed up to it. "Those union spies you're asking me about? They're mobbed up, too. Henry Ford pays the mob to infiltrate the factory to watch for any union activity.

"And the cops in Dearborn? Half of them are ex-Service Department goons. Bennett pressures Dearborn to hire them so they'll look the other way about policy books and prostitution around the plant. And you know why? So Bennett can get his cut of the proceeds."

"How do you know this?"

"You learn those things fast. And when you get behind in payments like me and Billy did, you figure it out extra fast."

"You have a good job, don't you? Why the gambling?"

"I wasn't always at Ford's. I used to work high steel in New York City. Then the Depression came and boom, all the building stopped and I couldn't find work no more. Meanwhile, our mother died and left Billy alone back here. I moved back to Detroit to take care of him. We were unemployed for a long time, but with the war coming, there's more factory work than there used to be. Here we are."

Billy throws the bedroom door open. He comes limping out from his room. He must have been eavesdropping. Says, "Jackie, Jesus Christ, what are you telling her?"

"Nothing but the truth, little brother."

Billy gets panicky. "No, no," he says to Eva, "you can't say nothing about this. Understand?"

Jack tells Eva, "He don't want word to get back to the Sicilians. Don't want them to think we're squealers. Right, Billy?"

"*I'm* not."

Billy hobbles toward Eva. Grips her hard by the arm. "But you I dunno about. So it's time for you to take a bunk."

Billy pulls Eva to her feet and gives her the bum's rush to the door as best he can with his injuries.

"Don't come back," Billy says. "And don't you repeat nothing you heard here, see?"

His sudden violence scares her. "But I can help you—"

"No! Don't you get me?"

He shakes her hard. Her teeth clack and her head wobbles.

Eva says she does.

14

CLARENCE BROWN

[Tuesday, April 1, 1941]

S takeout.

He sits in his car down St. Antoine from Darron's building. He settles in to wait. He heard rumors of strike activity at the Ford plant but nobody knows anything for sure.

He has a bottle of Coca-Cola with him. He hopes his bladder holds out.

It doesn't.

After an hour of waiting, Clarence has to urinate like a racehorse. A grocery, Washington's, is two doors down from Darron's on the corner of St. Antoine and Brewster. Clarence rushes in.

The grocer, Sidney Washington, knows him (everybody knows Mr. Clarence). He lets Clarence use his bathroom.

Clarence comes back outside. He stands in front of a hand-lettered sign on the grocery window:

Father Divine's Teachings
New Day
5¢

He looks up and down the street. Here comes Darron, a block away with his rolling diddy-bop pimp walk.

Clarence has an idea. He ducks back into the store.

He says to Washington, "Ask you a big favor?"

"Anything for you, Mr. Clarence."

"You know Darron Cummings? Lives two doors down?"

"Know him? I throw him out my store every other week for shoplifting."

"He's coming this way. Could you go out there and ask him to come in here for a second? Tell him you got a present for him."

"I got a present for him, all right. The back of my hand." He turns to his assistant. "Ernest, watch the counter."

Ernest nods and gives Clarence a broad smile. He is a handsome, dark-skinned young man. Sidney has taken him under his wing to teach him the business.

Washington goes out onto the sidewalk. Clarence hangs back inside the store. He hears Washington stop Darron, tell him, "Darron, come inside for a minute, will you? Got something for you."

Darron says, "Why, sure."

He follows Washington inside. Clarence waits beside the door. Darron gets half-way in the store and Clarence grabs him from behind.

Darron shouts.

Clarence has him cuffed behind his back in an instant.

"Aw, man," Darron cries.

"You're under arrest, son."

"I ain't done nothing!"

"The druggist you shot in the foot may disagree."

Clarence manhandles him out the door.

Darron turns back to the grocer. Sneers, says, "You fucker! I'll get you for this!"

Clarence wrestles Darron out of his car and into the sally port at the Hunt Street Station. Leaves him for processing with the duty sergeant and goes to fill out his arrest paperwork. If he's not arraigned later, Darron will be held overnight and arraigned in Recorders' Court in the morning.

The station isn't far from the Wayne County Medical Examiner at the corner of Lafayette and Brush. Clarence arrives at the Egyptian-style entrance to the building and heads toward the office. The first floor holds the offices and the crypt. The second floor has courtrooms where the inquests are held.

The coroner isn't in, but his assistant is. Clarence hasn't had many occasions to visit the morgue so he doesn't know the assistant coroner. He's a white man named Herman Weiskopf. He looks twelve, with slicked-back black hair and round rimless glasses.

Clarence flashes his buzzer. This may be a wild-goose chase. Still, he has to try.

"Was there a baby brought in yesterday," he asks Weiskopf. "Newborn, male, not more than a few days old."

Weiskopf says, "We get infants in here every day. If there's one thing we know how to do in this town, it's kill children."

"This would have been a white child."

"You might think that narrows it down," Weiskopf says, "but you would be mistaken. You'll have to be more specific."

"This child was found on Beaubien Street in Black Bottom. Wrapped in a blanket."

"A white baby in Black Bottom?"

"Uh-huh."

"That's new. You found him?"

"I did."

"Got a name?"

"No."

Weiskopf purses his lips. "Let me check our census."

He runs his finger down the lines on a blackboard on the wall behind his desk. Two dozen Baby Boy Does are listed. Roughly half are identified as White.

Weiskopf checks the names on the board against a list on his clipboard. Says, "Hmm."

Then he says, "Well, detective, I don't see any of them picked up on Beaubien. We don't usually get white children from around there. Two infants were picked up on John R. That's a block over. Maybe one of those?"

"Can I take a look?"

"Come with me."

Weiskopf leads Clarence back toward the crypt. In a long hallway lined on both sides with white-tiled drawers, Weiskopf says, "Space for 186 bodies," as though he is personally proud of this fact.

He pauses before drawers labeled B52 and B53.

He unlatches the door to B52. Pulls the drawer open. A small figure is dwarfed in a sheet. Weiskopf uncovers the body.

The child is white, but older than the baby he found yesterday. The child is also female.

"This child's a girl," Clarence points out. "I'm looking for a male."

Weiskopf slides the drawer closed and opens B53. On the table in the drawer rests another child, identical to the girl in B52.

"Another girl," Clarence points out.

"They're twins, these two. Picked up together. Found abandoned in a dumpster."

"Can I see what other babies you have here?"

"None of them were brought in yesterday, so . . ."

Clarence says nothing. Weiskopf opens seven more drawers where white infants and young children are laid out under sheets. None of them match the baby he held in his arms.

They lie here, unclaimed children, white or black or brown, abandoned and either murdered or dead from natural causes. They are waiting to be autopsied or, more likely, disposed of.

Jesus, Clarence thinks; all these children.

He leaves with Weiskopf's words echoing in his head: *If there's one thing we know how to do in this town, it's kill children.*

15

DENNY RANKIN

[Tuesday, April 1, 1941]

At the station, he tracks down the man charged in the third recent break-in he found when he was searching for crimes similar to the Mueller job. The guy has a strong alibi—he just got out of the pokey after a week inside.

Only one squad car is left on the Muellers' street in Palmer Woods. Denny sees two cops down at the end of the block. They're finishing up the canvas.

Denny brings his fingerprinting kit and rings the Muellers' doorbell. Shortly a white woman opens the door. She wears a maid's uniform, white blouse and skirt with a black apron. She has a wide face and probing eyes.

"Yah?"

You know you're hot stuff when you have a white maid, Denny thinks.

He flashes his buzzer, introduces himself. Says, "Is Mr. or Mrs. Mueller here?"

"No."

"How about the kids?"

"What you say you want with them?"

"I didn't," Denny says, and waits.

"Come in," she relents and steps aside. He walks into the foyer.

"Sorry," he says, "you are?"

"Easter."

"Pleased to meet you. You the one who called the police about the break-in?"

"Yah."

"Good work."

This does not soften her attitude. "Excuse please."

She turns and climbs the stairway to the second floor. He can hear muffled screaming, a high female voice skittering toward the edge of hysteria. A lower male voice trying to calm her down.

Then Easter's murmured voice.

She comes down the stairs to the foyer. "They prefer not to talk with you."

"I'm not asking," Denny says. "I'm telling you I need to speak with them. We can do it down here or I can go up and talk to them there. Or they can come down to the station. Their choice."

She gives him a foul look. Trudges back upstairs.

She returns with a young man. Skinny, maybe in his early twenties, sandy hair combed back. Denny smells his pomade, a sickly gardenia scent. The kid has on black slacks and a dark brown shirt with epaulets.

The only thing missing is the swastika armband.

He pauses half-way down. "What do you want?"

Denny shows his badge. "Heinz Mueller?"

The kid nods.

"I want to talk to you about what happened here yesterday. I'll want to talk to your sister, too."

"I'll talk to you, but my sister? Not going to happen."

"Why not?"

"She's in bed. She's sick. She can't come down. She doesn't want to talk to you."

"What's the matter with her?"

"Why? You a doctor *and* a copper?"

Denny beckons him down the stairs. "Come on down, Heinz."

Heinz waves Denny away. Turns to go back upstairs.

Denny leaps the three steps between himself and the twerp and drags him down by the back of his brown shirt.

The kid struggles but Denny holds him tight. Denny takes him into the sitting room and throws him into a chair.

"Do you know who my father is?" Heinz says.

"Don't you? Here's what's going to happen," Denny says. "The first thing I'm going to do is take your fingerprints so we can eliminate you from the investigation. Then I'm going to ask you a few questions and you're going to answer me. And if that's not okay with you, we can go down to the station and your father can come pick you up from there."

Heinz pouts but nods okay.

"Good fella," Denny says.

He starts taking a set of Heinz's prints. While he's working, he asks the young man, "Where were you when your house was broken into?"

"Out."

"Where?"

"At my friend's."

"Which is where?"

"On Bewick in Detroit. I stayed there the night before."

Denny knows the street. It's on the city's east side.

"When did you get home?"

"In the afternoon."

"What's your friend's name?"

"Bert."

"Last name?"

"Vogelmann."

"Did you have any idea the break-in was going to happen?"

"How would I?"

Denny stares at him. "That's not a no."

Heinz glares back. "No. Satisfied?"

Denny gives him a cloth to wipe the ink off his fingers. "What about your sister?"

"What about her?"

"Where was she yesterday morning?"

"Probably upstairs in her room. She's always in her room."

"Why don't we go up and ask her? I'll need her prints, too."

"I told you," Heinz says, "she's sick."

Denny hears the front door open and close.

Frieda Mueller appears in the doorway to the sitting room in a fancy hat and black lambs-wool coat. "Heinz," she says, "what's going on here?"

"Ma!" Heinz jumps up and runs to his mother. She puts a protective arm around him.

She asks Denny, "What are you doing here?"

"I'm trying to talk to your children about the break-in. As I told your husband I would."

"I told him Wanda's too sick to talk," the kid puts in.

"Do you have a warrant to be here?" Frieda demands of Denny.

"I don't need a warrant to speak with your son."

"Which stops this instant. And I'll ask you to leave my house. And not to return without my attorney present."

"Mrs. Mueller," Denny says, "it's almost like you don't want to know who broke into your home."

"I am not Mrs. Mueller. I am Countess Frieda von Schonburg-Glauchau. Address me properly, if you don't mind."

Denny sighs. He packs up his fingerprint kit.

The Countess shepherds him out to the foyer. Denny spies a young woman standing on the landing at the top of the stairway. She wears a powder blue silk robe. Her hair is dark and splayed across her face, which is waxen with no makeup.

"Hello," the young woman says. Breathless voice. "I heard you want to talk to me?"

"Wanda," the Countess says, "go back upstairs. Now."

Wanda starts down the stairs, one step at a time, like a model. All the time her eyes are on Denny. She gives him a dreamy look and wears a small, shy smile. "Here I am," she says, like a seductress. She looks drugged.

"Get back upstairs! I won't tell you again."

Wanda keeps coming down. She parts her robe to give Denny a view of her cleavage. She has no bra on, just the robe over a low-cut translucent nightgown. She locks eyes with him the whole time.

Her eyes are dreamy pinpoints. Drugged eyes.

The Countess turns to her son. "What's the matter with you?" she barks. "Take her back upstairs!"

Heinz hops to and intercepts his sister.

Who lets herself be guided back up the steps, but turns to give Denny a lingering look.

"My daughter," the Countess says, "has been sick."

"That's what your son said."

Easter the maid waits by the front door. The Countess gives her a nod and Easter opens the door for Denny to exit this nuthouse.

"Remember," the Countess says. "Never speak to any member of my family again without our attorney present."

Denny leaves the house with relief.

In his car, he opens the flask he keeps in his suitcoat and takes a hit. The whiskey warms him going down.

For the victim of a crime, Frieda Mueller—the Countess von Whatchamacallit—has no interest in helping the police solve it. On one hand, Denny has her and her husband obstructing him, and on the other hand he has Dwight Dietrich breathing down his neck to close it.

Plus the two delightful Mueller spawn.

The sun breaks through for a moment, then the clouds block it out again.

He takes another hit off his flask.

He thinks about another young woman with problems, Charlotte Wheaton.

She is sixteen and an only child. Phil asked for Denny's help. Denny needs to find out when she was last seen, and who she was with. Phil wouldn't know; he suspects Lena's closer to her daughter. Denny will need another conversation with her.

The Wheaton family—and the distance between Phil and the two women he lives with—gets him thinking about the gaps in his own life. Especially the chasms between himself and his wife and the two girls.

His life, quickly receding into his rear-view mirror.

He starts up. Heads north on Woodward.

He shouldn't do this, he knows.

Tells himself not to.

He does it anyway.

He feels the need to reduce the distance between himself and his family . . . in miles, if not in emotional proximity.

He goes west on Seven Mile Road. Takes a left on Roselawn, at the University of Detroit high school. Parks across the street from an all-brick two-story colonial in the first block. White shutters, curving front walk. In the gathering dusk, a gas light flickers yellow and blue in a globe on the front lawn.

Denny remembers when he put this light in. Hazel's brother helped him because he knew how to run a gas line from the basement and Denny didn't. Through the bay window he sees into the dining room. Both windows in the second floor are lit. The one on the right is the bathroom. The one on the left used to be their bedroom. Now it's just Hazel's.

Denny imagines the girls are in their rooms, playing before dinner. Alice and Rosemary go to Bagley Elementary School, straight up Roselawn at Curtis. Hazel and Denny bought this house after they were married because it was close to the school, which had a good reputation.

Before she threw him out, Hazel told Denny she was considering sending the girls to Gesu Catholic School up on Six Mile, then said she wanted to move. Jews were starting to move into the neighborhood from down around the 12th Street area—one now lived right across the street, a judge—and Hazel said it was just a matter of time before the entire neighborhood was filled with them. "You know how these people are," she said. The Rankins weren't Catholic, but she said she'd rather have her kids go to school with Catholics than Jews.

He knew lots of Jewish kids when he went to Central High School and they never bothered him. But he chose not to argue with her.

He watches the light go out in the upstairs bathroom and another light go on in the house—the girls' bedroom.

He feels unbearably sad, like a peeping Tom, snooping from outside his own life.

Denny Rankin, pariah.

Nobody wants him around.

He's a bad influence.

In retrospect, maybe confessing to Hazel about his involvement in the graft scheme was not the best course of action.

He misses the girls, though they don't miss him. He misses his wife, and doubts if she misses him, either.

Denny misses the stable, steady life he had with Hazel and the girls in this house in the quiet northwest Detroit neighborhood. Denny hopes this separation is only temporary; in his heart, he knows it's the beginning of the end for his family life.

He doesn't want to go to the door and listen to Hazel rail against him. Not after what he just lived through at the Muellers' house. He wants only to sit in his car and mourn the life he once had.

When he gets tired of feeling bad for himself, he starts up the car. Before he can ease away from the curb, a car pulls into the driveway of his house. A man gets out. He wears a fedora and an overcoat against the chill of the coming evening.

He climbs the front stoop and rings the doorbell. Hazel opens the door immediately; she was waiting for him.

She beams when she sees him. Denny can't remember the last time she gave him such a smile.

She takes the guy's hat. As he turns to close the front door behind him, Denny sees his long face and bald head.

He recognizes Barnett Hoosier. He's Hazel's supervisor where she works as a sales clerk at the Montgomery Ward's on Grand River and Greenfield.

Bald Barnett, she used to call him.

Now, before the front door closes, Hazel throws her arms around him.

She welcomes Bald Barnett into Denny's former home.

Now that he thinks back, maybe Denny was the one who called him Bald Barnett, not Hazel . . .

Briarcliff Road. The middle-class Green Acres neighborhood in northwest Detroit.

He parks outside a modest colonial. Lights on in the living room and in one of the second-floor windows. The other window facing the street is dark.

A car pulls into the driveway next door. The home of the Powells, Herb and Kathy. The brake lights flash and Herb gets out of the car. He gives Denny a long, searching look.

Who are you and what are you doing in my neighborhood?

For a moment, Denny thinks Herb might come over and ask him point-blank. Instead Herb goes into his own house. The light over his door goes out and other lights come on inside.

In a few minutes, the door to 20121 opens and a figure appears wrapped in a cloth coat. Hurries down the front walk.

Hops into Denny's car.

She brings the smell of cigarettes and her perfume with her. He remembers her scent, the crisp, slightly metallic aroma of lavender.

"Jesus Christ," she says. "What are you doing here?"

Lulu Hopkins. Red hair escaping from the cloche she has jammed on her head. Still a beauty . . . finely chiseled features, straight nose and a chin like the prow of a boat.

"I don't know what I'm doing here," Denny says, truthfully. What he doesn't say is, he was just at his former house and now—as though to torture himself further with what he's lost—or never had, as the case may be—he has been drawn here as if by a magnetic force.

"I hope you don't hope to come inside," Lulu says. "My husband's home."

"I don't want to."

"I asked you never to come here. I don't want to see you. How can I say this any other way but louder?"

"I didn't come for you. I wanted to see Larry."

She sighs.

"I'm his father," he says. "I have a right to see my son."

"You can't see Larry, Denny. We've been through this and through this. Why don't you go to your own house and take care of your own family?"

He tries to think of how he can let her know he doesn't live there anymore.

She's way ahead of him. "Wait, she kicked you out. I'm right, aren't I?"

He admits it with a nod.

"And you thought, what, you'd peep in on my family for a while?"

Lulu always was spectacularly astute.

Long before he met his wife Hazel, he knew Lulu when she was a jazz pianist appearing at Baker's Keyboard Lounge on Livernois. With her long fingers, her skill at the keyboard, her flaming red hair, and the louche way she carried herself around the jazz club, she enthralled him.

He told her she should sing along with playing—her voice was deep and mellow, like honey flowing—but she took it for what it was, his way of flirting. They started seeing each other. He was still a patrolman; he would come in after his day shift, or before his night shift. When they could, he took her out for a late dinner.

Then they started sleeping together. She lived in a room on Third Avenue and they spent the occasional night together after their shifts.

Until she got pregnant.

Denny offered to marry her—wanted to marry her, in fact—but she refused. She didn't love him, she said. She didn't even like him that much. And she couldn't see herself as the wife of a cop.

When her son—*their* son— Larry was born, they knew right away there was a problem. His eyes were far apart, his face was flat. The doctor called him a mongoloid and told Lulu she shouldn't even take him home—the boy should spend his life in an institution. She refused to put him in one. She quit work at Baker's and took care of him at home with the help of her mother.

She let Denny see him, but only with her there. The boy was so loving—and so vulnerable—Denny cried every time he had to say goodbye. From the extra money he got from Sam Block, Denny paid her expenses every week.

Until she met the guy she did fall in love with. He sold Cadillacs. A square john if there ever was one. She married him and joined the square john world. She thought it would be okay if Larry kept seeing Denny, until her husband said no; Denny couldn't see him anymore; this was the condition of her new husband adopting the boy as his own. He wanted Denny out of Larry's life, and out of hers.

Denny complained, but it was no use.

Larry doesn't go to school. During the nice weather, Lulu's mother takes him outside for walks. He was late walking and doesn't speak.

Nobody knows Denny observes them, walking down the sidewalks of their subdivision, strolling through Sherwood Forest, the next neighborhood over.

Now Lulu sits next to him on the front seat, scrunched up as far away from him as she can get while still being in the same car.

She says, "What's wrong with you?"

He doesn't know. Like he said, he doesn't really want to see her. He misses Larry, but he knows there's no chance she will let him see the boy.

What he wants tonight is to be wanted by someone.

It's not going to happen here, even though this house—and its prospect of a happy family, part of which is his—lured him tonight.

"Go, Denny," she says. "And *don't* come here again."

She gets out of the car. Slams the door. Trots back up the curved walk to her house.

Denny sees the curtain twitch in the dining room.

Larry peeks out.

His round, broad face. His mother's flaming red hair. Such a beautiful boy. The sight of him breaks Denny's heart.

He probably doesn't even remember me, Denny thinks. He probably can't even see me.

He waves at his son.

Sweet Larry waves back until Lulu pulls him away from the window.

He takes the elevator to his room on the fifth floor of the Wolverine. He stands at his window. Twenty feet away, in another wall of rooms at the hotel, an old geezer stares back at him in one of the windows.

The geezer grins a gap-toothed smile at their shared misfortune and pulls the shade down.

Denny sits on the bed.

Puts his head in his hands.

Barnett Hoosier.

Is she serious?

Bald Barnett.

Have they been seeing each other this whole time? Did she start seeing him before or after she tossed Denny out?

Was the graft trial an excuse to get rid of Denny? Or was the real reason because she had another man?

Denny wonders if Bald Barnett is a better influence on the girls than he is.

So the woman who's already (or still?) got another man, who doesn't want to live near Jews, called Denny a "bad influence."

When Denny graduated high school, he took a half-semester of college at Wayne University before he decided he couldn't spend any more time in school. He went to work for his grandfather, who owned a salvage yard; Denny's father died and his mother moved into her parents' home with Denny and his two sisters and brother. At the yard, Denny met a lot of Jews, the sheeny men, people called them, who collected trash with their horse carts in the alleys across the city. He got to know them; they were good men, hard-working, scraping by with the junk people threw out.

Denny's grandfather insisted the other workers at the yard treat the sheeny men with respect—no jokes about Jewing down the Jews—and the trash collectors responded in kind.

They were decent men whom history had always categorized as undesirable. Maybe because he felt undesirable himself, he grew to like them and empathize with their plights, hounded everywhere, even in this so-called "democratic" country.

Too bad Hazel never reached that point.

Hazel, who is now doing whatever she's doing with Bald Barnett, one-time figure of fun. She's with Bald Barnett, Lulu's with her husband (Denny can't even remember his name) . . . and here's Denny sitting by himself in the cell-like room in a hotel, with the prospect of many more nights like this stretching out to the end of his life.

He decides he can't spend another minute here.

He takes the elevator back downstairs. Next to the hotel is a bar, The Tropics. The place has a South Pacific theme: walls, ceiling, and bar lined with bamboo; papier-mâché tigers; the simulated pitter-patter of tropical rain on the roof of the Rainfall Bar. Next to the cocktail lounge sits a Tropics Native Village, a sad little re-creation of a white man's idea of a South Pacific native village. How often did native villages come with bandstands and a dance floor?

Denny has been here before, but the tackiness of it put him off. The prices, too. A martini here costs fifty cents, twice what it costs at any other joint in the city. Tonight, though, he doesn't care.

He splurges.

Two dollars later his head spins.

The barman is reading yesterday's *Evening Times*. Denny sees the headline:

COLBURN GUILTY!

As if tonight wasn't bad enough . . . thanks for the reminder.

The barman comes over. "You okay, pal? You look like you just lost your best friend."

"Truer than you know," Denny says. He throws a fin on the bar. "Just keep 'em coming until that's done."

Five dollars later the room tilts and whirls. There's no dance band tonight, but his head throbs like the hard pounding drums of Gene

Krupa.

He has been propositioned a half-dozen times by prosties. Not tonight, ladies. Couldn't get it up if he tried.

He stumbles when he tries to stand. He trips over his own feet and falls heavily on his shoulder to the floor.

He gets himself on his hands and knees, but can't manage the rest of the way up.

He feels himself being helped to his feet. Two men are by his side. They ask him where he lives. To his surprise he discovers he can talk; he tells them he's staying in the hotel.

They walk him slowly through the cocktail lounge and out to the street. Cold air smacks him in the face, but doesn't refresh him. If only the world would stop doing somersaults for a few seconds, he's certain he could regain control.

The men help him into the lobby of the Wolverine. They leave him in a deep leather chair. He passes out at once.

At some point during the night, he will have a vague memory of hearing his name. A voice, telling him he can't spend the night in the lobby.

He wishes he could respond. He really does.

No dice. He's out again.

He welcomes the blankness.

16

EVA SZABÓ

[Tuesday, April 1, 1941]

The night turns cold.
Rain turns to sleet.
Sleet turns to light flurries that melt on hitting the road.

Eva huddles up in a streetcar shelter on Michigan Avenue. Her arm smarts where Billy Fisk grabbed her and shook her when she visited the brothers' apartment earlier that evening. She looks around with suspicion. For the first time in her life, she worries about being out after dark.

Which might be the unintended consequence of this job: it has introduced fear into her life. It wasn't only Billy's attack on her, but seeing the endless line of walking wounded coming into the hospital at the plant . . . people who woke up with hopes and plans for the future, and who then went head-to-head with the massive Ford industrial monster and lost.

As everybody does.

It chews up everyone who comes in contact with it, whether it sends them away bleeding (or dead) like the men she sees every day, or just eats up their vitality in daily bites.

Now a car pulls up in front of her. She knows the car—recognizes its egg shape, its angled front—but still she has a frisson of fear when she sees it stopping. A sudden metallic taste blooms in her mouth.

The driver leans over. Opens the passenger door. Says, "Get in."

Eva does. The car takes off.

Elizabeth Waters behind the wheel gives Eva a side-long look. Eva sees Elizabeth take everything in . . . not just the look on Eva's face but the whole package—her clothes, her hat askew on her head, her shoes. The aura of fear radiating off her.

"Hey," Elizabeth says. "What's wrong?"

"Nothing," Eva says.

"You sure? You don't look too good."

Eva nods. Elizabeth looks unconvinced, but she continues west down Michigan. Both women are silent until Elizabeth pulls up to a Jolly Roger Donut shop.

Inside is warm, with an overwhelming smell of fried cakes and coffee. Elizabeth directs Eva toward a table. Only a handful of people in the place, mostly sad-eyed men, alkies trying to keep themselves upright with coffee and sugar.

Eva sits at a table away from anybody. Elizabeth returns with two mugs of coffee and two glazed sweet rolls on a tray.

"When was the last time you ate?" Elizabeth asks.

Eva has to think. "This morning." She realizes she skipped lunch.

"That's what I thought," Elizabeth says. "Here, have both sweet rolls. I'll get another one for me."

"No—" Eva begins. Elizabeth has already gone off to the counter.

By the time Elizabeth returns to the table, Eva has already eaten one of them.

"I could tell you were hungry by the look in your eye."

Eva smiles, says, "Thank you."

Elizabeth watches Eva eat for another few moments, then says, "Tell me what's going on."

Eva fills her in on what she has seen since their last conversation, last week. Elizabeth takes notes as Eva tells her about the strike. About her previous evening at the bar with Anton and his boys. About the kinds of injuries she has seen in the clinic, especially what Nadine said about some of the wounds seeming deliberate.

About what happened to Billy and Jack Fisk, and about her conversation with them tonight. About the widespread gambling in the plant. About Billy laying hands on her to ensure her silence.

Elizabeth says, "Being manhandled is not part of your job."

"I know," Eva says. "It shook me up, that's all. Surprised me."

"I told you, these men are rough customers. This is war to them."

"I know."

"You're only supposed to look for anything that contravenes the National Labor Relations Board's rulings against anti-union violence. You're not supposed to get involved with the fight for the union yourself. And the gambling problem at the plant doesn't concern you right now."

"I thought I was looking into anti-union violence. I didn't know it was about gambling."

"I get it. But the plan isn't for you to get hurt, regardless. Find out what you can, sure, but do it carefully. *Don't* engage these guys like that. *Don't* take chances."

Eva takes a sip of coffee and starts to work on the second sweet roll. Elizabeth blows across the mouth of her coffee mug and takes a sip. Says, "You shouldn't have even gone to their house by yourself."

"I know."

"No more risks, okay?"

"Got it."

Elizabeth drops Eva off at home. Inside, Ágnes has fallen asleep on the sofa in the living room. The radio plays.

Eva turns off the radio. The sudden silence rouses the old woman. Eva gently helps her stepmother up to her bedroom. Sleep-befogged, Ágnes says, "*Jozef bátyád itt volt ma este.*"

Your brother Josef was here tonight.

He's not my brother, Eva thinks; he's my stepbrother. He probably wanted money, which neither Eva nor Ágnes has. No wonder he didn't stay until Eva got home.

If he was even here. It might be a hallucination. Since her stroke she's been starting to see things from her early life . . . people who've been dead for years, homes she used to live in.

Eva gets her stepmother into bed and goes downstairs to clean up the kitchen. She sees no evidence her stepbrother has been here.

She goes up to her room. Exhausted, she gets into her pajamas and writes up the day's notes, even though she's already reported them to Elizabeth.

Despite the coffee she drank, despite the sugary donuts, despite her jitters earlier in the evening, she escapes into sleep as soon as she turns out the light.

17

CLARENCE BROWN

[Tuesday, April 1, 1941]

The night duty officer's phone rings. He picks it up, listens for a few moments, looks at Clarence standing in front of him, and hangs up. "Wilson wants you," he tells Clarence. "He's in his office."

William Wilson, the second-in-command of Clarence's squad, beckons Clarence inside. "Shut the door. Sit down."

Clarence sits.

Wilson says, "I hear you've been asking around about that dead baby you found."

"Yes sir."

"Think it was gonna come back to life?"

"No sir. Just curious why it's not showing up on the reports."

"Which reports?"

"Any of them. The ME's log, for one. They have no notification of a dead baby. None of our reports, either. I can't find an incident report about it. I'm trying to get hold of Clendening to ask him about it. But it feels like he's avoiding me."

"Don't you have any other work to do?"

"Yes sir. A full caseload."

"Then work your cases. Let this baby thing alone."

"That baby belongs to somebody, lieutenant. It was your child, wouldn't you want to know—"

Wilson cuts him off. "It's not our case. I sent it over to Homicide."

"Why don't we have a report on the boy? You asked me not to mention him, and I didn't. But where's the official record of him?"

"Let it go, Clarence. I'm not going to tell you again."

Home.

Bessie is not at her spot on the sofa in the living room. An electric stab of panic goes through him when he sees the empty room. He hears dishes clattering in the kitchen. He rushes through the house.

His fear turns to anger. She better not be walking around and making dinner, he tells himself . . .

He finds Malone Coleman in the kitchen, warming what looks and smells like stew.

"The lady who care for Miss Brown left this for us," Malone says.

"Where's my wife?" Clarence asks.

"In bed. She was tired. I helped get her ready and everything."

Clarence goes back through the apartment. Sure enough, Bessie is in bed. Sound asleep. A small smile plays on her lips.

Sweet dreams, baby.

Quietly he takes off his suit jacket and metal armor. Leans them against the wall in the bedroom and goes out to the dining room.

There Malone lays out plates for a late dinner.

Malone serves up rice and stew, with an open bottle of Coke beside Clarence's plate. The boy already has Clarence's number. He's a quick learner.

Malone stands beside the table while Clarence lowers his bulk into the chair.

Clarence points to a chair at the table. Malone sits.

Clarence says, "Miss Brown eat already?"

"She said she wasn't hungry."

Clarence takes a spoonful of the stew. Delicious—thick and sweet and cinnamony.

Miss Maxine sure can cook.

"Mr. Clarence," Malone begins.

"Don't talk with your mouth full. Swallow before you speak."

Malone chews. Swallows. He says, "Mr. Clarence, I want to stay here with you."

"We talked about this. I said you could."

"Yeah, but just for a little while, right? I want to stay here, Mr. Clarence. I don't want to go back to my mama's house."

"Malone," Clarence begins.

But Malone has his whole argument ready.

"I could take care of Miss Brown, I could take care of the house and keep it clean, I could take care of you."

"Boy your age needs a regular job."

"I could work at Ford's."

Clarence is unconvinced.

Malone barges on. "I don't wanna go back to that house. I never wanna go home to my mother. She ain't never gonna change, Mr. Clarence."

Based on what little Clarence knows about Malone's mother, Clarence has to agree. Women in her situation only change when they get worse or die.

"I want to stay here."

"Malone," Clarence says, "my wife, she's sick. She can't take care of you."

"I know. I could help you with her like I did tonight."

Clarence lays down his fork. "Malone, look at me."

"Yes sir."

"Miss Brown and me, we're too old to take on a boy your age."

"Please?"

Malone is so young . . . so mistreated . . . so full of possibilities if they haven't been stripped away already by his life closing in all around him.

Malone stares at him, eyes begging Clarence to say yes.

Clarence can't find it in his heart to turn the boy down.

Clarence says, "We'll try it. On one condition."

"Anything!"

"You got to find work. You want to work at Ford's, fine. But you can't be sitting around all day, getting yourself in trouble."

"I understand, Mr. Clarence. And I will. I promise I will."

He goes on trying to convince Clarence his plan is the best thing to do.

Clarence nods. He feels uneasy listening to all Malone's protestations. Clarence has heard all this before on the street . . . addicts and users and career crooks who'll say anything, promise anything with the same glib assurances if it'll keep them out of trouble or lead on to their next fix.

"We'll give it two weeks," Clarence says.

"You won't be sorry."

Clarence thinks: I'll be the judge of that.

Malone sleeps on the couch in the rec room in the basement. Clarence sits in the living room upstairs. Duke Ellington's "Cotton Tail" plays on the radio. Cootie Williams on trumpet, Ben Webster on tenor sax . . . it doesn't get better than this.

Bessie's been sleeping straight through. He checks in on her every few minutes to make sure she's still breathing.

Then he checks on Malone, sound asleep and snoring. He's kicked the cover off himself. Clarence replaces it and goes back upstairs.

The quiet domestic tasks make him think about DeMarco.

On the mantel is a photograph of DeMarco, Bessie, and Clarence. One of those formal photos taken at a studio in Lexington, where they lived back then. Clarence stares blankly out at the camera, as if he could see into the future and knows what awaits them all. Bessie and their son are smiling. They have the same gap-toothed grin, same round face and narrow nose. Same impish look in their eyes.

He turns the photo over. Bessie has written the date, 1919. DeMarco would have been seven.

Around the time when DeMarco started begging him for a piano, Clarence remembers. The boy was captivated by the piano player at their church and decided he wanted to learn to play it. Clarence had to tell him they couldn't afford a piano.

Instead Clarence talked to the piano player at church and arranged for him to give DeMarco lessons.

By the next year, the boy was dead.

He died in the final flare-up of the Spanish Flu. Clarence and Bessie spent another year in Lexington but it was too hard to stay there after DeMarco was gone. Everything reminded them of him—his room, their house, the neighbor boys outside playing without him.

They moved up to Cincinnati. There Clarence found work as a Pullman porter. They were making money, and he could finally afford to buy a piano. But by then of course it was too late.

Clarence had tried to get his son interested in baseball—

Clarence's own passion—he's behind on getting his team set up for the season, he remembers with a pang of annoyance at himself—and DeMarco tried, he really did. But he was skinny and frail, and the bigger boys pushed him around on the ballfield and never picked him for their teams.

No, DeMarco would have been a musician if he'd lived.

Or an artist; he loved to go out into the scrub field behind their house and come back with an interesting weed, or a lacy leaf chewed by bugs, or anything else catching his fancy. Then he'd draw it.

An artist. Or even a scientist.

He would have been one of those for sure, Clarence thinks. A smart, sensitive boy. Clarence would have seen to it that he got an education. He never would have turned into one of those bruisers like the other boys.

Or like his father.

Clarence closes his eyes and DeMarco's little boy smell, sweet, like candy, floats back to him . . .

A knock on the door interrupts his hour of peace.

In an instant he's up with one of his .45s in his hand.

"Who's there?"

"Sonny McGhee," a man's voice says. "From down the street."

"I don't know no Sonny McGhee from down the street," Clarence says. He tries to keep his voice low so he doesn't wake Bessie.

"Yes you do," the man says. "I'm the fella told you about that little baby in the basement over there on Beaubien."

"What are you doing here?"

"Come on, man, just open the door. It's cold out here. I got a question."

Clarence cracks the door. Keeps the .45 out of sight but handy.

He recognizes the man from the building where he found the baby.

"This time of night?" Clarence asks.

"I just want to know if you found anything out about that poor little child."

"Not yet."

The man pauses.

"Spit it out," Clarence says, "you got something else to say."

"Look here, I came to apologize."

"For what?"

"For being such a knucklehead the other day. I didn't mean to be so hinky. I know you were just trying to do your job. I'm sorry, Mr. Clarence."

Clarence opens the door the rest of the way. "Yeah, okay. I figured you were troubled about the baby, so . . ."

"I was. And I took it out on you. I feel awful I was disrespectful. I know you're the only one looking out for us. And I might have also had a little too much to drink, too, you know what I mean?"

Clarence replaces his gun in the holster hanging near the door. Holds out a hand for Sonny to shake. "You want to come in for a minute, get out the wind?"

"Don't mind if I do."

"Keep your voice down, though. My wife's asleep."

"Oh, okay," Sonny stage-whispers. Clarence points to the sofa where Bessie usually sits. He himself sits in his chair.

"All I got to drink is Coca-Cola and coffee," Clarence says. "You're welcome to either one if you want. I don't drink hard liquor."

"I wish I could say the same. I can't stay. Have to get back to my wife and kids."

"How many you got?"

"Pearl and me, we got three beautiful kids. Two boys and a girl. You?"

Once Clarence would have said he had a son but he died. Now he just says, "A boy. You all squeeze into those tiny little rooms where you stay?"

"You make do how you have to. Why I was going on about not having decent places to live."

"You were right."

"I know."

Sonny looks around at Clarence's flat. "You got yourself a nice place," he says.

"Thanks. What do you do for a living?"

"I work at the Rouge," Sonny says. "In the Foundry. That's where they put us, you know. Hottest, dirtiest places. Either that, or cleaning shithouses. War comes, I'm hoping to find defense work."

"War's coming. Ford switches over to all defense work, you will, too. Where you come from, Sonny?"

"Raleigh, North Carolina. I'm a graduate of Shaw University."

Proud of it.

"A college man."

"Yes sir. I moved north to get away from the south. You?"

"Same," Clarence says. "We're up from Kentucky, my wife and me."

"Up here, a colored man has a better chance of living out his natural life."

Based on what he's seen as a policeman in Detroit, Clarence doesn't necessarily agree. But he lets it go.

Sonny stands. "Got to get home. I just wanted to apologize to you properly, Mr. Clarence, like a man."

Clarence stands, too. "Thank you. I appreciate it."

"See you again, maybe."

"I'm sure you will."

18

DENNY RANKIN

[Wednesday, April 2, 1941]

He pours a cup of station coffee into a mug, but the smell of it turns his stomach. He dumps it down the sink.

The coffee is horrible under the best of circumstances, a muddy, foul-tasting brew. Now, after he woke up in the lobby of the Wolverine hungover with a raging headache, the joe's taste of turpentine and piss is too much to ponder.

When he woke up in the lobby, it took him a minute to figure out where he was. Light streamed in from outside; must be morning. At the desk the day man was giving him the maloik.

By the time Denny got his bearings, he had to make a dash for the toilet in the men's room off the lobby. He puked his guts out. He sat on the floor with his forehead against the ceramic bowl, sweating, panting, his head killing him, the taste in his mouth as sour as he can ever remember.

Here's why I shouldn't drink, he told himself.

Don't you ever do this again.

But like every other bit of advice he offers himself, he knows he will ignore it.

Now he sits at his desk. Tries to calm himself.

No one is in the detective squad room. Nobody to ask about the trial. No newspapers around, either.

He telephones a friend who's now a senior editor at the *Detroit*

News. Tom Glover. Tom used to be a reporter for the *Evening Times* and now runs the city desk at the *News.*

Tom picks up on the first ring. "Editorial, Glover."

"Tommy. It's Denny Rankin."

"Hey bud," Tom says. "What's up?"

Since he moved to the city desk, Tom has no time for shooting the shit during the day.

"Just wanted to know if anything's going on with the trial."

"Which trial?" Tom asks. "The trial over the Herman Gardens bribery scandal? Or the trial over the Wayne County corruption scandal? Or maybe you mean the Federal trial of Frank McKay on mail fraud charges? Or McKay's trial over the $500,000 liquor conspiracy? Or the Wayne County trial over selling jobs? Ask me about a trial in Detroit, you got to be more specific."

After auto production, Michigan's biggest industry is corruption and corruption trials. There's a cast of thousands.

"Tommy, you wag. You know the one I'm talking about."

"Yeah. They're in adjournment. Harry Colburn's sick. He supposedly had a nervous collapse after pleading guilty."

"I know how he feels."

"Defense says he'll be okay to start up again today with him in the witness box. The other thing I heard, Ferguson's going to hand down a lot more indictments from his grand jury."

Denny does not mention to Tom his name might be among those warrants signed by Circuit Judge Homer S. Ferguson.

"Look," Tom says, "gotta go. We're due for a drink soon, yeah?"

"We are indeed," Denny says.

"Let's plan on it. We'll catch up."

He hangs up.

There goes Denny's teetotal resolution.

There's nothing to be done now, he decides. He will or he won't be indicted and worrying about it isn't going to change it.

A line from the half-semester of college English he took at Wayne University runs in his mind:

"Use every man after his dessert, and who shall 'scape whipping?"

He has thought of the line often in his life as a policeman. As his first sergeant used to say, "Don't worry too much about it—they're *all* guilty of something."

He starts to shake his head to clear it but his headache discourages him.

Think about something else.

How about your job for a change?

That gets him going. He checks rap sheets for the Muellers. Nothing for any of them. If the two kids had juvie records, those would be sealed.

But Heinz's friend Bertrand Franz Vogelmann has a record. White male, DOB 5/12/18. Pimp conviction '37, five months served. Arrested 3/5/39 for criminal trespass at the Congregation B'nai David, a synagogue in the Linwood-Dexter area of Detroit. Fine paid, no time served. Last known address 2021 Bewick. He has a Chevy sedan, registration BA-30-11.

Heinz Mueller dresses like a fascist, Denny thinks, so it shouldn't be surprising if Bertrand Franz Vogelmann runs in the same crowd.

B'nai David. A massive brick building at 14th and Elmwood.

The heart of the Jewish section of the city. Here's the source of the exodus Denny's wife worries about.

Up a flight of outside steps and through one of the three doors under high arches. A narrow vestibule lined with heavy wooden doors. One set leads into a large nave. Curved wooden pews fill the bottom floor and the balcony around three sides. A wooden railing separates the altar—is that what they call it, an altar? Denny doesn't think so but he can't remember what it is; he knows little enough about his own vague Protestantism—from the rest of the seating. Behind the railing a dais stands between two large and ornate candelabras.

An impressive place, Denny thinks. He can imagine it filled with Jewish people chanting their ancient prayers in the strange, musical language of Hebrew.

He tries to think of who he knows today who's Jewish.

The only ones he's sure of are the Traub brothers, who own the jewelry store that was robbed. Considering how Jews are treated in this city of Henry Ford and Father Coughlin, Denny isn't surprised people don't broadcast it. He wouldn't.

He goes back out to the vestibule. One of the wooden doors bears the name "Rabbi Joshua Sperka."

Denny knocks. He thinks he hears a woman's voice. He thinks she says, "Come in."

He opens the door. A middle-aged woman sits behind a desk. She wears a white blouse with a Peter Pan collar. She has tightly permed dark hair streaked with gray.

"Can I help you?" she says.

He introduces himself, shows his badge. "I'm looking for the rabbi."

"Rabbi Sperka is conducting a prayer session," she says. "I'm Mrs. Adler. How can I help?"

On one of the other doors, Denny saw a nameplate for "Cantor Hyman Adler."

"Are you the cantor's wife?"

"I am," she says. "But my husband isn't here either. There's just me," she says with a small laugh.

"Were you here two years ago, Mrs. Adler?"

"Of course."

"Do you remember an incident when a young man was arrested for trespassing?"

"Do I remember. It was terrible. A *shanda*. A shame."

"If you don't mind talking about it, could you tell me what happened?"

"They came in a group. They should have arrested every one of them."

"What went on?"

"I don't know how much you know about the Jewish religion," she says. "But one of our holidays is called Purim. It celebrates the survival of the Jewish people at the hands of the Persians. Most every Jewish holiday celebrates a close shave, you know. The eve of Purim fell on Saturday, the fifth of March. We have a reading of the Book of Esther on the eve of Purim, which we do again on the first day. It's supposed to be a very joyous holiday for us.

"It was also the day a group of local Nazis decided to attack our synagogue. They ran in during morning services ringing bells and blowing whistles. They shouted 'Death to the Jews.' They wore swastika armbands and did everything they could to disrupt the service."

"What did you do?"

"Rabbi Sperka stopped the service and went to ask them nicely to leave. They knocked him down. Men from the congregation jumped up and tried to throw them out. Others protected the torah. I ran to call the police. By the time the police showed up, all the hoodlums had run off except for one, who was still wrestling with my husband. He's the one the police arrested."

She took a moment to calm herself down. "Why are you asking about this, if you don't mind?"

"Bertrand Vogelmann's name came up in another investigation. I thought I'd do a little digging into his background."

"I hear he got off with a fine, that bastard. If you could put them all in jail for good? *Halevai.* It should only happen."

19

EVA SZABÓ

[Wednesday, April 2, 1941]

She fixes Ágnes a soft-boiled egg for breakfast. She leaves a bowl of sauerkraut soup for her in the icebox for lunch. Eva makes herself a chicken sandwich to take with her.

"*Josef tegnap este itt volt*," Ágnes says around the egg. Josef was here last night.

"You told me. This what he wanted?" Eva rubs her thumb and two fingers together in the universal gesture for money. "If I'd been here, I'd have told him *nincs pénz*."

No money.

Ágnes points her spoon at the Maxwell House can in the Hoosier kitchen cabinet beside the sink. She returns to her egg and attacks it with an old person's feral intensity.

Eva checks. Inside the can is a small roll of filthy dollar bills rubber banded together.

Eva takes the roll out. Counts the bills twice. "There's fifteen dollars here. Josef left this?"

Ágnes nods.

"That's a switch." Eva can't imagine he would actually contribute money to their household.

Under the coffee can is a pamphlet. Eva asks, "Where did this come from?"

"*Josef tegnap este otthagyta.*"

"He left it last night? For what reason?"

Ágnes concentrates on finishing her egg.

Eva picks up the pamphlet. It's eight pages, printed on cheap yellowed paper stapled in the middle.

Does Jewish Power Control the World Press?
from
The International Jew: The World's Foremost Problem
being a reprint of a series of articles appearing in
The Dearborn Independent, 1920.

"What are we supposed to do with this trash?" Eva says.

Ágnes mimes sticking the roll of bills into her pocket. "*Azt mondta, ezek eladásából származik a pénz.*"

The money comes from selling them.

"Did you read this?"

Ágnes ignores the question.

Eva has no time to read it. She sticks the pamphlet in her purse, tells her stepmother goodbye, and leaves the house.

It's a busier day than it has been. Most of the patients are Negroes Harry Bennett brought in as scabs. Their injuries are from the vicious beatings the striking workers gave them as they tried to get through the picket lines into the plant—beatings with two-by-fours, picket signs, shovels, and tools the strikers took with them when they left.

Nadine treats them grudgingly.

In lulls she naps. She told the other nurses, the Marys, not to come in today.

Eva busies herself by reorganizing the medical files. At lunchtime she takes her sandwich to the empty post-surgical ward. She reads through the pamphlet Josef left at their house.

It claims Jews control newspapers everywhere in their quest to seize political and economic power across the world. It's a well-known plan, the pamphlet insists. It's detailed in something called the *Protocols of the Elders of Zion*.

The pamphlet comes from the series of articles Henry Ford ran in his newspaper. She was just a child when they ran, but she remembers her father talking about it. How it fanned the same flames of hatred for Jews in America that they tried to escape from in Europe.

All her life she has heard people complaining about Jews and how bad they are. How they run everything. And ruin everything. How cheap they are. How they'll cheat you whenever they can. Miklós Horthy's National Army back in Hungary launched the White Terror against anybody they considered part of the Bolshevik attempt to take over the country—peasants, intellectuals, and most especially Jews like her family. Horthy considered all Jews to be Bolsheviks. Whether they were Bolsheviks or not, Jews were tortured, raped, murdered by the hundreds, their bodies desecrated.

Her mother was a teacher caught up in a sweep through Budapest by the National Army in 1919. She was murdered for being Jewish in the wrong place at the wrong time, leaving infant Eva and her father by themselves.

As soon as he could, her father moved them to America in hopes it would be different here. He took as his second wife a woman from the old country, Ágnes, but she wasn't Jewish; he didn't care, so anxious was he to separate himself from the ancient hatreds of Europe.

But the more she reads and talks to people, the more Eva hears hatred raining down on the heads of the Jews in Detroit, just as it did—and is doing—overseas . . . the mild-mannered shopkeepers, the grocers, the men who drive their horses down the streets and alleys collecting other people's junk and who are called sheenies, that old disgusting term for Jews . . .

They don't seem like they control much of anything.

And now this, from her stepbrother? What could he be thinking, to bring this into our home?

Nadine sticks her head into the ward. "Done with your lunch yet? I need your help out here."

Eva sticks the pamphlet back in her purse and goes out to help Nadine. One of the Negro maintenance men has come in with badly burned hands.

20

CLARENCE BROWN

[Wednesday, April 2, 1941]

He cruises Black Bottom and Paradise Valley in his police car. When he joined the police department, Clarence was one of a handful of Negro police officers. He was assigned to this district, where Negroes were concentrated in Detroit. Now there are more Negro policemen and detectives, but he still prefers it here. He wouldn't abandon these streets for anything.

When he left home for work this morning, Bessie was in a bad way. The pain from her ankle sore was terrible. He wanted to take her to the doctor, but she insisted he go to work.

Malone says he will watch out for her until Miss Maxine comes.

Clarence is on his way home to check on Bessie when a woman steps into his path on Monroe Street. He stomps on the brake and swerves. Then twists the wheel in the other direction to keep from slamming into a parked car.

Stops his car. Jumps out.

"What the hell!" he cries.

The Negro woman stands in the middle of the road near the head of an alley. She wears a good cloth coat open to show a floral dress. Her hat is askew on her head.

She has blood on her hands. Blood on her dress.

Clarence trots up to her. "Are you alright?"

The woman looks dazed, in shock.

"Are you alright?" Clarence repeats.

When she doesn't—can't—respond, he grabs her hands. Looks her over. Her hands are bloody but she doesn't seem to have any cuts on them. He examines her dress and coat. Bloody, but no rips where she might have been slashed. This is not her blood.

The buildings around them are residential. No one will have seen anything, Clarence knows already.

He helps her into his car. "Can you tell me your name?"

She looks around, says, "My purse! I had it in the alley."

"Stay here," he tells her. He goes into the dark alley, searches around.

There, on the ground.

The purse.

All around it, blood on the concrete, leading off down the passage.

A shiny object catches his eye.

A bloody kitchen knife.

He wraps it in a handkerchief and brings it back to the car. The woman sits where he left her. She leans forward in her seat with her head in her hands.

"This yours?" Clarence says.

She shrinks from the knife. "No."

He sets the handkerchief and knife on the dashboard. Snaps open her purse. Her wallet identifies her as Florence Williams.

"Florence," Clarence says. This gets her attention. "Can you tell me what happened?"

"I was walking over there," she says. She is shaking. "When this man grabbed me. He dragged me in the alley."

She pauses for a breath.

"Okay, now. Take your time."

"He had a knife. That knife." She indicates the knife Clarence found. "He forced me into the alley with it."

"Then what?"

"He tried to pull up my skirt," she says, "and I pushed him and we fought and I got the knife away from him. And I stabbed him with it."

She looks at Clarence as if she can't believe she did this.

Clarence starts his car. He pulls into the alley. The headlights show the blood trail. Doesn't look like it's from a scratch, either; the trail proves substantial blood loss.

At the end of the alley, he stops at Macomb Street. He loses the blood trail in the road.

He goes left to Hastings, then heads north. Clarence guesses Florence's assailant will try to make it to Parkside Hospital.

He stops at every cross street. He judges the man will not be able to move very fast. Clarence watches for him.

He sees a man hobble across Gratiot. Clarence guns it.

The man doesn't have the energy to get away. He stumbles over a curb and falls. He lies still on the sidewalk.

Clarence pulls up next to him. Comes around the car and helps Florence out. Holding her arm, he guides her to where the man lies.

"Is this him?" he asks.

At the sight of him, she tries to pull out of Clarence's grasp. "That's him! He's the one!"

"Go back in the car," Clarence says. "I'll call for help. I'll see you get home safe."

Clarence puts a call through on his car radio for an ambulance. Then he goes to a phone booth to call his house. Malone answers.

"How's Miss Brown?" Clarence asks.

"Fine. Got a little pain, but I'm taking good care of her, like I said I would."

"Do me a favor, Malone, and make sure she has lunch? There's cold pork in the icebox. Maybe she'd like a sandwich."

"Yes sir, Mr. Clarence. I'll take good care of her, don't you worry."

Clarence takes Florence Williams's statement and drops her at her home on Hendrie Street. She says she lives with her two sisters and they will see to her.

Afterwards he stops at the hospital. Florence's assailant is named Walter Evans. Before Clarence even questions him, Walter confesses to an assault on another woman. He forced her at knifepoint into an empty building, then raped her.

Two cases closed at once. The nurse gives him a bag of Walter's personal effects. Not much here. A wallet, small change, a set of keys, and a folded flyer.

The flyer turns out to show a menacing-looking, heavy-lidded white man with a Jewish star on his watch fob. He lurks among three flags—the stars and stripes, the British flag, and the red Communist flag. The flyer has no other printing except the words, *"Hinter den Feindmächten: der Jude."*

He asks around on the nursing floor if anybody can read these words. A nurse recognizes it as German, but she doesn't know what it means except *Jude* means Jew.

Clarence goes back into the ward to see Walter Evans. "Where did you get this?" Clarence asks him. He holds up the flyer.

"White man in the street give it to me."

"Did you know him?"

"Never saw him before."

"Remember where he gave it to you?"

"Don't remember, exactly."

"Know what it says?"

"No. Do you?"

Clarence doesn't.

But he knows who will.

The Rexall on Hastings Street is open. Sol Weintraub must be back at work.

Sure enough, he stands behind the pharmacy counter.

"Mr. Clarence!" Sol says when he hears the door open and sees Clarence walk in. "Good to see you, my friend."

"Figured you'd be back at work again. How's your foot?"

Sol limps out from behind the counter to show Clarence. "They put on a cast with a platform on the bottom," Sol says. "The bullet went clear through. They told me I needed a cast on it to walk on, so they sewed me up and put one of these things on."

"Getting around okay?"

"Slower," Sol says. "But any day on this side of the grass is a good day. What can I do for you, my friend?"

Clarence unfolds the flyer he took from Walter Evans. Hands it to Sol. "Can you tell me what this says?"

Sol's face reddens. "What are you doing with this?"

"I took it off an offender. Can you read it?"

"Of course. It's German. It says, 'Behind the enemy powers: the Jew.' It's Nazi propaganda. It claims the Jews are behind the war."

Sol hands it back to Clarence. "Blaming Jews for starting wars is an old tradition in Europe. And not just there. You ever heard Father Coughlin's broadcasts? The priest from Royal Oak?"

"No."

"They took him off the air, the things he spouts. Like Hitler was writing his speeches for him. Every problem we have today? The Jews are behind them all. If we could only get rid of the Jews . . ."

He shakes his head. "I got news, my friend. Once they get rid of me, they're coming for you."

By the time Clarence rolls home to check on Bessie, both Bessie and Malone are napping, Bessie in her bed and Malone on the sofa in the living room.

Clarence tries to muster annoyance at Malone for not making an effort to find work, but can't. Malone is turning out to be a blessing.

Clarence stands at his kitchen counter and eats a bit of the left-over cold pork.

He heads back to the station.

Sol Weintraub's words echo in his head.

Once they get rid of me, they're coming after you.

Just what we need, he thinks: more crazy white people who hate Negroes.

21

DENNY RANKIN

[Wednesday, April 2, 1941]

Bertrand Vogelmann, the trespasser at the synagogue, lives on a block of tiny brick bungalows on the city's southeast side. Nobody answers the door at his address.

Denny drives up to Mack Avenue and goes west to Woodward Avenue. Heads north on Woodward to Palmer Woods and the Mueller home.

Denny hopes Mueller is at work at this time of day and the Countess von Whatchamacallit is busy with her social clubs. He wants to speak with Heinz by himself.

The Muellers' maid Easter answers his knock. She tells him nobody is home except her. Denny doesn't believe her but she will not let him in. No doubt acting on orders from the master of the house, Denny thinks.

He has no choice but to return to his car.

He keeps an eye on the house for another half hour. He sees no activity—no flicking of curtains, no shadows moving around inside.

He goes back to Seven Mile Road and heads west for a few miles, toward Phil Wheaton's house in Redford. A Packard is in the driveway, but he doesn't see Phil's police car.

Esther answers the door. Lena's sister-in-law. Denny reminds her of who he is and she steps aside. Lena's on a couch in the living room, leaning back against a pillow. Snoring softly.

"Did you hear anything?" Denny asks Esther. Keeps his voice down.

She shakes her head. Beckons him to follow her into the kitchen. "Coffee?"

"Sure."

She pours them both a cup. The ashtray on the counter overflows with cigarettes with lipstick blots on the butts.

"Anything new with you?" Esther asks.

"No. I was hoping to learn something about Charlotte. But if Lena's too upset—"

"She just fell asleep. She's been up for days, ever since Charlotte's been gone. I'd like to let her sleep."

"How well do you know the girl? An aunt might know more than parents."

"She's never confided in me."

"Never told you anything about her life? Boyfriends? Girl-friends? Any interests?"

"Honestly, I can't tell you about her friends. I know she has them because she's always going out. But I couldn't say who they are. They all look the same to me, these kids."

"Where does she go to school?"

"That I do know. Cass Tech."

A magnet school downtown, drawing students from around the city. A technical high school that also has art, music, drama, college prep programs.

"Doesn't seem like either Lena or Phil knows much about their daughter," Denny says. He immediately regretted the judgmental tone it struck. "Sorry, I didn't mean that as a criticism."

"Forget it. It's true." She sighs. "Do you have kids?"

"Two stepchildren," he says. "Girls."

"I have all boys," Esther says. "They're bad enough, God knows. But I'd say girls were more of a handful."

Denny can only nod. If girl children are a handful, girl stepchildren who can't stand you are an impossible burden.

His girls' father died when they were very young, and they never forgave him for deserting them—just as they never forgave their mother for marrying Denny, or forgave Denny for trying to take their father's place. Hazel didn't make it any easier by refusing to allow Denny to discipline the girls. So when they sneered at him,

"You're not our father," Hazel communicated that they were right . . . he really didn't have authority over them.

"Do you mind if I look at Charlotte's room?" Denny asks.

She leads him upstairs. A girl's room out of a fairy tale: everything pink. Pink throw on the bed, pink stuffed dog and cat on the bed, pinky and frothy dresses on pink-skinned dolls. The only thing not pink is the green-and-white Cass Tech pennant on the pink wall.

Denny makes a quick run through the drawers. Girl clothes, blouses, skirts, underwear.

"And there hasn't been a ransom note?"

"Nothing," she says. "No demands for anything."

"If you don't mind my saying so, Esther, you're remarkably calm about all this."

"What will worrying do? Besides, I'm an optimist. I believe things will work out for the best."

"My motto is exactly the opposite. I believe things start out fine and then get worse."

A photo of Charlotte in a pink frame stands on the pink dresser. Looks like it was taken a year or so ago; she is outside and the trees are just coming into blossom. She is a dark-eyed, dark-haired young woman staring straight into the camera with a go-to-hell expression. She has the same black Irish beauty as her mother.

"Can I borrow this?" he asks.

"Sure. Just bring it back. Preferably with Charlotte."

Cass Technical High School. An eight-story brick building on Second Avenue downtown. It looks more like a factory than a school—more like they stamp out parts for the automotive industry here than educate students. Even the name suggests it's preparation for work.

Near the entrance on the ground floor, he stops at a door marked Office. A handful of students sit on benches. The malefactors, waiting for their punishment.

My people, Denny thinks. He had his share of expulsions from high school: for fighting, talking back to teachers, skipping school. It was a wonder he graduated.

A clerk appears on the other side of the main counter. He flashes his buzzer and says his name. "I need to speak to someone about one of your students," he says. "Charlotte Wheaton."

He looks for a spark of understanding, appreciation, helpfulness—but doesn't get anything except a dead fisheye.

"Who can I talk to about her?"

Without a word, the clerk turns away from him and flips through files in an open drawer.

She takes out a folder. She looks at the top sheet and places it back in the folder. "Her counselor."

Charlotte's counselor is Dr. Alfred Bracciano. The clerk directs Denny up to Bracciano's fourth-floor office. It's at one end of a study hall with fifty students fidgeting at their desks and laughing behind their books.

Bracciano is a small, swarthy, intense, pear-shaped man in a glassed-in enclosure at the front of the hall.

Denny introduces himself, explains why he's there and what he's looking for.

"You think she's in trouble?" Bracciano asks.

"We're just trying to find her."

Bracciano leans over to the file cabinet beside him. Finds Charlotte's folder.

Bracciano says, "If you find her, let me know. She started the year in September—good student, good grades—but then she disappeared around October."

"You're saying she hasn't been in school since October?"

"That's what I'm saying."

Phil Wheaton told Denny she'd only been gone a few days.

"Do you know if she's close to anybody? Girlfriends? Boyfriends?"

Bracciano looks out at the students in the study hall. He gets up. Goes outside his office. Whistles. The student din abates. He calls: "Malinowski!"

A pretty blonde girl in the middle of the study hall raises her hand.

Bracciano waves her up.

She makes her way to his office. The noise level of the students rises again.

She follows Bracciano into his office. "Sit," he says. "Janice Malinowski, Detective Rankin, Detroit PD."

She nods at Denny.

"He's got questions about Charlotte Wheaton," Bracciano says.

Another nod.

"Janice, how are you?" Denny says.

"Okay."

"You're close, you and Charlotte?"

"I guess."

"When was the last time you saw her?"

She looks at Bracciano, who nods helpfully.

"This week," Janice says.

"Which day?"

"Monday. I stopped by her house after school."

"Have you heard from her since?"

"No."

"Is that unusual? Are you in touch a lot?"

"Usually every day. We used to be in the same classes."

"Dr. Bracciano tells me she stopped coming to school last fall."

Janice says nothing.

Denny says, "Reason I'm asking, Janice, Charlotte's been missing from home for a couple of days. Since Monday, as it happens."

He examines Janice's reaction to see if this is news or not. She remains poker-faced.

Denny says, "When you didn't hear from her, did you try to get in touch with her?"

"We're not joined at the hip, you know," Janice says, now testy.

"Okay." Denny pulls back. "Does she have a boyfriend?"

The girl looks at Bracciano again as though for permission to answer—or to prepare a lie, Denny guesses. She says, "No."

"And you don't know her whereabouts right now?"

"No."

"Okay," Denny says. "Thanks, Janice. Let Dr. Bracciano know if you hear from her?"

Bracciano sends her back to her desk with a flick of his head. "She's lying," he says.

"I think so, too," Denny says. "You'd make a good cop."

"A school counselor's like a cop, only different."

Bracciano looks through Charlotte's folder. Says, "Hmm."

"What?"

"There's a poolhall nearby. Before she disappeared, she was picked up there a few times for truancy. Might be worth checking out."

Denny agrees. He gets up to go. "One more thing," he says. "When she dropped out, did you get in touch with her parents?"

"Of course."

"What did they say?"

"Told me she was staying with relatives out of town."

Bracciano puts the folder back in his file cabinet. "You know what that usually means, don't you? A girl gets sent out of town for a while?"

"Indeed."

Among other possibilities, girls get sent to out-of-town relatives to have their babies.

22

EVA SZABÓ

[Wednesday, April 2, 1941]

The Rouge Tavern. Men laughing, drinking, celebrating what the walk-out means for them. Through the smoke eddying in the blue air over the tables she spots Anton at his usual spot. Kevin and Eddy are with him. Frank is missing.

"Hey," Anton says, "look who's here." He's smiling but the other two are stone-faced. "We missed you last night." He seems boozier than usual.

"I couldn't make it in," Eva says. "Can I sit down?"

"Sure thing."

She sits at the place where Frank sat last time.

"Where's your other friend?" she asks.

The three men share a look. Eva can't read it. The other two wait for Anton to speak.

"I guess you didn't hear," Anton says. "Frank got fired."

"When? What happened?"

"Just before the walkout. His union activity caught up with him."

Eva has to remind herself she's supposed to be anti-union with these guys. What would an anti-union remark be?

"There you go," she says. "The union comes through again."

Anton gives her a look, like he knows something about her she doesn't know about herself.

"How could he be fired if you're all on strike?" she asks.

"They can do whatever they want," Anton says. "Plus, it turns out Frank wasn't who we thought he was."

"What's that mean?"

"He got what was coming to him. He was a Red."

"How do you know?"

"Kevin here followed him one night after we left the Rouge. Saw him meet with a guy we happen to know is a Commie agent."

Why would Kevin follow him, she wonders. Do they follow her, too? And how do they know who's a Communist agent?

And did they tell someone about Frank, and that's what got him fired?

Instead of asking, she says, "Doesn't mean he's a Red."

"Baby doll, that's exactly what it means. Kevin heard him talking to the Commie. Frank was spilling beans nobody wants spilled."

Before she can stop herself, the question comes out. "About what?"

Anton gives a dramatic, long-suffering sigh. "Look, let's not talk about Frank, okay?"

The conversation comes to a dead stop. It's obvious Eva is inhibiting the men again. She is about to excuse herself when Kevin says, "Did you hear the game?"

Baseball. Men's gossip.

They go on to talk about the Tigers' win over the Louisville Colonels in Lakeland. A spring training game. Eva doesn't follow sports, but apparently a Tiger named Dixie Parsons was the batting star in a game that went ten innings.

The talk turns to the Stanley Cup playoffs and who will face the Red Wings in the finals.

She stops listening.

She's glad the awkwardness she caused has dissipated and the men talk sports as if she weren't there. Still, the weather around the table has changed; she feels less welcome here than ever.

She decides not to stay.

She finishes her drink. "Well," she says, "early day tomorrow. Gotta get going." She says her goodbyes and walks out of the bar.

She is dizzy. Not from being tipsy . . . she hasn't had that much to drink. Maybe it's the sudden fear she can't trust these guys.

She may already have said too much, judging by the look Anton gave her.

She hears the bar door open and close behind her.

Hears, "Hey, toots, wait up."

A guy she's never seen before follows her. Big, with eye-watering body odor even from several feet away.

He grabs her by the arm and leads her around the side of the building. She pulls away but his thick body presses her into the wall. Goes nose-to-nose with her. Blows his foul beer-breath into her face.

She says, "Stop it!"

She tries to push him away, but he's too strong. He comes right back at her.

"I seen you in there. You think you're too good for us? I know how to handle a twist like you."

She struggles, cries, "Let me go!" But she can't get loose.

She knees him between the legs. Slips out of his grasp.

He doubles over and pukes noisily and copiously.

She hears another man's voice. "Everything okay here?"

She runs toward the voice.

A camera hangs around the man's neck. She recognizes him—he's the one she talked to the first day of the strike. Hal, his name is.

"You okay?" he asks Eva.

She entwines her arm with his. "Let's get out of here."

Hal walks her to his car, an old Ford. "You okay really?"

"Let's just go."

With Eva in the passenger seat, he starts up and drives off.

"Have you been following me?"

"I was in the bar talking with strikers. I saw you come in, but when you sat down with those guys I decided not to bother you. I saw that guy get up and follow you out. My gut told me you might need help with him."

"I thank your gut. Not sure where this would have ended if you hadn't been there."

"You seemed to have it under control. Where to?"

She directs him to her house in Delray.

She sees Josef waiting for her on the front steps. She stiffens.

Hal sees him, too. Notes her reaction. "Everything good?" he asks.

"Yeah. You don't have to save me again. He's just my

stepbrother."

"I can stick around if you want me to."

"I can handle this guy."

"You sure?"

"Positive."

He reaches into his coat pocket and takes out a card. Hands it to her. His business card: *Harold Perlman, Free-lance Photographer*, along with his phone number.

"Hang on to it," he says. "If you ever need saving again."

"Thank you." She leans in to give him a quick peck on the cheek and jumps out of the car.

He gives two quick toots and drives off.

She turns to her stepbrother.

"Who was that?" he asks.

"None of your business."

"Somebody's going to be jealous," he sing-songs.

"What are you doing here?"

"Is that how to greet me? No, 'Hi Josef,' 'How are you, Josef.' 'It's good to see you, Josef'?"

When she doesn't respond—she doesn't care about the answer to any of those questions—he laughs. It's what crazy people do, as though alone in the world they're amused by their own cleverness. His dark good looks hide the lunacy in his heart.

He takes a swig from the whiskey bottle he's holding.

She asks, "Where'd you get that?"

"I brought it with me."

She goes up the steps past him into the house. Ágnes is in her chair, listening to the radio.

"Eva," she says, "*a testvéred éppen itt volt.*"

Your brother was just here.

"My stepbrother," Eva corrects her.

The storm door opens and slams. Josef comes inside.

Ágnes points to the Hoosier cupboard. "Yeah," Eva says, "I saw the money."

"*Nem, van több,*" Ágnes says.

No, there's more.

Eva goes into the kitchen and takes down the coffee can. Sure enough, there are more bills inside.

"You brought this tonight?" she says to Josef. It is more an accusation than a question.

He nods. "Anybody else might say thanks." He takes another swig from the whiskey bottle.

"Did you leave any more of your hate trash?"

"I just brought that one to show you. Thought you'd be interested in it."

"Really? Why?"

"You're a Jew, right?"

"So what? I need to know people hate me? Is this money part of that garbage you left here?"

"Yeah. A guy I know pays me to spread it around town. 'Garbage,' as you call it, means money for me. Just trying to share the wealth with my family. Besides, what you call trash other people call the truth."

This infuriates Eva.

"I don't want this money," she says. She takes the money out of the can and throws it at him.

Ágnes says, "*Nem, nem, nem!*" No, no, no! "*Ez kell nekünk!*" We need that!

"We don't need his filthy money."

The old woman starts to cry at the thought of losing all the money. Calmly Josef gathers it up and places it back in the coffee can. Sets it on the dining room table. "See what you're doing?" he says to Eva. "You're upsetting her."

Ágnes holds her hands out for her son. She cries for him with her twisted face.

He bends down to hug her. Gives Eva a smirk.

"Lots more where this came from, Mamma," he says.

Later. Eva helps her stepmother into bed. Josef has gone.

"Eva, *nem akarjuk azt a pénzt? Szükségünk van rá!*" Ágnes asks.

Don't we want the money? We need it!

"It comes from hate," Eva says. "I don't want it in the house."

Ágnes waves it away. Details, details. Eva has heard Ágnes complain about the Jews, even though she married one.

With Ágnes settled in bed, Eva sits by herself in the living room with her journal open in front of her. The can of money is still on the dining room table. They don't have Ágnes's seamstress income anymore, and what Eva gets from working at the factory she turns over to Elizabeth, who pays her a weekly salary.

But where does Josef get those terrible things from? And why is he even involved? He has always been a problem, even when her father Lazlo was alive. Minor scrapes with the police—thieving, vandalism, as though he had an anger inside him he couldn't understand or express except through violence and destruction.

He left home as soon as he could. Though in truth her father threw him out of the house several times for his filthy ways—drinking, whoring, smoking reefer. Now he still stays away for weeks at a time. Then he shows up like this, a conquering hero. He makes her sick.

And no matter what got him thrown out, what crime or misdemeanor, he's always welcomed back. First by her father when he was around, and now by Ágnes, who makes him feel—again—like he is her favorite child.

She hopes he'll disappear for another few months.

And if he should stay away forever, it wouldn't bother Eva either.

She writes up her day in her journal.

23

CLARENCE BROWN

[Friday, April 4, 1941]

The canteen at the Hunt Street Station. Exhaustion makes Clarence's mind fuzzy and his limbs hurt. He was up all night with Bessie. Her ankle was so painful it brought her to tears.

First thing that morning, Clarence took her in to see Dr. Jemison at Parkside Hospital. She didn't want to go, but Clarence insisted. The doctor told them the ankle would hurt as it healed, and gave her morphine tablets for the pain.

In the canteen, the few Negro officers sit in the back, confined near the kitchen. The whites are all up front.

He sees Roger Clendening. Sitting with a half-dozen other white cops. There they are, making the canteen safe for the white man.

Also making it impossible for Clarence to find out what he wants to know. Clendening will put on a show for his brother officers if Clarence approaches him.

Yet to ask to speak with him privately will also give him the opportunity to put on a show. Clarence can hear it: Who are you to order me around, boy? You got something to say, say it in front of my friends. What's the matter, afraid to talk in front of white men?

Which would be equally as bad. Especially since Wilson specifically warned Clarence off the case.

Instead, Clarence gets a Coca-Cola and sits with the Negro officers. When Clendening gets up to go, Clarence follows him out.

"Clendening."

Clendening stops. Turns.

"I knew you wanted to talk to me," Clendening says. "What's the matter, cat got your tongue in front of white folks?"

Uh-huh. Just as Clarence expected.

Clarence is bigger than Clendening, broader in the shoulders even without the armor underneath his suit coat. Clarence could break him in half if he wanted to, but it wouldn't solve anything.

Still, Clarence feels the urge.

Ignore it, he tells himself.

To keep himself from acting on it, Clarence says, "What happened to the child you took away on Monday?"

"What do you mean, what happened? It was dead."

"Where's the body now?"

"A little birdy told me it's not your problem anymore."

Clarence ignores him. So much of getting through the day is knowing what to ignore. "We don't have a report on him. I checked with the county coroner," Clarence says. "They don't have his body over there. Where is he? How did he die? How did he get in the basement of that building?"

Clendening reaches out to pat Clarence's shoulder. Clarence bats it away. "Don't put hands on me."

"Calm down, big man." Clendening starts to smile, a mocking little grin. "You seem a little tense."

"Where's that child's body?"

"Don't worry about it."

Clendening brushes by Clarence, who almost chokes on his anger. Don't let him see it, Clarence tells himself. And don't do anything you'll regret.

Clarence watches Clendening's back until he turns the corner out of sight.

Standing watching him is David Marshall, one of the other Negro detectives. Dave was indicted in the graft trial now under way. He was suspended pending the outcome of the trial.

Dave throws him a nod. The acknowledgement helps drain Clarence's anger away.

"Alright?" Dave says. He comes up and they shake hands.

"Clendening, man," Clarence says.

"I hear that. "

"What are you doing here? Heard you're on a forced vacation."

"Trial's on hold for another day. Thought I'd come down and see my brother in arms. Got time for lunch?"

Tipton's Luncheonette on Hastings in Black Bottom. The waitress, Miss Etta, shuffles over with a Coca-Cola as soon as she sees Clarence come in and sit down. She grimaces, as if her feet are hurting her.

"Mr. Dave," she says when she notices Clarence's companion. "Ain't seen you in a month of Sundays."

"You might say I been on sabbatical, Miss Etta."

"You still drinking your coffee black?"

"Black and strong, like I like my womens."

Miss Etta gives Dave a playful slap on the shoulder and totters off. Her ankles are swollen. She should have retired a while ago, but Clarence knows money's tight with her so she hangs on.

Money's tight with *her*?

With everybody.

"How you been, man?" Clarence asks.

"You know. Some days good, some days not."

"How's the trial coming?"

"They got nothing on me. I expect they'll dismiss the charges sooner or later."

"You'll still have to go up before the Board."

The Police Trial Board, where all the police who've been charged with a crime have to appear.

"Uh-huh," Dave says. "I also expect I'll just be reassigned. They'll take my suspension as punishment enough."

"You hope."

"I hope."

Miss Etta returns with his coffee. "Black and strong," she says, "just like I like my mens."

They share a laugh. The two men order the special of the day— roast turkey with dressing—and Miss Etta leaves them to their talk.

"What's shaking?" Dave asks.

Clarence tells him about the dead baby he found.

"White baby, you say?" Dave says.

"You haven't heard anything about it, have you?"

"No. Then again, I wouldn't. I'm not in on many conversations these days. I'll keep my ears open."

"Obliged," Clarence says.

Their food comes. They fold their napkins into their collars to protect their ties from the gravy the turkey slices are swimming in.

They eat in silence for a minute.

Then Dave says, "Say, Clarence, ask you a question?"

"Uh-oh, here it comes."

"You knew it was going to be something."

"Uh-huh."

"Would you do something for me?"

"If I can."

"Now, the Trial Board's going to clear me. I know that for sure. I also know they're going to transfer me out of Fourth Street."

"I'd bet on it."

"I know you like to work by yourself. But when I'm off suspension, will you ask to partner with me?"

"Happy to do it."

"Alright. Thanks, man."

"Why are you asking?"

"I have a feeling they're going to try and railroad me out the department."

"Why you think that?"

"Just things people said around me when they thought I wasn't listening. You know how it goes."

Clarence nods. Sadly, he does. He knows some white police still don't think Negroes are smart enough or good enough to be officers. Some whites they arrest don't want to be in the same police car or interrogation room as a Negro cop.

And some Negro officers try too hard to buddy up to the white police. That's why Clarence likes to work alone.

"I'll make sure they know I want to partner with you," Clarence says. "Not sure how much difference it'll make, but I'll try."

"I knew I could count on you," Dave says.

They tuck into their lunch.

24

DENNY RANKIN

[Friday, April 4, 1941]

On Ledyard Street, a block from Cass Technical High School in downtown Detroit, sits a small building with "Play-Mor Recreation" hand-painted on the front window. Inside, up front a tiny pool parlor with two tables. In the rear, down two steps, are three bowling lanes.

No one is bowling. A geezer older than Jesus sits smoking on one of the benches. A dwarf with an eye patch and a young man in Navy blue are trading strokes on one of the pool tables.

They keep playing when Denny comes in, but they give him the side-eye and share a glance.

The Heat is on the premises.

A ropey guy with a few days' grizzle slumps over the counter.

Denny badges him. Says, "You the owner?"

"Nah. Owner's a kike. He's probably sipping his Manischewitz in Florida right about now."

Denny shows him Charlotte Wheaton's photo. "Ever seen this girl here?"

"Never."

"Mind if I look around?"

"Your funeral."

Denny shows Charlotte's photo to the one-eyed dwarf and the sailor. Neither one knows her.

The ancient smoker stares at the photo of Charlotte with rheumy blue eyes. Says, "Yeah. I seen her here."

"You know her?"

"Nah. But Hooky, he knows her."

"Who's Hooky?"

"Kid who works here. Pinsetter."

"What's his real name?"

"Elmer something. Elmer, Elmo . . . last name's some Mick name. Stash, what's Hooky's last name?"

"Conroy," the counterman Stash says.

"Conroy," the old guy repeats.

"Is he here now?"

Stash says, "Nope."

Denny says, "When's he working again?"

Stash shrugs, says, "Schedule's in the office."

"Which is where?"

"Upstairs. Behind the lanes."

"Mind if I check?"

"Why you looking for him?"

Without answering, Denny gives him the fisheye.

"Your funeral," Stash says.

Denny follows a path down the left side of the empty alleys. A curtained doorway leads to the back. Denny sees the simple mechanics of the levers that raise and lower the pin setters, and a door leading to another level. He goes up a set of wooden stairs. One office, reeking of cigar smoke, has a desk cluttered with mail.

On the wall is a schedule of sorts, time slots beside names for the week. Pin boys, Denny guesses. One of the names on the schedule is Hooky. He's down to work Tuesday. Denny jots it in his notebook.

It's a date, Hooky.

He turns to go and a flyer on the top of the pile on the desk catches his eye. It's a full-color cartoon. It shows Uncle Sam being swatted in the face by a caricature of a long-nosed, bearded, yarmulke-wearing Jew with a smirking evil grin. The caption reads:

Should we let him get away with it?
The eternal enemy of the human race:
The Jew

In small print, Denny reads, "Join the National Workers League."
He folds the flyer and goes back downstairs.
He shows the flyer to Stash behind the counter. "Recognize this?"
"Never seen it before."
Big surprise.

He calls into the station for Elmer "Hooky" Conroy's last known address. It turns out to be a flop on Michigan Avenue. No names are listed on the mailboxes outside. He knocks on doors. Nobody answers.

He goes back to the station. Pulls out the flyer he picked up at the bowling alley. No indication where it was printed. He has heard of the National Workers League. It's one of the anti-Semitic groups sprouting up around town, fertilized by Father Coughlin's hateful radio broadcasts. What else they're up to, he doesn't yet know.

Denny badges his way into the United Artists Theatre on Bagley near Grand Circus Park downtown. The cashier is a white Southern woman with the unlikely name of Noviest Panty. She gives him a bright smile. He nods to the elderly ticket taker. Buys a box of popcorn at the concessions stand.

The stairs to the balcony are roped off but Denny steps over the rope and heads up.

Onscreen *The Bad Man* with Wallace Beery and Lionel Barrymore is showing. The theatre is mostly empty on this Friday afternoon and the dialog echoes in the huge auditorium.

Denny sits in the back of the empty balcony, a few rows under the projectionist's booth. Smoke from the smoking section on the main floor drifts up into the cone of light from the projectors.

He sits munching his popcorn.

In a few minutes, the door from the upper lobby opens and closes. Denny hears soft steps on the carpet. A burly figure in a blue wool uniform slips into a seat in the row behind Denny.

Aram Sarkisian. The chief of service, or head usher, of the United Artists Theatre. Also Denny's snitch. Denny doesn't know how he does it, but Aram seems to know exactly whatever's going on in the city at any given time. From his spot in the theatre, he's like a spider whose tingling web stretches all over town.

Now Aram reaches a ham-sized hand over Denny's shoulder and takes a fistful of popcorn from Denny's box. Denny holds it up, the better for Aram to grab it.

Aram leans forward so his head is next to Denny's ear. His cheap cologne smells harsh, like bug spray.

Aram says, "Noviest told me you were here."

Denny gets down to business. "What do you know about a break-in at a house in Palmer Woods? Family's named Mueller."

Aram shakes his big head. "Nothing."

"Heard of anybody pulling heists around that neighborhood?"

"Nothing in the grapevine. What was taken?"

"Jewelry," Denny says. "Also eight grand cash."

A low whistle. "Lot of scoots."

"Know anybody tossing around that kind of money?"

"Nope. I'd hear about it. The rocks, on the other hand . . . easy to move those without an ad in the paper."

"Put the word out?"

"You know me," Aram says. "We aim to please."

"Anything else shaking?"

"Nix. Quiet around town. I heard the Ferguson grand jury sent out the latest indictments."

If I haven't gotten one, Denny thinks, I'm probably in the clear for now.

Unless they sent it to his house on Roselawn . . . would Hazel send it on to the station?

Probably not. She'd probably throw it in the trash and hope the cops would come looking for him.

"Otherwise," Aram says, "you heard three of the graft defendants had their charges dismissed?"

"No. Who?"

"The Federman brothers and James Morano."

"Good news for them."

Denny gives a pair of sawbucks to Aram. "One's for you. The other's for anybody who might hear anything. Keep your eyes and ears open, eh?"

"Always do, boss. Always do."

Tom Glover lights a cigarette. He's grown visibly older, Denny thinks, since he took the editor job at the *Detroit News*. Denny has known him for years, since Tom was a brand-new reporter at the *Evening Times* and Denny was a patrolman. Now Tom is losing what gray hair he has left, and the circles under his eyes from working so hard have turned into dark puffy cushions.

Not that time has been any kinder to me, Denny thinks.

Tom's job promotion was part of what caused his wife to leave him, taking their three kids. She was already upset his investigative reporting was uncovering rats and snakes under the rocks of Detroit politics that put him in danger. (The Black Legion had marked him for death back in the '30s, but they were too inept to make it happen before the movement failed.)

Once he became an editor, his responsibilities doubled. True, he wasn't in the field anymore, but he spent more hours at his desk than ever. Tom's wife told him she didn't sign up for it—and boom, she was gone.

They sit at the bar at Jumbo's on Third Street. It's a new place, only open a year. The owner, Steve Demoff, comes by and schmoozes with Denny and Tom for a few minutes and leaves them to their whiskeys.

"Why do they call him Jumbo?" Denny asks the all-purpose authority newspaperman. "He's just a little shrimp of a guy."

"Not because of his height. Ever been here before?"

"Nope."

"If you were a regular, you'd know. It's his temper. It's legendary. It'll raise the roof once he gets wound up."

"Seems like such a nice guy, too."

"He is. Just don't cross him."

The barkeep comes over and recharges their glasses. They clink and drink. As Denny suspected, his teetotal vow was short-lived.

"So," Tom says, "the National Workers League."

Denny unfolds the flyer he took from the bowling alley. Flattens it on the bar. Says, "I can't find any information on where it's printed."

"Don't know that," Tom says. "What I can tell you is, these jamokes are crazy."

"This flyer gives me that impression. What do you know about them?"

"They started up a couple years ago. Originally formed by the German-American Bund to recruit enough white Christian workers from the auto companies so they could dominate the unions. They thought they could sabotage production through slowdowns and strikes.

"It worked for a while. They made inroads at Ford, Chrysler, Plymouth, Hudson, Packard . . . They also got into U.S. Rubber. They tried to convince the workers their Jewish bosses were smuggling Negroes into Detroit to lower workers' wages.

"After the auto workers figured out what they were doing and exposed them as a Nazi-inspired fifth column, they started focusing on pro-Axis racial propaganda. When they couldn't penetrate the unions anymore, the Bund allied with the Klan. Now the Klan is claiming the UAW and CIO leaders are all Reds. If and when the war starts, you'll see the Klan ramping up efforts to stir up racial trouble."

"Is the National Workers League behind the Ford strike now?"

"No. It's a genuine union stoppage. The Workers League, they're pro-Nazis. They'd like nothing better than to start a race war between Negroes and whites and Jews and everybody else. How'd you come across them?"

"I was looking for a missing girl. Turns out she's connected to another kid who works in a bowling alley not far from here. I found this there."

"Lots of these floating around nowadays. It was always in the air, but the Germans opened the floodgates for it. People like Father Coughlin gave everybody permission to be their worst selves."

"Who's in charge?"

"Of the National Workers League? Guy named Parker Sage. He runs it with Garland Alderman. Alderman's the national secretary. They're not pleasant people."

"Where can I find them?"

"They have an office downtown. I'll have to call you with the address."

They sip their whiskeys in silence.

Tom says, "How're Hazel and the kids?"

Fortified with another drink, Denny launches into the whole sad tale of the dissolution of his marriage.

He starts from the beginning, with his first meeting with Hazel while investigating a robbery at the Montgomery Ward department store where she worked (and still works). He takes Tom all the way through to their separation, the course of their relationship proving once again Denny's credo that things start out fine and then get worse.

Denny makes only a vague reference to his connection with the graft scandal. (No sense in saying too much about that to a reporter.) He concentrates instead on the growing distance between himself and his wife, a gap that Denny never knew how to recognize, let alone fix (having never had a good example of a loving couple in his alcoholic father and resentful mother); the demands of his job that pull him away from home at all hours and show him the worst of human nature . . . the usual outline of a couple growing apart with Denny filling in his specific details.

It's a story Tom Glover himself knows well.

The only difference between their stories is that Hazel has Bald Bennett, and Tom loves his wife and kids and his kids love him. Denny has only the police department and his monastic room at the Wolverine Hotel.

25

EVA SZABÓ

[Monday, April 7, 1941]

The least busy day so far as plant operations continue to shut down because of the strike.

Mid-morning, Eva gets a call.

Gloria, from the Administration Building. The pregnant young woman who fainted a week ago.

Whispering.

"Eva," she says, "are you alone?"

"Yes," Eva says. "Why are you whispering?"

"You got to get out of there. Right now."

"Why?"

"Two guys are on their way to see you. Tough guys from the Service Department."

"To see me? What for?"

"I don't know. I just heard them talking with Mr. Bennett. He said they got to find you. They're—"

The call cuts off.

Eva calls her back but her line is busy.

Nadine sticks her head out of one of the examining rooms. "No personal calls!"

Rather than explain, Eva just says, "Nadine, I have to go."

"What are you talking about?"

"I got to go."

"Right now?"

The entrance door to the hospital opens.

Eva stands frozen.

It's an injured man, holding his forearm that sticks out at an odd angle from the rest of his arm.

Shaken, Eva registers him.

Nadine comes up to take him back to the treatment room.

Eva throws on her coat and zips out the door.

Hurries down to the canal slip and along the bank. She takes the long way around the coal and ore storage area, then doubles back past the quenchers and the locomotive repair building.

She heads toward Gate #3 and Miller Road.

She thinks she's lost them, whoever they are.

She turns a corner.

The men cut her off.

One tall, the other short. Mutt and Jeff, she thinks crazily. They have dark jowls and suits with a bulge in front where they keep their guns for all the world to see. Mutt's fedora is dark, Jeff's is light.

They flank her. Honestly, they look like movie tough guys. The resemblance keeps Eva from being more afraid. She thinks this might be a joke.

Mutt says, "You Eva?"

Instead of answering she says, "What do you want? Why are you following me?"

"Tho many questionth," shorty Jeff lisps. He looks at his partner.

"Too many," Mutt agrees. They walk her backwards between the electrical furnace building and the sand pit.

They're like a comedy act, Eva thinks. She almost smiles. This must be a joke. Who could have arranged this? She tries to think who she knows with this kind of sense of humor.

They stop. Push her against the wall of the electrical furnace building.

Jeff in the light-colored fedora slaps her in the face.

Not hard enough to bring tears to her eyes, but hard enough to shock her.

Mutt says, "Got your attention now, sweetheart?"

Jeff slaps her again. This time it makes her eyes water and knocks her back into the wall.

"He don't usually hurt girls, but he will if he has to," Mutt says.

"We hear things about you. Matter of fact, we know all about you."

She's too surprised and frightened to answer.

"Here's a little advice," Mutt says. "Just one word: quit. Easy to remember. It'll be a lot more healthy for you."

"What are you talking about," she manages to get out before Jeff slaps her again. Harder this time.

"Oh, I think you know," Mutt says. "And by the way, we know about your father, too. He wasn't no union hater. I was you, I'd put your papers in today and don't come back tomorrow."

He pats her face—she flinches—and leads Jeff away like he's a rabid dog.

Nadine stands a little distance away, watching.

"What are you doing there?" Eva asks.

"You seemed upset, so I followed you. What was that all about?"

"I don't know. I got a call from Gloria in the Service Department and she said I had to get away right then. Then they found me. How did they know my name?"

"Listen, kid, those guys know everything. You must be on their shit list. Come on, let's go back upstairs."

In the clinic, Eva says, "They told me to quit my job."

"Why?"

"I don't know."

"Hey, you're shaking."

Nadine takes her to the Ladies lavatory. She sits Eva on one of the toilets and applies a warm compress of paper towels to her neck and the pink spot on her face where Jeff slapped her.

"Better?"

Eva nods. "Thank you."

Nadine applies Sloan's Liniment to her hands. She keeps a bottle in her pocket. The camphor smell fills the bathroom.

Eva has stopped trembling and gets herself under control. She splashes water on her face. Pats it dry.

Nadine says, "Okay?"

Eva nods.

Nadine says, "Why don't you take the rest of the day off? It's dead around here."

She doesn't have to tell Eva twice.

She hurries off the site, head swiveling all around to make sure nobody's following her.

How could those goons know her name? And about her father? Who could have told them?

Anton and the others must have given her away. She didn't fool them with her anti-union talk.

Late afternoon. The Rouge Tavern is like a crypt. Most of the men have joined the picket lines. Only a couple of guys are at the bar now, drinking away what's left of their day. Or their lives. The table where Anton and his pals sit is empty.

Eva gets a beer and grabs a seat at the table.

She's almost done with her drink when Anton and Eddy walk in. She watches Anton, looking for any sign he betrayed her—a blink when he sees her, a subtle change in the way he carries himself, anything.

There's nothing.

He greets her with a big smile. Seems genuinely happy to see her. Is he such a good actor?

Eddy stands stone-faced as usual.

"Hey," Anton says, "look who's here!"

He sits next to her, lays a glad hand on her shoulder. "You're almost done with your beer, there," he says. "Howzbout another one?"

"Sure."

"This one's on me."

Or on Eddy, because he gives Eddy a flick of his chin. "One for me, too," Anton says.

Eddy slinks off to the bar.

Anton says, "How's tricks?"

She decides to tell him about Mutt and Jeff to see how he reacts.

"I had an interesting visit today," she says.

"At the clinic? Yeah?"

"A couple of tough guys pushed me around a little."

"No," Anton says, suddenly concerned. An exaggerated frown replaces his smile. "What happened?"

"They told me I should quit my job. if I knew what was good for me. Slapped me around, too."

"Ah, no. That's rough."

She watches him carefully, looking for signs of lies. A tic, a blink, the slight rise of an eyebrow, anything.

Nothing there. His face is blank, like a slab of ice.

Maybe they weren't the ones who turned her in after all.

"I think they were from the Service Department," she says.

"Yeah, sounds like it, alright," Anton says.

Eddy comes back carrying three beers sloshing out of the glasses. He sets the drinks down, then sits next to Anton. He sees the looks on their faces. Says, "What?"

Anton says, "Our friend here got a visit from the Service Department today. They pushed her around a little. Told her to quit her job."

Eddy says, "Yeah?"

Like he couldn't give less of a shit.

Across the street from Holy Cross Hungarian Church is a phone booth. Eva shuts herself in. She dials Elizabeth's home number.

No answer.

She tries the office number. Elizabeth's answering service takes the call. Eva asks Elizabeth to call her as soon as possible.

She needs advice. She doesn't know how to handle this situation. The Service Department goons scared her, and she can't trust Anton and his boys.

She needs to talk to Elizabeth. Maybe it's even time to bring this thing to a close. Maybe Eva doesn't have enough experience to handle this. Elizabeth should have another operative on this job.

Or maybe they can just wrap it up, depending on what happens with the strike. It doesn't seem like things can just go back to the way they were; a line has been crossed.

Literally, she thinks, remembering the picket lines four deep and the rows of cars.

She spends another fifteen minutes waiting by the phone. Then she gives up and goes home.

All the lights are on in her house when she gets there. She hopes it doesn't mean Josef is here. She can't deal with him tonight.

Except she will have to.

He's on the sofa in the living room with Ágnes.

They listen to Guy Lombardo and His Royal Canadians on WJR.

"The Band Played On." They both wave their arms in the air, directing the orchestra.

Isn't this a heart-warming family scene, Eva thinks.

They don't even look up when she comes in.

"Hello," she says.

Ágnes sees her. Puts her arm around Josef and pulls him close. Very subtle.

Josef smirks at Eva.

"Did you bring any more of your filth?" she asks.

"This filth is making me money," Josef says. "And I'm sharing it with my family."

"I don't want that kind of money."

"It's green, just like every other American dollar. Buys the same things. The more the better."

Eva goes up to her room. Changes out of her work clothes. When she comes downstairs, Ágnes and Josef are still sitting with their heads together. No matter what her stepbrother does—and no matter what Eva does—he will always be Ágnes's pet.

"Ágnes," she says, "it's time to get ready for bed."

Ágnes mimes being hurt by this attempt to take her away from her son. *"Nem,"* she says, *"szeretnék több időt tölteni a bátyjával."*

No, I want to spend more time with your brother.

Of course you do, Eva thinks. The golden boy.

"It's time for bed. I have to get up in the morning and go to work."

Now Ágnes strokes her son's face, her face a sad mask of tragedy. When did she become such an actress, Eva wonders. She's a regular Greta Garbo.

Eva has lost her patience. Her anger at Josef and her fright over the threats from the goons during the day boil over into anger at the old woman. "Come on," she says to Ágnes, and grabs her arm to pull her to her feet.

Ágnes yelps in pain.

Josef springs to his feet. "Stop it!" He pushes Eva away. Eva stumbles backwards and falls over. She hits her head on the floor with a "thunk!"

She gets to her feet and goes after Josef, her sudden fury uncontrollable.

She slaps at him with broad swings. He punches her in the face and she goes down again.

Her nose gushes blood. She holds a hand against it and rolls onto her knees. Gets up on all fours. Gets her feet under her and reaches for a kitchen towel to stanch the blood.

Josef comes right up to her. Sticks his face into hers.

"You ever touch me again," he says, "I swear to God I'll kill you, you stupid bitch."

He gives her a push against the sink. Her feet give out from under her and she slides down.

Josef kisses his mother and swaggers out of the house, leaving Eva on the floor.

Her eyes burn with fury.

26

CLARENCE BROWN

[Monday, April 7, 1941]

W hen he gets home, Bessie is stretched out on the couch with her leg up on a pillow. She's reading a newspaper, but not the *Tribune*, her usual. She's reading the *Evening Times*.

He gives her a peck on the cheek and goes back to their bedroom to hang up his armor and change his clothes. He comes back out and sits in his chair. As days go, this was not a bad one.

He kicks off his shoes, asks, "Where's Malone?"

"I guess he's in the rec room in the cellar. I haven't seen him for a while."

"How's the ankle?"

"Same. How's your day?"

As a rule, he doesn't talk about his days as a policeman. Sometimes it's hard enough to get through them the first time; he doesn't want to relive them in the retelling, and Bessie doesn't push him.

Because he thinks she'll enjoy it, he tells her what happened when he was driving down Hastings Street in Paradise Valley. He got a radio call to see a man on Chestnut Street in Black Bottom.

The address was an old three-family wooden structure that leans to the right as if out of sheer exhaustion. Standing on the porch was Lott Turner, wearing a wool winter coat despite the weather; it was the warmest day of the year, in the upper 50s.

They shook hands and Lott led Clarence up a flight of stairs to his second floor flat. Inside was an immaculate living room. Lott took

Clarence through to the kitchen, also immaculate. Lott's common-law wife Lucille sat at the kitchen table. In front of her were three Mason jars covered with clods of dirt.

Clarence sat in front of the jars. "What have we here?"

"Our son Robert," Lott said, "was digging in the back with two friends and found these here glass jars. They filled with money."

Lott unscrewed one. Pulled out a handful of five- and ten-dollar bills.

"How much is here?" Clarence asked.

"Eight hundred twenty-one bucks."

The money was crinkly and old. The series dated back to the '30s. It's been buried a long time.

"We called you to ask what should we do," Lucille said.

Clarence knows if he takes the money down to the station, it will disappear. He says, "Let me check and see if there's any mention of this specific amount of money being missing in the last few years. Money's so old, I'm thinking there won't be. If nothing pops up, I guess it's yours."

Lott smiled broadly. "Just what I hoped you'd say."

Now Bessie shakes her head. "Almost enough to make me start digging in my own backyard."

"That kind of lightning doesn't strike twice."

"At least nobody took a shot at you today. That's a good thing."

He picks up a section of the newspaper she has dropped. "Finished with this one?"

She nods and he unfolds it to the front page. Beneath the main headline, toward the bottom of the page, he reads this:

"NEGROES KIDNAPPED MY BABY," WHITE MOTHER CLAIMS

And below, in a smaller headline:

PLEASE RETURN HIM, DISTRAUGHT WOMAN PLEADS

A near-hysterical Detroit woman, Mrs. Belle Baxter, 25, white, told police today her infant son had been kidnapped from in front of her sister's home.

Baxter said her newborn son, Jeremy, was in his carriage

as she was leaving her sister's home after a visit at 21511 West McNichols, when she realized she forgot her purse. She left him alone for less than a minute, she said, while she ran upstairs to her apartment to get her purse.

When she returned, the carriage with Jeremy was gone.

Baxter said she saw a Negro man running down the street pushing the baby carriage.

She hollered for him to stop but he took the baby out of the carriage and jumped into a late-model Ford waiting at the curb.

"If you have my baby, please don't hurt him. I miss him so much!" the mother pleaded.

Police are investigating. If any member of the public has any information about this kidnapping, please contact the Detroit Police Department.

No photograph accompanies the story.

"What's the matter?" Bessie says.

"You see this story about the baby got kidnapped by a colored man?"

"I saw it. People didn't have us to blame for these things, I don't know what they'd do. Why?"

"I found a dead white baby in a tenement in Black Bottom a week ago."

"You think it's the same baby?"

"I don't know for sure. But my gut tells me it is."

27

DENNY RANKIN

[Tuesday, April 8, 1941]

In the morning, the duty sergeant catches him before he gets upstairs to the detective bullpen. Says, "Rankin, we got a redball. All hands on deck."

"What's going on?"

"The jungle bunnies are restless," the sarge says with a grin.

A phalanx of Negro police, plainclothesmen, and citizens keep a crowd of two dozen white men at bay at the corner of Brush Street and Gratiot Avenue in Black Bottom. Cars parked in the middle of the street separate the groups. Store fronts along Adams are smashed: a tailor shop, a luncheonette, a drugstore, a grocery. Shattered clay pots and soil and yellow and purple daffodils and tulips litter the sidewalk on the front of a smashed florist's. Broken glass is everywhere.

The white men are screaming at the Negroes and wave baseball bats and two-by-fours.

Both sides are bloodied. There must have been a clash already.

An equal number of white policemen stand behind the white crowd, watching. They don't seem to be preparing for anything, as if they were bystanders.

For their part, the Negroes across Brush are angry and

determined. The police have their sidearms and billy clubs; the citizens carry nothing but broom handles, shovels, and their nerve.

Denny spots one of the white policemen he knows. Lieutenant Harvey Kendall.

"What's all this?" Denny asks.

"We got a standoff between those fellas with a suntan across the street and our white brothers over here."

"What's the problem?"

"Seen the *Free Press* this morning?"

"Not yet."

Before Kendall can reply, half a dozen whites make a dash across the street. They head toward a gap in the line of parked cars.

The Negroes beat them back. The skirmish is loud but over quickly.

The white men return to screaming from across the road.

Denny recognizes one of the bigger men in the line of Negro police. Clarence Brown, a detective assigned to the Hunt Street Station, which includes Black Bottom and Paradise Valley. Clarence was famous in the department for his home-made armor and his two pearl-handled .45s.

He seems to be in command of the men.

Denny crosses the street. All eyes are on him. He has pinned his badge to his coat but still there is no trust in the looks he gets. He knows. As far as they're concerned, he's the enemy.

Clarence steps forward.

"Detective Brown?" Denny says. "Denny Rankin."

The two men shake hands and the Negro police on that side of the street relax a bit.

Denny says, "What's going on?"

"There was a story in the paper last night. A white woman said a couple colored guys stole her baby."

"Jesus."

"So we got vigilantes hopping around, looking for an excuse to cause trouble. They started out smashing windows. A bunch of us got together and chased them off. Other groups are trying to get into the area from other streets. But we got them contained, too."

"I see the white cops are being as helpful as always," Denny says.

"They don't want to get our blood on their nice uniforms. I hear there's fistfights here and there around town. Couple people got pulled off streetcars. The usual. Nothing major. Yet."

Whenever there are racial fights in Detroit, gangs of whites appear out of nowhere and start pulling Negroes off streetcars.

Denny says, "You know anything about this baby story?"

Clarence gives him a forlorn look. He's big and bulky from his home-made armor under his coat. "Just came out last night. You know as much as I know."

Denny says, "Anybody talked to the mother who claims her baby was stolen?"

"Nobody, far as I know."

"The whole thing might all be just bullshit."

"Might be."

Movement down the block catches Clarence's eye. He mutters, "Shit." Then calls, "Malone? Malone! What are you doing here?"

Clarence turns to Denny. "Later, man. Gotta take care of this."

Clarence starts toward the young man he was calling to.

Denny eyes the whites who are making the disturbance. A few dozen, mostly in their twenties and thirties, their faces twisted in hated. They are very loud.

Denny thinks he sees Heinz Mueller among them.

Denny heads toward him. He can't tell if Heinz has spotted him or not, but by the time Denny makes the whites' side of the street, Heinz has disappeared.

"Nigger lover!" one of the white men screams in Denny's face.

Denny pushes him away.

"Who are you people?" he asks.

"White Americans who want to save our country from niggers and kikes!" another screams.

"Go home," Denny says.

"These are *our* streets! This is *our* city!" He shoves a flyer into Denny's face.

After shouting more slogans—"Keep America white!"—and pushing and shoving, they drift away, throwing curses back over their shoulders. The Negro police wait at their posts, and only gradually, when they are convinced the whites are gone for good, do they, too, leave. The civilians who protected their neighborhood linger.

They've learned never to trust a white man.

Who could blame them?

Denny looks at the flyer the guy shoved at him. It's the same one he found at the bowling alley. The same long-nosed, bearded, yarmulke-wearing Jew with an evil grin slapping Uncle Sam.

The same caption:

Should we let him get away with it?
The eternal enemy of the human race:
The Jew

The same sponsor: the National Workers League.

Easter answers the door at the Mueller home. "I don't let you in," she says.

"I'm looking for Heinz."

"Not here."

"Where is he?"

"I'm their cleaner, not their keeper."

He pushes past her into the house.

"I call police," Easter says to his back.

"I am police," Denny says. He looks around the downstairs. None of the Muellers are around. "When did you last see him?"

"He leave after breakfast. I don't see him since."

Denny takes the stairs up two at a time. All the doors on the second floor are locked. Only the bathroom door hangs open, but even this has a lock on the outside.

He goes back downstairs. "Tell Heinz I'm looking for him," he says to Easter on his way out.

She slams the door behind him.

28

EVA SZABÓ

[Tuesday, April 8, 1941]

Every time the door opens, she scrutinizes the visitor. Friend or foe? Another man wounded by the American industrial machine or a thug here to make good on his threat?

Even Nadine notices it. "You seem jumpy today," she says after lunch. "Everything okay?"

"Yeah. Everything's fine."

"Nervous after what happened yesterday?"

"I was. But I'm not anymore."

After she got Ágnes settled last night, Eva spent most of the previous night in bed staring at the ceiling. She felt like she passed a watershed, of sorts; never again would she let a man do violence to her. She was slight, with no fighting skills, so she didn't know how she would prevent it other than through her resolve. But she was determined she wouldn't allow a man to put hands on her like Mutt and Jeff and her stepbrother did yesterday.

"Ah," Nadine says, "those guys were just trying to scare you."

They succeeded; Eva thinks. But I'm never going to show it. And I'm not going to stop what I'm doing.

Nadine examines Eva's face for the first time all day. "What happened to you?"

Eva takes a compact out of her purse and looks at herself in the little round mirror even though she knows what she'll see: a bruise on her cheek from where her stepbrother hit her the night before. She tried to cover it up with powder from her compact but it was no use; the bruise showed through, dark and dangerous.

"I fell last night. Hit my face."

Which is, strictly speaking, the truth.

Nadine doesn't believe her. She says, "I've been there before, honey. You don't have to take that from a man."

Eva stays mum.

"I'll give you my two cents: leave him. He'll never change."

Now *she's* telling me to quit something, Eva thinks. Everybody wants me to go.

"It's not what you think it is," Eva says.

"Oh, it's exactly what I think it is. I told you, I been there. My first husband used me for a punching bag until I said to myself, 'No more,' and left him. Only thing that works."

"I'm not married."

"All the more reason not to put up with it. Men'll keep at it until you say enough."

Nadine reaches out and takes Eva's hand. Squeezes it.

Eva is too moved by her concern to say anything.

How to tell her it was her stepbrother and not her boyfriend?

For the rest of the day, Nadine treats Eva differently . . . her words are softer, more understanding.

Solidarity between battered women.

When Nadine goes out to get a worker settled in an ambulance, Eva dials Elizabeth Waters's office.

Elizabeth picks up right away.

"Eva, thank God. Sorry I missed you last night. Is everything all right? Your message sounded desperate."

Eva keeps an eye on the door.

"I got a visit at the plant from a couple creeps from the Service Department."

"What happened?"

"They told me I was talking too much about the union. They told me I should quit or else. Slapped me around a little."

"Oh Eva, I'm so sorry."

"They had me scared yesterday. But I'm better today." She won't mention her set-to with her stepbrother last night.

"No," Elizabeth says. "I'm pulling you out of there."

"I want to stay in. I hear rumors the strike's going to end soon. If it doesn't end by Friday, you can pull me."

"It's against my better judgment."

"If I got those two apes worried, I must be close to something."

Elizabeth pauses.

Eva thinks this was the right point to make.

Finally, Elizabeth says, "Okay. But if you smell any other trouble, you have to leave immediately. Just walk away. Drop everything and go. Promise me you will?"

"I will."

"You're going to make a great detective, kiddo," Elizabeth says. "You got what it takes. But you need to learn what kinds of chances you can take, and what kind you can't."

"I'm trying."

29

CLARENCE BROWN

[Tuesday, April 8, 1941]

"Malone!"

Malone stops and turns. Clarence catches up to him.

"What do you think you're doing?" Clarence says.

"Trying to help."

"How? By getting your head bashed in?"

"Naw, Mr. Clarence." Malone points across the line of cars that separated the angry white crowd from the Negroes protecting their neighborhood. "Not gonna let those white men in here. Not without a fight."

Malone rages. Not at Clarence, but at the whites who tried to run riot over Black Bottom.

Clarence calms himself. Forces himself to remember: for all his size, Malone is only a boy.

"This isn't the way to do it, Malone. You could have been hurt. Didn't you see those ofays? They had bats and clubs and who knows what all."

"That's how you were doing it."

"I'm a grown-ass policeman. I carry guns. It's my job. You're just a boy. No matter how grown you think you are, you're a kid."

Malone waves the thought away angrily and turns from Clarence.

Clarence says, "I'm not done."

Malone keeps walking.

Clarence takes two strides forward and grabs the boy by the arm. "I said I'm not done speaking with you."

"I'm done with you."

"Maybe you should go back home until you calm down."

"Maybe you should leave me the fuck alone. You ain't my father."

Malone pulls his arm free and keeps walking.

Clarence lets him go. Nothing can be accomplished with both of them this angry.

He's the adult, so he checks himself and watches Malone stomp off. They'll speak later, when they've both calmed down and their blood isn't up from the attacks on their neighborhood.

Damn. Clarence knows he handled this exactly wrong.

He let Malone transfer his anger from the white men—which he can't do anything about—to Clarence himself. Malone can do something about Clarence.

And Malone was right. You're too old to be anybody's father, Clarence tells himself.

Most especially a troubled kid like him.

With the crowd dispersed, he walks across the street to the white police.

Most of them are also gone. The situation commander, Lieutenant Harvey Kendall, remains to monitor things.

The two men give each other suspicious nods. "Brown," Kendall says.

"Lieutenant. Anything new on this kidnapped baby case?"

"Haven't heard anything."

"Who's in charge of it?"

"Why, you know something?"

"If my community's involved, I might be able to help."

"Cal Seidensticker's running it."

"Out of the Eighth? Why's it coming out of there?"

"That's where the abduction took place."

The Eighth Precinct station is on the west side, McNichols and Grand River, miles from Black Bottom. Detective Cal Seidensticker is a tall, bloated white man with a perpetual oily smile on his chubby face. Even when Clarence Brown shows up in the Detective squad room, Seidensticker keeps his smile in place.

"The famous Detective Brown," Seidensticker says. "Two-gun Brown."

Clarence doesn't extend a hand because he knows Seidensticker isn't going to shake it. Clarence feels all eyes are on him from the white detectives and uniformed police standing by.

"What can I do you for?" Seidensticker says.

"I hear you caught the stolen baby case."

"I did."

"You talked to the mother?"

"I did. She came down the station yesterday."

"She say what happened?"

"She left the baby alone for a minute while she ran back upstairs at her sister's and when she came down the baby was gone. She said she saw a colored gentleman get into a car with the child. Another colored gentleman was behind the wheel."

"The press got the story fast."

"Happened to be a reporter here. He heard what was going on and interviewed the poor lady."

"You get a description of the man? Or the car?"

"Not anything I could work with. Just he was colored," Seidensticker adds.

The oily smile says, *Like you.*

"How's the case coming?"

"It's coming," Seidensticker says.

Clarence asks, "Could I get her address?"

Now the smile wavers. "What for?"

"I'd like to speak with her. Maybe I can get a better description of the Negro she says took the baby. I might know who he is."

Now the smile returns. "Not going to happen, Sunny Jim." Sweet as pie. "The situation is under control. No need for you to get involved."

He turns away and leaves Clarence standing in the middle of the bullpen, all eyes still on him.

Clarence fumes.

Back in his car, he radios in for Detective Denny Rankin. After a few minutes, Rankin's call comes through on the two-way.

Clarence says, "Can you do me a favor?"

In ten minutes, Rankin radios him back with the address of the woman who made the stolen baby complaint. She has no phone.

Seidensticker gave it all to Rankin with no hesitation whatsoever.

Before he leaves the neighborhood, Clarence drives by the address listed in the newspaper. The mother, Belle Baxter, claimed she was visiting her sister's house here.

The address the newspaper gives for her sister, 21511 West McNichols, turns out to be the Redford Branch of the Detroit Public Library.

In a commercial section with no apartment houses—or single-family homes—nearby.

Rankin said the address for Belle Baxter is on Evergreen Road near Seven Mile Road, a neighborhood of single-story brick duplexes.

Clarence knocks on the door of the address Rankin gave him. A curtain twitches and a sour-faced middle-aged white man glares out at him.

A few moments later, the door opens. The white man stands there holding a shotgun pointed at Clarence's feet. The man says, "What?"

Clarence holds up his badge. Identifies himself. "I'm looking for Belle Baxter."

"Who the hell is Belle Baxter?"

"This is listed as her address."

"Ain't no Belle Baxter live here." Nasal Southern drawl.

"She's the woman just had her baby kidnapped."

"Ain't nobody here had no baby, neither, boy."

"What about the houses nearby?"

The guy slams the door in Clarence's face.

He stands on the porch for another few moments. The window curtain twitches again and the Southerner looks out again. He taps the barrel of his shotgun against the window and motions Clarence to move along.

Clarence tries the attached home, but an old white woman tells him there's no Belle Baxter there, either.

Same story in the surrounding duplexes.

The report from the woman whose child was "stolen" is probably as phony as a three-dollar bill.

And nobody checked it out? Seidensticker didn't send a prowl car past where she said the baby was taken? Wouldn't he have discovered it was a public library?

Or did he believe the woman's story just because it was plausible two colored men would have stolen a white baby in broad daylight. Only for the baby to reappear, dead, in a Black Bottom tenement.

Or maybe Seidensticker is part of a larger scheme.

This whole story stinks.

Clarence gets a radio call. Dispatch says there's a reported break-in on Brush Street.

Clarence is needed.

30

DENNY RANKIN

[Tuesday, April 8, 1941]

The one-eyed dwarf is still shooting pool at Play-Mor Recreation with the kid in Navy blues. The other table is in use, too, and a trio of ragged men sit looking on. Denny hears the clatter of pins in the bowling alley, then the rumble of the ball rolling back to the approach at the top of the lane.

The geezer he talked to last time is bowling. He looks like he doesn't have the strength to pick up the ball, but he throws a fast one down the lane and scatters the pins for a strike.

In the pin deck is a guy in his early twenties, with the burly look of a muscular kid starting to go to fat. Denny assumes he's Hooky Conroy.

Hooky gets the pins into the pin setter and puts his full weight on a bar and the pins lower and reset.

Denny goes down the walkway at the side of the lane and through the curtain leading into the back. Hooky can't see him because he's concentrating on the old bowler's ball bearing down; Hooky can't hear him because of the rumble of the ball rolling down the alley.

The ancient bowler rolls another strike. His game ends. Hooky resets the pins and turns the lane lights off.

Denny steps in. Flashes his shield. "Hooky Conroy?"

Hooky eyes the badge. "Yeah?"

"Step out here, Hooky, will you?"

"What for?"

"Step out."

Hooky comes into the hall and Denny spins him and leans him into the back wall. Pats him down. No weapons.

"Hey! What gives?"

"You know Charlotte Wheaton?" Denny asks.

"No."

"Never met her?"

"I said no."

"Don't lie to me, Hooky. It upsets my digestion."

"I'm not lying."

"Where is she?"

"How would I know where she is? I just said I dunno her."

Denny cuffs Hooky behind his back.

Hooky says, "What the fuck did I do?"

"Statch rape, for one thing."

"What? Who?"

Denny leads Hooky out from the pinsetter and walks him down the walkway beside the bowling lanes. "You got this all wrong," Hooky says.

"Do me a favor, okay? Shut up."

In the poolroom, Stash behind the counter watches with total unconcern as Denny frog-marches Hooky, like this is a daily occurrence.

The front door opens.

In walks Charlotte Wheaton.

She is small, with honey-colored hair and a heart-shaped face. Just like in her photo. Denny remembers her from the times he's been to dinner at Phil's.

She scopes out the scene in no time flat and turns and runs back out. Denny pushes Hooky on a bench—"Stay here!" he barks—and races out the door after her.

She's fleet. Denny starts after her but she's already across the street and down the block. He'll never catch her.

Denny goes back into the pool hall.

Hooky's not there.

Nobody saw which way he went, of course.

Only one direction he could have gone. Denny goes back into the bowling alley. Sees Hooky stumbling across the three lanes with his hands cuffed behind his back. There's an exit door with a panic bar beside the third lane. Hooky busts through it.

Denny clatters across the wooden lanes in his street shoes and follows Hooky through the door. This mook Denny can catch. Hooky's not as fast as Charlotte.

Denny overtakes him down the alley. One push from behind and Hooky goes face-first into the ground.

"Hey, come on, man, you can't arrest me."

Hooky, from the back seat of Denny's car. The side of his face is raw from the scrape on the ground.

"Is that so? Why not?" Denny says.

"Because you got it all wrong, man. She ain't with me."

Denny pulls into an alley off Peterboro. Turns to look at Hooky leaning forward in his seat, his hands still cuffed behind him.

"Who's she with?"

"A buddy of mine."

"Why was she coming to see you?"

"My buddy, he asked me to watch out for her."

"Why do you need to do that?"

"Her father's a cop. She knows he's gonna be after her."

"Who's your buddy?"

Hooky hesitates.

"No? Okay," Denny says, and puts the car in gear. "She's sixteen. Stat rape, Hooky."

"Wait—wait!"

Denny turns around and looks at him. A sheen of sweat now mixes with the blood oozing from the scrape on Hooky's face.

"Is she staying with you?" Denny asks.

"Just while my buddy's busy."

"I'll ask you one more time. Who's your buddy?"

"Guy named Bert."

"Not Bert Vogelmann?"

"Yeah. You know him?"

"I do."

He takes the flyer from his pocket. Unfolds it, shows it to Hooky. "This yours?"

Hooky shakes his head.

"I found it in the bowling alley office. Know where it came from?"

"It's Bert's."

"Where'd he get it?"

"From Charlotte."

"Charlotte?"

"Yeah. She got a bunch of them. She likes to spread them around."

Hooky directs Denny to his flop on Michigan Avenue. His room is on the top floor.

Hooky stands with his hands still cuffed behind him. Denny uncuffs him so Hooky can unlock the door. Hooky goes inside.

It's just one room. The bathroom must be down the hall. There's a sloppy bed in the corner and a table with one chair against a wall. On the table is a hotplate with a sauce pan. Looks like the leavings of lumpy oatmeal sludge in the bottom of the pan.

Groceries on the window sill . . . corn flakes, bread, peanut butter, jelly. On the sill outside the window a pint bottle of milk cools.

In a corner of the room are stacks of flyers and pieces of mail. The flyers are similar to the one Denny found in the bowling alley: caricatures of Jews with large hooked noses and Negroes with tremendous lips. All of them have the National Workers League stamped on them.

The mail is addressed to Parker Sage at the National Workers League, 13535 Woodward Avenue, Room 222, Highland Park.

"She ain't coming back here, man," Hooky says. "You scared her. She knows this is the first place you'll check."

And Vogelmann's will be the second place.

But we'll check anyway.

Vogelmann's bungalow. Denny leaves Hooky cuffed to the car door.

Nobody answers the front or side door. Both doors are locked. The garage behind the house has no door. It's an empty wreck, tilting backwards. Nobody here either.

The office of the National Workers League is in a four-story building on Woodward in Highland Park, a small city completely surrounded by Detroit. Vito's Barber Shop on the ground floor leaves everything around the entrance to the building smelling of Bay Rum.

It's a walk-up. Denny leaves Hooky cuffed to the car again.

The front door to the NWL is locked. Denny pounds on the door. No one comes. He jiggles the handle but no dice.

He takes Hooky to the station to spend the night in a cell. Denny books him on a misdemeanor disorderly conduct charge rather than statch rape, which is a felony.

Denny doesn't tell the young man, but he'll check his records. If Hooky's clean, he'll get released in the morning.

31

EVA SZABÓ

[Thursday, April 10, 1941]

She takes the streetcar home after work. Walks the two blocks from her stop by herself.

Yeah, maybe not such a good idea.

She is jumpy. Looking around. Flinching at every sound—the squeal of brakes, a car horn. Everything makes her think it's Mutt and Jeff come back for seconds.

She pauses at her front walk. Sees her stepbrother and stepmother in the house through the blinds.

No. She can't face either of them tonight.

She heads for the Rouge Tavern. It's quiet. The Andrews Sisters play over the PA. "Beer Barrel Polka."

She scopes out the place. Doesn't see the guy who attacked her. Also doesn't see Hal Perlman or Anton and Eddy. But Kevin McNamara sits at their usual table. She doesn't know Kevin well, and doesn't think he likes her much. It's a feeling she returns.

She decides to give it a try with him. She gets her Altes at the bar and goes over to Kevin's table. "Hey."

He looks up as if just noticing her. "Hey."

"Mind if I sit with you?"

"Free country," Kevin says.

"So far."

No reaction from him.

She sits across the table. Takes a thoughtful sip of her beer. Now Glenn Miller's on the radio. "Little Brown Jug." Must be tuned to the drinking station.

She says, "Where are your friends?"

"Out taking care of business. Might be around later." He stares off into the bar, deliberately ignoring her.

"Okay." Then she says, "How are you holding up?"

His head swivels in her direction. Gives her a sour look. "About what?"

"You know, the strike. Frank Ennis getting fired."

"What I care about him?"

"Does anybody know any more about what happened to him?"

He gives her a hard look. "What's it to you?"

"No, nothing. I kind of liked the guy. I was just getting to know him. I was sad to hear he got fired."

"Lots of people get fired. For lots of different reasons."

"I just assumed—"

"Don't assume nothing," Kevin says. "You don't know nothing."

Okaaaaay.

Time to go before this gets really ugly.

She gets up, says, "Sorry to bother you."

She walks over to an empty stool at the end of the bar. Gives her head a shake, runs a hand through her hair.

Maybe she really should stop asking these guys questions. She feels like she's pushing too hard.

Anton and Eddy still haven't arrived by the time she finishes her beer. Kevin still stares straight ahead.

Today she's uncomfortable about being in the bar by herself. It never bothered her before. She never feared for her safety before. Since her visits from Mutt and Jeff and the guy who attacked her outside the tavern, her nerves have been jangling.

She slides off her stool. Makes her way to the front door.

Outside she takes a deep breath of the cool night air. She starts walking down Dix toward home.

She doesn't get far before she hears footsteps scraping behind her. A metallic rush of fear makes her turn. "Who are you?" she barks.

"Now, now," the man says. He's in his sixties, white, barrel-chested, white-haired. Sad eyes in a basset hound face.

He holds his hands up to calm her. "Not gonna hurt you."

"Who are you?" she says again, loud, in case anybody's nearby and can hear her.

She looks around quickly. Nobody close. He's between her and the bar entrance.

Where's that photographer when you need him?

Her fear slides into anger. Who *are* these men who think they can do this to her?

"What do you want?" she demands.

He comes up close to her.

She backs off. "Stay away."

"You don't recognize me?" he asks.

"No. Should I?"

"I was a friend of your father's. Lazlo. I was over your house a few times. You don't remember? Bogdan Kowalczyk?"

She thinks back. Tries to place him. Maybe she does remember him. Except she remembers a woman who came with him. His wife?

"I was a friend of your father's," he says again. "He talked about you all the time. You were the apple of his eye. I wouldn't do nothing to hurt you. I promise."

"Did you used to come over with a woman?"

"Yeah. My wife. Hannah. She passed away. But we'd come over to play euchre, me and Hannah, and Lazlo and Ágnes. Remember now?"

"I think so."

"I ain't seen you for years. You're so grown-up."

"What do you want?"

"I heard you talking back in the tavern," he says. "You were asking about the guy got fired?"

"Frank Ennis?"

"Yeah."

"You know what happened to him?"

"I do."

"How do you know him?"

"I work in the Foundry. Frank worked there, too."

"What do you know about him?"

He gazes around. "We shouldn't talk here. Come with me."

He starts off.

She hangs back. Really not a good idea, she tells herself.

She hears Elizabeth's voice in her head telling her the same thing:

Not. A. Good. Idea.

He turns. Says, "No, it's okay. You can trust me."

"Famous last words."

"Please. You need to see something."

She thinks back to a time when she was a little girl walking home from school and a school bus pulled up next to her. The door opened and the driver said, "Come on, get in, your mother's waiting for you." She shook her head no and the driver said, "Hey, get that little girl!" A man started after her and she ran and ran.

Now the big man stands looking at her. His face is a mask of sorrow, with desolate eyes and deep lines on his forehead.

"Don't be afraid," he says. "Please. You can trust me. You need to see this."

Well, she tells herself, you did say you wanted to make your last days at the plant count. This may be an opportunity you don't want to miss.

Then again, it may be the last, stupidest decision you ever make.

She goes with him.

And hopes for the best.

He drives east on Dix, then north on Miller Road. At Gate #2 he pulls over. "Here's where it all happened," he says. "The massacre. Where your father was hurt."

"I know." Every time she goes past this spot, she thinks about March 7, 1932.

He pauses, as though at a shrine, then continues north on Miller all the way up to Warren Road. He heads west for what seems like miles.

"Where are you taking me?" she asks.

"You wanted to know what happened to Frank. I'm going to show you."

At River Rouge Park he turns right onto Outer Drive, which runs through the park. Goes right on Tireman and takes the bridge over the Rouge River.

He parks in a wooded area.

"Follow me," he says.

He takes a flashlight out of the glove box. He leads her through the trees to a small glade. Despite the setting, she is not afraid.

He stands beside an oak tree and shines the light on the ground. "If you're looking for Frank Ennis, here's where you'll find him."

"He's buried here?"

"What was left of him."

She stares at the plot of newly disturbed soil at her feet. "What happened?"

"First they shot him. Then they clubbed him to death."

"Who? Why?"

"Harry Bennett's boys. You know who he hires, don't you? Murderers, kidnappers, gangsters . . . those are the kind of men who work for Harry Bennett."

"Why did they kill him?"

"Because he was promoting the UAW."

"Lots of people do that."

"Maybe. But Frank Ennis was a Red. The Party's main recruiter at the plant. I heard Harry Bennett himself ordered this."

"And he had his thugs do it?"

"Then buried him here. Where nobody would ever find him."

"How do you know this?"

"I was there when they did it."

Eva takes a step back. "You helped them?"

He nods.

Suddenly being alone in the woods with Bogdan Kowalczyk seems a terrible idea.

She grows so cold she shivers.

"I don't understand why you're showing me this," she says. "Are you going to kill me, too?"

"No. I brought you here because I want you to see it's dangerous, poking your nose where it don't belong."

"Why are you doing this?"

"I told you. For your father. Lazlo. He was a good man, and he was a good friend to me. I owed him a lot."

"And you repaid his friendship by helping kill a union organizer?"

"No, by trying to keep his daughter safe. The wrong people know you're asking around about the union."

Right, she thinks; I had a visit from a couple of them.

"I'm here to tell you, you need to stop. Or you're going to wind up like the guy under the dirt here. Look. I'm a patriotic American.

You know what's the biggest threat to our way of life? Union Communists like Frank Ennis. You don't want people thinking you're one of them."

"You said you were with them when it happened? Who killed him?"

"I can't tell you."

"Can't or won't?"

He says nothing, just stands looking at her with his sad eyes.

"I think you need to take me back now," she says.

"I will. I won't hurt you. But the people who did this to Ennis won't hesitate to do the same to you just because you're a woman."

He says he will drive her home. At first she refuses; she doesn't want him to know where she lives. Then she remembers he visited her house.

Still, she has him drop her off at the Holy Cross Hungarian Church. She waits on the steps of the church until he drives away. She crosses the street and closes herself into the phone booth.

Elizabeth answers right away.

Eva tells her what Bogdan Kowalczyk said about Frank Ennis. About the burial site in Rouge Park.

First Elizabeth bawls her out for going with the man in his car.

After that, she says, "This is it, Eva. The evidence we've been waiting for."

"Don't we have to verify it first? And tell the police about it?"

"Sure. I'll take care of that. What you have to do is write it up. Then I'll take it to Maurice and see how he wants to handle it."

Maurice Sugar. The general counsel for the UAW, who gets Eva's reports from Elizabeth.

"And now," Elizabeth says, "it's time to go, Eva. No arguments."

Eva has been waiting for this. "I know."

"Tomorrow when you get into the plant, I want you to let them know you're quitting. We have what you went there for, and things are getting too hot around you now. No arguments. Understood?"

"Understood."

Ágnes dozes on the sofa. Josef is nowhere around.

Eva gently wakes Ágnes and gets her ready for bed. Before she turns the light out in her room, Eva asks, "Do you remember a friend of Papa's called Bogdan Kowalczyk?"

Ágnes doesn't say anything. Eva isn't even sure she understood the question. Or would tell her if she knew the answer.

For a second Eva is struck by how old the woman looks. Gray, stringy hair. Papery-thin skin over spidery blue veins. Rheumy blue eyes. Sunken cheeks where her teeth are missing. Her mouth down-turned at one corner, a lingering effect of her stroke.

Ágnes's eyelids flutter. Eva pats her shoulder. Turns out the light.

She gets into her own bed. She takes her notebook from the nightstand and writes up the events of the day.

She will miss working at the plant. She has been getting friendlier with Nadine Denton, the head nurse, and she has gotten used to the rhythms of the clinic. Most of all, she will miss feeling like she's a part of the battle for the union in her own small way.

The other thing was, she used working at the plant as a way to get distance between herself and Vincent Németh . . . which means she will no longer be able to put off the talk she needs to have with him about their future—or lack of a future—together. Knowing him, he'll think she quit because he told her to.

She pushes that thought out of her mind. Again.

She hopes Elizabeth really will come through with another assignment for her. Eva would have no problem answering phones and doing secretarial work. But she did have fun in the field (as Elizabeth calls the actual investigations that they do).

Before turning out the light, she resolves to talk to Elizabeth about this tomorrow.

32

CLARENCE BROWN

[Thursday, April 10, 1941]

After dinner, Clarence gets Bessie settled on the couch in their living room. Miss Maxine made an oxtail soup for them for dinner, and left a sweet potato pie for dessert. She's a treasure—though Clarence still has to speak with her about her sweet desserts, which Bessie isn't allowed to eat any more.

"Why you so down?" Bessie asks. "Still thinking about Malone?"

Clarence sighs, rubs a hand over his face.

"I am," he says. "Wish I hadn't lost my temper with him when he started to sass me on Tuesday. We didn't part on good terms."

"You did what you thought was right."

"I did. I shouldn't have yelled at him, though. He's so big, it's hard to remember he's just a boy."

"Not so much a boy anymore. He's almost as tall as you. But it's true, he needs to learn what's what in this world for a colored man."

They listen to the radio for a while. Clarence stirs himself, tells Bessie he has to go out for an hour. She promises to be careful while he's gone.

First he stops by Malone's aunt's apartment. He hears the children yelling while he's still outside the building. She comes to the door of her first floor apartment, harried and disheveled. She tells him she hasn't seen Malone for days.

"Matter of fact," she says, "I thought he been staying with you."

"You see him, you just give me a call, let me know he's okay?"

She promises she will.

Next he returns to Evergreen Road, where Belle Baxter said she lives. It's possible the address got garbled, he thinks, and she really does live around here.

He starts a canvas. Up one side of Evergreen for three blocks and down the other. Many don't answer the door to him. A colored man ringing your bell in the evening is not a welcome sight for most white people in this city. He has his badge out and holds it up to those people brave enough to come to the door.

Most of them make sure to lock the storm door before asking him what his business is. He doesn't reach everybody, but he talks to enough people to convince him of three things:

First, nobody knows anyone named Belle Baxter, or any white woman who lives in the neighborhood who has an infant son.

Second, everybody heard the terrible story about the Negroes who kidnapped a white baby yesterday. Everybody has a comment for the Negro detective about how Negroes are criminals and untrustworthy and how glad they are to keep them out of this neighborhood.

And third, Belle Baxter lied. She claimed she left her baby in his carriage on the sidewalk outside her sister's building while she ran up to get her purse. But the address she gave was the Redford Branch of the Detroit Public Library in a commercial district; there are no apartment houses anywhere nearby.

How could Seidensticker have gotten this so wrong? A tale of Negro men kidnapping a white baby would have brought out the cops in force to scour the neighborhood.

Unless he knew it was a lie, and he was in on it.

If Clarence hadn't found a dead infant, he would have thought Belle Baxter was made up to bring out the local white toughs, as it did this morning.

But there is a real dead infant in the middle of this. Who was he?

How did he die?

And where is his body now?

Malone Coleman still isn't back when Clarence makes it home.

You did what you could, he tells himself. You can't make people do what they don't want to do. You try. It's all you can do.

Maybe it's for the best. As the boy said, Clarence isn't his father.

And Malone won't replace DeMarco.

He helps Bessie get ready for bed.

He settles back in his chair in his living room and starts to plan a schedule for his baseball team—tryouts, practices, games. He's very late getting started this year. First time he's been this late. He could still salvage the season if he gets on his shake.

Too much going on, between taking care of Bessie and his cases and the dead baby.

Plus also too, he thinks, you're getting old. You pretend you aren't, but your years are catching up to you. You're feeling every one of them tonight.

As he hoped, getting lost in his baseball planning calms his mind.

33

DENNY RANKIN

[Friday, April 11, 1941]

The National Workers League door is unlocked. No one sits at the desk in the outer office. Denny hears a man's voice coming from further back. He follows the sound.

A guy's on the phone in another office. A heavy man with a pudgy oval face and dark curly hair. Broad forehead, deep circles under his eyes.

He spies Denny, says, "Call you back," and hangs up. "Who are you?"

Denny badges him. "Who are you?"

"Garland Alderman," the guy says.

"You run this place?"

"I'm the National Secretary."

Denny looks around. A photo of Hitler hangs on the wall beside a red and black Nazi flag.

Alderman says, "What do you want?"

"I'm looking for a girl named Charlotte Wheaton."

"What makes you think she's here?"

"She had your flyers on her."

"Don't mean she's here. Lots of people have our literature."

"Literature. There's a laugh. Do you know her?"

"Never heard of her."

"Mind if I look around?"

"You got a warrant, you can do whatever you need to. Got a warrant?"

"I can come back with one."

"Fine. Come back then," Alderman says. "Meantime, you'll have to excuse me. I got calls to make."

"Making the world safe for fascism."

"It's coming, pal. Before you know it. Better get ready."

Denny wanders back the way he came. He peeks into rooms as he goes. All the ones he sees are empty. Except there's a lot of Nazi paraphernalia. Photos of Hitler smiling and heiling from open cars, a box of swastika armbands, more flags, including little table-toppers. He strains to hear who Garland's on the phone with but can't make it out.

He picks up a few words: "Fatherland." "Tackle." "Movement."

Denny hears the phone hanging up. Garland Alderman comes out of his office. "You still here?"

"Thought you might change your mind about letting me look around," Denny says.

"You gonna leave or do I call my lawyer?"

The operator takes a few minutes to put Denny through to Alfred Bracciano, Charlotte Wheaton's counselor at Cass Tech High School. When he finally connects on the phone, Bracciano says, "Hang on, let me check."

Denny hears papers being shuffled on a desk. Bracciano comes back on the line. "No," he says, "neither Charlotte or her friend Janice Malinowski came in today."

"Can you give me Janice's address?"

She lives in Hamtramck, a small city entirely surrounded by Detroit. It has a large Polish population. Janice's street, Evaline, is a narrow road off Joseph Campau. He knocks on the door, waits, and knocks again. Hears a back door slam.

Denny trots around back and sees two girls run lickety-split through a gate in the back fence. He runs to his car and guns it down Evaline Street to Joseph Campau.

He swings right and makes for the next street, Edwin.

He sees them running up the alley between the streets, toward him.

He pulls over and gets out of the car. He hears them coming, huffing and laughing at how they fooled the dumb flatfoot. They reach the end of the alley and he steps out and grabs Charlotte in a bear hug.

Janice stops for a moment, as though trying to decide if she should help, then turns and flies down the street.

Denny doesn't care. Charlotte's the one he's looking for. She squirms. She kicks at his legs. He holds tight.

He walks her to his car. "I don't want to cuff you," he says. "I will if I have to."

"Let me go!"

"No dice, Charlotte. Time for a talk."

He gets her in the front seat and slides in beside her. He waits until she seems to calm down, then lets her go. She tries to make a break for it out the passenger door but he's too quick; he grabs her and holds tight.

"I'm not going home," she says. "You can't make me."

"Want to bet?"

"I hate you!"

"I don't care. Are you going to stop fussing and talk to me?"

"I don't have anything to say to you."

"Oh yes, you do. I have Hooky in custody."

"For what?"

"Abducting a minor. That would be you. Sexual relations with a minor. That would also be you. Resisting arrest. Want me to go on?"

"He didn't abduct me. I never had sexual relations with him. Are you going to send him to jail?"

"For a long time. Unless you talk to me."

She pouts. She has the mercurial temperament of a sixteen-year-old.

She takes a few deep breaths and quiets down. Flicks her pony tail at him. "What do you want to know?"

He takes the flyer from the bowling alley out of his pocket. "For starters, where'd you get this?"

"Where'd *you* get it?"

"Hooky's bowling alley. He told me Bert Vogelmann gave it to him. And Bert got it from you."

"How do you know about Bert?"

"I hear he's your boyfriend."

"He's more than that," she says. "I love him. We're running away together. We're going to get married."

"I'll kill him," Phil Wheaton says.

"No, you won't," Denny says.

"So help me God, I'll kill them, Hooky and Vogelmann both. I'll break every bone in their fucking bodies."

"No," Denny repeats, "you won't."

They sit in the Wheatons' small living room. Phil and Lena and Charlotte on the sofa and Denny on one of the wing chairs beside the fireplace. Lena has her arm around Charlotte, who has calmed down considerably.

"You won't find him," Charlotte says. Defiant.

"You bet your life I will," Phil says.

"No, you won't. He shipped out this week. He's in the Merchant Marines."

"Phil," Lena says. "Let her alone. If he's gone, he's out of our hair for a while."

Denny knows that's a lie. Hooky said he was minding Charlotte because his buddy Bert was busy for the day. Bert is still around.

Phil turns his rage onto his daughter. "How could you do this?" he bellows. He raises a hand to strike her. Charlotte cowers and Lena leans her away from Phil. Denny grabs his arm.

Denny wonders if this scene is typical. If it is, he gets why Charlotte wanted to run away.

"Go upstairs to your room," Phil tells her. Still with her arm around her, Lena walks the girl upstairs.

"Jesus Christ," Phil says. He's red in the face. "My little girl."

Denny has no reply.

Phil says, "Thanks a million, Denny. You found my little girl."

Phil starts to tear up. Where is this coming from, Denny wonders. He never used to be this emotional.

Denny waits until Phil has himself under control. He says, "Phil, we need to talk."

Phil wipes his eyes on his sleeve. Snorts up a load of snot. "Yeah?"

"I went to her school. Cass Tech. I talked to her counselor. He told me Charlotte hasn't been in school since October."

Phil says nothing.

"Want to tell me what's going on?"

"It's our fault," Phil says at last.

"Explain."

"We knew she was seeing Vogelmann. Last fall we told her to break it off. She said no. Said she loved him. Me and Lena talked it over. We decided the only way to split them up was to send her away. We sent her to live with my sister in Dormont."

"Where's that?"

"Outside Pittsburgh. Grace owns a big house. She's a widow, lives alone. Got lots of room. She said Charlotte could stay with her."

"What happened?"

Phil wipes his face again. "A week ago, we let her come back. She swore she was over this guy. We made her promise she'd go to school and finish out the year."

"But she wasn't over him."

"And she didn't go to school."

"Why didn't you tell me this?"

Phil runs a hand across his face. "I guess I was embarrassed. I didn't want you to think I couldn't control my own kid."

"Did you send her away because she was pregnant?"

This wrings a small, bitter smile out of Phil. "No," he says, "she wasn't pregnant. She was, I'd have killed them both."

34

EVA SZABÓ

[Friday, April 11, 1941]

The police cleared space around the gate. Coming through the picket lines, she notes a different mood this morning. The strikers are chattering and happy.

"What's going on?" she asks one of the men.

"The strike's over," he says. "The governor came up with a peace proposal. Looks like the union and Ford are going to accept it."

"Wonderful!"

"We might start back as soon as Monday if everything goes okay."

"I'm so happy to hear it," Eva says. Sounds like she's leaving the plant at a good time.

Nadine comes up beside her. She's almost giddy with the news. "Hallelujah. We'll be back to normal."

Nadine goes in the gate. Eva stays out to take the temperature of the crowd. She moves from group to group, asking them what they've heard about the strike settlement. From what she can gather, it was Michigan's Governor Van Wagoner who put the peace plan in front of the union and the company.

Someone comes up behind her.

Says, "We meet again."

She spins, frightened.

Hal Perlman, with his camera hanging around his neck.

She says, "Hi there!" She's glad to see him (and glad it's only him and not Mutt and Jeff). She had an urge to hug him, and she would except for the camera he carries. Instead, she says, "Isn't this great!"

"It is," Hal agrees. "Say, I should keep going. I have to keep taking photos."

Infected by the high spirits around her, Eva says, "Do you want to meet up later for a drink?"

"I'd love to. Can't tonight, though. I'm going to a Passover seder."

"A seder?"

"It's like a special holiday meal. I'm Jewish."

Without thinking about it, she says, "I know what it is. I'm Jewish, too."

"Want to come?"

"Seriously?"

"Yeah. The more the merrier. My aunt and uncle always have room for an extra person."

"Sure."

He tears a page from his notebook and scribbles an address. "Starts at five."

"Great," she says. "I'll see you there. Thanks."

He gives her a wave and walks off down the picket line, the camera already up to his eye.

She has reporting to do, too. She will need to let Elizabeth know about this latest development.

When Eva goes inside, she will have to turn in her notice to Nadine. Elizabeth said she would still employ her; Eva hopes that's going to be the case.

She puts it out of her mind. It'll take care of itself.

For now, happiness. She grabs a UAW sign off the ground and waves it around with others in the happy crowd.

A man comes up behind her. She thinks it's Hal again.

She says, "Back so soon?"

It's not Hal who grabs her by the arms. She struggles. Drops the sign she's carrying.

"Hate the union, do you?" a man's voice says into her ear. "In a pig's eye. You should have quit when you had the chance."

He covers her mouth. He drags her away. She fights back and tries to scream but he's too strong.

No one in the commotion of the strike's ending notices.

35

CLARENCE BROWN

[Monday, April 14, 1941]

Ordinarily Clarence dislikes spending time at the Hunt Street Station.

True, there are more Negro officers now than ever before, especially since the department formed a segregated squad of Negro detectives in 1937 to police the colored population. Clarence was part of this, along with a half-dozen other Negro officers. Since then, the level of antagonism toward him has diminished—though just barely—from what it used to be.

Still, he likes being out on the streets. Black Bottom and Paradise Valley are his patch, what he knows and where he feels most comfortable.

What he needs to do today, though, can only be done inside.

He puts a call in to a friend of his at the Eighth Precinct. Earl Perry. Another Negro detective.

"Can you do me a favor," Clarence asks. "I want to check on a woman named Belle Baxter. Anything you can find . . . address, arrests, anything at all on her record."

Earl says he'll do it right away.

Clarence hangs up and makes more calls to other detectives, both white and colored, in the other precincts around the city. If they can, they say they'll get started right away; everyone promises to do it as fast as possible.

Clarence starts his own search through the Hunt Street Station's files. He's pretty sure "Belle Baxter" is a phony name, as phony as the report she filed and the addresses she claimed. But he has to go through the motions.

It's tedious work. He goes back five years. He searches through vice reports, robbery reports, homicide reports, prostitution and disorderly houses reports . . . the only "Belle Baxter" he finds is a woman who died alone in a rooming house on Cass Avenue in 1939.

Later in the afternoon he gets a call from Junius Armstrong in the Corktown Precinct. Junius and Clarence were partners for a few months on the special Negro squad.

"Found her," Junius tells him.

He says a woman named Belle Baxter has been arrested multiple times for prostitution in the past three years. Her most recent arrests are at a disorderly house near the train tracks at Michigan Avenue and West Grand Boulevard. The home address on file for her is a rooming house on Michigan.

Clarence tries the rooming house first. The residents he talks to claim not to know anyone named Belle Baxter. Clarence doesn't know how reliable they are. They're all old white people, so far down on their luck Clarence doesn't even know if luck ever had any meaning for them. An old woman, two old men who live together, and a deaf old man who doesn't speak or use sign language.

Would they tell a colored policeman anything?

In the event she uses a different name, he asks if a young white woman lives here; maybe she was pregnant.

All the oldsters say no.

Would a young prostitute even live here? Clarence has his doubts. A phony address to go along with a phony name.

Next he goes to the brothel where Belle Baxter was picked up on her prostitution beefs. It's in an ancient house on Michigan Avenue. The doorman, white and an ex-boxer to judge from his misshapen nose and ears, won't let him in and won't answer any questions about Belle Baxter.

Clarence holds up his badge.

"No niggers," the guy says. "Especially cops." He shuts the door in Clarence's face.

A younger Clarence would have taken him on. Would have put his shoulder to the door and bulled it inside. Would have smacked this ofay around just on general principles.

Not so today's Clarence . . . not only older, but wiser, slower, heavier, less willing to get into it with younger men. Nothing will change, anyway. Clarence would bask in his own personal power for a few moments, then nothing in America would change as a result. Things would just go on as usual. Tomorrow this monkey might not close the door in Clarence's face, but he'd close it on another Negro.

So the wiser Clarence turns away. He knows there's another way.

She's still a beauty.

Rosita. She now calls herself Rosa Kennedy.

She rises with difficulty when the maid shows him into the living room. He recognizes the maid as Sophia, who worked for Rosita back in the day.

Rosita—he will never learn to call her Rosa; the closest he will get is Rosie, what he used to call her—is unsteady on her feet, even leaning on a cane. Clarence has heard she came down with some illness. This is the first time he's seen her since her marriage to Lester Kennedy. Lester owns a chain of funeral parlors in Paradise Valley and is a very, very wealthy man.

Now Rosie is a very, very wealthy woman.

Rosie used to be Madame Rosita, proprietor of one of the ritzier colored brothels in Detroit. Clarence heard she retired from the business when she got sick.

Lester Kennedy—formerly a long-standing client of hers—persuaded her to marry him. Now she lives in splendor in one of the larger homes in Conant Gardens, a three-story red brick house on Revere Street with a sunroom and upper porch. It's in the city's most exclusive neighborhood for wealthy Negroes.

As always, Rosita offers him her cheek to kiss. As always, he inhales her face powder's sweet smell of gardenia. Clarence loves things that don't change.

He never wants this to change. Her light skin is as wrinkle-free as it ever was. As he's heard many times in his life, black don't crack.

Now she also holds out her free arm, an invitation for a hug.

He wraps his arms around her and she laughs.

"Still wearing your armor, I see," she says.

"Got me this far."

She points her cane at a plush chair. He sits and she lowers herself onto the sofa.

"This is a welcome surprise," she says.

Sophia brings in a tea tray. Like everyone, Sophia has aged since the last time he saw her. Her hair has gone all gray and she's starting to hunch over. She was with the original disorderly house where Rosie started, and she stayed when Rosie took it over. When Rosie left the life, Sophia did, too.

"Mr. Clarence," she says.

"Sophia."

"You a sight for sore eyes." She keeps her mouth closed when she laughs. She's missing teeth.

"And you look as pretty as ever," he says.

She titters with a hand in front of her mouth and leaves them alone.

"Haven't heard from you for a while," Rosie says. "Thought you might have forgotten about me."

"Never."

He hasn't forgotten about her since they came into each other's lives back in the '20s, when he was new to the city and his son De-Marco's death still made him crazy with grief. And Rosie was there for the young policeman in a way Bessie never could be.

He almost left Bessie for her, except the guilt he felt was devastating and at the end he couldn't do it. He had to call it off.

"I know this isn't just a social visit," she says. "Much as I'm glad to see you."

"It isn't."

She pours them both a cup of tea. The cups are small and fragile in his huge hand. "We don't keep any Coca-Cola in the house," she says. "Or aren't you drinking that poison anymore?"

"I'm still drinking it."

"One of these days you'll be sorry," she says. "They're going to find sugar in you and then you'll have to quit."

"When the day comes, I will. Until then . . ."

He spoons three teaspoons of sugar into his tea and takes a sip.

Smiles. It's a toss-up which one warms him more, Rosie or the tea.

"How are you feeling?" he asks.

She gives a long sigh. She holds her cane up. "You heard about this?"

"I did."

"At least they know what it is."

"What is it? If you don't mind me asking."

"They call it multiple sclerosis. MS for short. It has to do with blockages on the nerves that keep the impulses from getting through."

"Anything they can do about it?"

She shakes her head. "It's incurable."

He doesn't know what to say. He can only gaze at her. Since the last time he saw her, she's put on weight. She's still beautiful.

As if she can read his mind—she always could—she says, "You don't look so bad yourself."

"Getting old," he says.

"We all getting old, big man."

"That's a fact."

"How's Bessie?"

He takes a moment before answering. He tries to gauge how she meant that question. Bessie is a long-time touchy subject between them. Rosie always knew Bessie stood in the way of her being together with Clarence. And she was right; Clarence would never leave Bessie.

He finally decides the question was serious, not mocking. "Got trouble with her ankle," he says. "She has the sugar. It's causing all kinds of problems."

"I'd ask you to say hello to her from me, but I'm thinking you're not going to mention we saw each other."

He has to laugh. "I won't."

"She wouldn't want my greeting anyway."

They cackle, a pair of old lovers who have been through the wars and survived and can still sit and have tea together.

They are quiet for a moment, each lost in thoughts of their old times.

"Rosie," he says finally, "I need your help."

"Figured as much."

'I'm looking for a woman named Belle Baxter."

"She in the life?"

"She is. At least used to be."

Rosie thinks for a few moments. "I don't believe I recognize the name."

"White gal. Got a few pops from a house on Michigan."

"Michigan and what?"

"Lawton. Edge of Corktown."

"I know just where it is."

"I went there fixing to ask about her, but I got turned away."

"I imagine you did," she says with a laugh. "They don't like our kind cluttering up their doorway."

"Know anybody there?"

"I know the owner. Bertha Johnson."

"Can you find out if she knows Belle Baxter? Or ask if she'll talk to me? I need to get to Belle."

"What's she done?"

"I found a dead white baby in a tenement over on Beaubien. A couple days later, a white woman named Belle Baxter claimed her baby was taken by a couple of Negroes."

"Think it's the same baby?"

"I do. Can you help me? For old time's sake?"

"Of course I will. For old time's sake." She gives him her smile, a lopsided grin that promises a world of happiness. He knows it's practiced, but he still feels like it's just for him.

"You're the best," he says.

"I know. You're the one always seemed to forget that."

36

DENNY RANKIN

[Monday, April 14, 1941]

Eppinger's Sporting Goods, 131 Cadillac Square, downtown. What the papers like to call a "Daring Daylight Robbery." Three knuckleheads robbed the store of eighteen guns in broad daylight.

Denny gets the scoop from Lou Eppinger, the owner. Three white boys who looked like they were around eighteen or twenty walked in just after the store opened and flashed handguns. They pushed the terrified clerk into the storeroom and made off with three boxes of Colt revolvers, six firearms to a box. They ran out the back door of the store.

Lou called the police immediately and a patrolman was there inside five minutes. He called it in and squad cars were out prowling for the boys.

According to the clerk, they took off on foot. Denny guesses with three heavy cartons of weaponry they wouldn't get far; they must have a car stashed nearby.

Within the hour, a patrol car radios in he has found a young man stabbed and bleeding outside the Mt. Elliot Cemetery. An empty box from Eppinger's is nearby.

By the time Denny gets there, the boy has been transferred to Receiving Hospital.

He goes to Receiving, only a few miles away. From the boy,

Denny learns he was one of the three who stole the guns. He's Jay Carstairs, and he's only seventeen. He was stabbed in a dispute with one of the other robbers. He gives them up without hesitation: Claude Fischer, 20, and William Toomey, 18. Carstairs says they are staying in a fleabag hotel on Fourteenth Street.

By the afternoon, Fischer and Toomey are both in custody and ready for arraignment in Recorder's Court. Denny recovers thirteen of the guns; the two punks have already sold the other five.

He questions each boy separately. They also admit to six gas station holdups prior to the Eppinger job.

They claim they're part of the Christian Front. The weapons were intended for the paramilitary training sessions for when the Christian nationalist organization overthrows the government of the United States and replaces it with a Christian dictatorship.

"Father Coughlin says it's going to happen," Toomey says.

"Not for you mooks," Denny says.

He's at his desk writing it all up when he gets a call from Arnold Jardine, one of the Homicide detectives.

Jardine tells him Edgar Vanarian, the dishwasher shot by the drunken policeman Thaddeus Ostrowski, has died of his injuries.

Ostrowski's charge will have to be amended. Jardine wants Denny to send over the file.

Denny finishes the report on the Eppinger heists. He looks at Ostrowski's file again before he sends it off to Jardine.

Again, it bothers him. According to the cop who took the initial report, Ostrowski shot at several civilians, and claimed to hit Vanarian "by accident." Denny is still not convinced the shooting was entirely random.

Ostrowski is out on bail awaiting trial. How the hell did he get bail? Denny wonders. Must be because he's a policeman . . . or was, at any rate. He's certainly not going to be one for long.

Denny arranges to get the file transferred. He drives out to southwest Detroit, where Ostrowski lives in a bungalow on Springwells Street. Ostrowski is already drunk when he opens the door for Denny.

Drunk at noon.

The alcohol seeps out of his pores.

Ostrowski's wife is also there. She introduces herself as Francine.

Denny sits with them both in the family's kitchen.

"Ted," Denny says, "I have bad news. The dishwasher you shot, Edgar Vanarian? He died today of his injuries from the shooting."

Ostrowski gazes blankly at Denny. Has Ostrowski understood what Denny just said?

"What does that mean?" Francine asks.

"It means your husband's charges will have to be amended. He's likely facing a manslaughter charge."

"What's manslaughter?" she asks.

"When you unintentionally cause the death of another person," Denny says.

"Will he have to go to jail?"

"It could mean a lengthy prison sentence."

She shoots daggers at her husband.

Who can't look at her.

"One of the Homicide detectives is going to come here today," Denny says, "and bring you in on the new charge. I wanted to catch you first. Have you thought any more about what happened?"

"It's all I been thinking about."

"Do you still claim you shot Edgar Vanarian by accident? You weren't deliberately shooting at him?"

"No sir," Ostrowski says. "I can tell you absolutely I wasn't deliberately shooting at him. I never met the man."

"Were you shooting at someone else?"

"No."

"What were you doing so far from your home precinct?"

"I was drunk. I don't remember why I did what I did."

"How did you get to the Woodmont?"

"Streetcars."

"Why did you go there, specifically?"

"I'd been there before. It was a nice place . . . clean, quiet. I wanted to get away from the station."

"And so nobody would see you get shitfaced?" his wife puts in.

He can't say anything else.

Denny asks Francine, "Do you two have any children?"

"No," she says. "One bit of good news. No kids I'd have to take to prison to visit their daddy. Lucky us."

Ostrowski's hands are trembling. His life is ruined. Ditto Francine's.

Denny leaves the poor bastard there.

At the station, there's a message from Noviest Panty. The cashier at the United Artists Theatre.

He calls her back.

She tells him Aram Sarkasian wants to see him.

Aram waits for him in the balcony. *Andy Hardy's Private Secretary* plays onscreen. Judge Hardy is having a come-to-Jesus talk with Mickey Rooney as Andy Hardy.

Denny sits in the row behind Aram. "What do you have?"

Aram leans back. "Nothing about the Palmer Woods break-in."

"You got me here to tell me you got nothing?"

"Possess yourself in patience, boss. I heard you're also working a shooting down here a couple weeks ago. I heard the shooter's a copper. I heard the guy he shot died."

"Bad news travels fast."

"I heard the copper's coming up on a manslaughter beef."

"Still right."

"I heard there's an eyewitness."

"Yeah? What's this eyewitness say?"

"He says you got the wrong guy in the pokey."

Denny says, "Where can I find this eyewitness?"

The Mayflower Café on Woodward hasn't fixed the broken front window. A piece of cardboard blocks the broken pane.

Inside smells of cigarette smoke and bacon. The counter is empty except for an old man who sits hunched over a coffee and newspaper. Denny stands at the register and the old guy looks up.

He stands and comes over. His stained white tunic says "George" in red script over the pocket. He reaches for a menu, says, "Yes sir. Sit anywhere."

Denny badges him. "You the boss?"

"That's me."

"There was a shooting out front the other day. Edgar Vanarian was shot. I understand he works here?"

"He washes dishes."

Denny doesn't want to tell him Vanarian is dead. He doesn't know if Arnold Jardine has informed any next of kin Vanarian might have. Instead he says, "Were you here when it happened?"

"Sure. We just finished the lunchtime rush."

"Did you see it?"

"I was in the back. I come out when I hear all the commotion."

"One of your employees saw it?"

"My busboy. Hubert."

"Is he in? Can I speak with him?"

"I get. You sit."

George points to a booth. Denny sits. George goes to the back of the narrow restaurant. Calls "Hubert!"

The "busboy" comes out. He's a grown man, a middle-aged Negro who drags his leg with a limp. He comes out with an empty dishpan, ready to clean a table.

"This policeman wanna talk about what you saw out front," George says.

Hubert gives Denny a suspicious look. Denny throws him a friendly nod back.

Hubert sets his dishpan on the floor and slides in the booth across from Denny. Denny reaches out a hand. "Denny Rankin."

Hubert shakes it. "Hubert Taylor."

"You want a cup of coffee?"

"No, I'm good."

"I hear you saw the shooting."

Hubert nods.

"Can you tell me what you saw?"

"Well," Hubert says, "I was mopping up by the front door and I hear this pop pop pop pop. Which I knew it was gunshots. So I look outside. I see this cop coming across the street, shooting his gun off."

"From what direction?"

Hubert points south, toward the Woodmont Bar.

George sets a cup of coffee in front of Denny. Denny raises a hand in thanks.

Denny says, "Did he look like he was chasing somebody?"

"He was staggering around like he was drunk off his ass. But yeah, I suppose he might could have been chasing somebody."

"Could you tell who?"

"Hard to say. I saw Edgar go down. He just left the restaurant.

His shift ended at two. He was standing by the door having a smoke, waiting for the streetcar. But I don't think the guy, the policeman, was shooting at him. Matter of fact, I don't even think he shot Edgar."

"Wait a minute," Denny says, "what did you say?"

"I don't think it was the cop shot Edgar."

"Who did?"

"There was another cat out there, shooting back at the cop. Pop pop pop pop." Hubert holds a finger and a thumb out like he's shooting a gun.

This was new. None of the witness reports mentioned this.

Denny says, "Could you see who else was shooting?"

"No. He was coming from the same direction. Running across the street. Looked like the cop might have been chasing him."

"And you saw him shooting back at the cop?"

"Yes sir. Looked to me like he was shooting at the cop, who was shooting at him. The guy, he runs by the front of the diner. Then he turns and gets off a shot, 'pop!' And Edgar, he steps out the doorway just then 'cause he wants to jump on the streetcar that's coming. He caught the bullet right in the chest."

"This second guy—did you get a look at him?"

"No. Happened too fast."

"Can you tell me anything about him?"

"He was white. And tall. I couldn't see his face because he didn't turn toward me."

"Anything else you can think of?"

"Yeah, he was wearing one of them coats like sailors wear."

"Heavy blue woolen thing?"

"Yeah."

A peacoat.

"Let me make sure I got this," Denny says. "You're saying there were two men shooting, the cop and this other guy. And you think the other guy was the one who shot Edgar Vanarian."

"What it looked like to me."

"Why didn't you tell anybody?"

"Nobody asked. Soon as this happened, George shut down the shop. Sent us all home."

Hubert notices George at the cash register giving him the eye. "Can I get back to work now?" Hubert asks.

"We're going to need you to come down to the station and make a statement about what you just told me."

"Yeah, okay."

Denny thinks for a moment, says, "Don't come down until I tell you to, okay?" Denny takes out his notebook. "Hubert, write down your address for me."

Hubert does.

"Telephone?" Denny asks.

"I look like I can afford a telephone? Lucky I got a roof over my damn head."

Hubert picks up his dishpan, nods goodbye to Denny, and limps back to the rear of the restaurant.

George, who has been listening, says, "Everything okay?"

"Not really," Denny admits.

This changes things.

All the patrolmen's reports were wrong. The cops who were first on the scene must have let all the witnesses go, or else never questioned them carefully. They saw the aftermath of a drunken brother officer's shooting spree, and assumed they knew what happened.

Denny thanks George and goes outside the restaurant. He stands where Edgar Vanarian stood. If Hubert is right, Ostrowski didn't shoot Vanarian after all.

The Woodmont Bar is a block away, across Woodward Avenue. He remembers what the bartender there said: Ostrowski was sitting and drinking by himself, then suddenly jumped up and ran out the door.

Was he waiting for the man in the peacoat? Was he ginning up his courage with booze, then when he saw the guy he was looking for he ran out the door and chased him across the street?

Edgar Vanarian took the shot in the right side of his chest. Denny visualizes what could have happened:

Peacoat walks by the Woodmont. Ostrowski sees him and stumbles out. Peacoat sees or hears Ostrowski coming for him and takes off across Woodward and runs by the Mayflower with Ostrowski coming after him, shooting. Peacoat turns to return fire. Edgar Vanarian steps out to look for his streetcar. Vanarian turns toward Peacoat—facing north—and takes the bullet. Peacoat keeps running—

And why does Ostrowski stop? Instead of continuing to chase

Peacoat?

Ostrowski must have seen the dishwasher fall, and a twinge of awareness must have penetrated his drunken rage and made him stop and wait around for the cops.

But why isn't Ostrowski telling the truth? Is he protecting Peacoat?

And who wears peacoats?

Navy men.

Or sailors.

Like sailors in the Merchant Marines?

And where has he just heard about a Merchant Marine?

Bert Vogelmann, beloved of Charlotte Wheaton.

He needs to see what Ostrowski says about all this. By the time he drives to Ostrowski's, Detective Arnold Jardine has already taken Ostrowski in for rebooking.

"My louse of a husband," Francine Ostrowski says. "I hope they lock the bastard up and throw away the key."

"They probably will."

Denny gets to Jardine's station. Jardine has put Ostrowski back in the system for manslaughter. Jardine already left to start his night's drinking at Nancy Whiskey.

Where he's yukking it up with other cops. Denny slides onto the stool next to him at the bar.

"Rankin!" Jardine cries. "Come to celebrate?"

"Before you get too far gone," Denny says, "I got to tell you—you might have the wrong guy."

Jardine's drunken gaze is already unfocused but he tries to zone in on Denny. "The fuck you talking about? Ostrowski admitted it."

"Except I just talked to a witness who told me there was another shooter in the street. Witness says this other guy plugged Vanarian, not Ostrowski."

Jardine holds his hands up. "Wait, wait, wait—Rankin, this ain't your case no more, right? You don't come in here and tell me how to work my case."

"I'm telling you, you got the wrong man in custody."

Jardine slides off his stool and gets ready to go at it with Denny. Steps right in his face. "Don't tell me what I did and did not do."

One of the other cops holds him back. "Arnie, forget it. Let it go. This guy's got nothing to say about it."

"What," Jardine says to Denny, "suddenly you're a homicide dick?"

"I'm just telling you," Denny says. "You do whatever you want with it."

Jardine grabs his crotch. "Hey Rankin? Here's what I want to do with it, right here."

The other cops laugh.

Jardine goes back to his beer.

Denny leaves them to their blunder.

37

ELIZABETH WATERS

[Wednesday, April 16]

She hears her phone ringing from down the hall. Her heels echo on the marble floor.

It's still ringing as she opens the outer door to her office.

Waters & Associates, Confidential Investigations.

So far she doesn't have any associates, but it looks better on the door. And makes clients think the firm is bigger than it is.

Elizabeth Waters works in the Barlum Tower in downtown Detroit, in the offices of attorney Maurice Sugar. When Elizabeth worked for him as a researcher and then an investigator, he gave her a desk to use. Since he became the general counsel for the UAW, he's hardly ever around. Now head of her own firm, she rents one of the offices in his suite.

Maurice took his long-time secretary Inez Reynolds with him when he moved to the UAW offices. When Elizabeth needs secretarial help, she contacts one of the secretarial services in the building. They also act as her answering service.

So she doesn't need to run to the phone because the service will pick up the call. She drops her purse and coat on the visitor's chair in her office. She sets a coffee from the diner downstairs on her desk.

Papering her desk are notes she writes to herself for things she needs to do. The building is filled with attorneys who give her work.

She calls her answering service to get her messages.

A handful of calls, tasks to add to the notes on her desk:

An attorney wants her to interview a witness in an automobile accident to verify the witness's statement.

Another attorney wants her to do a background check on a guy accused of larceny by conversion; he charged an old woman $100 to make repairs to the roof of her house, which he never did.

Another attorney wants her to canvas the scene of a shooting to see if she can uncover any more witnesses than the police found.

Another call comes from a personal injury attorney named Max Rubenstein. He's looking for a good investigator; he was referred to her.

The final call on her list puzzles her. It's from the Lincoln Park police. Would she give them a call at her earliest convenience?

First she calls Max Rubenstein. They agree on an appointment in the afternoon. Elizabeth has heard of him; he has a rep as an honest guy. Sounds like they'll get along.

Next she calls the Lincoln Park PD. Gets put through to Detective Sergeant Curtis Pixley.

"Thanks for calling back," he says. His voice has a smoker's rasp. "Hang on a sec."

She hears papers shuffled.

"Here we go." He has a coughing fit. He comes back on the line and says, "Do you know a woman named Eva Szabó?"

Her stomach flips over. "Yes."

"She was found unconscious early this morning. Your business card was in her purse."

Exactly what Elizabeth was afraid would happen.

She asks, "Is she alive?"

"She is," Pixley says. "But she took a pretty good pounding."

"Where is she? I want to see her."

Wyandotte General Hospital, Biddle Avenue, miles south of Delray, where Eva lives. A nurse directs Elizabeth to an open ward filled with the smells of urine and soiled clothes.

"Are you a relative?" the nurse asks.

"I'm her sister," Elizabeth lies. They probably won't let her see Eva if she's not a family member.

The nurse points to a bed at the end of the ward.

The detective was right; Eva has been pummeled. Her face is purple and swollen. Her head is wrapped in gauze. Her left leg is in a cast and raised in a traction device. She is unconscious but breathing regularly.

"My god," Elizabeth murmurs.

The nurse comes up beside her. "She turned up early this morning. She's in pretty bad shape, as you can see. You'll have to ask the doctor about anything else."

"Where's the doctor?"

"He made his morning rounds already. He won't be back until the afternoon."

The nurse goes off to attend to another patient.

Elizabeth stands beside Eva's bed. Rests a hand on Eva's shoulder. Elizabeth says, "This is my fault."

Eva does not reply. She's out cold.

Her chart hangs on the iron rail at the end of her bed. Elizabeth looks it over.

Eva was brought in at 4:34 this morning. She has been unconscious the entire time. Fractured skull and jaw, missing teeth, fractured ribs and left tibia. Numerous cuts and bruises on her face and torso.

Prognosis: critical.

Possible brain damage from the skull injury.

Elizabeth braces herself on the bed rail. She feels burning vomit surge into her throat. She swallows it back.

"Miss," the nurse says with a hand on her arm, "are you alright?"

The nurse brings her a glass of water and Elizabeth sits with her head in her hands in a wooden chair beside Eva's bed. Guilt overwhelms her. She knows this happened to Eva because of the assignment she was on. And Eva was on the assignment because of Elizabeth.

Alright, Elizabeth told Eva to be careful—but if Elizabeth hadn't given her this job—had never come into her life—Eva wouldn't be lying in bed, beaten unconscious with who knew what kind of long-term damages.

The nurse returns. "Better?"

"Yes, thanks. How did you know who she is?"

"The ambulance brought her in with her purse. She had her ID from the Rouge plant."

"Where's her purse now?"

"The police have it."

"The police in Lincoln Park?"

"Yes, ma'am."

Detective Sergeant Curtis Pixley could have been sent up from Central Casting. A big man with a large, blond, crew-cut head. Badly-shaven pale jowls are beginning to droop and the back of his thick neck bulges over his shirt collar. He smells of cigarettes from the overflowing ashtray on his desk.

"Do you know the area?" he asks.

"No."

"There's a vacant lot in southern Lincoln Park near where the railroad comes through," he says. "That's where we found her. You saw her at the hospital?"

"Yes."

"Then you saw how bad she looked. Really worked her over. Looks like she's been outside for a few nights."

"Any idea who did it?"

"Not at this time."

"How did you know where she was?"

"Anonymous tipoff. Phoned into the department sometime after midnight."

"By the people who did this to her?"

"Could be."

"At the hospital they said you have her purse."

Pixley swivels in his seat and retrieves the purse from the credenza behind him. "We knew to call you because your card was in here."

"She cares for her stepmother. Has anybody notified the family?"

"I sent a car to her address. Nobody came to the door."

Elizabeth will have to go there and make sure Eva's stepmother is okay.

"Can I take the purse?" she asks.

"Sorry, no. We have to keep it for now as evidence. Best I can do is let you look through it."

He sits watching her as she empties the leather purse on his desk. Folded-up handkerchiefs blotted with lipstick. A comb and brush.

Her wallet with a few dollars still in it. This was obviously not a robbery.

There's a compact with face powder and a cylinder of lipstick. Her Ford plant ID. Assorted change. A matchbook from the Rouge Tavern. Elizabeth's business card. A slip of paper with a scrawled address in Detroit without a name. A folded pamphlet on yellow paper.

Elizabeth opens it.

Does Jewish Power Control the World Press?
from
The International Jew: The World's Foremost Problem
being a reprint of a series of articles appearing in
The Dearborn Independent.
1920, The Dearborn Independent

"What's she doing with this?" Elizabeth mutters to herself.

"Beg pardon?" Pixley says.

"I was just wondering where she got this."

Pixley takes it from her. Looks it over. "I've seen these by the dozens," he says. "They're all over town."

He hands it back to her. Voice lowered, he says, "Between you, me, and the fence post, at least Henry Ford had the guts to tell the truth about these Jews."

38

CLARENCE BROWN

[Wednesday, April 16]

A message comes through to his radio car.

Urgent: Call Rosa Kennedy.

He's near Tipton's Luncheonette, where there's a payphone on the wall outside.

The call gets picked up right away. "Kennedy residence."

"Sophia, it's Clarence Brown. How you doing?"

"Oh, Mr. Clarence. Miss Rosa's expecting you. Just a minute."

Clarence hears the sounds of footsteps and the phone being walked into another room. Hears Sophia say, "It's Mr. Clarence."

Rosie comes on the line. "Still looking for your Belle Baxter?"

"Don't tell me you found her already?"

"I was going to tell you, but if you'd rather I didn't . . ."

"I knew you were the right one to ask."

"You never really get out of this life, you know. Except once, at the end."

"What do you have for me, Rosie?"

"Got a pencil? Go to this address and ask for Jewel."

It's one of the aging mansions in Brush Park, an imposing, narrow Victorian home with a spire on one side of the façade and a cupola on the other on Watson Street.

At the turn of the century, Brush Park was home to lumber barons and other white elites of the city. Then German Jews moved in. As often happens in Detroit, when they moved in, the original residents moved out, and when the Jews moved out, Negroes started moving in, just like in Black Bottom.

Clarence stands on the imposing front porch. A curtain inside the front door twitches, and the door swings open. A beautiful, fine-boned, light-skinned woman says, "You must be Clarence."

"I am. Would you be Jewel?"

"I would be." She opens the front door all the way. "Come on in." Her voice is deep, honeyed, inviting, practiced.

He follows her through the hallway into a massive sitting room. Plush sofas and chairs. Paintings on the walls of nude Negro and white women. In the corner a shiny, black grand piano. Everything in the room screams CLASS.

"Have a seat," Jewel says.

He sinks into one of the chairs.

She arranges herself in another plush chair. "How do you know Rosie?" she asks.

"We go way back," he says. "She told me you know where I can find Belle Baxter."

"I do. Except her real name's Lucy Taggart."

"If she's not Belle Baxter," he says, "how do you know who I'm looking for? I've never seen her, and I'm pretty sure Rosie's never seen her."

Jewel lights up a smoke from a bejeweled cigarette box. She blows a perfectly round smoke ring toward the ceiling. "This is really just a small town, detective. It may seem like a big city, but it's small."

She takes another drag.

"Rosie, she asked around. When she asked me, I asked my girls. It turns out one of my girls is the favorite of a copper named Clendening. Know him?"

"I know the mug."

"He runs a string of girls at Bertha Johnson's house," Jewel says. "They take care of him, but every once in a while, he likes some strange. So he comes over here. Likes to talk after he gets his ashes hauled. Got a favorite over here. He talked to her about how there's a con going with one of his other girls who said a colored man kidnapped her baby."

"Sounds like my Belle Baxter."

"Clendening, he's a real chatterbox. Said the guy who planned it was hoping to start a race war with it. Matter of fact, he bragged about it."

"Did he say who planned it?"

"If he did, I don't know."

Though it's cleaner than it used to be, Hamtramck is still a tough town. For years, policy shops and brothels operated without fear of the cops. It was well-known the bookies and madams paid off the mayor and the police department of both Hamtramck and Wayne County to let them operate openly.

A grand jury a few years ago launched an investigation that trapped dozens of police and politicians. Clarence knew a few of the cops who had been caught and suspended; the friend he had lunch with at Tipton's, Dave Marshall, was one of them. Now the trial for almost three dozen of them was under way.

Jewel said Lucy Taggart worked in a house off Caniff and Conant Streets in Hamtramck. She said the girls who worked in nearby houses get together at a diner on Caniff before their nights started. Jewel thought at this time of day, late afternoon, Clarence would have the best luck finding Lucy there.

At the rear of the diner sit half a dozen women, white and colored, smoking and drinking coffee. Clarence approaches. Smoke from their cigarettes hangs in a drifting cloud over the table. The conversation dies. They all look at this large Negro man standing beside their table.

"Is it getting hot in here, or is it me?" one of the women asks the others.

"No, I feel the heat, too," another woman says.

Clarence shows his badge, says, "I'm looking for Lucy Taggart."

"I dunno nobody named Lucy," the first woman says. She looks to be the oldest and the one in charge of the others. She turns to them. "Anybody know Lucy?"

They all shake their heads, except for one woman. Her gaze drills into Clarence. She stubs out her smoke and keeps staring at him. White, in her thirties but with a lot of wear and tear. Dark eyes and bottle blonde hair pressed into waves.

Clarence guesses this would be Lucy.

"I didn't know they were letting spades be policemen nowadays," another of the women says.

"Oh, yeah," the first woman says. "Now when they say 'The jig is up,' they really mean it."

This brings mocking laughter from the others, except for the one still staring at Clarence.

To her he says, "How about you and me have a little talk outside, Lucy?"

"You got the wrong girl, smoke."

"Going to make me arrest you?"

"Get lost."

"On your feet."

Clarence takes out his handcuffs. "You're under arrest."

"For what?"

"Obstruction of justice."

He grabs her arm and pulls her up.

"This is bullshit!" she cries.

She weighs nothing. The women at the table explode in anger.

He turns her around. Cuffs her hands behind her back. "This your purse?"

The women are yelling too loud. She doesn't hear him. He grabs the handbag off the back of her chair.

He pulls the woman out through the restaurant.

Outside he hauls her around the corner and into the mouth of an alley.

Throws her against the brick wall of the back of a store.

"This is bullshit," she says. "I ain't done nothing."

"Shut up."

He opens her purse and takes out her wallet. Her driver's license IDs her as Lucille Taggart.

He snaps her purse shut and drops it on the ground. She spits in his face.

He makes a show of getting out his handkerchief and wiping the spit off.

She spits in his face again.

He spins her so she faces the wall. She squirms and struggles. He holds her in place with a hand on her back.

He wipes his face again. "Here's your choice," he says. "I can arrest you for prostitution, resisting arrest, assaulting a police officer, making a false police report, and anything else I can think up, or you can tell me what you know about the missing baby you reported."

"I ain't telling you nothing."

"How many pops you got for prostitution? Four? Five? What's going to happen when I put all that other shit on you? With police corruption trials going on every day, think the judge'll go easy on you? Think he'll care your pimp's a cop with cops indicted left and right every day?"

"I'll tell Roger about you. He'll kill your black ass."

Roger.

Roger Clendening, the detective who runs whores in the City of Detroit.

Clarence sighs.

"Here's what I know," he says. "I know you made a false report about your baby being kidnapped by a couple of colored guys. I'm pretty sure you didn't think it up by yourself."

She is still silent.

"Whose idea was it? Clendening's?"

"I dunno. He never said. I had the feeling another cop was putting him up to it, but he never gave me a name."

"How about the baby? Whose was it? Is there a mama out there missing her child?"

"It wasn't no real baby, ya dumb dope," she says. "It was all made up. It was imaginary, see?"

"There was a real baby, Lucy. And he was dead. I held him in my arms. He was ice cold."

"You're lying."

"I found him in a cellar in Black Bottom. Child never had a chance in the world."

"You're lying," she says again, not quite so sure now.

"You didn't know? Clendening just told you to make the report and you thought it was all for show?"

"Clendening, he gimme twenty bucks to make the report and then drop out of sight. I dunno why. I didn't ask. He just told me there wasn't no real baby, it was just a goof. I believed him."

"He lied."

"How do you know it's the same baby?"

"I'm certain it is."

Clendening drove the infant's body away from the house in Black Bottom. If Clarence had any doubts that was the baby "Belle Baxter" reported missing, this allayed them.

Her tough armor melts away. She says, "Jesus. I didn't know there was a real kid. I swear. Clendening said it was just a goof."

Clarence watches her. She could be telling the truth. Her distress looks real.

"Look," she says, "it was just a way to make a quick double saw. Clendening swore to me I wouldn't get in any trouble."

"He lied about that, too," Clarence says.

"What are you going to do to me?"

In truth, Clarence doesn't know. If he takes her in, it will let Clendening and whoever else is involved know that Clarence is onto what they did.

It'll also let the assistant commander of his segregated squad, Lieutenant William Wilson, know Clarence ignored his order to leave this alone.

Either way, it won't end well for Clarence Brown.

His other option is to let Lucy Taggart go and hope she'll fade back into the life while he figures out his next step.

Trusting this woman seems like a bad choice.

Taking her in would be even worse.

He goes with the lesser bad choice. He unlocks the cuffs. Sticks them back in his pocket.

She turns around, suspicious.

"I'm letting you go," he says. "If I find out you told Clendening or anybody else about this, I'll be back for you."

"You're letting me go?"

"Go back inside."

"You're saying nothing's coming back at me for this?"

"Just keep your mouth shut. Tell the girls you gave me a blow job and I let you walk."

"Don't have to tell me twice."

She scoops her purse off the ground and teeters around the alley corner and goes back into the diner without even a thank you.

Some people have no gratitude.

39

DENNY RANKIN

[Wednesday, April 16]

He stands outside the Woodmont Bar and looks down Woodward to the Mayflower Café. Runs through the scene in his head again.

The drunken copper Ostrowski sits by the window, drinking and fuming, if the barman was right. He's watching Woodward Avenue, sees someone who makes him jump up and run out of the bar. He winds up in a shootout across Woodward.

Edgar Vanarian, the world's unluckiest dishwasher, stands in the diner doorway having a smoke. He hears shooting, maybe sees two men run across the street, one chasing the other, exchanging gunfire.

Vanarian sees his streetcar coming so he steps out from the doorway (in the middle of a gunbattle . . . perhaps also the world's stupidest dishwasher). Gets plugged.

Hubert Taylor, the diner worker, sees Ostrowski shooting at another gunman.

True, he's shooting wildly, because he's plastered. But the other gunman is returning fire.

If gunman #2 is firing back, he didn't hit anybody else because nobody else turned up injured . . . but what happened to the bullets?

At a break in traffic, Denny trots across the street. He turns, extends his hand as if he were shooting. Tries to imagine where the bullets would have gone from the second gunman.

A car barrels down on him with a shrill horn. He jumps up on the sidewalk.

Think this through . . . a man runs out of the Woodmont shooting at another man, who shoots back.

Denny tries to judge trajectories.

Standing where he stands—or even running from the Woodmont—a man shooting from there would hit what?

The Woodmont itself.

Back across the street, he examines the cream-colored enamel steel panels of the outside wall. He sees a crack and indentation in one of the panels.

He looks closely. A bullet. It might still be there.

Maybe so, but it would be damaged beyond usefulness.

On the side of the Woodmont, facing north, toward the Mayflower, is a billboard for Stroh's Bohemian Beer. It's next to a parking lot.

Denny badges the attendant who comes over to him. Denny says, "Were you here when there was a shooting across the street?"

"Yeah."

"See what went on?"

"Nah. I was in my hut when it started. Soon's I figured out it was gunshots, I ducked down. I didn't come out till I was sure it was over."

"Then you didn't see anything."

"Nope."

Denny examines the billboard. Anybody shooting while running wouldn't have been able to aim properly. Not with Ostrowski shooting at him. Just as Ostrowski was described as shooting wildly, this other guy would have been, too.

One bullet hit the front of the Woodmont façade. Could another have hit the billboard?

Denny runs his hands over the surface of the poster. The advertisement is pasted on a wooden board.

He finds holes puncturing the surface of the bottom of the ad down in the slogan, "It's Fire Brewed."

He takes a penknife and scores the paper around the holes. Digs out the bullets.

Denny doesn't recognize them. From a foreign gun. Slightly damaged, but not too damaged for the forensics guys to ID the type.

These might not even be from the Ostrowski shooting. They could have come anytime. But it also could have happened when the mystery shooter fired at Ostrowski.

It might not prove much, but at least it would be a start.

The forensics lab stands deserted except for Rooney, the director's assistant.

"Rooney," Denny says. He puts the bullets wrapped in a handkerchief on a lab table. "Are these too damaged to ID?"

Rooney gets a magnifying glass and takes a close-up look with his rabbity eyes. He nods. "Too damaged to make a comparison with."

"Do you recognize the ammo?"

"Oh yeah. No doubt. These are 124 grain. See that little rim around the base of the bullet? Even though the bullet's damaged, it's your clue right there."

"Can you tell what kind of gun it comes from?"

"I'd say a Walther P38. German pistol. They're brand new—just started mass production last year. Sweet little weapon. You found the bullets around here?"

Denny nods.

"Whoever fired them must have a pretty good line to Germany to get these so fast. Want me to take a closer look at them?"

"Maybe later," Denny says. He scoops up the ammo. "By the way, I never got a copy of the forensics report on the Mueller break-in. Did you ever finish it?"

"You never got it? Yeah, I'll run it down for you and send it over."

In the detective's squad room, he searches for Edgar Vanarian's forensics report from the medical examiner. When he can't locate it, he asks the bureau secretary what happened to it.

She tells him Arnold Jardine from Homicide had everything connected with the Ostrowski shooting sent over.

"Including the forensics report?"

"Yup. He has it all," she tells Denny.

40

ELIZABETH WATERS

[Wednesday, April 16]

A light glows behind the curtains in the front room of Eva's house. Elizabeth rings the doorbell.

She hears the news of the day on the radio inside. The Germans mined a Suez Canal port to keep American aid from getting through to the British. In the ongoing graft trial, Carl Staebler, formerly of the Wayne County Sheriff's office, denied ever taking payoffs from bawdy houses or policy shops despite the wealth of evidence to the contrary.

A young man swings the door open. It occurs to Elizabeth she doesn't know much about Eva's life . . . whether she has a husband or a boyfriend, or anything else about her family beyond her father's dead and her stepmother's disabled.

The young man looks younger than Eva.

He says, "Yeah?"

"Do you know Eva Szabó?"

"She's my stepsister. What of it?"

"I have some news about her. May I come in?"

"Who are you?"

"Elizabeth Waters. I'm a friend of hers. Is your mother home?"

He steps aside and she pushes past him.

An old woman is lying on the sofa, her arm dramatically thrown across her face.

"Mrs. Szabó?" Elizabeth asks.

When she gets no response, she says again, "Mrs. Szabó?" Eva's stepbrother says, "Ma!" and the older woman opens her eyes.

"*Nem kell kiabálnod!*"

She notices Elizabeth standing there. "*Ki vagy te?*" the old woman says.

Elizabeth looks to the young man. "What's she saying?"

"She said I don't have to shout. Then she said, 'Who are you?' She understands English but she don't like to speak it no more."

"My name's Elizabeth Waters. I'm a friend of your daughter. Can I sit?"

Eva's stepmother keeps looking at her. The kid nods toward a chair and Elizabeth takes a seat.

"Have the police spoken to you today?" she asks.

The older woman looks to her son.

"We ain't talked to nobody," he says.

"Then I have bad news for you. Eva's in the hospital."

The old woman looks at Elizabeth with dull eyes.

"She was very badly beaten," Elizabeth says. "She's alive. And she's being well taken care of."

"*Hol van ő?*" Mrs. Szabó says.

"She wants to know where she is," the young man translates.

"Wyandotte General Hospital," Elizabeth says. "Do you want a lift there? I'll drive you."

"What do you say, ma? Wanna go see her?" the kid says.

The old lady waves away the suggestion. Makes a sour face. Beckons her son to come closer to her. He sits beside her and she puts her arm around him and pulls him close.

"I guess she don't want to go," he says, like he just won an argument.

"Look," Elizabeth says, "Eva might have something of mine. Can I take a look at her room?"

"Upstairs," the kid says.

On the second floor, she finds two bedrooms; she guesses which one is Eva's—the one with a small library on top of the dresser. Otherwise, it's a spartan room with only one photograph on the wall. It's a picture of a babe in arms and a man and woman; Elizabeth assumes it's a photo of Eva and her parents. On top of her nightstand is a small menorah. Elizabeth didn't realize Eva was Jewish.

She finds a notebook in a drawer in the nightstand. She flips through it to make sure it's Eva's and she buries it in her coat.

On her way out, she asks Eva's stepbrother if he's sure they don't want a lift to the hospital.

"Nah, we're good."

Which tells her everything she needs to know about Eva's family.

41

CLARENCE BROWN

[Thursday, April 17, 1941]

He makes sure Bessie sits comfortably on the sofa before he leaves the house. He sets a pillow under her bad ankle and tunes the radio to the news.

Once again, Malone did not come back last night.

At roll call he sits with the other colored police. He gets a run. The information is garbled: a man was bit on the lip by another man who was holding a knife on a girl.

Doesn't make sense.

He's partnered with Francis Pitts, another Negro detective. The address is on Theodore Street. It turns out to be a one-story shotgun shack. It looks like it's been here since before the Civil War.

"Mind if I take this one?" Francis says. "Ain't had an arrest for a while. I could use one."

"Be my guest," Clarence says.

Francis knocks on the front door. There's yelling coming from the rear of the house. A woman's voice and two men.

"Let's go," Clarence says.

Francis shoulders in the door and they enter the apartment.

Francis leads them through a narrow hallway to the kitchen. They see two men struggling over a gun. A woman beats one of the men on the back with her fists.

Francis yells, "Stop!" Clarence rushes forward to break them up.

One of the men stops struggling and the other man takes the gun and shoots Clarence point-blank in the middle of the chest.

The force of the shot sends him reeling.

The gunman turns the gun on Francis but Francis has his .38 out and shoots him in the belly.

Francis attends to Clarence. His armor stopped the shot. Clarence has the breath knocked out of him but he's okay.

Francis calls an ambulance for the man he shot.

"He shot at us," the woman said. "He just came in here and shot at us!"

"You don't know this guy?" Francis says.

"Never saw him before," the other man says.

Clarence picks himself up from the floor. There is a hole in his overcoat from the bullet. Another hole for Bessie to patch.

"Alright?" Francis asks.

Clarence adjusts his armor. Says, "I'll live." To the man and woman, he says, "This your house?"

They say, "Yes," in unison.

"We got a call about a man got bitten on the lip. Did you make that?"

The man says, "We didn't make any call. Matter of fact, you hadn't got here when you did, we'd be dead."

"Then where's the man with the knife and the bite?" Francis asks.

It turns out dispatch got the street number wrong. Instead of 819 Theodore, the right address was 918. Francis goes off to the hospital with the man he shot. Clarence goes down to 918.

There he finds another trio. He gets the story straight. There was a man holding a knife on a woman, and another man bit him on the ear to make him drop the knife. The man who was bitten sits on the floor against the stove in the kitchen pressing a bloody towel against the side of his head.

Off to the hospital with another guilty victim.

Clarence is parking his car back at the station when he sees Roger Clendening come out of the building and get into his squad car. Clarence stays in his car and follows him.

Rain starts. First a drizzle, then within seconds a heavier downpour. In moments the street floods.

Clendening takes Gratiot to Beaubien. Turns on Monroe. Pulls over in front of the New Hellas Restaurant at the corner of Monroe and St. Antoine in Greektown. Leaves his car double-parked with a "Police Business" card and runs through the rain into the restaurant.

Clarence parks on St. Antoine. Splashes through puddles on the curb to the restaurant.

Clendening sits by himself in a far corner of the place. He faces the door but doesn't seem to see Clarence because Jimmy Anthony, the owner, stands in front of him. The two chat.

A waiter comes up to Clarence. Before he can tell Clarence no colored are allowed, Clarence badges him, brushes by him. The waiter doesn't like it but he stands back.

Clarence crosses the dining room floor to Clendening's table. Clendening looks up in shock. Jimmy Anthony looks at him in disbelief. Clarence badges him, too, and sits at Clendening's table. Jimmy walks away shaking his head. What's the world coming to?

Clendening wonders, too. "The fuck are you doing here?"

"Thought I might grab lunch."

"Don't grab it here. I'm waiting for people. And don't plan on being served anytime soon."

"Who are you meeting?"

"None of your business. Beat it."

Clarence leans in. "You're right. None of my business who you meet. Or why. Know what is? Your little scheme with Lucy Taggart."

"I dunno nobody named Lucy Taggart."

"How about Belle Baxter?"

Clendening stares at him. "Say," he says, "what are you trying to pull here?"

"What kind of stunt are you trying to pull with Lucy? Trying to start a race war? Have her make a false claim about Negroes stealing her baby? Then what's your plan? You going to whip out the dead baby and say the colored folks killed him? Start a real race riot?"

"You dunno what you're talking about."

Clarence leans in. Grabs Clendening's tie and pulls him across the table, nose to nose. Clarence tightens the tie around Clendening's neck. Clarence is trembling with fury.

"Was this your idea?" Clarence says.

Clendening turns purple.

"I'll choke the life out of you right here, you don't tell me what I want to know."

Holding the tie with one hand, Clarence pulls a .45 with his other hand and holds it against Clendening's leg under the table.

Clendening starts to sputter.

"Before that happens, Roger, I'll shoot your goddamn dick off."

Behind them the door to the restaurant opens. Clarence turns his head.

He recognizes Joseph Zerilli, Detroit mob boss, and Salvatore Lucido, his top gambling lieutenant. "Joe Uno" and "Sammy Lou." They chat with Jimmy Anthony.

Clendening sees them, too. He shakes his head at Clarence.

Clarence holds on.

"Your lunch meeting?"

Clendening nods, struggles.

Clarence holds him tight.

"Where's the dead child's body?"

Clendening tries to speak but he can't get the words out. Clarence eases his grip on Clendening's tie.

"In the morgue," he says.

"I checked the morgue. He wasn't there."

"Not the city morgue. The morgue at Receiving."

"What's his name?"

"He's logged in as Baby Doe. I swear I don't know his real name."

"Who does?"

"I dunno."

Clarence shakes his tie. "Who put you up to this?"

Clendening's eyes widen. Clarence turns to see Jimmy Anthony pointing in their direction. The gangsters start toward them.

"Who put you up to this?" Clarence says again.

"Wheaton," Clendening chokes out. "Now Jesus Christ—go!"

"Phil Wheaton? In Robbery?"

Zerilli and Lucido are on their way across the room. They stop to chat with other diners.

Clendening is frantic. He nods.

"What's he got on you, he could make you do that?" Clarence asks.

Without answering, Clendening grabs Clarence's arm. Grits his teeth. Forces out: "You got what you wanted. Let me go or on my mother's life, you're going to be a dead nigger."

Clarence lets Clendening go. He holsters his pistol. Stands. Straightens his coat and walks out past the two hoods.

Hears Clendening coughing behind him.
The gangsters stare after Clarence.
Clarence knows exactly what they're thinking:
What's this fucking moolie doing in here?

42

DENNY RANKIN

[Thursday, April 17, 1941]

A Walther P38.

A brand-new German gun.

Whoever fired the bullets must have a pretty good line to Germany to get these here so fast, Rooney at the forensics lab said.

And all the pro-Nazi shit flying around the city?

That must come from a really good line to Germany, too.

But whose?

Denny knows there is no shortage of pro-Nazi feeling around the country. Even the great and powerful Henry Ford admires Hitler. Hitler returns the admiration; he mentioned Ford in *Mein Kampf* and a portrait of Ford hangs on Hitler's wall.

Last winter, the German-American Bund sponsored a mass meeting at Madison Square Garden. It was explicitly pro-fascist and anti-Semitic. One of the main speakers, Denny remembers, was the leader of the Bund, a traitor named Fritz Kuhn. Last year, Kuhn went to prison for tax evasion and embezzlement, but before that, and before he assumed the leadership of the Bund, he worked for Ford Motor Company at the River Rouge Plant.

Kuhn worked in the Chemistry Department at Ford.

The same department where Prentiss Mueller works.

Whose son strolls around in fascist duds.

And is a good friend of Bert Vogelmann, who is coming into focus for the Edgar Vanarian shooting.

It's turning into a tangled web, but they're all connected.

Time for another trip to the Muellers' Palmer Woods home.

A new model Packard pings in the driveway. A car Denny hasn't seen before.

He parks down the street from the Mueller house. Radios in the registration number to the station for an ID. The car belongs to Dr. Fred W. Thomas. Address in East English Village.

Denny waits.

In another half hour, a man busts out of the Mueller house like it's on fire. He carries a doctor's black bag. He jumps in the Packard and tears off.

On a whim, Denny follows him.

Dr. Thomas—if that's who this is—gets to Woodward Avenue, takes a right. Goes south on Woodward, headed toward downtown. In about five miles, he takes a left on Mack Avenue, heads east. Goes past Gratiot Avenue, Mount Elliot, East Grand Boulevard, Van Dyke, Cadillac Boulevard.

Still in the Detroit city limits, Thomas turns right onto Garland Street. A quarter of the way down the second block he pulls over in front of 3521 Garland.

It looks like a rooming house. A frame building, three stories, wide covered front porch with two rocking chairs.

Thomas gets out of his car and heads inside the house.

Denny pulls up behind him. He gets out and starts toward the entrance to the house when a car screeches to a halt beside his.

A guy in a fedora and gray suit opens the passenger door and steps half out of the car. Flashes a big gun. Says, "Get in."

Denny does a quick calculation: a quiet residential street, not much traffic, no bystanders, Denny's service weapon in his shoulder holster . . . Would this guy take the chance of shooting him?

The guy lifts his gun. Says, "You no speak-a da English? I said get in."

Denny figures a stupid guy with a gun is nobody to argue with. He gets in the car.

They roar down Garland.

"I'm a Detroit Police Department detective," Denny says from the back seat.

The guy who ordered him into the car turns around. "And I'm the frickin' king of England. Pleased to meet you."

"If you let me take my badge out of my coat pocket—"

The guy shows his gun again. It's a .38 police special. "Move an inch and you're one frickin' dead detective sergeant."

Denny holds his hands up in surrender. Sits back.

Thinks: these guys must be G-men.

Nobody else would be this rude.

They head downtown. The car weaves through the city's streets, past Grand Circus Park, down Washington Boulevard, turning onto Michigan Avenue.

They pull into a closed-off parking lot. The two thugs hustle Denny out of the car and in through a sally port in the back of the building. Then into an elevator and up to the twenty-sixth floor.

They pass a sweat room. "Inside," one of them says, and pushes Denny into the room. A standard interview room, a table and four chairs. Two-way mirror.

Odd they didn't take his weapon or his badge.

Denny takes his badge out and lays it on the table in front of him. And waits.

In another half-hour, two other men enter the room. One is tall and rangy in a suit. Early thirties. Dark, suspicious eyes. Long nose. Receding chin. Plastered down hair.

The other man could have been a few years younger. He has the same straight-laced demeanor as the first man, but with a ruddy raw Irish face. Red hair, thin lips, blue eyes.

They sit across the table from Denny. Without saying anything, the older man picks up the badge. Looks at it and pushes it back across the table to Denny.

"Put it away," he says. He has a mild western drawl. "We know who you are."

Denny stows the badge. Says, "Mind telling me what's going on?"

"I'm John Bugas, special agent in charge of the Detroit FBI office." Bugas looks at the man seated beside him. "This is Special Agent Duhamel."

Denny says, "Would have been nice if the goons who picked me up identified themselves."

Bugas ignores the comment. Says, "How do you know Fred Thomas?"

"I don't."

"Why were you following him?"

"He might have a connection to a case I'm working on."

"What's the connection?"

"I'm trying to find out."

"What's the case?"

"A break-in in a house in Palmer Woods. If you already know who I am, you know I'm attached to DPD Robbery."

Bugas stares him down.

Denny tries to remember what he knows about this guy. FBI reputations—like Hoover's—tend to be manufactured by the press. But this guy's the real thing. He recalls Bugas was briefly a hero for capturing a kidnapper down south—Louisville, maybe—about six or seven years ago.

"You probably also know whose house it was," Denny says. "I went over there today and I saw Thomas running out like his pants were on fire. I decided to follow him."

"Why?"

Denny shrugs. "Hunch."

"Do you know where he led you?"

"A house on Garland, is all I know. Where your goons grabbed me before I could find out anything."

Bugas gives him the malocchio for another few moments, then exchanges a look with the other agent.

Bugas gets up and leaves the room.

Duhamel reaches a hand across the table. "Doug Duhamel."

Denny shakes. "The hell's going on?"

"In the last few years, the Bureau's changed our focus from crime to national security. We've been looking at pro-Nazi groups and individuals around the area and generating lists of their known associates. We've uncovered connections between Dr. Thomas and Fritz Heiler, the German Consul in Detroit, as well as links to Fritz Kuhn and Gerhard Heinz Kunze, leaders of the German-American Bund, which is connected to Hitler's Germany."

"Which means . . .?"

"Thomas is a German agent. The house where we picked you up?" Duhamel continues. "It's a rooming house owned by a couple named Emma Elise Leonhardt and Carl John Heinz Leonhardt. They have German roots. They're known to be the founders of the Nazi movement in Detroit, and their house is a known meeting place for Nazi sympathizers."

"Sounds like you've got this well in hand."

"We're keeping an eye on them," Duhamel says. "Detroit's a prime target for enemy sabotage, with all the industry."

"Why are you being so open about this with me? Usually you guys are tight as a tick's ass with information."

"You've been seen around places where pro-Nazi groups congregate."

"Like the Mueller house?"

"For one. You've also been seen at the National Workers League."

"And what, you think I'm one of them?"

"If we thought that, we wouldn't be sitting down with you. We'd keep you under surveillance. No, what this tells us is, our interests are converging. We're hoping you'll share with us what you know about the Nazi threat as you learn it. And that's why we're loosening our tick's asshole."

"I could have done without that image."

"All the same, what do you say?"

"Fine with me. If it's okay with your boss."

"He just wanted to check you out for himself."

The agent reaches across the table again. They shake hands.

Denny says, "Mind if I ask you a question?"

"Fire away."

"What do you know about Prentiss Mueller?"

"He's another one with close ties to pro-Nazi groups."

"For example?"

"The German-American Bund. The Christian Front. The National Workers League."

Denny huffs in exasperation. "Seems to me like you guys know a lot more than I do."

"Every bit of information helps. We're talking about the security of the United States of America."

They both rise. Duhamel says, "We'll give you a ride back to your car."

"You just reminded me," Denny says. "I'm looking for anybody who might be bringing new German small arms into the country. Any thoughts who that could have been?"

"My first thought is the German Consul General. Fritz Heiler. He's got his diplomatic pouch . . . you could bring anything over in that. You'll never get in to see him, though."

"Nobody else?"

"There's a lot of subversive activity going on," Duhamel says. "A gun could come from almost anywhere. Are you looking for anything in particular?"

"A Walther P38."

"What's your interest?"

"Might be part of one of my cases. What do you know about it?"

"I know it's a nice weapon."

"You've fired it?"

"I have."

"Where?"

"Here," Duhamel says. "Interesting story. The German Consul, Heiler? Turns out he presented the Grand Cross of the German Eagle to Henry Ford here in Dearborn. It's the highest award Germany can give a foreigner. They gave it to Ford three years ago.

"The two got friendly, and Heiler sent a prototype of the Walther P38 to the old man as a gesture of friendship. He brought it in with his diplomatic pouch. Heiler bragged it would revolutionize small arms fighting."

"And how did you get to fire it?"

"One of our operatives found out Ford had it. We asked if we could examine it. He wasn't happy about it, but he loaned it to us. I'm the special agent in charge of counter-espionage in the Detroit office. Couldn't keep me away from it."

"Where's the gun now?"

"We gave it back to Ford."

"Any chance Heiler sent more than one gun? And Ford only let you see one of them?"

"Ford would have told us, I'm sure. The old man is many things," the agent says, "but more than anything he's a patriot."

43

ELIZABETH WATERS

[Thursday, April 17, 1941]

She sleepwalks down the hall to her office. Drowsy, cotton-brained. She was at the hospital most of the night with Eva.

The on-call doctor told Elizabeth to go home because Eva was not in danger of dying. Still Elizabeth stayed.

She left after three in the morning. She drove back to her apartment in Palmer Park. The elevator operator used to be an irascible old fart named Mr. Fox. He died five years ago and a younger guy replaced him, a ferret-faced kid in his twenties. He was sound asleep behind his desk, so she took the elevator up to her floor herself.

She intended to go through Eva's journals. Eva had been sending in written summaries of what she had seen up to last week. What Elizabeth retrieved from Eva's room were the diary pages she kept as her original drafts.

Elizabeth started reading the diary but fell asleep before finishing the first entry.

Now, at the office in the morning, she checks her answering service messages—nothing urgent—and makes a pot of coffee. She doesn't want to be disturbed; she locks the front door.

She starts through the journal again.

Eva's handwriting is small and precise, difficult but not impossible to read.

March 10, 1941

My first day at work.

Excited and scared, but most of all worried I'll disappoint the boss. She's going out on a limb for me, and I so appreciate that. There must be a hundred other girls she could get to do this job, but she asked me. I have to succeed.

The thing I'm most worried about, though, is leaving Ágnes alone all day. I know she can get around by herself and even prepare her own food, but still I feel guilty. I know Josef will not help out (right now I don't even know where he is, the bum!) and the neighbors would give her a hand if she needed it. But I keep thinking it's my job to do. Even though I'm sure Ágnes wouldn't do the same for me.

Anyway.

The first day wasn't bad. I spent most of the day in the personnel office, filling in forms and signing things. Every time the administrative assistant put a form in front of me, she'd say, "Sign your life away." I didn't make it over to the hospital until later in the day. Nadine was cold to me at first, but I expect she'll come around.

The other nurses seem nice. Both are named Mary. Nadine calls them Mary 1 and Mary 2. I already forget which is which.

A couple of doctors rotate through the shifts. The one who was supposed to be there today, Dr. Fletcher, never came in. When I asked about him, Nadine just smiled and said, "You'll find out." The Marys tell me he has a drinking problem, so it's just as well he doesn't touch the patients.

I didn't learn much here today, except I did hear a secretary in the personnel department complaining about how awful the union is. (She was talking about the United Auto Workers). I asked why she said it, and she said the unions are filled with Communist Jews.

I hope I can start gathering information from the men tomorrow.

March 11, 1941

My first full day in the hospital. It's a good thing I'm not squeamish about the sight of blood, because there's going to be lots of it. Papa worked at this plant, so I always knew it was a dangerous place. I guess I never realized how dangerous it is, and how lucky or careful he was . . . he never got a serious injury until the Hunger March, and it wasn't from the factory but from the police thugs.

I got a good (and safe) job here, but I'm not sure I'm going to be able to pick up as much information as I thought. I'm never alone. Nadine and the Marys and occasionally the doctors are always around. I'm never left alone with the men who come here and I can't really ask them about what happens to them or if anyone has kept them from talking about the UAW.

And they're not allowed breaks, and they're not supposed to talk to anybody except as part of their jobs. There's no place to go, really, where I can just sit and listen or even talk to anybody. Everybody is very cautious about what they say when they're in the hospital. Somebody is always listening.

March 13, 1941

I think I discovered the best way to be helpful. The men come here when they're injured, so even if I don't get to talk to them directly, I can see what kind of injuries they get, and if they're worth reporting. Some seem accidental, but some seem deliberate. One man from the Foundry came in today with his whole arm burned. I heard Nadine ask him what happened and he said he got too near one of the furnaces but when I talked with her afterwards she said the kind of burns this fellow had could only be gotten by holding his arm near the furnace way past the time he could stand it. Another man must have held him there.

Still, it's exciting. I feel like a spy. When I walk around the buildings, I feel like I'm bearing a secret with me everywhere.

March 17, 1941

I was going to keep this strictly a record of my notes for the report, but something happened last night I have to put down before I forget.

My stepbrother Josef came over yesterday (Sunday) for the first time in ages. The last time I remember seeing him was right after Papa's funeral, which has been a couple of years. But there he was, big as life, when I got home from grocery shopping. Ágnes was so happy to see him . . . I don't remember her ever being as happy to see me as she is to see him. She smiled with the side of her face that isn't droopy, and clapped her hands and even laughed! I can't remember the last time I saw her laugh. She sure never laughs when I'm around.

I asked him what he wanted and he said, What's the matter, aren't you glad to see me? And I said, No, not particularly. And he just laughed. He sat on the couch with his arm around his mother for a few hours. Then just like that he got up to go. He didn't even say goodbye to me even though I had made a pot of chicken soup for dinner with the bones I got from the butcher.

He was also wearing one of those swastikas like the Germans wear. He wore it on a chain around his neck.

This also made me angry. I said, "What's the matter with you? Why are you wearing that thing!"

And he just looked at me and shook his head like I was the stupidest girl in the world. He said, "I'm not Jewish."

"I said, 'That doesn't matter, I am. And that's a symbol of hate,' and he said, "No, it's a symbol of hope. Our only hope for the future." He said I better understand that if I know what's good for me.

Even before we left Hungary, when mama died, Papa stopped admitting we were Jewish. But I could never do that. It would feel like losing mama again.

After Josef left, I tried to tell Ágnes what those crooked crosses meant but she thought I was just out to get Josef so she pooh-poohed me. Josef always was her favorite.

I'm sorry this doesn't have more to do with the Rouge plant, but I just have to get it out.

March 19, 1941

Today I decided the only way to get to speak with the men at the plant is by going out to the bars where they drink after their shifts. They know they're not supposed to talk about the union during workdays at the plant, but maybe when they're away and have a few drinks in them, they'll open up a bit.

That's what I thought, anyway.

So I went to the Dix Bar and Grill. I went by myself, which was a very big step for me. I never used to go to bars alone. But there I was today, walking in just like I owned the place. Of course, I had to screw up my courage to the sticking point, but I finally was able to do it enough to walk in there. I know Papa used to go to bars like this after work. I loved it how I was following in his footsteps again. I only wish he could have been here with me.

The place was like a crypt. Only a handful of men were scattered around the room, plus a few at the bar. But nobody was talking to anybody. I remember thinking, Is THIS why people go to bars? To sit by themselves and suck on a beer bottle, then throw it away and start again?

It was exhausting, trying to catch a name from anyone. Just a roomful of dog-tired regulars who looked like they hadn't slept in their own beds for a month.

Or bathed in a month, either, for that matter. Did you ever smell a beat old guy who's been doing manual labor all day? Not pleasant.

I ordered a beer and stayed until I finished it. A couple times I tried to start up a conversation with a pair of rummies at the bar. But they thought I was a whore. One of them even asked me how much I charged for a handjob.

But I swear, during the whole time I was there, not one person came over to me and said anything to me, except for the bartender and even he just asked me what I wanted. I didn't think this is going to be a useful place so I won't be back.

March 31, 1941

What I'm learning more and more is, the Rouge plant is a terrible place to work. I understand about the need for it, but the kinds of injuries I'm seeing are beyond belief.

By now I'm starting to see patterns. Many of those injured in the Foundry are Negroes. They are concentrated there, which seems to be one of the most dangerous areas. Men come in damaged by frequent explosions, thick soot, and the heat. Henry Ford had a reputation for supporting Negro employment, but the conditions for the Negroes who work there are brutal.

Then today this one guy came to the hospital with a foot that looked like hamburger. He said he dropped a piece of glass on it (he works in the Glass Plant). I haven't been to the Glass Plant yet, but I didn't see how a plate of glass winding up on his foot could cause such damage.

Tonight I decided I would try another working-man's bar. See if maybe I might unlock more conversation than I have in the previous weeks. I went to the Rouge Tavern. I was getting impatient.

It was hopping, compared to the place I went last week. Lots of men, lots of music, lots of noise. Particularly conversations.

I met a guy named Anton Luedke, who was there with his friends. To tell you the truth, they looked like gangsters. Anton is not tall but he's wide and he has big arms and shoulders, like he's been doing manual labor his whole life. The other guys are named Eddy Singleton, Kevin McNamara, and Frank Ennis. Anton seems to be in charge of them. At least the other guys defer to him.

He also seemed interested in me. I still don't know how I feel about it. I haven't had a boyfriend for ages, and to be perfectly honest I don't want one. There's this one guy—Vince Németh—who acts like I'm his girlfriend. I met him at the market where I worked, and it turned out he's a friend of my stepbrother.

I told Vince I wasn't interested in having a boyfriend right now, but it didn't seem to faze him. He still acts really possessive. And he hates me working in the plant, and he doesn't hesitate to let me know. I try to tell him nicely that he doesn't have any say in the matter, but he mostly ignores me when I talk like that.

But to have another man even seem like he was interested, like the guy in the bar . . . well, it was a new sensation, to put it mildly. I love what I'm doing—but honestly, coming home to my stepmother every night isn't much of a life. And now my stepbrother has started to show up, which just makes things that much worse.

Maybe that's why I'm so happy about this opportunity and I don't want to fail at it.

April 1, 1941

I saw the boss tonight and I talked about everything I saw and heard from today. The men at the plant went out on strike and it was crazy. This guy, Frank Ennis, talked to me—or talked at me—on the streetcar to work, before I knew what was happening at the plant. I got nervous because I thought he might have figured out who I am, but I kept it safe, I think.

I definitely need to speak with him. The other guys said he's a union organizer, so he probably has lots of stories about violence directed at the union workers. I'll have to get him alone and talk to him.

April 2, 1941

I went to the Rouge Tavern again. Anton told me one of the guys who hang around together—which I've started thinking of as Anton's Gang—got fired. The guy named Frank Ennis. Anton said Frank got what was coming to him.

Frank seemed like he was a dedicated union guy. Then how could Anton say he got what was coming to him? Anton told me Frank was a Communist. Is that what he meant when he said Frank got what was coming to him? Lots of the men in the union movement are Communists . . . I don't understand.

And what's that say about Anton? I thought he was a union guy, but it looks like I'll have to re-examine my opinion of him.

I thought Frank would be a good person to talk to about what he knew about violence against the union organizers—and now he's gone. Anton said he was fired because he was a Red, but I'm not convinced. I'm going to try to track him down and ask him what's going on. I pressed Anton about what happened, but he couldn't—or wouldn't—tell me anything.

April 7, 1941

A terrible day.

Two Service Department goons came to see me and threatened me if I don't quit. They scared me. I got a call from Gloria, the woman I helped in the Administration Building. She told me there were people after me from the Service Department and I needed to get scarce. I tried to run but they found me on the plant site. There was a short one and a tall one, and I kept thinking about them as Mutt and Jeff but there wasn't anything funny about them. They roughed me up a bit—nothing very bad, just a few slaps. But they scared me. Which I'm sure is what they had in mind. They told me I should quit, which of course I'm not going to do.

I know I'd recognize them again if I saw them. Jeff, the short one, had a lisp and a crooked nose, like it had been broken. Mutt, the tall guy, had a scar running down the side of his face.

I was frightened, until I realized this is what the men fighting for the union have to put up with all the time. I go in to my job every day and play secret agent while these guys are really the ones who put their lives on the line.

The boss said I should walk away from the job, but I said no, give me until the end of the week. It feels like there's still more to find out. If I don't find anything out by Friday, I promised I'd quit.

Then that night I had a fight—a knock-down, drag-out fight—with Josef. So two men hit me today. If these men think they're going to cow me into submission, they're sadly mistaken.

I'm going to fight back even harder.

Elizabeth puts the diary down. On one hand, she's impressed Eva was so dedicated to her assignment. But she is saddened, too—because reading Eva's notes was like walking through the mind of a woman who is too young for the spot Elizabeth put her in. Elizabeth also forgot how young and inexperienced Eva was. She'd never had a boyfriend, and the attention this guy Anton was showing her seemed to be turning her head.

Still, this business with—what was his name? She reread the entry for April 2nd—Frank Ennis—this business with Frank getting fired jumped out at Elizabeth. Eva, too, must have known it was fishy because she zeroed in on it with Anton. And Anton was evasive.

Eva said Anton told her Frank Ennis was a Communist. She was right, there was no shortage of Communists in the labor movement.

She hears a noise at the door to her suite.

The handle of the door. It's turning.

Not turning like a client who wants in, but slowly, like whoever is behind the door doesn't want anybody to know they're trying to get in.

She always keeps a .22 pistol in her purse. She takes it out now. Turns out the light in her office. She opens her inner office door. A dark shape fills the other side of the pebbled glass of the outer door.

She can't make out who it is. It's just a silhouette, lurking and turning the door handle very quietly.

She sidles up to the door and stands to the side of the glass with her pistol ready.

After a minute she hears scraping on the door handset.

She remembered to lock the door. But whoever is on the other side is trying to pick the lock.

Maurice Sugar told her the door lock is virtually pickproof.

That "virtually" left a small but important margin of error, she thinks.

She stands with her gun poised to blow the head off whoever comes through the door.

After a minute of trying and failing to gain entry, the intruder gives up and the shadowy form on the pebbled glass fades away.

She waits a full minute, then she unlocks the door and throws it open.

The corridor is empty.

44

CLARENCE BROWN

[Thursday, April 17, 1941]

He badges the woman on the Admissions desk at Detroit Receiving Hospital. Asks to be directed to the morgue.

It's in the basement. He makes his way down cement-block hallways with steam pipes and electrical conduits running overhead. At the morgue reception desk sits a woman with steely blue eyes behind wire-rim glasses. She looks up at him standing there as if she just discovered him on the bottom of her shoe.

"Detective Clarence Brown, Detroit Police," he says. "Are you the morgue administrator?"

"Dr. Cavanaugh is our director."

"Is he in?"

She takes a long moment to think up an answer to his question. Almost as if she considers not telling him.

Finally, she decides she may as well answer him. "Hang on."

She lifts the phone and pushes a button. "There's a Negro police detective here to see you."

She listens for another long moment, then hangs up. "Go straight back and make a left at the end of the hall. Dr. Cavanaugh's office is on the right."

The walls are subway tile with a pungent smell of bleach. At the end of a small jog is the office of the morgue director.

Clarence knocks once on the closed door and goes inside. The office is cramped, with every horizontal surface filled with stacks of files. Dr. Cavanaugh himself is a small, very white man in a lab coat. He rises with his hand out as Clarence approaches.

Clarence shakes his hand, which is damp and limp as a fish. Cavanaugh himself looks haunted with bleary blue eyes behind horn-rimmed glasses and a tiny Hitleresque mustache.

Clarence badges him, tells him his name.

"I'm looking for the remains of a white male infant logged under the name 'Baby Doe.' He would have been brought in a few weeks ago."

Cavanaugh adjusts his glasses on his nose. "Do you know how many unclaimed, unnamed, dead white male Baby Doe infants we have here?"

"I do not."

"I'd say roughly thirty."

"How is that even possible?"

"Infant mortality isn't as bad as it used to be, but it's still bad. You get children who are orphaned or deserted, who then die without anyone to care for them. You get mothers who abandon their children. Fathers who abandon the mothers, who then feel like they have no choice but to leave their sick or dying children at churches or hospitals."

"I need to be able to look through your files for my particular baby Doe."

"No can do. Not without a warrant."

"There can't be that many who came in in the past couple weeks?"

"It wouldn't matter if there was just one. I can't let you look through the medical records—never mind the cold drawers—without legal permission."

Which Clarence knows he will never get. He's not even supposed to be here now asking these questions.

He says, "You can't even let me know if any dead white male infants were brought in?"

"Oh, yeah, sure, there were. There always are, every day, day in and day out. More than that, I can't say."

Clarence sits in his unmarked across the street from the main police station. The Robbery Division is on the second floor.

Phil Wheaton's desk is up there.

Wheaton, who Roger Clendening said was behind the scheme with the dead child.

Clarence asks himself: do I confront *another* detective in the Detroit Police Department?

Almost ten years ago Clarence shot and killed the then-chief of DPD detectives, Ray Lindenauer. It would have been the end of his career if he hadn't proven Lindenauer was a bad cop, and he was part of an attempted assassination of not only Mayor Frank Murphy but Clarence himself.

Still, it ended his chances for advancement.

If he went after another detective now?

It would be the end of the line in the DPD. If not in law enforcement in general . . . he doesn't see how he could ever get a job as a policeman again. Not up north, anyway.

Well.

He asks himself: would that be so bad?

If he left police work, he and Bessie could leave Detroit. Go back down to Kentucky, maybe, where they come from. He was too old to work the jobs he had before they left to come north—when he was young, he worked as a tanner in Lexington; after DeMarco died, Clarence and Bessie moved across the river to Cincinnati, where the best-paying jobs for Negro men were. Clarence became a Pullman porter.

A chance encounter with a Detroit clergyman on a train one day led to his joining the Detroit Police Department, which was then looking for men like himself to keep the growing Negro population of Detroit in line.

Maybe now that they're both older, being where they lived with DeMarco would bring Clarence and Bessie more peace than pain.

Anyway, here he was, in his fifties, tired, sick of this job, his own health failing.

He's tired of hoping things will change and being disappointed if the changes are incremental and often subtle instead of sudden and immediately visible.

And those changes are obstructed by every white person around.

Clarence's neighbor Sonny McGhee was right: until the Negro gets justice, there will never be peace either in this city or in this country.

Once upon a time Clarence thought when—not if—the Negro in America got justice, it would be in part because people like him did everything they could to make it happen.

More and more, he's starting to believe real justice will never come.

But what does he tell his boys on the ballfield? Even if you're behind, you can't leave the field. You have to play the game to the end.

It takes more courage to do that than it does to win the game.

Now, he wonders if watching the station with Wheaton inside is more courage or more stupidity?

He thinks of that poor infant wrapped in a blanket. That baby never had a chance to decide for himself . . .

Someone has to speak for that child.

Everyone is telling him not to do it.

Which means he's the one who has to.

He needs to find out more about Phil Wheaton.

Who does he know in Robbery?

More importantly, who does he *trust* in Robbery?

He radios in to the dispatcher. Tells him to get hold of Denny Rankin.

It's urgent.

45

DENNY RANKIN

[Thursday, April 17, 1941]

Back at the station, he has two messages. One is from Captain Dwight Dietrich.

Denny calls back right away.

Dietrich says, "What's going on with the Mueller break-in?"

"I'm starting to zero in a possible motive."

"You don't have anybody in lockup yet?"

"No sir."

"Christ on a bike. Speed it up, will you? I told you, Mueller's got powerful friends in the department. They want it solved and I want it solved. If you're not the man to do it, I'll get somebody else."

"It's moving along, captain."

"It needs to do more than move along. I need it cracked. Then I need you back on rotation. Did you forget your promotion's on the line? I'll give you two more days. If you haven't closed it by then, you're out. I'll get fresh eyes on it."

Denny says nothing. This isn't like Dietrich to be so shook. The bosses must be leaning on him.

Dietrich hangs up.

Denny doesn't understand. This guy Mueller's a low-level suit at Ford's. Where's the heat to solve this coming from?

Either: (1) Mueller is higher up than Denny thinks he is.

Or (2) the case being open is a threat to someone. To who? Higher ups? But nobody can shut it down; it has to be legit closed and off the books.

Denny remembers it wasn't supposed to be his case in the first place. Phil Wheaton was supposed to take it. Was Phil planning (or ordered) to take whatever steps he needed to close it? Is this why Mueller was distressed to see Denny and not Wheaton coming out to work it that first day?

Either way, Denny tells himself, I'm not giving this up. He calls Rooney in the forensics lab. "Rooney, where the hell is my forensics report for the Mueller break-in?"

"What are you, kidding me? I sent that over right after we talked yesterday."

"You sent it somewhere, but not to me."

Denny hangs up, goes to ask the division secretary to find the missing report.

His second message is from the Dispatcher. Detective Clarence Brown wants to talk to him. ASAP.

After five minutes of patching calls through, Denny connects with Clarence.

"We need to meet," Clarence says.

Denny says, "You're sure he said Phil Wheaton?"

"Positive."

Clarence has just told him what Clendening said in Greektown: Phil Wheaton was behind the dead infant in Black Bottom.

"Any chance he was bullshitting you?" Denny asks.

"You had a .45 pointed three inches from your willie, would you be inclined to bullshit?"

"Not when you put it like that."

Miss Etta shuffles over with their lunch. Coca-Cola and a sweet roll for Clarence, a hot hamburger sandwich for Denny. They sit in Tipton's Luncheonette. Denny is the only white man in the place.

"Let me make sure I got this right," Denny says. "Phil Wheaton told Clendening to get this hooer to make a false claim about Negroes kidnapping her child? That's what she said?"

"Yeah."

"Why would he do that?"

"My guess? To start problems between Negroes and whites."

"But you found the baby's body and that threw off their plans," Denny says.

"Yeah."

"Jesus Christ. What a country."

"I was downtown a little while ago," Clarence says. "I almost went up and braced him."

"Who? Wheaton?"

"Yeah."

"And said what?"

"Nothing that wouldn't have got me shot in the head. You know him. What's the best approach here? Go to the Trial Board?"

Denny considers it. The Police Trial Board is looking at the cops who were being investigated over the graft scandal. At first blush, that would be the approach to take.

Except the head of the Trial Board is Bill Wannamaker, who used to command Homicide when Wheaton was there.

"I'd say no," Denny says. He explains the link between Wannamaker and Wheaton.

Denny says, "Speaking of links, I'm also finding connections between Wheaton and pro-Nazi groups in town."

"Got his fingers in lots of pies."

"Let's both do some more digging and see what those are."

Clarence agrees.

He finishes off his Coca-Cola and signals Miss Etta for another.

It's hard for Denny to square what Clarence told him about Phil Wheaton with what he himself knows about the man. True, Phil lied about Charlotte's whereabouts, but before that they'd been friends. Denny and Hazel had been to Phil's house for dinner; Phil was a family man who loved his wife and daughter. He was a mediocre detective, but so were most of the humps in the bureau, who couldn't solve a crossword puzzle let alone a crime, so . . .

There were holes in the story Clarence told him. Clarence got his information from a crooked cop and a worker in a brothel. How reliable are they?

Denny goes back to the precinct house. His first instinct is to find Phil Wheaton and have it out with him. But he and Clarence Brown agreed to put off any confrontations.

And anyway, Phil's in the field. It's just as well.

He started out the day looking for the source of the Walther P38 before he got sidetracked at the Mueller house. He gets back to it.

Still no sign of life at Bert Vogelmann's bungalow. He's now in the frame for the Ostrowski shooting. Plus he connects with Heinz Mueller, the little rat-bastard Nazi. And Vogelmann has his own anti-Semitic history at B'nai David.

Time for another talk with young Heinz.

No cars are in the Mueller driveway. Denny rings the bell. He knocks on the door.

Rings the bell again. Waits.

Nobody comes.

He rings again, and again nobody comes. He starts back down the front walk and hears the door pulled open inside the house.

Wanda Mueller stands framed in the doorway.

She has on a prim skirt with a sweater with one of those round collars his wife puts on her daughters to go to church. Wanda's face is heavily made up, with dark raccoon rings under her eyes and bright red lipstick.

She's not as dazed as she was the last time Denny saw her. The fog is starting to lift.

The seductive smile is gone. She scowls as she opens the door to him, as though she has been waiting for someone else. "Yes?" Same breathless voice, low this time, as if she were humming the word.

"Is your brother here?"

"No," she says, and goes to close the door. As she does her legs give out from under her and she goes down in a heap.

He pushes inside. A caramel-colored striped tweed suitcase stands beside her on the floor.

He calls out, "Hello? Anyone home?" He hears nothing.

Denny half-carries, half-drags her through the long foyer into the sunken living room. He lays her on one of the couches. He guesses this is Dr. Thomas's handiwork.

"What does Dr. Thomas have you on?" he says.

She's conscious but he gets no response. She moans. He goes into the kitchen and fills a glass full of cold water. Brings it back to her. Props her head up so she can take a sip. She drinks in too much all at once and sputters it out into his face.

"Are you getting ready to leave?" Denny asks.

As if remembering what she was about to do, she starts to gather herself to stand.

"Hold it," he says. "Where are you going?"

"Anywhere but here."

"You're going by yourself?"

"A friend's picking me up."

"You look a little green around the gills."

She gulps. "I'm going to throw up."

He grabs a potted philodendron from a nearby coffee table and sticks it under her nose. She throws up into it.

It tapers into dry heave and he gives her a handkerchief. "Wipe your mouth. Are you on medication?"

This time she nods.

"From Dr. Thomas?"

"He says they're iron tablets."

"I'm guessing they're more than iron tablets. You look drugged."

"He says I'm anemic since the baby."

"What baby?"

He waits for her to continue but nothing more comes. She sits up on the side of the couch with her elbows on her knees and her head in her hands. She burps.

He sits beside her. "Wanda," he says, "look at me."

With an effort, she turns her head.

"What baby?"

"I had a baby."

"When?"

"Three weeks ago."

"Do you want to tell me what happened?"

She takes another sip of water.

"I was pregnant," she says. "I went into labor early. There was a problem."

"Did you go to the hospital?"

"No. Daddy called Dr. Thomas."

Fred Thomas, the German agent the FBI questioned Denny about.

"And what happened?" he asks.

"He came over and delivered it. It was a boy. Except Dr. Thomas said it didn't live very long. He tried to save it, he said, but he couldn't."

"What happened to the baby?"

"They took him away."

"Who?"

"I'm not sure. I think Bert was here."

"Bert Vogelmann?"

She nods. "I think maybe he was the one took Franklin away."

"Franklin?"

"My baby. I named him after the president."

"You named your baby after Franklin Roosevelt?"

"Yeah."

"Did your family know?"

"I didn't tell them."

"Did your father know about taking Franklin away?"

"Uh-huh. He was here when it happened."

"Where's Franklin now?"

"No idea." She takes a close look at him. "Who did you say you are?"

"Detective Sergeant Denny Rankin. I'm with the Detroit Police. I saw you the last time I was here."

"I don't remember."

"I'm not surprised. Do you know where Bert Vogelmann is?"

"I haven't seen him since that day."

"Is he Franklin's father?"

"No." Wanda wrings her hands. "I can't tell you who is."

"If you named your baby after the president of the United States, I assume you don't share your family's beliefs about the Nazis?"

"I used to. But I don't anymore." She struggles to her feet. "Come on. I want to show you something."

Denny helps her down the stairs to the locked rooms in the basement. She is weak but moving on her own.

She opens one of the doors and stands back. Says, "Daddy doesn't think I know about this, but I have a duplicate key to the locks."

Facing Denny is a massive red and black Nazi flag, taking up the whole wall in the room. On shelves along the wall are stacks of speeches, propaganda pamphlets, circulars, buttons, posters, stickers, letters, 16 mm film cannisters, and posters on stakes for picketing. In German and English, with and without a swastika. The materials warn about the Jewish threat, portraying Jews as subhuman and dangerous enemies of the German Reich and democracy across the world.

On a table in the center of the room is a copy of a newspaper, *The Free American and Deutscher Weckruf und Beobachter*. It proclaims itself the official organ of the German-American Bund with the headline, "We Cannot Win this War for England."

A flyer beside the paper headed "America First Committee" lists organizations that endorse it:

American Destiny Party
American Guards
American White Guards
Blackshirts and Italian Fascist Clubs
Christian Mobilizers
Ethiopian-Pacific League
Flangists
Gray Shirts
Ku Klux Klan
Kyffhaeuser Bund
National Copperheads
National Workers League
Patriots of the Republic
Save America First
Save Our America Clubs
White Russian Fascists

He's heard of America First. A new group headed up by Charles Lindbergh. They don't want the country to enter the war, but a hefty layer of race hatred underpins their objections.

But these other groups? He had no idea this was so widespread.

On a bookshelf are copies of a magazine, *Today's Challenge*. Denny skims the table of contents. "Can the Jewish Problem be Solved?" "Are We a Dying People?" "America's No. 1 Problem." "War is the Enemy of Democracy."

There are also copies of Father Coughlin's *Social Justice*, the same paper Denny saw upstairs next to where Frieda Mueller was sitting on the day of the break-in. Issues of *The American Vindicator*. The

Detroit National Workers League Newsletter. They call for immedi-
ate impeachment of FDR for throwing "our young American
manhood into the BLOODY JEW REVENGE WAR IN EUROPE."

"What does your father do with all this?" Denny asks.

"He gives it to people to distribute."

"Where does it come from?"

"A lot of it comes from Germany. A lot comes from the Christian
Front, here in America."

The organization Father Coughlin promotes; they want a white
Christian America. The boys who stole guns from Eppinger's belong
to the Christian Front; they took the guns to arm the group.

Denny picks up a few pamphlets. They come from a publishing
company in New Jersey: Flanders Hall, Inc. Like everything else in
this room, they are virulently anti-British, anti-Jewish, and pro-Nazi.

"Ever see any guns down here?" Denny asks. He's thinking of the
Walther P38.

"Never. Just this stuff."

They both turn at a sound from upstairs. Heinz's voice. "Wanda?
You home?" They hear his footsteps creaking across the floor in the
drawing room overhead.

She goes pale. "Oh God," she says. "I was hoping to get away
before he came home. Please don't tell him I'm here."

Denny tells her to stay quiet.

He goes upstairs. "Hello, Heinz."

"What are you doing here?" Heinz asks. "You're not supposed to
be here."

"I want to talk to you."

"Where's Wanda?"

"You won't be seeing Wanda again."

Heinz stares at Denny for a moment. Then he turns and races out
of the house.

Denny's right on his tail.

Heinz jumps behind the wheel of the Ford idling in the driveway.
He peels off and Heinz is gone before Denny can ID the license.

Back in the dining room, Wanda sits at the table with her head
resting on her arms.

"Are you alright?" Denny asks.

She picks her head up. "Yes."

"Do you want me to stay with you until your friend comes?"

"She was supposed to be here by now."

As if on cue, a car pulls into the driveway. Denny hears steps running up to the front stoop, then the doorbell.

Denny helps Wanda to the front door with her suitcase. Wanda pulls the heavy bag through the open door.

Charlotte Wheaton stands on the porch.

As surprised to see Denny as he is to see her.

"What are you doing here?" he asks.

"Helping Wanda escape from this nut house," Charlotte says.

"How do you know each other?"

"We met at the National Workers League."

"That was when I was still a believer," Wanda says. "We stayed friends. But let's go! Let's go before somebody comes back!"

"Out of the way," Charlotte says. She brushes by Denny and helps Wanda down the front steps to her car. It is not her father's police unit, but a beat-up Chevy sedan.

"Where are you taking her?" Denny asks.

"Someplace she'll be safe," Charlotte says. "I'm not telling you where. And don't you follow us, either."

Charlotte gets Wanda settled in the front seat. She slides behind the wheel. She backs the car out and speeds away.

On the way back to the station, he stops at a pay phone. Leaves a message for Clarence Brown at the Hunt Street Station:

"The package we talked about today? The one you found? It might have been dropped off by a mug named Bertrand Vogelmann."

46

ELIZABETH WATERS

[Thursday, April 17, 1941]

Satisfied the office doors are still locked against intruders, she returns to Eva's journal.

The entry for April 8th talks about Eva's meeting with Bogdan Kowalczyk, which Eva has already described for her.

Elizabeth closes the journal. Her heart aches for Eva. This poor girl, all she wanted to do was impress Elizabeth and all Elizabeth was concerned about was getting enough information to satisfy Maurice Sugar.

We all want to satisfy somebody, she thinks. Life is a gigantic food chain, only instead of the higher levels feeding on us, each one of us yearns for the approval of the next ones higher up on the chain; we willingly feed them.

I should have stopped this in its tracks, she thinks. If only I had gone with my instincts.

What's done is done. All she can do now is move forward. Most of all, she wants to find who left Eva for dead.

Mutt and Jeff, maybe?

Even if they did it, how would she pick them out of the dozens of ex-cons, dirty cops, washed-up palookas, and other assorted low-lifes that make up the Red-bashing, union-bashing Ford Service Department?

Elizabeth used to be a sympathizer of the Communist Party, too.

Her former—what was he? lover? partner? boyfriend? betrayer?—
was a member; it's how they met. He was British, Clive Sinclair-
Smith. He wrote a book about Sir Oswald Mosely, founder of the
British Union of Fascists. Clive came to Detroit in the mid-30s to
speak about the growing fascist threat in Europe. He was a dozen
years older than Elizabeth, but in the way these things happen they
fell in love.

Instead of returning to London, he stayed and moved in with her.
He said he saw America as being ripe for the kind of fascism that
was sweeping through Germany. He wanted to study it. Maybe
write another book about it.

She thought they were happy. She was happy, at any rate, happier than she could remember being.

After a few months together, he said he had to go out of town for
two weeks to research his new book. He was secretive about where
he was going; she didn't push him to know.

He called her a few times at the beginning of the first week, but
then she didn't hear from him again. He didn't return after the two
weeks were up.

She got no calls. No telegrams.

She was worried. She came up with a thousand scenarios for
what happened: his plane went down. His train derailed. He had an
accident on the road.

The Nazis he was researching got to him.

Three more weeks went by before she got his letter. In it, he said
he went to visit his wife in England—wait, *his wife*?!—and he realized he missed her and their children—*their children*?! He decided to
stay in England with them.

Thanks for the memories, etc.

She was devastated. She couldn't sleep, she couldn't eat, but most
of all she couldn't look at herself in the mirror. Couldn't take in the
fool who had fallen for Clive, and who had let herself start to fanta-
size about a life together with him.

Gradually her revulsion for herself faded. In the aftermath,
though, she associated Clive with the Communist Party, and her hatred of him turned her away from Party politics; she began to see the
Party's promises as empty as Clive's had been. Her disgust with men
in general as represented by Clive in particular turned her away
from men and women. Her first big love in college was another

woman, who took her own life, which devastated Elizabeth at the time; in the years since, she's had relationships with men as well as women. After Clive, that all stopped. She became reclusive, concentrating on the battle for union representation and on her investigation agency.

Now she rereads Eva's journal.

She can't let this go. If she's going to find whoever beat Eva, she decides she needs to trace Eva's contacts.

Starting with Anton, Kevin, and Eddy.

47

CLARENCE BROWN

[Thursday, April 17, 1941]

D riving around.
   Thinking.
   He picked up Rankin's message about Bertrand Vogel-
mann. Now he has two names to investigate.

If the chain of events that led to Vogelmann ditching the baby's
body in Black Bottom started with Phil Wheaton, how can he get
more information on Wheaton?

Easier said than done. He trusts Rankin, but he doesn't trust
many others in the department.

And not many trust him. Certainly not the white officers who
would be the ones he'd need to get information from.

He hates to do it, but he might have to speak with John Hays, the
supervisor of Clarence's segregated squad of Negro detectives.

He couldn't talk to the squad's assistant supervisor, William Wilson, who specifically told him not to pursue this child's case.

Does he have any other options?

The other cop he's close to is Francis Pitts.

Would he know anything about what goes on in Robbery?

A call comes through on his car radio.

A Negro boy's body has been found in Paradise Valley.

Unlike his wife, Clarence is not a praying man. He knows begging
an invisible man in the sky for favors is futile. He can only throw a

vain hope out into an indifferent universe that the boy who was just found is not Malone Coleman.

It's not Malone.

It's another mother's son, abused and discarded like so much trash.

They even found this boy in a trash can in an alley off Adams and Hastings Streets. Henry Yee, the owner of Duck Yee Laundry, went behind his shop to throw away empty boxes and discovered the boy stuffed into a trash can.

A trash can.

It was a weathered gray galvanized steel trash container. The boy's small body had been bent and twisted so it fit inside.

The coroner and his assistant, Herman Weiskopf, arrive shortly after Clarence gets there. Clarence doesn't know the coroner but recognizes his assistant, Herman Weiskopf. Weiskopf and Clarence lay the can on its side and gently extract the body.

The police photographer takes his pictures, then leaves.

"Poor child," the coroner says. "He's still in rigor. Death occurred within the last twenty-four hours."

The boy looks to be eight or nine. Bruised, bloody face. Not from a beating, though. Most likely from the mistreatment his body got from being jammed into the receptacle.

Clarence doesn't recognize him.

That doesn't mean much; the population of Black Bottom and Paradise Valley is constantly shifting.

"Are those tire tracks I'm seeing?" Clarence points to scuff marks across the boy's jacket and legs.

"I'd say so," the coroner says. "From the looks of him, he was run over, then stuffed into the garbage can. I'll know more when we do the postmortem."

"Thrown away like a piece of trash," Clarence says. He checks the boy's pockets. No ID, but two quarters in one pocket. "When'll you get to him?"

The coroner gives him an unhappy look. "All I can tell you is, he has to wait his turn."

Clarence examines the can. He smells a particularly pungent odor. It's one he hasn't smelled in a while.

The coroner says. "I'll let you know if I find anything useful."

Weiskopf prepares the boy for the ride back to the morgue. Clarence goes over to Henry Yee, standing outside his back door.

Yee says, "Not my can!"

"This isn't your trash can?"

"No! Not my can!"

"Do you know whose it is?"

"Nobody I know. No cans back here. That mine."

He points to a garbage dumpster, a large green rectangle.

Clarence asks, "Was the lid on when you found it?"

"Lid on. Took off to see. Found boy."

"When was the last time you were back here?"

"Last night. When I close."

"And this wasn't here then?"

"No."

"When do they collect your garbage here?"

"Two day ago."

"Who collects your garbage? The city?"

Another nod.

"Did you hear anything unusual back here?"

"Busy, don't hear nothing. Terrible," Henry Yee says. "Terrible."

Clarence can only agree.

He looks around the site where the boy was found. Francis Pitts shows up. "You on this one, too?" Clarence asks.

"Yeah," Francis says. "I hate these."

Clarence fills him in. Asks him to organize a canvas of the area.

"Tell you right now," Francis says, "nobody been gone seen nothing."

"We still have to ask."

At the station, Clarence reviews reports of missing children. He knows Negro families don't usually go to the police to report their children are missing; they know the police won't look for them. Sometimes the police are the ones responsible for sons and daughters going missing.

These are our lives, Clarence thinks; to too many people—all too often, to ourselves—we're expendable. Unnecessary.

He tries to counter such a notion with his baseball league and his recreation room for the neighborhood kids and his general presence on the streets, but it's like bailing out the ocean with a thimble.

He remembers with a pang how behind he is on arranging this year's teams. He has to get busy.

As he suspected, there have been no Negro boys reported missing in the last week. They'll have to spread the word house-to-house in the neighborhoods. Clarence expects it won't take long for the boy's name to surface.

Francis Pitts calls in from his canvas. "Just as I predicted, nobody saw nothing."

"Meet me at the morgue. I want to take another look at the boy."

Francis is there when Clarence arrives. The dead boy still hasn't been logged in ("We're backed-up," Weiskopf apologizes), but Clarence and Francis take another look at him on the gurney in the hallway, lined up with the half-dozen other bodies dropped off that day.

Weiskopf unzips the bag with the boy's body. Clarence leans in.

"What are you thinking?" Francis says.

Clarence leans close. Takes a whiff.

Restricting the body in a bag has concentrated its odor. It's more noticeable now than when it was outside. "What's that smell like to you?" Clarence asks Francis.

Francis leans in for a sniff. Wrinkles his nose. "Smells like shit. The boy defecated when he was run over?"

"He did," Clarence says, "but that's not all."

Francis leans in again and sniffs. Shrugs.

"Cow shit," Clarence says. "Manure smells different from human shit. It's made out of different things."

"Take your word for it," Francis says. "I'm city born and bred. You the country boy."

"Who uses cow manure?"

"Farmers?"

"Farmers," Clarence repeats. "And where you going to find farmers in the city of Detroit?"

"Eastern Market? Neighborhood gardens?"

"Exactly. I'll check out the market in the morning."

"Want me with you?"

"Not necessary. I'll call you if I find out anything. Check out the gardens in the area. Keep canvasing the businesses on the street."

Francis turns to leave.

"Wait," Clarence says. "Got a second?"

He pulls Frances into a storeroom.

Closes the door.

"Do you know a copper named Phil Wheaton?" Clarence asks. "White, works Robbery."

"Heard of him," Francis says. "Don't know him personally."

"Ever heard any rumors about him?"

"What kind?"

"That he's crooked?"

"Man, every cop on this force got rumors he's crooked. Most of them are true."

"Seriously," Clarence says, "you never heard anything about him sounded like it might be true?"

"I can't tell you anything, big man."

"Know anybody who does know him?"

"What do you want to know?"

"I heard things about him. I just want to find out more about it."

"I heard he's tight with Clendening."

"I heard that, too."

But he sure as shit can't ask Clendening what he wants to know.

"You think of anybody might know something, you tell me, right?"

Francis says he will.

48

DENNY RANKIN

[Friday, April 18, 1941]

Easter, the Muellers' white maid, opens the door to their Palmer Woods home. Denny stands on the front porch with a harness bull behind him.

Stone-faced Easter says, "Yah?"

"I'm here for Heinz," Denny says.

Heinz comes around the corner from the dining room. He dabs his mouth with a linen napkin. He is in his fascist uniform. "You're not supposed to be here."

Denny says, "I'm here to put you under arrest."

"For what?"

"Inciting to riot."

"That's ridiculous."

Denny steps aside and motions for the bluesuit he brought with him to place the young man in custody.

"Easter," Heinz says, "call my father. Tell him what's going on." To Denny, Heinz sneers, "I'll be out before lunch."

Denny needs to make this fast. Prentiss Mueller probably has an attorney already on the way.

Heinz slumps in the sweat room. Denny asked Burner Buntzen

to join him to have a witness to the interview.

"This is a bullshit charge," Heinz says.

"Watch your mouth," Burner Buntzen says.

Denny says, "Where were you on Tuesday, April 9th?"

"No clue. Where were *you*?"

Denny says, "I was at the near-riot on the corner of Brush and Gratiot outside Black Bottom. I saw you there."

"Wasn't me."

"You were trying to egg your friends into attacking the Negroes and stores of Black Bottom and Paradise Valley. You ran when you saw me."

"Nope. Must be a case of mistaken identity."

"I'm charging you with Escape, Obstructing Justice, Disorderly Conduct, Disturbing the Public Peace, and Conspiracy. Also obstructing police."

Heinz laughs out loud. "You got no proof I was there. And you can't prove any of those other bullshit charges, either."

Denny changes tack. "Where's Bert Vogelmann?"

The question throws Heinz momentarily.

He recovers quickly.

"Probably in the middle of the Atlantic Ocean. He's a Merchant Marine."

Denny suspects Heinz is lying about where Bert is, just like the lie Charlotte told him about Bert's whereabouts.

"I haven't seen him in a couple weeks," Heinz says. "His parting gift was breaking into my house and stealing my father's money and my mother's jewelry."

"How do you know it was him?"

"He told me."

"He told you he broke into your house?"

"Yeah."

"Why would he confess that to you?"

"You'll have to ask him, won't you?"

"Why didn't you tell the police?"

"He's my brother-in-arms. I wouldn't betray him."

"A brother-in-arms in what? Fascism?"

"You wouldn't understand."

"What's his relationship with your sister?" Denny asks.

"You bastard, leave my sister—"

Burner Buntzen reaches across the table. Gives Heinz a hard cuff across the face. Burner says, "Watch your language, you little punk."

Denny changes up, says, "Are you a member of the National Workers League?"

The new switch-up catches Heinz by surprise again. "Sure."

Like, isn't everybody?

"What about Bert Vogelmann?"

"He is, too."

"What about your father?"

Heinz scoffs. "You kidding? He helps fund it."

"When was the last time you were at the League offices?"

"Last week."

"What did you do there?"

"There's a meeting every other Thursday."

"What do you talk about?"

"Returning this nation to its white Christian roots."

The kid seems emboldened, as if he now has the strength of the group behind him.

A quick knock comes at the door. Captain Dwight Dietrich, with a slick-looking shyster in a shiny suit. Heinz's lawyer, no doubt.

"Interview's over," the shyster says. To Heinz, he says, "Come on. We're done."

"And I'll see you," Dietrich says to Denny, "in my office."

"I told you the Mueller job was urgent," Dietrich says. "Did you hear me tell you?"

"I heard."

"And didn't you tell me you understood?"

"I did."

"Then what are you doing talking to that little shit?"

"He's a friend of the guy who's coming into focus for the break-in. I was hoping the boy could help us find him."

"You finally got your priorities through your thick mick skull?"

"My people are from Edinburgh, sir."

"It's too late. You're off the case."

"Captain—"

Dietrich holds a hand up. "I don't want to hear it."

"You gave me one more day."

"And I'm taking it back. Time's up. Wrap up your file and let me have it. And oh, by the way, I got another complaint about you."

"From who?"

"Homicide. You did the intake on the Ostrowski shooting?"

"I did."

"And then you were supposed to turn it over to Homicide to pursue."

"Yes sir. I did that."

"Why are you now interfering with Detective Jardine's handling of the case?"

"I wasn't interfering, I—"

Dietrich waves his words away. "Shut up. Here's what's going to happen: you're going back on rotation and leaving the homicides to the homicide dicks. It's not your job, do you understand me?"

"Yes sir."

"Now get out of my sight. And kick the Mueller kid loose before you do anything else."

49

ELIZABETH WATERS

[Friday, April 18, 1941]

The Rouge Tavern.

Elizabeth and Gladys Hart find a table in the crowded barroom. Gladys used to live down the hall from Elizabeth at the Trocadero Apartments in Palmer Park. Gladys married one of her many, many beaux and moved out. Elizabeth thought it best not to come to this place alone. Gladys has always been up for a night out, especially when her husband is out of town, as he is now.

Elizabeth tips the barmaid to point out Anton Luedke. The woman nods her head toward a table in the back with three men. "The mouthy one," she says.

"Lizzie, what are you planning to do?" Gladys asks. Her voice is gritty, rougher than ever. She always has a cigarette in hand.

"I'm not sure. Eva mentioned them in her diary. I wanted to take a look at them before I do anything."

If Luedke's doing all the talking, the others must be Kevin McNamara and Eddy Singleton. They look like ordinary working Joes.

"I'll be back," she tells Gladys. She strolls over to the men's table. Luedke stops gabbing and sizes her up. Says, "Well, well, well. What can we do for you, doll?"

"I'm guessing you guys work at Ford's."

"We do indeed, pretty lady," Luedke says.

"I'm supposed to meet a girl here. She works at Ford's. Name's Eva Szabó. I never met her so I don't know what she looks like. You wouldn't happen to know if she's here tonight, would you?"

Luedke makes a show of thinking.

"I know it's a big place," Elizabeth says.

"No," Luedke says finally. "I don't know anyone by that name. Either of you guys?"

The others shake their heads without even making a pretense of considering it.

"No," Luedke says. "We dunno her."

"Pardon my manners. I'm Beatrice Davis."

Her standard *nom de guerre* when she's undercover in the field.

Luedke sticks his hand out. "Pleased to meet you, Beatrice. I'm Anton Luedke. My pals, Kevin and Eddy."

"Very happy to meet you, I'm sure," she says. She shakes Luedke's hand. The other two don't offer to shake. They sit and regard her sullenly.

"Sorry to bother you," she says. "My friends call me Bea."

"No trouble at all, Bea," Luedke says. "Say, why don't you have a seat with us and we can maybe help you find her?"

"I would, except I'm with a friend."

She points to Gladys, who wiggles her fingers at the men.

"She can join us," Luedke says.

Elizabeth says, "Maybe another time."

"Anytime, doll," Luedke says. "Anytime at all."

Elizabeth returns to her table. "Any luck?" Gladys asks.

"They claim not to know her at all. Which is a goddamned lie."

"What are you going to do?"

"Now I know what I'm dealing with, I'm going to finish my beer and call in reinforcements."

Elizabeth drops Gladys back at her home in Dearborn. She makes a call from Gladys's house, then lets Gladys persuade her to have a nightcap.

"In the old days, with hubby gone, I'd be out kicking up my heels all night long," Gladys says. "Now I'm just a boring old lady who turns in early."

"Honey, one thing you will never be is boring."

Elizabeth turns down a second drink. They hug goodnight and Elizabeth heads back down Dix.

She notices a pair of headlights pulling out behind her when she leaves Gladys's driveway. She takes Dix to Schaeffer and the car is still behind her.

She takes Schaefer up to Ford Road and the headlights are still there. She flashes back to her sojourn in Dallas, Texas, where Maurice Sugar sent her to collect evidence in the National Labor Relations Board case against the Dallas Ford Assembly Plant. There Service Department thugs flogged, tarred and feathered, tortured, and beat union members and organizers with blackjacks, whips, brass knuckles, steel rods, and clubs. They tailed Elizabeth, too. They never stopped her; she assumed they were just trying to frighten her.

It didn't work then, and it's not working now. That's when she bought her .22 pistol . . . just to stay safe.

She turns left into a driveway beside a massive castle-like building. Fordson High School, named after Henry Ford and his son Edsel.

A single car is parked in the lot alongside the school. She makes out the turtle-like shape of a Dearborn Police Department unit.

She pulls over beside the cop car and looks back. The headlights belong to a Ford, she sees. It pauses by the side of Ford Road and then roars off.

She hops out of her car and into the cop car.

"Hey," she says.

"Hey."

The uniformed policeman behind the wheel is Eugene Rumson. She's used him as a source of information in the past. She knows he's not connected to any of the Ford goon squads. He's in his early sixties, with a full head of silver hair and a white mustache, and because he's not connected to Harry Bennett he'll never rise higher than a patrol officer. That's okay with him.

"How's tricks?" she asks.

"Same shit, different day. You?"

"Same," she says. "Listen, did you find what I asked you to?"

"I did." He pulls a sheet of paper from his breast pocket. "Pretty unsavory crew you got yourself mixed up with."

"Tell me what you know."

"All three of them guys are plants."

"Meaning?"

"Ever hear of Charles E. Spare?"

"Sure. Runs a detective agency. On the shady side, as I recall."

"He doesn't do much detecting. What he does, he provides labor spies for the Service Department over there." He aims a thumb in the direction of the Ford Rouge plant.

"All three of those jokers are management spies," she says.

"Yup. I talked with a buddy at the Cadillac plant. He knows them. Or at least this Luedke fella. Says he was caught trying to sabotage the line over there, slow down the production. When they found him, they bounced him out."

This is where Eva's inexperience failed her, Elizabeth thinks. She found exactly who she was looking for—anti-union spies—but she didn't know it, or realize the danger she was in from them.

This is where I failed her, too, Elizabeth tells herself. I should have kept closer tabs on her. Eva might not be lying in the hospital.

"Couple other things about this Spare character," Rumson says. "You remember the Black Legion trial in 1936?"

The mention of the Black Legion takes her back even further, and reminds her of Ben Rubin, a man she knew at the time. She and Ben and a Negro detective named Clarence Johnson were involved in trying to stop a plot by the Black Legion to assassinate then-mayor of Detroit Frank Murphy. Elizabeth and Ben were also briefly—very briefly—involved with each other.

"Well, the Wayne County prosecutor who was in charge of investigating Black Legion activities," Rumson says, "was a guy named Duncan McCrea. You might have seen his name in the papers."

"He's on trial in the Wayne County graft corruption scandal."

"That's him. His chief investigator in the Black Legion affair was Charles E. Spare. Who's also the top man in the Michigan KKK. So look what you have."

Eugene counts on his fingers. "Luedke's connected to Spare, the KKK, and Ford."

And also to Eva Szabó.

"All part of the same web," she says.

"You got it."

She sits and looks out into the night.

"Thanks, Eugene. You're a man of many talents."

Rumson gives her a two-finger salute.

50

CLARENCE BROWN

[Saturday, April 19 – Monday, April 21, 1941]

First thing Saturday morning, Clarence parks at Eastern Market between Riopelle and Russell on the near east side of the city. This is the hub for the city's wholesalers and food processors, and for surrounding farmers who bring their wares for sale.

He walks around the area but doesn't find anything helpful. None of the truckers he speaks with say they haul manure in a garbage can.

He calls Francis Pitts on his car radio. Says, "I'm at Eastern Market. Looks like a dead end here. Find anything in the canvas?"

"Maybe," Francis says. "Nobody remembers seeing the boy."

"Naturally."

"But I talked to a guy works in a club a couple blocks down. Said he was outside having a smoke night before yesterday. Said he saw a truck going like hell down the alley Thursday. He can't remember the exact time. Said he noticed the truck because nobody ever comes down this alley except for trash pickup, and this guy was too late for a pickup."

"He say what kind of truck it was?"

"An old dark Ford pickup. Maybe black, maybe dark blue. He didn't get the license plate, but he said he noticed there was a fish on the passenger side door."

"A fish."

"Yeah. Drawing of a fish."

"Any special kind of fish?"

"Like a fish jumping out of the water. Like it was caught on a line. Said he noticed it because he likes to fish."

"Where was this?"

"A few blocks down from where the kid was found. On Hastings."

"You went all the way down there?"

"I did," Francis says. "That was my boy, I'd want somebody do the same for me."

The Tropicana Show Bar.

One of the clubs in the district owned by Robinhood Rowe. The king of the area's policy handbooks as well as owner of a half-dozen entertainment spots. Quincy is his real name, but people call him Robinhood for all his philanthropy in Black Bottom and Paradise Valley—food relief, donations to churches and parks, and so on.

Clarence pulls up in the alley behind the show bar. He scopes out the area: trash bins, dumpsters, crates of rotting vegetables.

The back door to The Tropicana is propped open. The club isn't open for business yet, but there's activity in the kitchen. Clarence smells garlic.

He fills the doorway. A Negro man in a chef's hat stops stirring a pot of garlicky food. "What you doing in my kitchen?"

Clarence flashes his buzzer, says his name. The chef immediately backs down. "Oh Mr. Clarence," he says. "Didn't recognize you in the glare in the doorway. How you doing, sir?"

"Doing alright. Say, I'm looking for Cletus Simpson."

"What that lazy-ass motherfucker done now? He in trouble?"

"Just got to ask him questions."

"About the boy y'all found yesterday?"

Clarence nods.

"Cletus!" the chef shouts. "Where you at?"

"In the basement," another of the cooks says. "Went down for a load of lettuce."

"You got a minute to wait?" the chef asks Clarence. Clarence nods.

Clarence stands back while the food preparation continues:

chopping, dicing, pounding.

In another minute, a door opens and a Negro man carrying a box of lettuce comes into the kitchen.

The chef says, "Cletus. This policeman wants to talk with you. What you done now?"

"I ain't done nothing," Cletus says. He drops his box on a counter.

Clarence badges him, says, "Let's talk outside."

Cletus follows him out to the alley.

"I hear you spoke with another Negro detective, name of Pitts," Clarence says, "about the boy we found in the alley."

"I did."

"Tell me what you told him."

Cletus repeats what Francis told him. Clarence just wants to make sure he got the information right.

"And the fish on the side of the truck?"

"Yeah," Cletus says. "Jumping high out of the water, look like a trout fighting like hell."

"But you can't remember any name?"

"Tell the truth, I can't read too good. I seen a name, wouldn't recognize it anyway."

"Anything else you can remember you might not have told Detective Pitts?"

"I remember the truck was dirty as shit. And oh yeah—there was tools sticking out the back end."

"What kinds of tools?"

"Big long brooms and rakes and shovels and whatnot. And a lawnmower."

Brooms and rakes and shovels and lawnmower.

Who uses those implements? And also has manure in the back, and a garbage can?

He goes into the station. Sits down at his desk with the Michigan Bell Yellow Pages and Polk's Detroit City Directory.

An hour later he finds what he's looking for.

*   *   *

Monday morning. The white woman behind the desk in the tiny

office on Greenfield Road introduces herself as Estelle Fisher, wife of John Fisher, owner of Fisher Landscaping.

There's only one truck, she tells Clarence, and her husband is the only one who drives it. Yes, there's a leaping fish emblem on the doors. Right now he's out on a job in Grosse Pointe. The owner of one of the large estates there is putting in a large garden.

"The homeowner thinks war's coming," she tells Clarence, "and he's making a garden for when there are war-time shortages."

"I bet that includes a ton of manure."

"Oh, you wouldn't believe how much."

Clarence and Francis Pitts drive out to the mansions off Lake Shore Road in Grosse Pointe Farms. A white man in a flat cap holds a shovel while he directs a trio of white laborers. They're working manure into the soil, preparing an acre of land facing Lake Saint Clair for planting.

Clarence pulls up as far as he can in the driveway, behind a dirty Ford pickup truck with a lunging fish on a line over the words "Fisher Landscaping." The pickup bed holds a mound of pungent manure and three empty garbage cans like the one the boy was found in. There's a dent in the right front of the hood.

"John Fisher," Clarence hails him.

Fisher stops what he's doing. Glares at the pair of Negro men who are approaching him. Clarence would bet they are the only colored men within miles, the Grosse Pointes not being known for their racial tolerance.

Clarence badges him, introduces himself and Francis. "Do you know why we're here, Mr. Fisher?"

"No."

"It's about a child we found in a garbage can behind a building in Paradise Valley," Clarence says. "Ring any bells?"

Clarence opens his coat so he can get to his .45s if he needs to. And to show Fisher the shovel he holds will be no match for Clarence's firepower.

Fisher hands the shovel to one of his men. "How is he?" Fisher asks.

Clarence stares at the man in disbelief as Francis goes around behind him and cuffs his hands together.

"It was an accident. A terrible, terrible accident."

Fisher sits at the table in one of the sweat rooms at the Hunt Street Station. Clarence and Francis sit across from him.

Clarence says nothing. In the lengthening silence, Fisher says, "I was coming out of the Calumet Club."

Clarence knows it. A titty bar on Third Avenue.

"Were you drunk?" Clarence asks.

"I'd had a few. I thought I was okay to drive. I got behind the wheel and started out. Next thing I know, I feel this 'thump.' I get out to see what's going on, and there's this little colored kid, lying on the ground. I didn't see him, I swear! He came out of nowhere."

A knock comes at the door. The door opens and one of the uniforms beckons to Clarence. Clarence motions Francis to see what the uniform wants and Francis leaves the room.

Clarence says, "So what did you do?"

"I panicked. I'm not proud of it. I picked him up and put him in the back of the truck in one of the empty cans I was bringing back from the job site. I took off. I wasn't thinking straight, I tell you. I just started to drive and I got as far as Paradise Valley. I realized I couldn't take him home with me. I stopped and left him in the alley behind a restaurant. I figured he'd be found soon enough. I didn't know he was dead, I swear to God."

"He probably wasn't," Clarence says. "If you'd taken him to the hospital, he might still be alive. Thing I don't understand is why you put the lid on the trash can when you left him."

Fisher says nothing.

"Almost seems like you didn't want him to be found," Clarence says.

Fisher buries his head in his dirty hands.

Francis comes back into the room. Hands Clarence a sheet of paper. He leans over and whispers in Clarence's ear. "We picked this up from the canvas of the neighborhood. We know who the boy is."

Clarence skims the paper.

"The boy you ran over?" he tells Fisher. "Melvin Samples. His mama sent him to the store with fifty cents in his pocket to get potatoes for dinner. Thanks to you, he never made it."

Clarence lays the paper on the table. He gazes at Fisher. He's not really even angry anymore, just terribly sad.

Clarence says, "He wasn't but eight years old."

"I like your style," Francis says to Clarence after they book John Fisher.

"Yeah?" Clarence sits at his desk. He feels more discouraged than he has been in a long time. "Why?"

"You solved this in, what, a day?"

"Won't bring Melvin Samples back."

"No, but it'll get justice for him."

"All we can do is get justice after the fact. We don't prevent nothing. We just clean up the mess when it's over. We're nothing but janitors."

Francis says, "I think you're tired, big man. Why don't you go home?"

Clarence nods his agreement.

"Go home, get a good night's sleep, feel better in the morning," Francis says.

Clarence stays where he is. He believes if he gets up right now, at this moment, he will never come back to the police station.

He's not quite ready to do that.

He sits a while longer before he can make himself move. The thought of Bessie in the house waiting for him by herself finally gets him going.

51

DENNY RANKIN

[SUNDAY, APRIL 27, 1941]

A guy roughly the size of an icebox opens the door at the Mueller house in Palmer Woods. Denny badges him. The mug sneers and goes to slam the door in his face.

A voice behind the big guy says, "Wait."

Prentiss Mueller.

He's standing in a doorway off the front hall. "It's alright, Hancock. He can come in."

Reluctantly Hancock steps aside so Denny can enter. The big man has a boxer's lumpy nose and cauliflower ears.

"Come in, Detective Rankin," Mueller says. He waves Denny into his study, all wood and dark red leather. "Have a seat."

"Who's the palooka?"

"Hancock? After everything that's happened, I felt we should have more security around here."

"Looks like a tough customer."

"That's the idea."

"Borrow him from the Service Department?"

"He has the look, doesn't he? But no, I got him from a local detective agency."

Mueller seems calm today. Even cocky. He knows Denny wasn't able to hold his son. Thinks he got one over on the stupid flatfoot.

He doesn't know Denny's been screwed over by better men.

Including his captain.

He did what Dietrich asked and gave the Mueller file to him. Dietrich turned around and handed the case to Phil Wheaton.

No surprise there. That's who was supposed to have it in the first place.

But Denny won't give up on it. Too much isn't making sense.

Mueller says, "What can I do for you?"

Smug. Smarmy.

He must know Wheaton's on the case. Now their original plan—whatever it was—can go off without Denny's interference.

Denny says, "I want to follow up on a conversation I had with your daughter."

"My daughter."

"She told me she gave birth three weeks ago. Fred Thomas delivered the baby."

Mueller sits back. Intertwines his hands over his belly. His vulpine face breaks into a smile. With his long yellow teeth he is not a pleasant sight. The smile doesn't reach his eyes. "She told you this, did she?"

"She did."

"And why are you interested?"

"I believe that infant's body wound up in Black Bottom."

"Detective Rankin," Mueller starts out with a chuckle, "your skills at detecting constantly surprise me. Or should I say your lack of skills? They should call you a defective, not a detective."

Denny has never seen Mueller smile. The effect is ghoulish.

"Let me tell you about my daughter," Mueller says. "The first thing you should know is, she's had long-standing mental problems. She has great difficulty distinguishing her fantasies from real life. Always has.

"The second thing you should know is, my daughter has never had a baby. One of her latest fantasies is that she was pregnant and delivered a baby. The baby didn't live long before someone whisked it away from her. Is that about what she told you?"

"Why would she have that particular fantasy?"

"Who knows why schizophrenics think the way they do? The only true part is, Dr. Thomas is treating her."

"Is he a psychiatrist?"

"No. But he has access to the medications she requires to maintain even a nodding acquaintance with reality. And he's a personal friend. He's treating her very well, in my opinion. He's using the latest discoveries in modern medication for schizophrenia. And she seems to be responding excellently."

"Except for the part about fantasy pregnancies."

Mueller raises a shoulder. "She backslides. Nature of the beast. If that's all you came to ask about, I'd appreciate if you would let me get back to work."

Out of spite, Denny says, "Where is your daughter today, Mr. Mueller?"

Mueller smiles again, but it's a hard smile. A false one. "Upstairs."

Denny knows that's a lie. He saw Charlotte Wheaton driving her away.

Denny says, "I'd like to talk to her. Verify what you're telling me."

"Not possible. Go away."

When Denny doesn't move, Mueller says, "Or should I call Hancock? You're right about him being a rough customer. Would you like to see him prove it?"

As if they had rehearsed it, the security guard sticks his head inside Mueller's study and says, "This guy bothering you, Mr. Mueller?"

"Thanks, Hancock. I believe he's just leaving."

Denny drives to the station house. Outside, a newsie hawks copies of the Sunday *Free Press*. He buys one.

The headline:

GRAFT CASE IS GIVEN TO JURY

He skims the article. The jury got the case at 5:12 p.m. yesterday. They deliberated until midnight, then adjourned until Monday.

This first trial is heading into the endgame.

Denny folds the paper, tucks it under his arm, and goes up to the Robbery Division.

Where more news greets him.

Phil Wheaton closed the Mueller case.

Already.

A trio of detectives sit around Phil's desk. Phil has a Florsheim up on an open drawer. Denny sees a bottle of hooch inside the drawer. Phil is regaling them on how he closed the case.

Phil sees Denny, waves him over. "Heard the news?"

"Just now," Denny says. "Congratulations."

Phil holds his coffee mug up in acknowledgement.

"How'd you do it?"

"Good old-fashioned police work, my son."

"Who was it?"

"You put me on to him. I was just telling the boys here. I went back and checked into B and Es around the neighborhood. There was a break-in a couple weeks before with a similar MO. Wealthy area, high-end shit stolen. I reinterviewed a guy you already talked to. Come to find out he was in jail but a known associate of his was out and around. He gave up his associate in a jiffy—and there's your villain. I got a confession out of him in record time, thanks to ace detective work and my assistant Brassie Mae."

He pulls a set of brass knuckles out of his pants pocket. Caresses them.

Burner Buntzen, says, "Another big win for the Philster."

Laughter all around.

Denny sees a report from forensics on Phil's desk. "That the Mueller forensic report?" Denny asks.

"Yup."

"How'd you get it? I've been asking for it for weeks."

"Must have got routed to me by mistake."

"Bullshit."

Phil shrugs.

Denny chases down Phil's arrest write-up. He's charging Herbert Henry Anderson, white male, DOB 5/10/1889, 5'6", 136 pounds, Cass Avenue address. Held for arraignment in the lockup downstairs.

Denny slips away to the lockup. He doesn't want to talk to Anderson, he just wants to get a look at him.

As soon as Denny eyes him, he knows it's the wrong guy.

Herbert Henry Anderson is feeble. Wild hair. Overgrown salt-and-pepper beard. Emaciated. Arms like twigs trembling in the wind. He's sitting on a cot, staring at Denny through the bars with sad, sad eyes. A rumdum living a hard life. This guy couldn't have pulled off the Mueller heist without taking a long-term rest cure first. He wouldn't have had the strength to cut through the back screen and climb into the house through the kitchen window.

Phil closed the case by finding a fall guy. Framing this poor alkie and calling it a win.

This isn't going to fly. Even if Phil got this sad sack to confess, there can't possibly be enough physical evidence to convince a jury.

Unless Phil plants it.

Denny goes back upstairs to his desk. He finds Captain Dietrich in the squad room, congratulating Phil Wheaton.

Dietrich gives Denny a scowl across the room. Dietrich tips his head toward Wheaton, as if to say, *See what good policework looks like?*

52

ELIZABETH WATERS

[Monday, April 28 – Thursday, May 1, 1941]

My candle burns at both ends;
It will not last the night;
But ah, my foes, and oh, my friends—
It gives a lovely light!

These lines tumble through her mind every morning. She rolls out of bed having slept too little. Stares at her bleary-eyed reflection in the bathroom mirror and can almost measure the bags forming under her eyes. Burning the candle: taking care of her own business during the day, and at night drinking at the Rouge Tavern. At best she gets four hours sleep. It's not enough.

When she wraps up her jobs during her long days, she goes either to the hospital to visit Eva Szabó or to the Rouge Tavern.

Eva's recovery has been slow, but it's happening. The surgeons wrapped her broken leg in a cast and wired her broken jaw. They shaved a section of her head to suture a gash. It's going to be a matter of taking the time to heal. Elizabeth assured the hospital she would take care of the bills for Eva's medical care.

Eva's stepmother and stepbrother haven't visited. Her stepbrother moved back to the family home to take care of Ágnes; her stepmother was the first thing Eva asked about when she regained consciousness.

She's a better stepdaughter than Ágnes deserves, from what Elizabeth can see. Ágnes cares more for the son than the stepdaughter. This doesn't stop Eva from worrying about the old woman.

Eva's a little younger than Elizabeth's child would have been, if Elizabeth had had the baby instead of getting a scrape in California during her stay out there when she was in her twenties. Seeing Eva recover, Elizabeth thinks about what would have happened if she'd had the child all this time.

She tries to explain this not by her maternal instincts sputtering into life at this late date, prompted by the sight of the young woman whose condition Elizabeth feels responsible for. Rather, as she grows older and more solitary, she feels it's part of a general sense of nostalgia for a part of the life she never lived.

She's not unhappy; on the contrary, she feels herself content, well in place.

At least for the time being. Like everyone else, she knows war is coming to America, and she knows it will upend everything. What happens afterwards is anybody's guess.

When she's not visiting Eva, she spends her evenings at the Rouge Tavern, getting to know Anton and Kevin in hopes she'll find a clue to what happened to Eva. (Eddy seems to have disappeared; the others won't tell her what happened.)

Anton fancies himself a lady's man and tried it with her the first few evenings. But she put him straight right away. She's not looking for a man, she doesn't want a man, and so on. She senses he doesn't believe her. She feels like he's biding his time and he'll make another try for her.

Well, that's his problem.

Meantime, she doesn't care. She transforms herself into one of the guys on her nights at the Tavern to ingratiate herself with these men. Her cop friend Rumson told her who these guys really are; her sense is they are—or can be—the key to finding out what happened to Eva.

Soon she is joining in their conversations, badmouthing Jews ("filthy kikes"), Negroes ("goddamn niggers") and Catholics ("Papists and Jews run the whole goddamn world").

She knows she's playing a role. She gives herself another month to see where this all leads.

It doesn't take that long.

*   *   *

One night not long after she starts drinking with them at the Tavern, toward the end of the evening she asks, "Who wants another round? I'm buying."

Luedke polishes off his beer and slams the glass on the table. "We can't. And neither can you."

"Why?"

She thinks Luedke's winding up for another come-on. She prepares herself to deflect it.

But he says, "We got a meeting to get to."

"What kind of meeting, this time of night?"

She hopes she's not coming across as too much of a snoop. That's what called out Eva.

"We belong to this organization," Luedke says. "Me and Kevin, we go to these meetings every other week."

"Is it boys only?"

"Nah, lots of women in it."

"What are we waiting for?"

They pile into Luedke's old Ford. He slides into the driver's seat with Kevin next to him. Elizabeth gets in the back seat.

Anton bombs up Fort Street toward downtown Detroit. The two men are flying—laughing, shouting. She's keeping her reserve up. She doesn't know where they're going and she wants to stay clear-headed.

Besides, she's carrying her .22 in her purse. She's pretty sure she can take these guys if the balloon goes up.

They go north on Woodward Avenue. They pass the big rectangles of Hudson's Department Store. They pass the entertainment district with all the theatres—the Madison on the right, the Adams, the United Artists, the Michigan on the other side of Grand Circus Park, the State, the Fox—and keep traveling north.

They pass the Hotel Detroiter, formerly the LaSalle, where the radio commentator (and her boss at the time) Jerry Buckley was murdered back in 1930. He died scant seconds before she would have blundered into the gunfire that killed him.

Eleven years ago now. Another lifetime.

Several lifetimes, in fact.

They pass the Maccabees Building where she used to work as assistant to the creative staff at WXYZ Radio.

They pass the main library and the Art Institute. They continue north into Highland Park.

They pass Davison Avenue and now Anton circles the block around Grand Street. He parks on the side street and the three of them troop back to number 13535 Woodward. They go up the stairs to the second floor.

She hears a rumble of activity in a large meeting room set up with folding chairs. Elizabeth sees maybe four dozen men seated in front of a dais. A huge red and black Nazi flag hangs from the front wall.

Anton and Kevin find seats. She sits beside Anton. She scans the crowd and notices a young white man sitting with a camera on his lap. He's holding a notebook. A student? A reporter?

He's sitting apart from the others, near the back.

Beside him is a middle-aged white man who has cop written all over him. For the photographer's sake, she hopes he's a cop . . . this looks like the kind of crowd that would turn on a journalist in a minute. The far right agrees with Hitler: journalists are the enemy of the people.

Anton leans closer to her. Whispers, "You're gonna love this."

In a few minutes, a man in a suit comes up to the podium. He waits for the buzz of conversation to abate. He clears his throat and begins.

"Heil Hitler."

The group heils him back.

"Evening everybody," he says. "For those of you who don't know, I'm Garland L. Alderman. I'm national secretary of the National Workers League. Welcome."

The crowd murmurs its greetings back.

Alderman says, "I want to start by reading you a note from George Deatherage, the leader of the American Nationalist Federation—our nation's official fascist party—and national commander of the Knights of the White Camellia. He writes:

"'I say to you all assembled today the 'Jew Deal' being rammed down our throats by President Rosenfeld will come to nothing. And corpses of Jewish scum will litter the roads and fields of our great nation before we will lift a finger against the valiant fight on behalf of our Aryan civilization our German brothers are waging against the forces of Judeo-Bolshevism.'"

The audience meets this with clapping and nods of approval.

Anton looks to Elizabeth. Winks at her. Elizabeth nods back.

Alderman says, "I know we all wish George could join us tonight. Next, I'm happy to introduce somebody from one of our sister groups, the Silver Legion. Here's William Cassidy."

To applause, a man stands beside Alderman. He wears a silver shirt and blue tie with a red L over the heart.

"Good evening," he says. "Silver Legion leader William Dudley Pelley sends his regrets he couldn't be with you tonight. I want to welcome you to the Christian Commonwealth that Leader Pelley will form as we save America from the Jewish Communists, just as Mussolini and his Black Shirts are saving Italy and as Hitler and his Brown Shirts are saving Germany.

"I implore you to join our movement to fight this greatest of all fights against Jew domination of all we hold noble and sacred. We're recruiting volunteers for the swastika nation—see me at the end of the night."

More applause, including from Anton Luedke and Kevin McNamara. Elizabeth glances back at the man with a camera, who is scribbling frantically on a notepad. Beside him, the policeman frowns.

She catches his eye. He is grim. He's not entering into the spirit of this any more than she is.

Alderman gets up again and introduces the next speaker: Parker Sage, treasurer of the National Workers League.

Sage receives the applause of the group humbly. He takes a moment, then begins.

"Britain is almost finished. Churchill is done. In six weeks, the Japs will be in Australia. The English will be broken completely. There won't be a kike left in the American nation a year after that. You won't be bothered by the lousy nigger and Hebe problem we have now, no sir."

The young journalist is still taking notes. The cop sits stone-faced.

The speaker goes on about the Jewish conspiracy to push the country toward war. Only the courage of fellow Christian nationalists keeps America's sons from dying for the international Jew.

She knows she is supposed to be one of them, but she can't abide any more of this.

She slips out of her seat and goes out to the empty corridor. She goes down to a door marked *National Workers League.*

The door is unlocked.

She peeks inside. The office is unoccupied.

She slips in and closes the door. The file cabinet is not locked either. She opens a drawer and flips through the files hanging inside.

In one folder is a stack of little cards. She reads:

Christian American Workers!
Join the National Workers League for the Purpose of Protecting the Jobs, Happiness and Welfare of the American Gentile.

She slips one of the cards into her pocket. Along with her .22, she brought her small Ansco Pioneer camera in her purse. She pulls out a folder labeled "Membership." She spreads it out on a desk and quickly takes a snap of the pages.

The door to the office opens.

She freezes.

It's the guy from the meeting sitting beside the kid with the notebook. The one she pegged as a cop.

He parts his suit coat to show her a gold badge on his belt. Raises a finger to his lips.

She nods. He gives her a thumbs up to reassure her, then spins his finger in the hurry up sign. He closes the door, leaving her alone.

More applause from down the hall, louder this time. The speaker must be finished. She needs to return to the meeting room before Anton and Kevin get suspicious.

Nervous now, she puts the folder back into the file drawer without shooting all the pages.

She slips down the hall and back into her seat. Anton says, "Little girl's room?"

She brings a finger to her lips behind a sly smile. A lady doesn't speak of such things.

Garland Alderman returns to the dais.

The crowd grows quiet.

"Now we get to our special guest of the evening," he says. "Welcome Titus Moran of the Christian Front."

Applause.

A short, apple-cheeked man comes up to the front of the room. He motions for quiet. "Hey, folks," he begins.

"The Detroit branch of the Christian Front formed almost exactly a year ago. We had our first meeting at the Book-Cadillac downtown. Over fifty people attended. I think many of you here tonight were there back then.

"Now, I know you're as disappointed as I am we haven't started our revolution like we planned. On January 27 this year, the coup d'etat was supposed to begin. Our plan was to seize gold from the U.S. Customs House and federal reserve banks, and blow up bridges, utilities, railroad stations, and Jewish-owned newspapers and stores. We were going to assassinate members of Congress, and force the government to send in troops.

"The public would see how much money was being spent to protect the Jew and they'd rise up to overthrow the Jew-led government of Franklin D. Rosenfeld and install a white Christian government with General George Van Horn Moseley in power."

Elizabeth turns to look at the photographer, who still writes furiously. Beside him, the detective has returned to his seat. He's staring at Moran.

"Little did we know an FBI informer was in our midst and our plot was foiled by a government raid. But the good news is, after a sham trial, almost every man arrested was acquitted!"

This brings an appreciative murmur from the crowd.

"You might think it would spell an end to the Christian Front, but you'd be mistaken. We are still in the battle for this nation's eternal soul, under the guidance and approval of our spiritual leader, Father Charles Coughlin.

"We're based in New York City and Boston, but we've spread into Cleveland, Cincinnati, Chicago, and of course Detroit."

More approvals from the audience.

"Now I know you heard my friend Bill Cassidy talk about the Silver Shirts. I'm here to tell you you can be part of both the Silver Shirts and the Christian Front, and it will only make our total movement stronger! So if you're interested in joining our new plans for a Christian coup d'etat, then we'll welcome you with open arms. We can start with smaller revolutionary activity and make sure the government keeps its nose out of our business!"

More applause. Several of the men, including Anton beside her, "heil" Titus Moran with outstretched arms.

"We've been stockpiling weapons," he goes on, "and when the time is right, we're going to take back our country. Come see me if you want to join in!"

In the enthusiastic response Moran gets, the click of a camera comes from the back of the room.

Garland Alderman jumps up. "Hey—no pictures!"

"Get him!" Moran cries. He points to the young man with the camera who has just snapped a photo.

Two men who have been standing at the side of the room leap after him.

One shouts, "Get him! He's a Jew."

The photographer races out the door with half a dozen men in pursuit.

Garland Alderman steps back to the dais. "They'll catch him," he says. "And he'll be one sorry kike. Meanwhile, this is as good a time as any for a break."

Anton and Kevin head toward the coffee urn at the side of the room. They look like they want to talk with the speakers. Elizabeth sidles back to the cop. He pats the seat beside him.

"I can't be seen talking to you," she says. "Tell me who you are and I'll be in touch."

He slips a business card to her. "I want to see the pictures you took."

She glances at the card. Detective Sergeant Dennis Rankin. DPD Robbery Divison.

She retrieves her own card from her purse and shoves it at him. She joins the crowd massed at the front of the room.

The next time she turns around, the cop has disappeared.

"What did you think?" Anton asks her above the din of conversation. Loud male voices, charged up.

"Wonderful," she says. She echoes the words of Detective Pixley from Lincoln Park. "So good to hear the truth about these Hebes."

"Thought you'd like it," Anton says. "And believe me—we're just beginning."

"Let's hope."

You better be careful, she cautions herself.

You're getting too good at this.

53

CLARENCE BROWN

[Tuesday, May 6, 1941]

He picks up a run to a restaurant on Woodward near downtown. The owner, Gus Petrakas, is holding a man who he claims robbed him last month.

Clarence expects to find bedlam when he gets to the diner a few blocks from the Fisher Body plant on Piquette. All is suspiciously quiet. Petrakas is a short white man sitting at his counter, smoking and chatting with one of his waitresses.

Clarence identifies himself, says, "What's the trouble here?"

Without a word, Petrakas gets up and beckons Clarence to follow him into the back of the restaurant, through the food preparation area and into a storeroom.

There he sees a Negro man on a chair in the middle of the room with his hands tied behind him and a gag in his mouth. A young white man in a cook's hat stands beside him holding a carving knife.

"What the hell is going on here?" Clarence demands.

"You see this guy here?" Petrakas says. "You see this guy? This guy robbed me last month and now he comes back and orders food!"

The man who is tied up is shaking his head.

"Jesus Christ," Clarence says. "Untie this man. Right now."

"Not until you arrest him," Petrakas says.

Clarence gives him his full 6'3" cop glare. "Untie him."

Grudgingly Petrakas nods to the guy in the chef's hat, who cuts the man's bonds and undoes the gag.

Clarence expects an explosion but the guy just says, "Thank you."

"What's your name?" Clarence asks.

"James Carter."

"Did you rob this man's restaurant?"

"I most certainly did not."

"I identify him," the Greek says. "He hold me up!"

"Did you make a police report?"

"Yes."

"What was the date?"

"Wednesday, March 12th. The policeman who took the report was a colored cop. I don't remember his name."

"What do you have to say for yourself, Mr. Carter?"

"I've never seen this man before," Carter says, "and I've never been anywhere near this restaurant."

"Liar," Petrakas says. "I saw him do it. I'd swear on my life this is the guy."

Clarence tells Carter, "I'm going to have to take you in until we settle this. And you," he says to Petrakas, "don't let me catch you tying anybody up again. Understand?"

Petrakas holds up both hands. The picture of innocence.

Clarence puts James Carter in the back of his police car and takes him to the station.

Clarence puts him in a holding cell and finds the incident report. Sure enough, Detective Francis Pitts took the report—the "colored policeman." A man entered the restaurant and held up the cashier with a gun. Carter matches the description in the report, though it could be a thousand other Negro men.

Clarence brings Carter up from the cell to sit at his desk. "James," Clarence says, "can you account for your whereabouts last March 12th between one and one-thirty in the afternoon?"

"At work. I own a confectionary store on St. Antoine."

"Can anyone vouch for you?"

"My wife. I'm usually there all day. I'm out today because I was looking for something new to sell at my store."

"Okay, James," Clarence says. "Ordinarily I'd hold you while I checked your story. But you've had enough humiliation for one day.

You're free to go. I'll take you back to your store."

"That fucking Greek hasn't heard the end of this," Carter says. "I'm going to sue him for false imprisonment."

After driving Carter to his store, Clarence stops home to see Bessie.

Malone Coleman is there.

He and Bessie are laughing together in the living room, where Bessie reclines on the sofa. Malone sits in the chair where Clarence usually sits.

When Malone sees Clarence, he stands. Tries to keep a straight face but whatever he and Bessie were laughing about makes it impossible.

"Hi, baby," Bessie says.

"Hey," Clarence says. "Malone. Good to see you. How you doing?"

"Alright," Malone says. "Just came by to say hello to Miss Brown."

"You don't have to explain. I told you, you're always welcome here. What are you doing with yourself these days?"

"Getting by. Got my boys I hang with."

"Anybody I might know?"

Malone gives him a tight little laugh. "No doubt."

"Where do you stay?"

"Here and there."

"Still got a bed for you here, you want it," Clarence offers.

"Nah, I'm good. Well," he says to Bessie, "gotta get going."

"Don't go on my account," Clarence says. "Stay a while longer. I just stopped in to see how my wife was doing."

"Nah," Malone says. "Got places to be. See you later," he tells Bessie.

She holds her arms out for a hug. Malone bends over to wrap her in his arms. He gives a grudging nod to Clarence, and goes out the door.

"The boy seems to have a problem with you," Bessie says.

"Guess so. How long's he been here?"

"Couple hours."

"What were you talking about?"

"Just chatting about my ankle and everything."

"You were in a pretty good mood when I came in."

Which I crapped on immediately, Clarence thinks.

"He's a stitch, Clarence."

"Couldn't prove it by me. Boy didn't have a word to say to me. You doing okay?"

"I'm fine. Malone made us a sandwich for lunch. You hungry?"

"No. Nothing I can do for you?"

"You might could come over here and give me some sugar," Bessie says with a grin.

Clarence drives back to St. Antoine. He parks and walks the streets. His streets. And the people he has given his life to.

He walks up Hastings, crosses Clinton to Beaubien, then up Brush across Gratiot into Paradise Valley. Shopkeepers wave to him through their plate glass windows. Men and women on the sidewalks nod and step aside for big Mr. Clarence to pass.

He can't get the sight of Malone laughing with Bessie out of his mind.

He doesn't begrudge Bessie her friendship with Malone, but damn . . . what's Clarence done to make the boy so cold to him? He thinks back over all his talks with Malone. Clarence just wanted to let him know he'd always be there for him if Malone needed him.

It must have been connected with the attack on Black Bottom when the story about the dead baby came out. All Clarence wanted to do was make sure Malone was safe. Malone took it the wrong way . . . he must think Clarence didn't trust him to make a good decision.

And okay, maybe it's how Clarence came off. He's so used to dealing with knuckleheads, he treated Malone the same way without even thinking.

He decides to be on the lookout for ways to make it up to Malone.

Back at his car, he gets a radio call: the dispatcher gives an address in Black Bottom, says, "Shots fired."

Clarence takes off at once.

Usually "shots fired" brings the cavalry. Clarence rolls up at the address and finds no cars.

Well, they probably figured shots fired in Black Bottom, ho-hum. Wake me when it's over.

The address is a one-story shack off St. Aubin. Clarence pulls one of his .45s. Advances toward the house.

The front steps and porch have fallen through. He goes around the back. An open door leads into the kitchen at the rear of the house.

Inside, the basement door to the cellar hangs off its hinges. He walks over, peers into the cellar darkness. Tries to hear if anyone's down there.

He hears nothing down there, but with a sudden rush of feet on the floor someone comes up behind him and gives him a shove down the steps.

He slides down. His home-made armor takes the brunt of the tumble, but his gun skitters away and he hits his head on the dirt floor at the bottom of the staircase.

He's dazed. The breath's knocked out of him.

One revolver is still in his holster but it's pinned under him.

Footsteps follow him down the stairs.

Roger Clendening stands above him. He holds a sheet of paper. Says, "Recognize this?"

Without waiting for an answer, Clendening says, "Found this in your desk drawer. Looks like notes about a little body you found in one of the dumps around here? What do you say? Sound familiar?"

The notes Clarence typed up the day he found the dead baby. And then hid at the back of his bottom drawer.

Clendening looked through his desk.

Clendening holds up the papers and flicks a Zippo. Sets the page on fire. He lets the burning paper drop to the stair, where he crushes the ashes under his heel.

He steps over Clarence to the basement floor. Kneels beside him. Says, "Nasty knock on the head you got there, big fella."

He pats Clarence's face with the gun.

Clarence says nothing.

Clendening says, "Be glad it's just a bump and not a bullet rattling around inside your skull."

He puts the barrel of his gun against Clarence's forehead.

"See how easy it was to lure you here? Throw your nigger ass down the stairs? I could put a bullet in your head and leave you for the rats and you wouldn't know what hit you. Boom. Light's out."

Clarence glares at him. He says nothing.

He's helpless in this situation but he's not going to give this ofay the satisfaction of showing it.

Clendening says, "Here's what I have to say. This crusade you're on about the dead kid? It stops now. Get me?"

"Fuck you."

Clendening cocks his revolver. Presses the barrel hard into the center of Clarence's forehead. Clarence refuses to give Clendening the satisfaction of closing his eyes; he stares at Clendening with eyes burning with hatred.

"I should shoot you right in the fucking head right here and now," Clendening says.

"Why don't you?" Angry. Defiant.

"You keep up with this, I will," Clendening says. "And after I kill you, I'll kill your wife. And I'll sleep like a baby with two less coons in the world. Get me?"

Clarence blinks. Swallows.

Bessie . . .

"Get me?" Clendening snarls.

Clarence nods.

"I'd kill you in a minute, you black bastard," Clendening says. "I mean it."

He stands. Says, "I'm glad we had this little talk."

Clendening steps over Clarence on the damp dirt of the cellar. Deliberately lets his foot catch Clarence's arm.

Clendening pauses on the first step. "By the way, I hear you talk to anybody about this—Hays or Wilson or *anybody*—you just signed your death warrants. Get me? This is over."

He continues up the stairs.

Clarence hears him walk across the floor above him.

Hears him leave the house.

He slowly gathers himself. Brushes the dirt off his clothes. Adjusts his armor. Finds his .45 in a damp corner of the cellar. Picks up his hat.

Sits on one of the steps until his heartbeat returns to normal and his eyes no longer see the world through a red haze of fury.

Thinks to himself: Over?

Oh, no. This is not over.

This has just begun.

54

DENNY RANKIN

[Thursday, May 8 - Thursday, May 22, 1941]

Once Dietrich takes him off the Mueller case, Denny goes back on the robbery rotation.

He finds no shortage of cases to occupy his time.

Four men hit a numbers clearing house and make off with $4,000, half of it in dollar bills. They're still at large.

Two men walk into a corner store on Leland and Rivard Streets, order a Pfeiffer Jumbo beer, and pull a gun on the proprietor; their take from the register is only $4.00. They shoot the proprietor but he lives and identifies them from mug shots.

A policeman is shot during an attempted robbery of Naftalin's Restaurant on West Bancroft Street; the assailant is still at large.

An unknown man enters a home in the Boston-Edison district, threatens to kill the homeowners, and steals the homeowner's pants containing his wallet with $11 and jewelry—watches, rings, and pendant drop necklaces. When Denny catches him, he grills him about the Mueller break-in but the guy wasn't part of it at all; he was in jail when it happened.

Two young men rob the Duco Coal Company on St. Aubin Street of almost $300. They brag about the operation. Denny catches them with information from his snitch Aram Sarkisian, head usher at the United Artists Theatre.

Denny arrests four boys who are acting suspiciously outside

Pocock's Drug Store on Cameron Avenue; upon investigation, Denny learns the quartet is responsible for a crime wave of more than thirteen store robberies.

The thing is, he can't let go of the Mueller job.

He has a policeman's instinct that it involves the National Workers League. The night he went to the League meeting he got an eye-opening—and chilling—introduction to them.

Denny said he would get in touch with the woman he met, Elizabeth Waters. He does some checking and discovers she is a private eye with radical leanings. She was connected to the Ray Lindenauer situation ten or so years earlier. Lindenauer was the chief of detectives in the '30s who was involved in an assassination attempt on then-Mayor Frank Murphy. Clarence Brown thwarted the attempt, shooting and killing Lindenauer in the process. The shooting was investigated and ruled an act of self-defense by Clarence—in large part because Elizabeth Waters testified as a witness.

But that made Clarence even more of a persona non grata than he ever was.

Now Elizabeth Waters works as a private investigator. Her clients include the UAW. She was a known Red but in the last few years the Special Investigations Bureau lost interest in her. They were still the Detroit Police Department's Red Squad, but they had their eyes on others—now mostly in the union movement.

He told her he would get in touch with her, but he has yet to do it. For now, he's concentrating on his secret surveillance of the Mueller house.

He is careful not to be seen around there; he only goes late at night when he can't sleep. He watches the house from down the street. When Heinz leaves, Denny follows him to the National Workers League or out to debauches with his friends.

He never sees the daughter, Wanda. Presumably she's still hiding wherever Charlotte Wheaton took her outside the house.

He also surveils Bert Vogelmann's home, but never sees any activity there.

When he's not pursuing robbers or tracking down members of the National Workers League, Denny Rankin spends his off-time in The Tropics, the ridiculous South-Pacific-themed bar next to the Wolverine Hotel where he stays.

His wife still refuses to let her girls see him. Occasionally his late-night surveillance includes their house on Roselawn. Barnett Hoosier seems to spend most of his nights there.

Ultimately it's too painful for Denny to watch; he stops going. He stops peeping-tom on his son Larry, too; it hurts too much to know his son will need so much help as he gets older, but Denny will never be there for him. Larry will never even know Denny is his father.

The first graft trial concludes. The jury delivers guilty verdicts on twenty-four of the remaining defendants, including former prosecutor Duncan McCrea and former Wayne County sheriff Thomas C. Wilcox. Now the appeals begin.

The prosecutor, Chester O'Hara, says he's already prepping for the next trial.

That one starts on May 15th. It seems like the rest of the cases will move away from the gambling and vice conspiracy. But Circuit Judge Homer Ferguson's one-man grand jury is still moving forward, handing down indictments. Denny isn't in the clear yet.

The longer the graft trial drags out, the closer the country edges toward war, the more Denny drinks.

The more he drinks, the deeper he sinks into his loneliness and despair.

Denny stops turning down the working girls when they sidle up next to him, sitting alone at the bar with drinks capped with silly little umbrellas.

Going with them isn't satisfying, and is all too temporary. But it helps to relieve the long hours of his nights and the void growing in the pit of his empty heart.

55

ELIZABETH WATERS

[Friday, May 23 – Friday, June 23, 1941]

After the National Workers League meeting, Elizabeth makes her way deeper into the pro-Nazi underbelly of the city. Anton Luedke acts as her guide. After fending off his awkward passes, she settles into the easy connection of acquaintances who drink together and hate the same people.

Keeping up with Luedke's drinking is no problem for Elizabeth. Once a morphine addict following an automobile accident in her youth, she quit drugs in favor of alcohol once Prohibition ended. More readily available than morphine, in sufficient quantities alcohol led her to the same destination as morphine: oblivion.

Luedke prides himself as a drinker. He's no match for Elizabeth. And she knows a tidbit about Luedke.

He and his cronies weren't any more Ford employees than Eva Szabó was. Like her, they were playing a part. Their job was to disrupt the movement to unionize Ford. They failed, and they're back working for Charles Spare. They tell her they do security work for Spare's detective agency, but she knows what they're really up to:

Provoking disputes and discontent to sabotage the industries where they are now planted, like Detroit Edison, Chrysler, Cadillac, and the Michigan Central Railroad yards. She's biding her time as she figures out what to do with this information.

One evening, Luedke tells Elizabeth to meet him at the German Restaurant at East Jefferson at the foot of the bridge to Belle Isle. There he introduces her to the owner, Max Stephan. A short, balding, oval-faced man with wide-set blue eyes, Stephan and his wife Agnes take to Elizabeth immediately. They welcome her not only to the restaurant, but to the secret rifle range at the back of the building.

Stephan tells her he's from Germany. He had been a sergeant in the Great War, then a guard at a military prison, and, after the war ended, a member of the German National Police. He owned a pub in Germany and emigrated to Canada to take advantage of alcohol smuggling from Windsor during Prohibition. Once Prohibition ended in 1933, Stephan and his wife used falsified papers to obtain naturalized American citizenship and opened his restaurant.

He's well-known in German circles in Detroit. Because his restaurant is a meeting spot for German emigres and organizations—the Schwaben Society, a German-American social group; the German-American Societies in Michigan; the German-American Bund—Elizabeth meets the city's leading Nazi sympathizers. Stephan introduces her to John Schreiber, the German-American Bund leader in Detroit. She meets Charles W. Chill, secretary of the central committee of the German-American Societies in Michigan.

And she meets Theodore Donay, owner of the German-American Europe Import Company on Gratiot near Mack. Of all the people she meets at Stephan's restaurant, Donay seems to be the most outspoken and vicious pro-Nazi anti-Semite of them all.

At Stephan's restaurant, she also meets Theresa Behrens, secretary of the International Center of the YMCA. The job brings her into contact with recent immigrants, whom she eagerly recruits into Hitler's activities in America.

She doesn't meet only German pro-Nazis. She finally meets Parker Sage, who in addition to being treasurer of the National Workers League, also leads the Pontiac America First Committee chapter. She meets Charles Spare, who runs the detective agency employing Luedke and McNamara and who also heads the Michigan klavern of the Ku Klux Klan.

Luedke introduces her to Fritz Heiler, the German Consul.

She begins frequenting the German Restaurant without Luedke.

She spends evenings singing German songs, drinking German beer, and listening to rabid anti-Semites talk about increasingly violent means of overthrowing the government of the United States and ridding the country of its Jews.

Many of the people she meets have German roots. During the evenings when she is there, she tries to talk seriously with them about why they are such strong supporters of Hitler—not to challenge them but as a way of pretending to gather more arguments against democracy and the Jews.

Mostly it comes down to hatred for FDR (whom they all refer to as President Rosenfeld, swearing they know for certain he has Jewish ancestry through the Delanos); fierce anti-communism, for which they see Nazism as the only reasonable alternative; and an even fiercer hatred of Jews.

Everyone mentions Henry Ford's series "The International Jew" in his *Dearborn Independent* as a source of their beliefs; none of them admits to knowing an actual Jew.

Elizabeth travels to Pontiac to meetings of Parker Sage's America First Committee. She visits Theodore Donay's store. She meets members of the German-American Bund. She attends a KKK meeting with Charles Spare. She visits the rooming house owned by Emma Elise Leonhardt and Carl John Heinz Leonhardt, which Luedke said is the headquarters of a Nazi spy ring; she has tea with the residents.

She goes with Luedke to the National Shrine of the Little Flower Catholic church in Royal Oak to meet Father Charles Coughlin; afterwards, in an empty ballfield in Livingston County northwest of Detroit, she watches a training session of an armed detachment of the Christian Front, the pro-Nazi militant group inspired by the hatred Coughlin broadcasts on his radio shows. Coughlin denies a connection with the group, but everyone knows he's its spearhead.

She doesn't know if she's closing in on the people who hurt Eva. In all the Nazi sympathizers, she keeps watch for Mutt and Jeff—a tall guy partnered with a short guy with a lisp. She hasn't seen them yet.

But all these pro-Axis sympathizers and their vicious hatred begin to repulse her, both with the danger they pose and with their own lunacy.

Even so, she stays with them, convinced they will lead her to the men who beat Eva and left her for dead.

56

EVA SZABÓ

[Monday, June 16, 1941]

She has been in the hospital for over two months. The doctor told her the first month she was in and out of consciousness; they didn't know if she would have lasting brain damage.

Now she has begun to heal. The sutures are gone from the wound to her head. The cast is gone from her leg. Her bruises are fading away. Her ribs are still sore but no longer wrapped.

She sustained a fractured jaw. The doctors wired it but the wires are off now. Still, she has to be careful when she eats and speaks.

She had a few teeth knocked out, several others loosened. She will need dental work. But first things first.

"Headaches any better?" the doctor now asks.

"No."

She suffered a concussion when her attacker cracked open the gouge on her forehead.

She doesn't remember anything about the attack. The last thing she clearly recalls is being at the Ford walk-out. She has a vague memory of a chaos of sounds and laughter from men, and loud-speakers and car horns. Nothing is remotely clear. But now she thinks she might be regaining a glimmer of a memory.

She has been having physical therapy to keep her leg and arm muscles moving. She is weak from lack of eating and inactivity.

Elizabeth Waters has come to see her every day. At first, Eva was terribly upset when Elizabeth saw her; Eva blamed herself for the shape she was in. She still does, despite all Elizabeth's efforts to assure her she isn't responsible for what happened to her.

Ágnes and Josef do not visit. Josef stays with his mother.

On one of her trips, Elizabeth told Eva not to worry about the hospital bill, which by this time probably totals in the hundreds of dollars. Elizabeth promised to take care of it.

Eva said, "I don't know how I can ever thank you."

"No need," Elizabeth said. "Don't worry about it. Just get better."

Now the cheery physical therapist appears at Eva's bedside. "Guess what time it is?"

When Elizabeth gets to Wyandotte General on Monday, Eva is still in the therapy room. It's a small gymnasium with parallel bars, medicine balls, wheelchairs, and mats. Eva stands with her elbows on the parallel bars, propping herself up.

She sees Elizabeth and flashes a smile. Eva has to learn to walk again like an infant. She places one foot in front of another and slowly makes her way down the track.

"How's she doing?" Elizabeth asks the therapist standing by, ready to catch Eva if she falls. He is a cheerful man in a white collarless shirt and white pants.

"Wonderfully well," he says. "She's got a lot of guts."

He says this loud enough for Eva to hear. It brings another smile, even though Eva sweats from the effort.

She gets to the end of the bars and collapses into a wheelchair.

"Nice going!" Elizabeth says.

Eva is huffing and puffing. "Thanks."

"I think you deserve a break," the therapist says. "Take a few minutes and visit. Then we'll get back to it."

Elizabeth pushes Eva to a corner of the room. Elizabeth sits beside her on a pile of mats.

"He's right, you know," Elizabeth says while Eva catches her breath. "You do have a lot of guts. I don't know if I could go through what you're doing."

"You do what you have to," Eva says. "I'm glad you came. I was hoping you would."

"Here I am."

"I think I'm remembering more."

"About that night?"

Eva nods.

Elizabeth leans in. "Tell me."

"It's not much."

"Anything could be helpful."

"The police told me they found me in a vacant lot in Lincoln Park."

"Right. Are you remembering how you got there?"

"I remember riding in a car."

"What kind of car?"

"I don't know."

"Who was with you?"

"I'm not sure. I have a vague memory there were two men. I remember being in a sort of cold room, too. I remember the smell of meat."

"Meat."

"Raw meat. And blood. And it was cold. Freezing cold. And I was in a chair. Tied to a chair."

"Sounds like you were in a meat locker."

"That's all I remember."

"That's great, really. Great start."

They're both quiet for a few moments. Then Eva says, "So am I done?"

"At the plant? Yes. You're done. But right now you're not ready to do anything else."

"No, I know. But what about when I'm back on my feet again? Will you still need me?"

"Absolutely. I'll have a lot more work for you. No more grocery stores or candy counters for you."

"I'm glad to hear it."

"Now rest. I'll see you tomorrow." She bends down and gives Eva a gentle hug.

Eva watches her go. The physical therapist comes back over. "Ready for more torture?" he says with a grin.

His joke is not as funny as he thinks it is.

57

CLARENCE BROWN

[Monday, June 16, 1941]

He keeps his encounter with Clendening to himself.

He doesn't mention it to Bessie, or Denny Rankin, or either of his superiors in the department. Or to any of his colleagues in the segregated unit.

Not out of fear of Clendening.

No, he keeps it to himself until the white-hot rage he feels abates enough for him to make a cold, hard plan on how to respond.

Because he knows he's not going to let what Clendening did go unanswered.

In the meantime, he stays mum and lets Clendening think he's cowed. For the time being he works his cases. He says no more about the dead child he found in the tenement, and pauses his investigation into Phil Wheaton.

One evening after dinner, Bessie says she'd like to go for a walk.

"A walk?" he says.

"At least a ride in my wheelchair. It's such a beautiful evening."

He's happy to do it. She spends too much time in the house, even with her visitors from the church Sisterhood and other friends from the neighborhood.

She agrees to wear the shawl Clarence insists on. He helps her into her wheelchair with a sliding board he made for her when he built the ramp from the porch to the sidewalk.

People are out on their porches up and down the block. Clarence and Bessie stop to talk; everyone asks after her.

Lilacs have begun blooming. She holds her hand up to indicate she wants to stop and pick a sprig.

"Won't last," Clarence says.

"I'll enjoy it while I can."

They turn the corner and continue walking down Beaubien. Further down the block, Clarence sees Sonny McGhee on the steps of the building where he found the dead infant, bundled up and thrown away like a piece of trash.

Sonny is fingerpicking a battered guitar. He sings an old blues tune in a sweet baritone.

Clarence knows the song well.

Poor boy, long way from home.
Poor old boy, I'm a long way from home.
Poor boy, I'm a long long way from home.
Please don't mistreat me, please don't do me wrong.

Broke and hungry, ragged and dirty too
Broke and hungry, ragged and dirty too
Broke and hungry, ragged and dirty too
Just want to know, can I go home with you?

Big bell ringin', little bells fairly tone
Well, big bell ringin', little bells fairly tone
Big bell ringin', little bells fairly tone
I'm a lonely, lonely, long long ways from home.

What makes you baby hold your head so high?
Tell me baby, what make you hold your head so high?
Tell me baby, why do you hold your head so high?
Well, the way you hold it, that's the way you die.

Sonny finishes with an impressive blues guitar riff.

Clarence and Bessie clap along with the other neighbors on their porches.

"You got you some chops, Mr. McGhee," Clarence says. "Ever been on stage?"

"In my misspent youth," Sonny says with a smile. "I worked with a guy who played the mouth-harp. We traveled around the south until we got tired of getting thrown out of juke joints. Say, who's this beautiful young lady?"

"You never met my wife?"

"Never had the pleasure."

Clarence introduces them. Sonny tips his flat cap. "My pleasure."

"Likewise," Bessie says. "I could sit here and listen to you all night."

"I thank you kindly."

Clarence peers at Sonny's face. It's bruised. One eye is almost closed.

"What happened there?" Clarence asks.

"Guess you didn't hear."

"Tell me."

"Last night my wife and me were going to visit her sister. She lives in Hamtramck. Before we got there, this group of white punks attacked us."

"Oh no."

"They beat me down to the ground and then started on Pearl. Would have beat her too, except a couple of colored men saw what was going on and chased them away."

"Did you make a police report?"

Sonny snorts in derision. "Police was standing right there. You think they did shit?"

"Jesus, man, That's terrible."

"Bad shit brewing over there. Reason we went, Pearl's brother-in-law Marvin was getting cigs at the Okey Dokey Smoke Shoppe and the owner pulled a gun on him and threw his ass out the store. White punks chased him away with stones and bricks. He had to leave his car, it was so bad. He came back later with a friend to pick up his car and the police arrested them. His friend took his gun with him for protection. The cops arrested them when they both said they owned the gun. Pearl's sister called us to come over and that's when they got us."

"How's she doing? Pearl's sister."

"Battered and bruised, like me. But nobody gonna run us out of

Detroit."

"Pearl's brother-in-law and his friend, they still in custody?"

"No, they got released on bail."

"What's going on over there?"

"I'll tell you what's going on. A few colored families moved onto Newton Street. That's where Pearl's sister lives. And them Polacks, they don't like it one bit. This their way of showing us we not welcome. None of us."

"Sorry, my friend," Clarence says.

"It's this city, man. Hell, it's the whole damn country. I said it before, I'll say it again. When is the colored man gonna find peace?"

58

ELIZABETH WATERS

[Tuesday, June 17, 1941]

Her last job of the day: interviewing a bicycle rider who was knocked off his bicycle by a car running a stop sign. One of the teachers at Burton School on Cass and Peterboro in Detroit, he was heading home to his apartment on Peterboro and a car ran the stop sign and t-boned him. Knocked him into the street and drove over his bike, bending it in half.

The teacher called Max Rubenstein, who was just starting out in private practice. Max had talked to Elizabeth a few months earlier because he was looking for an investigator and she agreed to work this case as a try-out.

The teacher, Richard Mockton, is a man in his fifties, slight and bearded. His face is abraded where his head hit the concrete when he flew off his bike. His arm is in a sling, and he says a couple of ribs are broken. He wants to sue the man who was driving the car.

Elizabeth's job is to see if there's enough for a case. She interviews Mockton and takes photographs of his damaged face and arm. She walks out to the site of the accident, not three buildings away from where Mockton lives. The intersection is clear; no tree branches obscure the stop sign or the streets. Mockton says the man who hit him was driving in a car with a woman by his side. He was probably paying more attention to her than to the road.

Elizabeth thanks him and tells him she will report back to the attorney, who will then be in touch about the next steps.

At her office in the Barlum Tower, Elizabeth finishes up her report and drops off the roll of film of Mockton's injuries at an all-night developer. In the morning she'll pick up the film and deliver it to Rubenstein, whose office is three floors above hers. From what she can see, the bicycle rider has a good case.

She turns out the light on her desk lamp and sits in the dark. Her office faces south. Off to the right she can see the lights of the Penobscot Building on Griswold, and below that the Guardian Building, its nest of searchlights on the roof probing the night sky.

Should she go to see Eva Szabó, go to the Rouge Tavern, or go home to her apartment?

She is too tired to decide.

She leans toward going home.

She stands to work out the stiffness in her hip. When she was young, during her single year at Oberlin College, still grieving over the suicide of her best friend Sarah Kirschner, Elizabeth began spending less time in class and more time with the wastrels who used their allowances for bootleg booze in Cleveland. One night she went out riding with a stockbroker's son from Cincinnati who, pie-eyed drunk, rolled his car off the road. He walked away unharmed, but Elizabeth came out of the accident with a severely broken leg that was never fixed properly and caused constant pain in her hip.

She walks around her office until the pain subsides. Back at her desk, she shovels her pen and notepad into her purse when a business card falls out of the notebook. It's from the cop she saw at the meeting of the National Workers League.

Dennis Rankin. Detective Sergeant. His phone number is there, too.

She was going to let him see the snaps she took at the National Workers League meeting.

On a whim, she dials him.

He answers on the second ring.

They meet at Cliff Bell's, a music bar on Park Avenue near Grand Circus Park in downtown Detroit. Dimly lit, plush red upholstery. A pianist plays quiet jazz on the bandstand.

Elizabeth sips a daiquiri. Denny Rankin works on a gin and tonic.

"I haven't been here in ages," she says.

"Likewise. I don't get out much."

"Tied to your job?"

"Always."

"Which explains why you were at your desk so late today."

"Is it stranger that you thought I'd be at the station this late, or that I actually *was* at the station this late?"

"I was on the job, too."

"You're a peeper," he says.

"I prefer private investigator. But yeah, that's me. Speaking of which, these are for you." She hands him the photos she took in the National Workers League meeting. "You said you wanted to see them."

"Thanks. Can I hang onto them for a while?"

"Sure. I don't have copies, though. And I didn't have time to get all the way through the alphabet, so it's not the whole list."

"No problem. I'll keep them close."

He places the envelope inside his suitcoat pocket. Says, "What brought you to that meeting?"

"I was on a case. How about you?"

"I was working a home break-in in Palmer Woods. The home-owner's part of the National Workers League and I was trying to find out what else they're involved in. One of the family members told me about the meeting. I wanted to see what was what."

"'Was working.' Past tense. Did you solve it?"

"No. I got pulled off it."

"What happened?"

He takes a sip of his drink.

"I wasn't solving it fast enough for the bosses. They wanted it closed pronto. The boss gave the case to somebody else."

"Was it frustrating?"

"The worst."

"If you don't mind my asking, if you're off the case, why do you want the photos?"

"Officially I'm off the case. Unofficially . . . I'm convinced there's more going on here. They pinned it on a rumdum who no more pulled the job than I did. I hate to see the wrong guy go down for it. Plus, there's a connection with all the Nazi anti-Semitic flyers and pamphlets I've been seeing around town."

"Are you Jewish?"

"No. But I feel for what they're going through in Europe and over here. What did you think of that Workers League meeting?"

"Chilling. I met a lot of the people there over the past month. I agree with you . . . it seems like there's a Nazi fifth column hiding under every rock in this city."

"That's why I can't let it go. Everybody connected with the house that got broken into seems like a Nazi collaborator. Detroit's an ideal spot for saboteurs. All the heavy industry around here. When the war starts, espionage will be even more intense."

"*When* the war starts?"

"Inevitable. My opinion."

"I tend to agree. I meant to ask," she says, "who was the kid you sat next to at the meeting?"

"The photographer? Name's Hal Perlman. I asked him why he was there—he seemed way out of place."

"Why was he there?"

"Said he feels compelled to document what's happening with the local Nazis."

"He took his life in his hands, taking that picture."

"Yeah. Gutsy kid."

"They didn't catch him, did they?"

"He outran them," Denny says. "He's a free-lancer. Sells his pics to *Life*, *Look*, anyplace he can. He was telling me he's been going around documenting the Ford strike and the labor fights."

Their conversation decides her. Tonight she should go to the Rouge Tavern. She hasn't been there in a few nights. It might be time to check in with Anton Luedke to see what's going on with him and his cronies. She has not had any success in finding out who beat up and almost killed Eva.

She can take Fort Street and be there in twenty minutes.

Out front on Park, an awkward moment.

"Well," he says. She senses he wants to ask to see her again.

This was fun, she has to admit . . . but she's not interested. She short-circuits his question by holding out her hand. She says, "Thanks for meeting me."

He shakes. Snaps back to being Detective Sergeant Rankin. "I'll be in touch once I've looked over the photos."

"Fine. Good night."

She doesn't look back, but she knows he's watching her go.

The Rouge Tavern is livelier than she's seen in a while. Anton and Kevin are at their usual table at the back of the barroom. Another man sits with them. Elizabeth hasn't seen him before.

"Bea," Anton says, using the fake name she gave him. "We were waiting for you."

"What's up?"

"We gotta get going." Anton stands along with his friends. "C'mon," he says.

They head out the door. Elizabeth follows. "Where are we going?"

"There's another get-together tonight," Anton says. "You'll want to be in on it."

Outside the three men pile into Anton's Ford.

She takes a look at them waiting for her.

Thinks about what happened to Eva.

Thinks: no.

Drive yourself.

She says, "I'll follow you."

"Suit yourself," Anton says.

He leads her down Fort to Woodward Avenue, then north. Anton turns right on Elizabeth Street, at the Woodmont Bar. Across Woodward, the State Theatre's red box office glows under the lights of the marquee. *I Want Wings* and *Honeymoon for Three* are playing.

Anton leaves his car in the lot behind the bar. Elizabeth parks beside him. The four of them go into the Woodmont.

It's dim inside, long and narrow with a bar the length of the left wall, a line of tables down the middle, and booths along the windows facing the street. At the far end of the room, three tables are pushed together. Ten men are already seated there.

Anton works the room, greeting people, shaking hands. Kevin follows in his wake, sour-faced as usual.

They land at the tables pushed together. "You're a real star here," Elizabeth says.

Anton says, "This is our joint."

"I thought the Rouge Tavern was your joint."

"That's our work bar. This is our real bar. The League office is down the street. The boys meet here to drink and talk. And plot." He gives her a wink.

A barmaid takes their drink orders. Pitchers of Stroh's all around.

Elizabeth recognizes Garland Alderman and Parker Sage, the officers of the National Workers League. She recognizes another man—Charles Spare, head of a detective agency and the top of Michigan's KKK.

The barmaid comes back with their beer. Alderman calls everyone to order with a toast. He holds up his glass. "To a white Christian America."

The others repeat the toast.

"Alright, now," Alderman says, "there's a lot to talk about. As you probably know, in May, the war-mongering president authorized a thousand new homes for defense workers in Detroit. For the past few months, the Housing Commission's been looking at locations for those homes. Of the thousand new housing units, a couple hundred are supposed to be set apart for niggers.

"Here's the thing," Alderman continues. "I got a pal in the Housing Commission. He just shot me the word. The government's going to make an announcement in another couple days. The Housing Department picked land for the colored housing that's right between a Polish Catholic community and Conant Gardens, which is a colored area. You get what this means, don't you?"

"Whites and coloreds living side by side," one of the men around the tables says. "Never gonna happen."

"There's already too much race mixing in this city," another grouses.

Alderman says. "Boys, we're either going to stop the construction of this housing or make sure it's dedicated to whites if it's the last thing we do."

The others pound the table in agreement.

The front door at the other end of the bar flies open and a white kid runs in and looks around. He heads toward the back.

"Did you hear?" he says to the group. He's in his teens, in a rumpled white shirt and wrinkled pants. "There's a wild time going on in Hamtramck. We're kicking some nigger ass!"

One of the men at the table says, "Where?"

"Joseph Campau. Near Newton."

Another man jumps up and says, "Where all the jigth are moving in."

He is short and stout. Elizabeth remembers Eva's diary . . . one of the men who slapped her around was short and had a lisp. The other man was tall with a scar down the side of his face.

Just like the guy sitting next to him now.

Mutt and Jeff.

In the dim light of the bar, she didn't even realize they were there.

"Come on," the tall one says. It's Mutt. He stands.

"Now hold it, hold it," Alderman says before they run off. "This is exactly what I was talking about . . . niggers moving in and displacing white Americans. This might be an opportunity, here. We need to talk about it."

The tall man says, "No more talking. Let's show those niggers where they belong."

"You go, if you want to," Alderman says. "The rest of us, let's stay and talk about how to use this."

Mutt and Jeff rush out the door, leaving Anton and Elizabeth and a half dozen others.

"Who's there?" Parker Sage asks.

"Now it's just guys from the neighborhood," the kid says. "It started at the Smoke Shoppe on Sunday night. Every night more of us are coming to fight."

Charles Spare says, "I can get a couple carloads of boys for tomorrow night. We'll kick those boogies all the way the hell back to Africa."

The boys he's talking about are likely members of the KKK.

"Okay," says Alderman. He points at Spare. "You get your fellas in line for tomorrow."

"Roger."

"We'll get some fellas over there, too," Parker Sage says. "Cops won't lift a finger to stop us."

Anton pipes up. "I'll talk to Harry Bennett. I'll get his Service Department guys. Those mugs are tough customers, believe you me."

"Perfect," Garland Alderman says. He rubs his hands together in anticipation.

"We'll show those niggers," one of the other men at the table says. It's the first time he's spoken up tonight. Elizabeth doesn't know him. Long, thin face. Blue eyes, a sharp nose, and chin belonging on a larger man. A dark mop of hair under a Navy beret. Short-sleeved work shirt with the tattoo of an anchor on his forearm, like Popeye. "We ain't going to let them replace us."

Elizabeth sits with Anton after the others leave. She's driving, so she limits herself to the one beer. Anton is not so careful. When he gets drunk around her, he gets handsy. She keeps her distance from him.

Still, she has questions.

She says, "Who were those guys who ran out?"

"The tall guy's Mickey Smith. Little guy's Carmine Sant'angelo. He don't look it, but he used to be a boxer. Tough little wop, too. Wouldn't want to tangle with either of them in a dark alley."

"What do they do?"

"Mickey works for Harry Bennett in the Service Department. Carmine's around whenever Bennett needs extra weight. Get this, Carmine, he works for a couple of Yids. Ain't that rich? You know Tom's Quality Meats, over there on 12th Street? He works there. Says those Jews are a bear to work for. Big surprise, right?"

"What's he do?"

"He's a butcher. He slices up meat. Good practice, eh?"

"What about the guy who spoke up at the end? With the sailor cap?"

"Bert Vogelmann. Be careful of him. He's crazy as a loon."

Home. The Trocadero Apartments in Palmer Park.

She changes out of her work clothes and makes herself an Old Fashioned. Sits on the couch under her bookshelves and sips it. The accumulated tension in her neck and shoulders starts to ease.

Mutt and Jeff.

Mickey and Carmine. Carmine, the short guy with a lisp, is a butcher. He's around cold storage lockers where they hang meat.

Where they beat up young women, too?

When they're not beating up Negroes . . .

As soon as they heard about the ruckus in Hamtramck, they flew out the door. They just can't stand the idea of Negroes and whites mixing, these savages.

And now with the new defense worker housing for Negroes, there's even more trouble brewing. Sounds like they're going to do everything they can to stop it.

People need to know about this.

She mentally goes through the list of who she knows who can impede their plans, or direct her to someone who can.

Who represents that district?

She takes another drink.

She can't think tonight. Too many voices rattling around in her head.

Save it for tomorrow.

59

DENNY RANKIN

[Wednesday, June 18, 1941]

Denny sifts through the photographs Elizabeth Waters gave him.

They show the membership of the National Workers League. He sees familiar names with addresses and phone numbers. Garland Alderman and Parker Sage, of course. Heinz Mueller is also on the list, as are his parents, Prentiss and Frieda.

As is Dr. Fred Thomas. Denny was following him when the Keystone Kops from the FBI collared him. Denny hasn't run across a tail lately, but he is wary now of being followed.

Denny recognizes other names on the list, including ones Special Agent Duhamel of the FBI mentioned: Emma Elise and Carl John Heinz Leonhardt, owners of the house that's a mail drop for Nazi spies.

Other names Duhamel didn't mention are there, but have the same address as the Leonhardts.

Also on the list of the National Workers League is Thaddeus Ostrowski, the disgraced Detroit Police Department patrolman who killed Edgar Vanarian.

There's nothing after the letter T. He remembers Elizabeth telling him she didn't finish photographing the list.

Ostrowski was remanded to the Wayne County jail. Denny considers going to see him and asking about belonging to this group.

Immediately he drops the idea. Ostrowski wouldn't tell him the truth—he hasn't so far—and Denny would have no good reason to believe him regardless of what he said.

He might get the truth from Ostrowski's wife Francine.

Who seemed, last time Denny spoke with her, already as pissed-off at her husband as a woman could be.

"You again," Francine Ostrowski says.

"Can we talk about your husband?"

"Why? What kind of trouble you bringing to my door now?"

He doesn't reply. She turns away and leaves the door open for him. He comes in. Follows her to the kitchen.

There is a cup half full of coffee on the counter. Without asking, she takes a cup out of the cupboard and fills it from the battered aluminum percolator on the stove. "How do you take it?"

"Black is fine."

She brings her own coffee cup over and they sit at the kitchen table.

She sighs. "Now what?"

"I want to ask you a question about Ted."

"Why don't you ask him?"

"I don't trust him to tell me the truth."

"Welcome to my world." She takes a sip of coffee. "Fire away."

"Have you ever heard of the National Workers League? I have information Ted was a member. I have a witness who says he might have been shooting at someone other than Edgar Vanarian."

"The guy Ted shot?"

"Yeah. I think it was an accident. I think he was shooting at another member of the League. I want to know what you know about it."

She says, "Come with me."

Denny follows her down the basement. On one dank wall is a set of wooden shelves. She turns a light on over the shelves and steps back. "This answer your question?"

Another cache of pro-Nazi pamphlets, flyers, and magazines. The same stuff he found in the Mueller basement.

As the newspaperman Tom Glover said, this is all over town.

Denny says, "He got this from the National Workers League?"

"Yeah. There's a whole network of people passing this stuff around town."

"Are you part of it, too?"

"My father fought the Germans in the Great War. I have no use for those people."

"What's he supposed to do with all this?"

"Distribute it. Leave it around. Sell it, if he can."

"Has he ever been in any anti-democratic demonstrations?"

She scoffs. "Only if he had to walk through one to get to the liquor store."

"Did he ever talk about this?"

"He knows I hate it. He keeps mum."

"Did he ever mention a couple of guys named Garland Alderman or Parker Sage?"

"Not in front of me."

"How about Prentiss Mueller?"

"Same."

"Charles Spare?"

"I told you, he never talks about it in front of me."

"One more name. How about Bertrand or Bert Vogelmann?"

This one makes her think.

"What?" Denny prompts.

"I do remember Ted was on the phone a couple weeks ago. I thought I heard that name. Only he was saying, 'Bert.' I dunno who he was talking to."

"When was this?"

"I can't remember exactly."

"Please try."

"What I just say?"

"Okay, okay," Denny says. "Thanks for your help."

"Is any of this going to help my husband get out of jail sooner?"

"It's possible."

"I wish you said that to start with. I wouldn't have told you a goddamn thing."

Back at the station, he calls the Michigan Bell police information number. "Detective Dennis Rankin, badge number 4969. Requesting a list of all calls to and from this number, TUxedo 3678, from March

30th to April 1st."

Ten minutes later the phone clerk comes back on the line. "Four incoming calls," she says. "All from UNiversity 2670, all on the evening of March 31st. No outgoing calls during this time."

"Got it. Thanks."

UNiversity 2670 was a familiar number.

Denny looks it up to make sure.

Yes. It's the number for the Mueller house in Palmer Woods. A call made from there to Ted Ostrowski late in the day on March 31st. The day of the Mueller break-in.

According to Francine, Bert was a subject of the conversation.

Denny's guess: Prentiss Mueller called Ted Ostrowski about Bertrand Vogelmann.

What did the dishwasher at the Mayflower Café say? The guy who looked like he was shooting back at Ostrowski wore a peacoat, like sailors wear.

Or the Merchant Marines.

Was Mueller giving Ostrowski orders to shoot Vogelmann?

Why would he do it? Vogelmann was part of his cadre.

Maybe Mueller was punishing Vogelmann.

Not for stealing an imaginary baby from his delusional daughter.

More like for stealing $8,000 in cash from him.

60

EVA SZABÓ

[Wednesday, June 18, 1941]

I *woke up this morning gasping for breath. I was back there again, in a black room, cold, stiff, the heavy smell of death around me.*
    I could sense but not see the sides of beef hanging on hooks around me, drifting in the cold air from the vents.
    I told Elizabeth about it. I think she believed me. Though to be honest, I don't know if I believed it myself. It was like a nightmare at the time. I don't know how long I was kept there. It might have been a few hours, it might have been overnight, it might have been a week . . . time lost all meaning.
    And yet—so much still remains a blank. I don't remember anything after going outside and celebrating the end of the strike with the men.
    The cold room felt like what death would be. . . no afterlife, no heaven, only a never-ending frigid blankness.
    Interrupted periodically by two men—yes, Mutt and Jeff, I'm getting more certain it was them—who came in to beat me.
    But they never answered me when I asked what I did to deserve this.

She is so focused on writing her journal entry she doesn't notice the figure who stops at her bedside. Frightened—everything frightens her these days—she looks up into the face of Vincent Németh.
    Her brother's friend who thinks Eva is his girlfriend.
    Holding a paper bag with grease stains.

He says, "Hey." Holds up the bag. "These are for you."

"Thanks," she says. She takes the bag. Inside are half a dozen Hungarian kifli cookies, rolled, crescent-shaped treats with a walnut filling. She lays the bag on the bed.

"I remember you saying those were your favorites."

"That's very nice," she says, certain she never said any such thing to him. "Thank you."

He sits on the edge of her bed. She eases away from him.

He examines the wounds on her head and face. He frowns. Says, "They really did the job on you, didn't they?"

"They really did."

She's still having trouble speaking.

His gaze sends a chill down her back.

They did a job on her?

Why would he say "they"? Did he know there was more than one? For the first time, she considers he might be involved with what happened to her.

She says, "Do you know who did this?"

"How would I know?" he asks with wounded innocence.

He doesn't say anything more. He stands and smooths the sheet on the bed where he sat.

He opens his mouth as though to say something. She hopes he won't—she doesn't want to hear anything he has to say, especially if he tells her how this wouldn't have happened if she had left the plant like he wanted her to.

She just wants him to go.

Instead he asks, "Can I sit here with you for a while?"

"I'd rather you didn't. I'm really tired. I need to rest."

When he doesn't move, she says, "I wish you would leave."

"I'll just keep you company. I won't disturb you. I'll just sit here. I'll be quiet."

She sighs. He is not going to leave.

Here's Vincent not taking the hint again. If you can call "Go away" a hint.

He drags a chair over and sits.

She turns her head away on the pillow. Closes her eyes.

She evens out her breathing and pretends to sleep.

After a while, he gets up and tiptoes away.

When she is sure he's not coming back, she calls a nurse over and hands her the bag. "Would you like these?"

The nurse opens the bag. "Smells delicious! Don't you want them?"

"Take them," Eva says.

The nurse takes the cookies away. Eva closes her eyes and tries to go to sleep for real.

She wakes in a panic.

(I'm always in a panic lately, her conscious mind thinks.)

She dreamed about Hal Perlman.

She dreamed he was being chased down the street by men wearing Nazi uniforms.

All because she never made it to the seder he invited her to. When she didn't show, he went out looking for her but ran into the pack of them, roaming the streets like wild dogs.

She knows it's just a dream, but it frightens her.

All the more so because he probably has no idea what happened to her. Nobody at the plant knows. He knows where she lives, but between her non-English-speaking stepmother and her Nazi-sympathizing stepbrother, they'll never tell him where she is.

The next time the nurse stops by her bed to check on her, Eva asks her to please get in touch with Harold Perlman, a photographer, and let him know where she is. His phone number is probably in the directory.

The nurse says she will.

61

CLARENCE BROWN

[Wednesday, June 18, 1941]

Bessie had a bad night. Clarence was planning on going into Hamtramck to see what was going on there, but he couldn't leave her; he stayed home with his wife. In the morning, he wants to take her to see Dr Jemison, but she feels better, and one of the women from her church Sisterhood will sit with her. They are praying together when he leaves them.

The Negro section of Hamtramck is only the last street on the south end of the small city completely surrounded by Detroit. Newton Street. Barely even in Hamtramck. People are out sweeping up broken glass. Windows in the houses are broken. Basement windows are kicked in.

He stops to ask a woman sweeping up what happened.

"Those white punks again," she says. "This time they wore masks. Cowards. Afraid to even let us see what they look like."

"How could you tell they were white?"

"They only covered their noses and mouths. They broke into houses and trashed them until we got together to fight them off."

"Anybody hurt?"

"A few people. An older couple, man and his wife, got roughed up. Now I ask you: who roughs up old people?"

"And the police?"

She spits on the ground. "They was standing right there. They did nothing. Nothing! I myself went up to one and asked him to do something. They could see what those punks was doing right before their eyes! You know what he says to me? He says, 'You people always asking us to protect you. You all need to learn to protect yourself.'"

"I'm so sorry, ma'am."

"Nothing for you to be sorry about. You not causing this."

He shows her his buzzer.

"I'm a Detroit police detective. I know what y'all are going through, believe me. I do."

"Unless you coming back tonight and arresting all them white boys, your good wishes ain't going to make no difference."

"They're coming back again?"

"They said they were. 'We'll see you tomorrow, auntie.'"

Clarence helps her sweep the broken glass from her windows into a trash bin. Sonny McGhee had given him his wife's sister's address. It's at the middle of Newton, a narrow, white wood-framed house with all the windows on the ground floor broken.

He rings the doorbell. A man opens it an inch on a chain. An older man with a ring of white hair around a bald top. His cheek and forehead are bruised. White tape binds the bridge of his eyeglasses. One of the lenses has a star fracture.

"Marvin?"

Marvin gives him a suspicious nod. Clarence shows his badge, says his name. "I'm a friend of Sonny McGhee."

Marvin waits. He is no friend of any policeman right now, no matter the color.

"Checking up on how you are," Clarence says. "Sonny told me you had trouble Sunday night."

Marvin stays silent.

Clarence says, "Can I come in, sir?"

"Rather you didn't. Nobody here got nothing to say to you. These Polish people, they trying to drive us out. But I ain't leaving, no matter what they do to me and my family. I only got one time to die, and I'd rather die here."

Marvin closes the door in Clarence's face.

Clarence waits a few seconds, then, as sad as he's ever been, he steps down from Marvin's front porch.

He goes back to his car. Drives up Newton to Joseph Campau, the main street through Hamtramck.

Just one section where Negroes are starting to move is what's causing all this. Go back to where you belong, the white punks are saying.

We are where we belong, Clarence thinks. Everywhere we are is where we belong. Except whenever restrictions on Negroes loosen, whites seem to fight them every step of the way.

His car radio crackles. A man took a baseball bat to his wife, who then stabbed him.

Clarence thinks: this is who people think we are. Beating and stabbing each other. They don't see the picture he sees everyday: the desperation of people so locked out of their own futures they turn their anger inward, against themselves and each other.

Clarence radios he's on his way.

At the end of the day, Clarence stops home before going back to Hamtramck to face whatever this night will bring. A woman stands on his porch. Light-skinned, care-worn. He does not recognize her.

She says, "Mr. Clarence?"

"Hello."

"Mr. Clarence, I'm Mary Coleman. Malone's aunt?"

"Oh sure. We talked on the phone. How you doing this evening?"

"Not too good. It's Malone. Could you give him a message for me?"

"I haven't seen him in weeks, Miss Coleman."

"I thought he was staying with you."

"He was. He took off on his own a while back. I don't know where he is."

"The thing is, Mr. Clarence, one of his friends lives in my building. He told me Malone's fixing to go up to Hamtramck tonight. You heard about what's going on?"

"I have."

"This boy, Malone's friend, told me him and Malone and them are going to start trouble with these white boys been raising hell."

"And you want me to make sure he's alright?"

"Yes sir. If it ain't too much trouble. I can't ask anybody else, and with the other children I'm taking care of . . ."

"I'll do what I can. I was going up there anyway to see if I can help calm things down. I'll keep an eye out for him."

"I'd be obliged, Mr. Clarence. If you do see him, you might also tell him his momma hasn't been home in weeks. If he's staying away because of her . . . he can come on home."

"I see him, I'll let him know."

Bessie is standing in the living room.

She has a crutch under one arm, but she is standing. The sight of her on her feet brings tears to Clarence's eyes.

"What's all this?" he asks.

"Doing my exercises. The physical therapist told me I need to spend more time on my feet so my muscles don't fail on me."

"I'm happy to see you standing upright."

"I do it through the day," Bessie says. "You just don't see me because you ain't hardly ever home during the day. And I'm too tired come evening."

She starts toward the kitchen.

"Wait, wait, wait," he says. "Where you going?"

"Make you dinner."

"Oh no you're not. You're going to sit back down and I'll make you dinner. You're not going to start taking care of me again."

"You sure?"

"Positive. Go on, now. You sit back down. I'll change your dressing and then I'll get dinner ready."

"When the good Lord was passing out husbands, he saved the best for me."

"Go on, now. Just sit back down and I'll get you set up."

After dinner he helps her to the sofa. As she said, once the sun goes down, she gets too tired to do much of anything.

He turns on the radio for her. He puts his armor and suitcoat back on. "Where are you going?" she asks.

"There's bad things happening in Hamtramck."

"I heard. Those Polacks."

Her use of the term surprises him. She never uses derogatory language against anyone.

She asks, "You going down there?"

He nods.

"Why you can't let the police in Hamtramck take care of this?"

He gives her a despondent look. She knows the answer already.

"Clarence, you got to save every colored person in Michigan?" she asks.

She knows the answer to that question, too.

He will.

If he can.

62

ELIZABETH WATERS

[Wednesday, June 18, 1941]

She tries Denny throughout the morning, but he's in the field. She leaves messages. After lunch she tries again. This time she catches him at his desk.

"I just got back," he says. "I haven't gone through my messages yet. What's up?"

"Do you know what's going on in Hamtramck?"

"I haven't heard any news about anything. Hang on." She hears his chair screech, papers turning. "I'm looking at today's *Free Press*. Don't see anything about Hamtramck. What's going on?"

"Whites are going crazy over there. They're terrorizing Negroes who moved into their neighborhood."

"What do you mean, terrorizing?"

"Beating them. Stoning them. Breaking into their houses."

"It's a Hamtown police problem. We wouldn't get involved unless it spread over to Detroit."

"It may. I was sitting around the Woodmont last night with the crème de la crème of Detroit's fascists."

"Moving down in the world, are we?"

"They were talking about throwing gas on the fire."

"I'd say let the police know, but that would be useless. They won't do a thing to help. Except maybe tell the Negro families to go back where they came from, which is what usually happens. And just what the whites want. The mayor's a crook. He did time in the pokey for contempt of court over the gambling graft scandal, and he was brought up on a federal charge in the twenties over fraudulent citizenship papers. He's thick with the police commissioner. I can't think of anybody in the local government who'd be helpful."

"Maybe their representative?"

"That's Rudy Tenerowicz, I think. Good luck with that."

"Whatever happens, I'm going down there tonight."

"Hamtramck?"

"Yeah."

"Why?"

"At the meeting last night there were these two guys, I'm pretty sure they were the ones who beat up Eva. They said they'd be there."

"Who's Eva?"

"She was working for me at the Rouge plant and somebody abducted her and beat the crap out of her."

"How's she doing?"

"They hurt her. She's recovering. But I want to bring these mugs to justice."

"What are you going to do when you find them?"

"I'm hoping that's where you come in. I want you to arrest them."

"I can't just arrest them without evidence of a crime. If I see them breaking the law, that's a different story."

"Then will you come with me tonight?"

He agrees at once.

They will meet at a diner on Joseph Campau.

She has not had a chance to pursue the memories Eva told her about—the smell of meat, being cold in a food locker. And now there's another danger—a developing race riot.

Who can she warn about this?

She calls the operator, gets Tenerowicz's number in Washington. He's in Detroit, they tell her. They give her the number of his Detroit office and she leaves a message for him to call her.

She tells him it's very important.

63

DENNY RANKIN

[Wednesday, June 18, 1941]

Elizabeth says, "I left a message for Tenerowicz. I'm sure I won't hear from him."

"Never can tell with these guys."

The waitress comes over with Denny's bowl of cabbage soup. He has not eaten since breakfast. Elizabeth only orders coffee. They're at the Polish Village Café on Yemens Street. The place is almost empty. Newton's only a mile away but people are staying home tonight.

"You're not hungry?" he asks.

"I can't eat. Too nervous."

"You're sure these jamokes are going to be there?"

"Not positive. But from what I heard them say, tonight's going to be the night."

He finishes his soup. Pays the tab. They go out into the warm night. It was a hot day, in the mid-80s. The heat and humidity linger even as the day wanes.

Denny drives them down Joseph Campau. They cross the railroad tracks. Once they get past the Dodge Main plant, they see an increased police presence. Hamtramck cops stand on the sidewalks. Intermingled with them are whites, both kids and adults. Mostly male, as far as Denny can see.

A cop car blocks the road at Smith, a street away from Newton.

A copper stops them, looks inside the car, waves them back. "Can't get through," he tells them.

Denny turns down Whiting toward Conant. A parking space opens up and he pulls in. Takes his shotgun out of the trunk.

The end of the street at Conant is open. They head toward the intersection.

They hear voices raised. The crash of glass. White youth are pouring into this end of Newton, carrying clubs and baseball bats. Their faces are twisted in fury.

As Elizabeth and Denny look on, two cars full of white men barrel down Conant. A police vehicle blocks the end of Newton, but Denny and Elizabeth watch a cop move the police car so the other cars can swing around into Newton. She recognizes Charles Spare as one of the passengers.

Elizabeth says, "The KKK. They said they'd be here. And the cops are just letting them go in."

They walk down Conant unhindered. They turn the corner.

Newton Street is a battleground. An overturned car is on fire in the middle of the road. White men pour out of the cars that just arrived. They carry shotguns and clubs. They jump into hand-to-hand rumbles with Negro residents. They're carrying guns, too. Denny hears the exchange of gunfire. Most of the fighters are too hyped-up to hit anything. Stray shots are going everywhere.

Shotguns shoot out what windows remain unbroken, mostly on the second floor. Men kick in doors of the houses, pull people—men, women, even children—out into the street and beat them.

"This is chaos," Denny said. "We'll never find your guys."

The violence stuns Elizabeth. She starts walking down Newton as though drawn by the screams and bloodshed.

Denny grabs at her—"No!"—but she pulls away and keeps walking.

Her skin color protects her from the marauding whites. The Negroes have their hands full with the white men.

Racial skirmishes are nothing new in this town. When Denny was in uniform there were skirmishes every week, at Belle Isle (where the races mixed and where the presence of a coast guard station meant white sailors joined in the fistfights that flared up constantly), in all-white neighborhoods where courageous Negroes dared to move, in factories and plants, wherever Negroes transgressed the racial boundaries established by white Detroiters in their neighborhoods and communities.

But this is war, a race war, organized and deliberate. Another in the seemingly endless upsurges of racial violence in this city. Where does all this hatred come from?

And how will it ever abate?

He walks with Elizabeth down the street. He sees her head swiveling from side to side; she's looking for the men who beat her friend. He has his eye out, too, for Heinz Mueller and Bertrand Vogelmann.

He walks past three white men beating a young Negro man.

He jumps into the fray. He clubs the whites with the butt of his shotgun and pulls them off the frightened, bloody Negro, who Denny sees is just a boy.

Elizabeth stops. She looks across one of the lawns. Something else further down the street catches her eye. She starts running in that direction.

64

EVA SZABÓ

[Wednesday, June 18, 1941]

She dozes, a light, dreamless sleep.
A noise beside her bed brings her awake.
Her heart pounds.
A shadow drifts around her.
For a moment she thinks it's Mutt and Jeff.
How did they find me?
Her vision clears and she sees Hal Perlman standing there.
His handsome features pulled together in a deep frown of concern.

"Hey," he says.

"Hey."

"It's conventional at this point to say, 'You should see the other guy.'"

"I came off way worse than the other guy, believe me."

"Jesus Christ, Eva."

He steps forward and takes her hand. "Does that hurt?"

"It's possibly the only spot on my body where I don't hurt."

He pulls up a chair. "Do you know who did this? Or why?"

"I suspect I know who. I don't know their names."

"There was more than one?"

"Yeah."

"But why?"

"It has to do with the union."

"You're not part of the union, are you?"

She pauses before answering.

Can she trust him?

She decides she can.

He's not carrying his camera (the first time she's seen him without it) but she remembers him talking about his own project of documenting the union's fight for recognition.

She hopes he's as good a man as he seems.

She says, "I wasn't just the hospital receptionist. I was working for a private investigator. I was supposed to collect information about illegal anti-union activities."

"And by 'collect' I assume you don't mean jumping in the middle of a union-management fistfight?"

"It was supposed to be secret. And nonviolent."

"And they found out about you."

"I guess so. Not sure how."

The chai symbol she wears on a chain peeks out of the neckline of the hospital gown. She notices Hal looking at it. Well, she has already told him she's Jewish, but she tucks it back in.

He reaches down and gently pulls the chai out of her gown. "You don't have to hide this with me."

She lets the chai stay visible.

He says, "Are you sure this all wasn't for another reason?"

"Like what?"

"Like the fact you're Jewish?"

She is silent as she considers it.

"There's a lot of hatred of Jews nowadays," he says. "It's the other thing I want to document. All the darkness closing in on us."

"I suppose it's possible," she admits. "My father brought me over from Hungary to escape it. Except it's followed us here."

"It's everywhere. I've come to believe anti-Semitism is an inherited condition for gentiles," he says. "Passed down from generation to generation. Periodically people fight against it, but in the end scratch a goy and you'll find an anti-Semite not far below the surface."

'I'm afraid you're right. So yeah, I suppose it's also possible that's why I was attacked. But how would they know I'm Jewish?"

"They can tell. For some of them, it only matters if they think you are."

"Pretty sure it was the union," she says. "Being Jewish might have been the icing on the cake."

He hangs onto her hand. Now she brings his hand to her painful bruised cheek.

"Thank you for visiting me," she whispers.

"When you didn't come to the seder," he says, "and weren't around afterwards, I figured there was a problem."

"Did you go to the plant hospital and ask Nadine about me?"

"I did."

"What did she say?"

"She said she knew you were getting threats for some reason and she hoped you were safe. I'm just glad to know you're alive."

She turns her head to kiss his palm. He cups her face with it.

He leans down and kisses her on the lips. A soft kiss, gentle, like the touch of a butterfly's wing.

A nurse passes, scowling. "Eva needs her rest," she says, shooing him away.

"I'll come back soon," Hal tells Eva.

And he is gone.

She misses him already.

65

CLARENCE BROWN

[Wednesday, June 18, 1941]

Sounds of battle fill the air.

Shouts. Gunfire. Breaking glass. The cracking of wood as door and window frame shatter. The bellowing of young white men calling the Negro residents of Newton by the worst racial slurs.

As Clarence watches, the young Poles who live around here in Hamtramck who are trying to force the Negroes out are joined by men who arrive by car and pour in the street with handguns, clubs, baseball bats . . . while the police stand by at either end of the street. They don't keep people from getting in (Clarence can see certain cars get free passage onto the street), but they keep the Negroes inside.

Where they can be shot and beaten. Like fish in a barrel.

Let them try that with Clarence.

He walks down Newton from Conant. The police gathered at the corner who are letting the riot unfold approach him until they clock the badge pinned to his suitcoat lapel and the .45s at his waist. They step away and let him go unimpeded but not before sharing smirks with each other.

He sweats with his suitcoat on and, underneath, the metal plates he wears as armor. He can't get very far without wading into the rumble. With his height and his girth and his twin pearl-handled .45s he's intimidating; these white boys know better than to take him on so they scramble away from him.

He keeps his eyes open for Malone, but doesn't see him in the chaos.

He does see Elizabeth Waters running toward him.

Followed by Denny Rankin.

Clarence met Elizabeth nine years ago, when circumstances threw them together to stop a plot to assassinate then-mayor Frank Murphy. Clarence saw her get shot by the head lawyer of the Red Squad, Horace Howcroft; Clarence picked her up off the street in front of the mayor's home and drove her to the hospital.

"Clarence," Elizabeth says, "do you believe this?"

"What are you doing here?" Clarence asks her. And to Rankin, "And you, too?" He shouts to be heard above the din.

"I'm looking for two white guys who beat up my friend," Elizabeth says.

"Could be anybody here," Clarence says. "You'll never find them in this."

Two white kids, tow-headed, vicious teenagers, come running at Clarence, screaming. One swings a baseball bat, the other a wooden plank.

Clarence and Rankin both cry, "Halt!"

The boys keep coming.

Clarence steps in and clocks one over the head with a .45. Rankin takes the other down with a roundhouse swing of his shotgun.

"Those the ones?" Clarence says.

"No." Her voice quakes. She seems appalled by the violence.

Rankin takes Elizabeth by the arm. "Let's get out of here. He's right—you'll never find anybody tonight."

Elizabeth turns to Clarence. "What are you going to do?"

"I'm going to keep searching for my kid. He's supposed to be here. I want to make sure he's safe."

"If you see two white guys," Elizabeth says, "one tall, one short, like Mutt and Jeff, they're the ones I'm looking for."

"I'll watch for them. But—"

More gunfire around them. Broken windows. A house at the end of the block begins to burn.

"Don't stay, man," Rankin says.

"I got to find my boy."

Rankin and Elizabeth make their way back the way they came. Rankin breaks up fights, throwing whites off the Negroes they're attacking.

The streetlamps have been broken so the only light on the two blocks that make up Newton is the glare from the flames. Clarence walks from one end to the other. He doesn't see Malone.

There's a paddy wagon at St. Aubin Street, at the end of Newton. Clarence sees a half-dozen Negroes being loaded into it.

Of course, he thinks.

We're the ones getting arrested.

Bessie dozes on the sofa in the living room when he gets home. He tries to be quiet but she wakes.

She takes one look at him and says, "Oh my lord. What happened?"

He tells her what he saw tonight.

"I told you to be careful."

"I'm back in one piece, aren't I?"

He takes off his suitcoat, soaking wet with sweat. He hangs his gunbelt on the peg by the door and takes the damp metal plates over his head and stows them in the closet.

His legs shake from exhaustion. But he's not done yet.

He calls Mary Coleman on the phone in the niche in the dining room. Malone's aunt.

"Hey," he says, "it's Clarence Brown. Look, I went down to Hamtramck but I didn't see Malone. I tried to find him, but it's crazy bad down there. Impossible to find anybody."

"You think I should check the hospitals?"

"You could. Colored boys were being arrested—"

"*They* were being arrested?"

"That's how it goes. Malone might have been one of them. I'll check tomorrow when I get in. They won't sort this out before then anyway."

Mary sighs. "Mr. Clarence, I appreciate it. Thank you so much."

"If I find him, I'll let you know."

"I'll do the same if I hear from him."

He lets himself fall into his chair in the living room. Bessie eyes him with concern.

"Clarence," she says, "how much longer you gonna do this?"

"Long as we have to. It's got to change one day. It's got to."

"No, I'm talking about you. How much longer you going out there and face riots and shootings and stabbings and people who hate the ground you walk on? You not getting any younger."

"That's the truth. Tonight I feel my age."

"Just saying."

"I know. How are you doing?"

"Better than you, I'm thinking."

66

ELIZABETH WATERS

[Wednesday, June 18, 1941]

At the end of the block, the white police stand around and give Elizabeth and Denny the fish-eye as they leave Newton Street.

Elizabeth can't help herself. "Why aren't you doing anything?" she demands of one uniformed cop.

He gets right up in her face. Denny holds up his badge, says, "Step away." Pushes the guy back.

The cop says, "These people are always asking for protection. Next thing you know, they're beating up Polish kids. They want to live here, they better learn to protect themselves."

"Let's go," Denny tells her.

"These goddamn useless cops. What good are they?" She turns around to yell at the police, who are standing around laughing at her. "What good are you?"

She shakes with anger.

Denny walks her back to his car.

"Let's get as far away from Hamtramck as we can," she says. "I've had enough of this place."

He takes her back to the restaurant to pick up her car. She follows him to Conant. From there he goes east to Warren and drives to the east side.

He takes a right on Cadieux, drives south a few blocks. Pulls into the lot of the Cadieux Café. She parks beside him.

"Ever been here?" he asks.

"No." She is still upset at what she's just seen.

"It's a Belgian place. You can play feather bowling."

"What in Christ's name is feather bowling?"

And why would I care about it now? she thinks but does not say. Denny says, "You'll see."

The front door is open and a giant floor fan blows hot air inside. It's a large room with tables and a bar at the far end. She hears men's voices coming through a doorway to the left.

He shows her the feather bowling alley. It's a long, wide, concave dirt lane. With great concentration men are rolling thick wooden disks the size of small cheese wheels down toward a feather stuck upright at the end of the lane.

Elizabeth rolls her eyes at the efforts. They find themselves a table in the large room. Denny goes to the bar and brings back an Old Fashioned for her and a St. Sixtus Belgian beer for himself.

She takes a long drink.

She says, "I've never seen anything like this in my life. It was like Kristallnacht."

"I've seen it all too often."

"You would," she says, "you're a cop. But I don't see it much."

"Hundreds of thousands of Negroes and Southern whites coming into the city looking for work?" He shakes his head. "A dangerous mix. Negroes are routinely pulled out of streetcars and beaten, sometimes for no reason other than they're there. Pulled out of their cars and beaten and their cars set on fire. Racial fights break out routinely on Belle Isle . . ."

"And we're supposed to be the great arsenal of democracy in the world."

"This thing tonight? You won't even read about it in the papers," he says. "Unless you read the *Tribune*."

The *Detroit Tribune*. One of the city's Negro newspapers.

She drains her Old Fashioned.

"Another?" he asks.

She shakes her head. "I'm driving. I just needed a drink to steady my nerves."

"You didn't see the two mugs you were looking for?"

"No. But I thought I saw another guy I recognized. He was at the bar with the National Workers League guy last night."

"You went someplace else last night after we said goodnight?"

"I wanted to check in with the guys I've been keeping an eye on. I think they're connected with what happened to Eva. They took me down to the Woodmont downtown. It's evidently 'their' bar."

"The Woodmont Bar and Grill?"

"That's the one. Why?"

"That place is involved in one of my other cases. An on-duty copper got drunk there and started shooting up the street. Who was your guy?"

"First name's Bert. I didn't get his last name."

"Describe him."

"Tall, six-one or -two. Dark hair. At the bar he had on a sleeveless undershirt and denim workpants. One of those berets like French sailors wear. Tattoo of an anchor on one forearm. Like Popeye."

"Bert Vogelmann. I'm looking at him for a shooting. Possibly a robbery, too. I bet that was him."

"Pretty chaotic, but I'm pretty sure it was the guy from last night."

"You said the local fascists were meeting?"

"Yeah. A kid ran in with news about what was going on in Hamtramck. Before that, they were talking about disrupting the new housing project for defense workers."

"Why?"

"It's going to be for Negroes. They don't want them living near whites."

"Jesus. What a country. Who else was there?"

She names the men she recognized: Charles Spare, Garland Alderman, Parker Sage.

She says, "I need to tell someone about what they're planning."

He fishes in his coat pockets. Brings out a business card and passes it across the table to her.

"Doug Duhamel," he says. "This guy's the local FBI special agent for counter-espionage. What you're telling me sounds like something he'd want to know about."

"Thanks." She pockets the card. "One of the other guys I was looking for works at a market on the east side. I'm going there tomorrow."

"What are you going to do when you find him?"

"I don't know," she says. "I might be able to get the attention of police in Lincoln Park. That's where Eva turned up."

"I know a detective there. Guy named Pixley."

"I've had the pleasure."

"Then you know how far you'll get with him."

"Detective Pixley makes a brick wall seem enlightened."

He drains his beer. "I'm going for another. You?"

"Oh, why not."

He retrieves their drinks. They clink glasses. She feels herself starting to relax; her shoulders loosen and the tightness around her head eases.

He says, "Feeling better?"

"Yeah."

And she's surprised to admit to herself she is.

He says, "How long have you been a private eye?"

"Around eight years."

She gives him the short version of her story: her escape from a privileged upbringing in Grosse Pointe, her year at Oberlin College, her stepfather's usurpation of her inheritance when her mother died, her travels west to put Michigan behind her, her return to Detroit, her job as assistant to the creative department at WXYZ, her flirtation with the Communist Party, her connection with Maurice Sugar, her brief association with Ben Rubin, her slightly longer association with Clive Sinclair-Smith and his London family that he conveniently forgot to mention.

"I don't often talk about Clive," she says. She doesn't often talk about any of this. Why is she doing it now, with this guy?

"Quite a journey," he says.

"Yeah, it's not over yet. Your turn."

He gives her his own abbreviated bio: an alcoholic father who drank himself to death; a frustrated, resentful mother who moved with her four kids back to her own alcoholic parents' house; Denny's graduation from Central High School and then a half-semester at Wayne University leaving him at what is politely called "loose ends"; his job in his grandfather's salvage yard until he couldn't stand the filthy, noisy, horrible work any longer; his sweet handicapped son Larry, whom he is never permitted to see, and his sadness at being distant from the boy; Larry's mother, who wants nothing to do with him; Denny's two brothers and sister, scattered across the country, as far away from Detroit as they could get; his joining the police because his uncle was a cop and it seemed like a good way to make a living; his failing marriage.

"Has it been a good living?" she asks.

"It started out okay. But you know, day after day you see the worst of humanity. On both sides of the badge. It wears on you."

"Why do you stay?"

"Don't know where else to go. You know, when I first joined, I thought I was going to do big things for people. Great things."

"An idealist under that rough exterior."

"Now I know those intentions don't mean anything. They're impossible to accomplish, anyway. You get up and go to work and hope for the least awful day possible you can make it home without pushing your already-shaky principles beyond the breaking point."

"So much for big dreams."

"I'd settle for learning how to live decently in this indecent world."

"Tall order."

"Besides, there are no big things. What's important are the small things, the tiny things we do for each other, person to person. That's what matters. What lasts."

She looks at him, sitting there staring into his beer.

She thinks she has misjudged him.

When she grew disenchanted with the Communist Party, she had a similar feeling. The large narrative of progress at the core of Marxism seemed to her to be a hollow promise. A hoax. Unattainable by the band of murderous mutant monkeys that constitute the human race with their unshakable hatreds and prejudices.

And yet there are some parts of the ideology she hasn't been able to shake. The belief that police are protectors of the status quo, an occupying force protecting the capitalist state. The ones she's met are no better than servo-mechanisms, but this guy seems different . . .

Now they share a look. She knows what they are both thinking: what's going on here?

If she were younger, she would invite him back to her apartment and take him to bed. Sadly, she's not that young anymore. She's lived long enough to know things aren't that easy anymore.

She feels as if she can peer into his brain and see that same thought running through it. If he were younger . . .

He surprises her by saying, "You look tired."

It's not what she expected him to say—she thought a pass would be coming her way, not a prelude to ending the evening.

But she realizes she's exhausted. She nods.

"Maybe we should call it a night."

"Probably a good idea."

Outside they pause at their cars. The same awkwardness they felt outside Cliff Bell's settles over them.

"Thank you for coming with me tonight," she says.

"It turned out to be a good idea."

Is he talking about Hamtramck, or what came after?

"Well," she says, "goodnight."

"Be careful driving. I hear the cops in this town are brutal."

In her apartment, she gets ready for bed.

Except she can't sleep, of course.

All she can hear are the screams of people being terrorized, the sounds of shattered glass as carloads of white hoodlums break into their homes.

And Denny Rankin and their unexpected conversation tonight.

After another hour, she gives up and gets out of bed.

Makes herself a cup of tea and takes it out to the living room.

She has a large apartment with a picture window that gives a luxurious view of the park. When she first moved into this building—four stories, awning-covered balconies, architectural nooks and crannies, and stunning decorative brick work in the Moorish style—she could barely afford it. Now she could afford a home of her own but she doesn't want to move, doesn't want to be tied down to a place she has to keep up.

Or tied down at all.

To anything.

Or anybody.

Even Denny Rankin, whose face she conjures in front of her, a ghostly apparition.

It's what's left over from the time she spent wandering after her single year of college at Oberlin. She would have stayed if she could have afforded it. As she told Denny, her stepfather refused to give her any of her late mother's money. He kept it all.

When she left school, she traveled to Ann Arbor, Chicago and Los Angeles and points in between, back to Ann Arbor, and then finally back to Detroit. She was tired of traveling. Tired of meeting herself where she landed.

The best thing that happened to her was meeting Maurice Sugar, who took her under his wing and gave her the direction she craved in the labor movement.

In between were the men—and occasionally women—she was briefly (always briefly) involved with. First was Sarah Kirschner, another student at Oberlin—her first real love, who killed herself in between semesters that first year, which traumatized Elizabeth for a long time. Then came the writers, artists, musicians, and drifters she met—and often fucked—in her travels.

After she nearly bled to death when the drunk LA doctor with the jim-jams aborted her pregnancy, she decided it was time to come back east.

She met Maurice Sugar at socialist meetings around Detroit. After the Ford Hunger March in 1932, she began working for him as a researcher.

The work he had her do was inherently useful, and also, at times, dangerous. When she went to Dallas, Texas, in 1937, she knew Service Department thugs were tailing her. It's why she bought her .22 pistol.

In 1940 the National Labor Relations Board charged Ford with violations of the Wagner Labor Act at the Dallas plant. Elizabeth testified at the NLRB hearings.

Her efforts collecting evidence for Maurice also helped prove collusion between then-United Auto Workers President Homer Martin and Harry Bennett when Bennett tried to gain control of the union. The union subsequently ousted Martin as president.

It didn't endear her to Harry Bennett and his Service Department goons, either in Texas or up here.

She sips her tea. Stands at her living room window, looking beyond her reflection into the darkness of the park. She used to do this and look out at the pitch-black park as though looking into her blank future. Has her blank future turned into an equally opaque past?

She remembers one time when she was standing here and saw a young man, Ben Rubin, drifting like a ghost among the trees. She had a quick fling with him, and then—younger, Jewish, on the run from gangsters and police alike—he moved up to northern Michigan and got a teaching job thanks to Maurice's good offices.

They were supposed to stay in touch, and he tried, she had to give him credit. He tried.

It was Elizabeth herself who preferred not to. He wrote a few times, she wrote back once or twice, and they saw each other one time when he came down to Detroit for a weekend. But by then both of them had burrowed into their separate lives, Elizabeth's down here and Ben's up there. They spent Saturday night together, but by the morning they were both anxious to be anyplace else but together in her bed.

Or maybe I'm just projecting my own thoughts onto him, she thinks now, as I was doing with Denny Rankin earlier tonight. Maybe Ben badly wanted to stay with her, wanted to rekindle what they once had for a short time. And when she eased him out of her apartment, he realized there was nothing to stay here for.

After the debacle with Clive, she decided she wanted nothing more to do with either men or women. She turned into one of the detectives in the hard-boiled world of pulp fiction . . . a Philippa Marlowe like in *The Big Sleep*, a solitary warrior tilting at windmills.

She makes another cup of tea. Takes it to the sofa. Sips at it until it gets cold, then sets it on the coffee table. She stretches out and, finally, nods off to sleep.

She dreams of glass breaking.

67

DENNY RANKIN

[Thursday, June 19, 1941]

As he suspected, the *Free Press*, the *Detroit News*, and the *Evening Times* carry nothing about the trouble in Hamtramck the night before. One of the papers carries a small notice about two white youths "sustaining injuries," but without context.

Phil Wheaton is not at his desk when Denny gets in. Out making the city safe from crime, no doubt. Or should he say safe *for* crime. The image of the poor sap who's taking the fall for the Mueller job still haunts Denny.

During the morning, he has to go down to the lockup to see one of his collars. The custody sergeant stops him, says, "Hey, Rankin, remember that geezer Wheaton collared a couple weeks ago?

"Yeah. Why?"

"Wheaton gave him the bum's rush out of here so fast, the geezer left his personal effects. Now he's in the county jail. You're going to see Wheaton, I'll give them to you to pass along."

The sergeant hands over a paper sack with the poor Joe's name on it. Herbert Henry Anderson.

Denny takes the sack up to his office. Dumps it out on his desk.

A raggedy-ass wallet. A few loose pennies and a nickel. A beat-up pocket watch. Inside the cover, the inscription, "To Herb with love."

At least Herb once had a love life. Denny wonders what

happened to it.

Probably what happens to everyone's.

Love is like the flu, he thinks: when you feel it coming on, you pretend it isn't happening; then there's a certain pleasure in giving yourself up to it; then it makes you feel so bad you wish you were dead; and when it's over, you're a little better protected against it happening the next time.

You're too old for it, he cautions himself.

It's the last thing you need.

It's why the attraction he feels toward Elizabeth Waters worries him. It's too soon to call it love, of course. But he senses the allure that tells him it's a possibility. She's smart and beautiful, and she has that mystique of being inaccessible that always spells trouble. It's what drew him to Hazel, a still-grieving widow with two young children who would never have the time to devote exclusively to him. Just his type. So he fell hard for her.

That's how it is with Elizabeth. Except he suspects she might be feeling the same thing for him.

No, he tells himself. You are definitely too old for this.

He turns to business. Opens Herbert Henry Anderson's wallet. No money or identification. A few business cards, including one from Phil Wheaton. A few liquor store receipts. A folded-up sheet of paper.

Another anti-Semitic flyer.

At the center of a six-pointed Jewish star is the usual rough caricature of a hook-nosed Jew. Every point of the star is an octopus's grasping tentacle with the words "Roosevelt," "Jew Morgenthau," "Communism," "World Domination," "Unions," and "The Jew Deal." At the bottom of the flyer Denny expects to see the words National Workers League, like the flyer he found in the bowling alley. But this one has "Christian Mobilizers" printed at the bottom, with a post office box in Hazel Park.

What's a down-and-outer like Herbert Henry Anderson doing with this? And who or what are the Christian Mobilizers?

He dials a number.

"Glover."

Tom Glover from the *Detroit News*.

"It's Denny Rankin."

"Denny Boy. What's up?"

"Got a quick question. Ever heard of the Christian Mobilizers?"

"I have indeed."

"What can you tell me about them?"

"It's a splinter group of Father Coughlin's Christian Front. Started by a mook named Joe McWilliams out of New York."

"I have a flyer from them with a P.O. box number in Hazel Park. Do they have a local headquarters?"

"They do. Lemme think. It's run out of a printer's shop. Hang on."

Denny lights up a smoke. Tom Glover returns in half a minute. "Got a pencil?"

American Lithography on East Nine Mile Road in Hazel Park, an inner-ring suburb across Eight Mile Road, the northern border of Detroit. Lots of Southern white transplants live here. Denny's heard it called Hazeltucky.

The smell of ink hangs heavy inside the building. A woman sits at a desk in the front office. Behind her Denny hears the clanking of presses. Through a doorway he sees massive rolls of paper on pallets.

"Good morning," the woman sings. Late middle-aged with a head full of tight curls. "How can I make you smile today?"

"I bet you get lots of different answers to that one."

She lets out a cackle. "Bud, I heard 'em all."

He shows her the flyer he got from Herbert Henry Anderson's wallet. "Recognize this?"

She examines it. "Yup. We did this."

"Designed it in-house?"

"We print it here. Got a guy who does the design for us. It's a very special client." She winks.

"I'd like to meet him."

She leans forward, brings her hand to her mouth as if sharing a secret with him even though they're alone and she's yelling to compete with the presses in the back room. "Kind of hush-hush. I shouldn't really be talking to you about it. Let me get the boss man and he can tell you more."

She gets up and peeks in the doorway into the pressroom. "Ken!"

She yells twice more and then comes back to her desk. "He's on his way."

A man heaves himself into the doorway. Tall, bulky, in an inky full-length apron and a cap made out of newsprint on his head.

"Yeah?"

Gravelly voice.

"This fella's got questions about this." She holds up the flyer.

He takes it. Looks Denny over. "You want it reprinted, or . . ."

"If I wanted to get one like this made, I hear you got a guy who can do it."

"Yeah."

"How would I get in touch with him?"

Ken squints at Denny. "I know you?"

"I'm with the American Destiny Party," Denny says. He picks a name out of the air, the first one he remembers from the stash in the Muellers' basement.

As luck would have it, Ken the printer knows the group. "Oh yeah," he says, "Joe McWilliams's group. He was going to run for Congress on the American Destiny Party but he couldn't get enough signatures to get on the ballot. Formed the Christian Mobilizers, too. You know Joe?"

"Yeah," Denny lies, "we met in New York a couple years ago."

"Good man."

"The best." Denny holds up the flyer. "So your guy, he did this from scratch?"

"You bet. Kid's got talent. Hang on, I'll get his number."

Ken lumbers over to a desk in the corner of the room. It's piled high with invoices. He rummages through it and finds a card. He copies down the information on a sheet of note paper and hands it to Denny.

"Kid's name is Brian Murray," Ken says. "I want to get hold of him, I call this number. Tell him Kenny Boyle sent you."

"Much obliged."

"I run the Michigan chapter of the Christian Mobilizers. You should think about joining us."

"I will," Denny says. "I definitely will."

Denny calls the number Boyle gave him. If he can make contact with the designer, he could get closer to finding out who's behind these.

A squeaky-voiced woman answers the phone.

She says it's the Ford Motor Company advertising department.

She tells Denny Brian Murray is on the other wire at the moment. Would he like to leave a message?

Denny leaves the number of the Wolverine Hotel. Giving the Detroit Police Department line would guarantee he'd never hear back. "And tell him Kenny Boyle said he could help me with it."

"You got it."

68

EVA SZABÓ

[Saturday, June 21, 1941]

She's dressed in her robe in a wheelchair in the courtyard outside the Wyandotte General Hospital. The nurse brought her out here to get some fresh air. It's another hot day; the temperature has been climbing even in the time she's been outside. Fortunately, the nurse who wheeled her out left her in the shade of a towering elm.

Her leg is out of the cast but both it and her head still hurt.

She dozes in the heat.

She dreams.

The tall one, Mutt, comes to her again. In her dream, she has a sharp remembrance: he is asking her a question. The same question over and over.

And when she won't answer again, he's going to hurt her. Again and again.

She screams. She wakes herself up in a full-blown panic. She tries to run but realizes she is buckled into a wheelchair. She begins rocking it from side to side; if she can knock it over, she will have a chance to crawl out and make her escape from the man coming towards her.

"Eva," the man says.

She hides her head in her hands.

Like an ostrich, she thinks.

If I can't see him, then he can't see me.

"Eva."

He reaches out to lay a hand on her shoulder. She is about to scream again but she lifts her head. His face comes into focus. It's Hal Perlman, not one of the men who hurt her so badly.

"It's me. Calm down, okay? I'm not going to hurt you."

He rests the shopping bag he's carrying on the ground and squats down to look her in the eye. "It's me. Okay?"

She reaches out, as if to prove it's really him. He takes her hands and holds them until she comes fully around.

"Oh my," she says. "Oh, Hal, I'm so sorry."

"Another bad dream? Do you need water?"

"I'm okay now. But I remembered another thing. They were asking me questions."

"The men who kidnapped you?"

"Yeah. They were asking me questions—no: one specific question—and I wouldn't answer it. And when I wouldn't, they beat me. But I can't remember what the question was."

Hal puts his arm around her shoulder. She smells the sweet, clovey scent of bay rum on his face. She realizes he has a suit on. He has his wavy hair slicked back.

"Did you hear the news?" he says. "Harry Bennett signed the union agreement yesterday. The men are going to vote to ratify it tomorrow at the State Fair Coliseum."

"Wonderful!"

"I thought so, too. They expect the vote's going to be unanimous to approve."

Best news she's heard in a while. "I bet it will be, too."

She pats his arm, still around her. "I'm glad to see you," she says.

"Ditto."

"What are you all dressed up for?"

"I have a photography shoot today." He pulls away and stands. "And I want you to come with me as my assistant."

"How can I be your assistant? I can't even walk by myself."

"I'll push you. And I can use your wheelchair to tote my camera bags."

"Where's the job?"

"At one of the mansions along Lake Shore Drive in Grosse Pointe

Farms. The guy's some auto bigwig. He's throwing a birthday party for one of his kids. He hired me to photograph it."

"Gee, my father never hired a photographer for me."

"An oversight, I'm sure."

"Yeah."

"It's going to be mostly outside, and I thought it would be a chance to get out of the hospital. And, incidentally, give me a hand. What do you say?"

"I don't know if I'm up to it."

"Only one way to find out."

"And I don't have the right clothes."

"As luck would have it, I bought you some on the way here." He opens the shopping bag and shows her a skirt and blouse. "I guessed on the size. And anyway, you'll be working, not one of the guests. I guarantee you'll look terrif."

She thinks for a moment. She realizes she's afraid to go out in public after what happened to her.

Then she decides it's exactly the reason she should do it. And Hal will be with her . . .

"Can you take me in so I can get changed?" she asks him.

"Your wish is my command," Hal says. He puts the shopping bag with her clothes in her lap and pushes her back into the hospital.

69

CLARENCE BROWN

[Monday, June 23, 1941]

What he finds out about Malone Coleman:
As he suspected, Malone was caught up in the sweep of Hamtramck on Wednesday night. Because of Malone's age, Clarence would have expected him to be sent to the Wayne County Training School. Because of his race, however, the Training School would not accept him. On Saturday morning, Malone is still in the holding cells at the Hamtramck Police Department.

"Has he been processed yet?" Clarence asks the duty sergeant.

The sergeant looks through paperwork on his desk. Says, "Don't see nothing on him."

"You been keeping this boy in the holding cells since Wednesday night and you haven't done anything with him yet? Where are the others you grabbed?"

"Shipped off to the Wayne County Jail. We're waiting for this one to find a bed in a children's center that takes coloreds."

"I'm taking him," Clarence says.

"You run a service home?"

"I run a service home for this kid. You haven't processed him yet, he's walking out with me."

The duty sergeant says, "One less headache. Be my guest."

Malone still won't say anything to Clarence even as Clarence walks him out of the police station.

"All you got to say is thank you," Clarence says. "I don't expect a conversation, but 'thank you' goes a long way."

"I ain't axe you to come get me," Malone says.

Still surly, even after—maybe especially after—his ordeal in jail.

"You rather I left you to rot in there? A colored boy in the Hamtramck jail? You happy with how they been treating you so far?"

Malone has no answer to this.

Clarence drives on in silence.

Finally Malone says, "Where you taking me?"

"Back to your aunt's. She said your mama hasn't come around in a while. You'll be safe there."

Malone's tough reserve melts instantly. "No, Mr. Clarence," he says, "don't take me back there. I won't go back there. Please!"

"Why not?"

"Ain't just my mama I'm scared of. It's the man who stay with her when she come home. He beat me, too."

Clarence pulls the car over.

"I'm not lying, Mr. Clarence, I swear. Please don't make me go back there."

"He beat the other kids, too?"

"No, sir, just me. On account of he say he got to keep me in line."

The boy's shedding real tears.

Is he this good an actor?

Clarence pulls back into traffic.

He takes Malone back to his own house, his wife's question about saving every Negro life in Michigan echoing in his ears.

Bessie is thrilled to see Malone. Malone is equally thrilled to see Bessie. While they have their reunion, hugging and chatting, Clarence feels like he's an outsider, standing there in his suit coat and metal plates.

He leaves them to their own company. He goes back out to the streets, where he feels most comfortable.

It's another scorcher, in the low 90s.

Clarence drives past 975 Beaubien. Where Sonny McGhee lives. And where Clarence found the dead baby.

He beats back the cold fury at Roger Clendening that grips him yet again.

He never found out what happened. Denny Rankin told him he thought a man named Bertrand Vogelmann left the child in the building. He hasn't had time to follow up on it, between taking care of Bessie and his job and Malone . . . and the hundred other things that come between us and our plans.

He stops at a call box. Gets through to Rankin. "Hey," he says, "remember the name you gave me, Bertrand Vogelmann? Who maybe left the baby's body?"

"Did you find him?"

"I was about to ask you."

"No, he's gone to ground," Denny says. "Elizabeth said she thought she saw him the other night in Hamtramck. Let me try to run it down and let you know."

They agree to get in touch later.

Clarence continues his patrol.

He gets a call on his radio car. Shooting at Washington's Market, corner of St. Antoine and Brewster.

He speeds down the streets, afraid for what he will find. Remembers Darron Cummings's chilling last words to the grocer who helped Clarence nab the young thief: *I'll get you for this.*

An ambulance takes off as he pulls to a stop. The store window is blown out, the shards of shattered glass sprinkled over the apples and oranges in the bins out front.

Clarence runs into the store.

He doesn't see what he fears. Darron Cummings is nowhere in sight. Sidney Washington stands off to the side talking with a uniformed officer. The old grocer sobs.

"Mr. Washington," Clarence says. "What happened?"

"Mr. Clarence," Sidney gets out, but he can't get any further.

Clarence turns to the bluesuit for an explanation.

The cop says, "Grocer's behind the counter, Darron Cummings comes in with a shotgun. Tells Washington he's going to drop him for turning him in. Washington pulls a pistol from under the counter and takes a shot at Darron first."

Sidney seems to be in one piece except for being shaken up. "Did he get him?" Clarence asks.

Sidney buries his face in his hands.

The cop says, "Missed him. Darron shoots back and accidently plugs the grocer's kid."

Not the young man with the wide smile. Ernest, his name was.

"How is he?" Clarence asks, not wanting to hear.

The cop shakes his head.

"Where's Darron now?"

"Gone with the wind."

70

ELIZABETH WATERS

[Monday, June 23, 1941]

When she gets to her office, the answering service has a surprise for her.

Congressman Rudolph Tenerowicz returned her call. It came in an hour ago. He's in his Detroit office. There may still be a chance to reach him.

She catches him in.

"Miss Waters," he says. "How can I help?"

He's had a checkered career: a medical doctor, he was the mayor of Hamtramck in the early thirties until he was indicted for vice conspiracy and served time in prison. When he was pardoned by the governor of Michigan, he was elected mayor again. And now he's a congressman. As with Hamtramck's current mayor, a stretch in the slammer is good preparation for being a Hamtramck politician.

"Thanks for returning my call, Dr. Tenerowicz. I'm calling as a concerned citizen for a couple of reasons."

"Always happy to listen to a citizen."

"There's a scheme in the works to derail the federal defense worker housing for Negroes in Detroit."

"What do you mean, derail?"

"The same people causing trouble in Hamtramck are going to make sure Negroes never move into the new housing units."

He stays quiet for a few moments. Then he says, "Have you ever heard of the neighborhood composition rule?"

"No," she says.

"It's a guideline from Harold Ickes. The Interior Secretary. It says new federally-funded housing projects have to maintain the racial balance of the areas where the housing goes. In white neighborhoods, the housing has to be for whites only. In Negro areas, the housing should be for Negroes. In mixed areas, the housing can be designated as mixed. In theory.

"In practice, mixed housing is never really mixed. It's dedicated to either white or Negro families. The area the housing authority picked for the new housing in Detroit is between a white Polish neighborhood and a nearby Negro area. If it's designated for Negroes then the Poles are going to be upset. Things are going to get ugly very quickly."

The National Workers League, Elizabeth thinks, wants to make sure the new housing doesn't go to Negro workers and their families even though it's already been decided. As Alderman said, they're going to do everything they can to make sure Negroes don't move near a white neighborhood.

"Thanks," Elizabeth says. "That's helpful."

"My pleasure."

"So I'm telling you about this group's plans to disrupt the project?"

"Yes?"

"My question is, what can you do about it? How can we make sure this group doesn't stop the development?"

"Miss Waters," Tenerowicz says, "what if I told you the plan to house colored people in the defense housing project in the proposed location is being objected to by Negroes themselves?"

"I don't understand."

"Just today," he says, "I received a letter—a very impassioned letter—from the Negroes who live in Conant Gardens. As you may know, that's near where the Federal Housing Authority in their wisdom chose to put the new housing."

Conant Gardens, one of the few other places in Detroit besides Black Bottom and Paradise Valley where Negroes can live.

"The members of the Conant Gardens Community Association are worried new Negro housing so close to their homes will lower their property values. They're afraid that will stop any money coming in to build new homes in the area."

"What are you saying? They don't want the housing units built there either?"

"It's not the building of the units they object to. The problem is designating them as Negro housing."

Now it's Elizabeth's turn to be silent as she tries to grasp this.

"Just let me get this straight," she says. "I'm telling you the Ku Klux Klan and others are planning to disrupt the future building of housing for Negro defense workers, and you're telling me you're not only okay with it, but you agree they should do it?"

"I'm just telling you how the situation stands right now. I'm not convinced the Housing Authority's decision is final. It's possible Negroes won't be moving into the new housing project after all. If so, the trouble you're warning me about will never happen."

"But—"

"Look, miss, my schedule is full this morning. If you have any more information for me, please let my aides in the Detroit office know. Thank you for your interest."

He hangs up.

Translation into plain English:

Miss Waters, fuck you and the horse you rode in on.

Tom's Quality Meats. 12th Street and Forest in Detroit. The store where Anton Luedke said Carmine Sant'angelo works.

A small grocery store. Busy, with women doing their daily shopping. Elizabeth goes to the meat counter, which at this hour is two deep with shoppers. An array of meats, pinkish-red flesh and pale ecru bones fill up the shelves behind the counter glass.

Behind the meat counter is an open doorway. It leads into the rear section, where the meat locker would be.

She goes back outside the store. Walks around the block to the alley. She sees a Star Bakery Shop truck parked behind Tom's. The driver loads a handcart with loaves of braided bread and cinnamon pastries from the back of the truck.

Elizabeth peeks into the rear of the store. The meat locker appears to be on the right, a room with insulated walls and a heavy metal door.

She continues inside. Acts like she belongs there. Workers

bustling around nod to her.

In for a penny, in for a pound . . . she walks over to what she assumes is the meat locker. Opens it and looks inside. A blast of cold air hits her, along with the rich, bloody smell of beef and pork.

"Hey—what are you doing?"

A short man in a butcher's apron approaches her. "Who are you?" he says. "What are you doing here?"

He's built like a fire plug. He stands with his hands on his hips, challenging her. The name "Tom" is embroidered in script on the bib of his apron. Is he the Tom who owns the place?

"I'm looking for Carmine Sant'angelo," she says.

"What makes you think you'll find him in there?"

"I heard he was a butcher here."

"He ain't. I dunno nobody named Carmine Sant'angelo. Who'd you say you were?"

"A friend of his. He told me he worked here and I was passing by."

"You better pass right on out again," the guy in the apron says.

He stands watching her, making sure she leaves the premises.

She walks back around to the front of the store, where she left her car. She only got a brief glimpse of the meat locker, but she saw enough to doubt what Eva had told her. The locker was small, for one thing, without enough space to allow two men and a woman tied to a chair. It was also filled from wall to wall with hanging carcasses of beef. Again, there would be no room for two men and a chair.

Of course, this might not be where they held her. Elizabeth remembers Tom's might have another store.

She goes inside the store and leans over to ask the cashier, "Is there another Tom's location?"

"There is, honey," the cashier says. "On Kercheval. Over there on the east side."

Elizabeth parks across Kercheval from the grocery. This store is bigger and newer than the original place on 12th Street. She decides to try her rear-door ploy again. She goes around to the back. The large receiving door stands open in the heat.

The layout is similar to the other Tom's. The bustle around the storeroom is the same: workers shuttling crates of fruit and vegetables on hand trucks. Different faces, though.

She strides in, nodding to the workers who pass her. The meat locker is in the same place as in the other store. She takes a quick look around and unlatches the door.

Another blast of cold air. This locker is larger than the other store's. Sides of beef hang on hooks, but there is an open space in the center of the locker with a butcher's block.

A folding chair leans against one wall. She pulls it into the center of the room. Yes, there would be room for the chair and two men, as well as the butcher block cutting board.

But why would they bring Eva all the way over here? And why keep her in the meat locker?

She lets herself out of the chilly room. Wanders around the back room. Sees a timeclock beside timecards in a holder. Rifles through the timecards.

Sees one for Carmine Sant'angelo.

Who turns out to have been working during the late evening of June 11th. In fact, as she studies the timecard, she sees he was working overnight. He seems to work overnight quite a bit. Maybe it's when he gets the meat cutting done for next day at the store.

He could have picked up Eva at the Rouge plant and taken her directly here.

Why would he do that? Assuming Mickey Smith and Carmine Sant'angelo snatched her from the demonstration at the Ford Rouge plant, they wouldn't have taken her right here while the store was open. What would be the purpose of taking her here? And what was the purpose of snatching her in the first place?

She hears men's voices outside the locker. She hurries out. Goes around to the front of the store. Asks the cashier, "Is Carmine Sant'angelo in today?"

"No," the cashier says, "he only works overnights."

Overnights . . . when the store is closed.

Elizabeth asks, "Are you open on the weekends?"

"Closed Saturday and Sunday," the cashier says.

Eva was snatched on Friday . . . that means she could have been kept here Friday night through Monday morning and no one would know.

71

DENNY RANKIN

[Monday, June 23, 1941]

On his way out of the Wolverine Hotel in the morning, the desk clerk waves him over.

"Message for you, Mr. Rankin."

The clerk hands Denny a phone message slip. Brian Murray, the pro-Nazi graphic designer. It's a different number than his office. He must be calling from home.

The call came through fifteen minutes ago. Denny trots out to the phone booth on the corner. Brian picks up right away.

"Brian," Denny says. "Denny Rankin. We connect at last."

"Finally," Brian says. "You got my number from Kenny Boyle?" Light voice, high, girlish.

"Yeah. He said you might be able to help me."

"What's going on?"

"I got hold of a pamphlet, shows a Jew in the middle of octopus tentacles. Boyle says it's your work."

"One of my better ones, if I do say so myself."

"It's brilliant. I was thinking of a similar piece. How the Jews are pushing us to war to save their brethren in Europe."

"Tell you what, I hope Hitler finishes the job first."

Denny lets the comment go by. "I have a rough version of what I had in mind. I sketched it out. Can you design it and lay it out?"

"When do you need it by?"

"Soon as possible."

"Can't," Brian says. "Nothing personal. Right before you called, I got off the phone with a pal of mine. He's got a rush job for me, and he's a steady client."

"What's the job?"

"There's a community meeting tomorrow about a public housing project for spades in Detroit. The spades who already live in the area called the meeting and invited all the white homeowners around where they want to put the housing. They think because they have something in common, they're all going to get along. Good luck with that! So my pal's group wants to make sure the whites are represented at the meeting. I'm putting together a flyer for them to get the word out."

"I might be interested in this," Denny says. "What's the group?"

"The National Workers League. They're trying to bring together a group of white homeowners to torpedo this project. Or at the least move it to another part of town."

Denny says, "I'm definitely interested. Where is it?"

"Pershing High School. In Detroit."

"Who's the guy you're doing it for?"

"Guy named Bert Vogelmann. He don't run the group, he's just part of it. So yeah, so, anyway," Brian says, "I'm not going to be able to take on any outside work just now. Maybe call me next week?"

"Count on it, Brian. Thanks."

Again Vogelmann's name surfaces.

Denny goes to Vogelmann's house on Bewick. Seems like he's been here half a dozen times already. Again no one answers his knock.

This time he tries the neighbors on either side of Vogelmann and the ones across the street. Next to Vogelmann's house an old man in a sleeveless undershirt shuffles to the door in carpet slippers.

Says he doesn't know who Vogelmann is. Hasn't seen anybody go in or out of the house next door. Can't help.

Denny goes to three houses on either side of Vogelmann's, and the ones across the street from his house. Same story. Oldsters shuffle to the door. Don't know Vogelmann. Can't help.

Who else might know where Vogelmann is?

He can think of at least one young woman.

First he needs to make a call. Elizabeth Waters would want to know about the meeting at Pershing. He calls her number, but gets her answering service. He leaves the information, time and place. Says he hopes to see her there.

Lena Wheaton answers the door in Redford. Denny sees a range of emotions cross her face: surprise, concern, apprehension. She finally settles on annoyance.

He asks, "Can I come in?"

She hesitates a moment too long, which tells him she really doesn't want him to come in. But she steps aside for him to enter.

He follows her into the kitchen. The house is quiet. Her husband's car is gone from the driveway.

"Phil's not home," Lena says.

"Actually I'm here to speak with Charlotte."

"Well, there's a slight problem."

"Okay."

"She's gone again."

"Define gone."

"She's not here. She's somewhere else. I got up yesterday and when she never came downstairs, I went to wake her and she wasn't in her room. She hadn't slept in her bed."

"And you haven't seen her since . . . ?"

"Not since Sunday night. We all listened to the radio together and she went to bed. She wasn't here in the morning."

"She didn't say anything to you or Phil?"

"Not a word."

"Any idea where she might be?"

"I had to guess, I'd guess she's with Bert Vogelmann. But I couldn't begin to say where."

"I just left his house. Nobody was there."

"Then I don't know where she is."

"You don't seem terribly upset by this."

"What's to be upset about, Denny? If she's just going to keep running away to be with this boy, I'm not going to stop her. Short of locking her in her bedroom, which I'm not about to do."

He goes to the Mueller house. Easter tells him no one else is home.

He says, "Have you seen Bert Vogelmann in the last couple days?"

"No."

"Where are Heinz and Wanda?"

"Who knows?"

Her tone says she doesn't care, either.

It seems like everyone is getting fed up with the antics of all these kids, Denny thinks.

He goes out to his unmarked. He is about to head toward the home of Charlotte's Cass Tech friend Janice Malinowski when a call comes through his car squawk box.

"Armed robbery," the dispatcher says. "Willis Theatre, Willis and Hastings. See the manager."

Vogelmann will have to wait.

The Willis Theatre is on Hastings Street in Black Bottom. By the time Denny gets there, an ambulance crew tends to a Negro man sitting in the back of the ambulance with a white cloth around his head.

Denny pushes through the neighborhood onlookers. The medical team has already taken care of the man's medical injuries. They don't look severe. Abrasions, cuts on his forearm and face. Split lip.

Denny says to one of the uniforms, "Where's the manager?"

The uniform points out a round butterball of a man standing outside the foyer. He's a white man in a shiny black suit with a black bow tie and a heavily starched white shirt over a bulging belly.

Denny goes up to him. Shows him his badge, says, "Detective Sergeant Denny Rankin."

The man says, "Howdy. Keith Musser." White hair, tremulous jowls. Clicking his false teeth nervously.

Denny says, "What can you tell me about what happened here?"

Musser points to the ambulance. "That feller there? My assistant manager. I sent him around the corner with fifty bucks in bills and told him to bring back change—small bills, rolls of quarters and dimes and nickels."

"From where?"

"The Club Three Sixes. Robinhood Rowe owns it."

Denny knows him. A local gangster.

Before Musser can continue, another car pulls up. Clarence Brown gets out. He approaches Denny and Musser. Nods to Denny, says, "Keith" to Musser.

Musser says, "Mr. Clarence."

Of course they know each other, Denny thinks. This has been Clarence's patch for years. He must know most people.

"I heard the call on the radio," Clarence says to Denny.

Denny catches Clarence up on what Musser has just told him.

"Like I was saying," Musser continues, "we have an arrangement with Robinhood. When we need change, he helps us out. On the way over there, my guy got jumped by a guy with a gun. The guy pistol whips him and steals the money."

"Do you know who did it?" Denny asks.

"No, but the ticket taker saw it happen," Musser says. "It was right after the show opened today. Raymond—he's my ticket taker—was looking out the front of the theatre. He saw the whole thing."

"I'll speak to him," Clarence says, and heads inside the theatre.

Denny goes over to the ambulance where the assistant manager sits.

"How you doing, buddy?" Denny asks.

"Been better," the assistant manager says.

"I'm Detective Rankin, Detroit PD."

"Melvin Montgomery."

They shake.

"What happened here, Melvin?"

The assistant manager is shaken, but he tells the same story as Musser.

"Do you know who did this?" Denny asks.

"No sir."

"Would you recognize him if you saw him?"

"Sure would."

"Okay. We'll ask you for an ID once we nab him. You're sure you don't need to go to the hospital?"

"Positive."

Denny goes inside the theatre lobby. Inhales the aroma of popcorn from the candy counter.

The ticket taker Raymond stands at the ticket box. He's a big hulking white man shifting from foot to foot. "Hello," he says with a high piping voice. "Welcome to the Willis."

Denny continues into the foyer. There Clarence stands at the candy counter, listening to two girls, Negro teenagers in pink striped uniforms and aprons. One looks ready to break into tears.

Clarence spies Denny and excuses himself. Walks Denny into the lobby.

Clarence says, "One of the candy girls IDed the thief. He's her boyfriend. She told him the assistant manager makes regular runs to get change and the boyfriend decided to hijack him."

"Let me guess. The one who's near tears."

"That's her."

"You got his name?"

"Turns out it's a bum I know. Guy named Darron Cummings."

"The candy girl gave it up so fast? You make this detective thing look easy."

"I got him in my sights for a few other things. Found anything about Vogelmann?"

Denny tells him about Charlotte Wheaton's latest disappearance. "I have a few ideas about how to find him," Denny says. "Pretty sure he's with a girl named Charlotte Wheaton. You know Phil Wheaton?"

"I do."

"Charlotte's his daughter."

"Small world."

"We find her, we find Bert Vogelmann. How about we meet up tomorrow and we'll track down this mug? Get answers to both our questions."

"Sounds like a plan," Clarence says. "Meantime, I'll keep after Darron."

72

EVA SZABÓ

[Tuesday, June 24, 1941]

Another dream.

Or nightmare, as the case may be.

She is back in the meat locker. She sees the two men who abducted her.

She hears the question they asked her over and over.

She pops awake, remembering what they asked her.

She has to tell Elizabeth about it.

She wheels herself down to the nurses' station to use their telephone. She calls Elizabeth's home number. No answer. She calls Elizabeth's office number.

The answering service picks up. Eva leaves a message to call her as soon as possible. "Tell her I remembered something important."

Hal Perlman stops by to see her after lunch. Elizabeth has not called back.

He says, "Feel like being a photographer's assistant again?"

"Where?"

"There's a community meeting tonight to talk about housing for Negro defense workers. I thought I'd go, take photos on spec, maybe sell them to *Life* or *Colliers*. I could use your help."

"I don't know."

"I guarantee it'll be more interesting than a little rich girl's birthday party."

He waits for her answer, eyebrows raised.

He's cute, Eva thinks. So earnest. And I did have fun the other day.

But she's waiting for Elizabeth to call.

"I better not," she says. "I'm waiting for a call."

"This thing isn't until tonight. What do you say?"

She thinks more about it. She thinks Elizabeth will call back before then. And she doesn't want to give up the chance to spend more time with him. Says, "Okay. You convinced me."

"Great," Hal says. "I'll be back to get you around seven."

73

CLARENCE BROWN

[Tuesday, June 24, 1941]

Clarence and Denny are both tied up with case paperwork until afternoon, so they meet for a late lunch at Tipton's Luncheonette. Denny orders the blue plate special, corned beef hash and coffee. Clarence gets a Coca-Cola.

Miss Etta greets Denny with a smile.

Clarence says, "She doesn't show that smile to everyone."

"Must be my natural charm."

Clarence snorts. "Nobody got that much charm. Miss Etta's a tough cookie."

Denny's food comes immediately and he digs in.

"Here's my thought," he says between bites. "Last time Charlotte was missing, she was shacked up with Bert Vogelmann. I'm thinking they're together again. We'll try the place where I found her last time, and go from there."

From Tipton's they head into Hamtramck. The city is quieter today than the last time they were here. You wouldn't know from the calm pedestrian traffic on the sidewalks there was a race riot, unless you drove down the street where it happened and saw the ragged aftermath.

They pull up in front of the Evaline Street house, off Joseph Campau. A haggard white woman in a floral apron answers the door. She gives Clarence the eye. For a moment he forgot he's the enemy; she reminds him.

Denny introduces them both, asks who she is. She says she's Mrs. Malinowski. Denny says, "We're looking for your daughter, Janice. Is she here?"

"No. She should be in school. Why? Is everything alright?"

"Do you know Charlotte Wheaton?"

"Sure. Why?"

"When was the last time you saw her?"

"Ah jeez," the woman says, "not for a while."

Denny thanks her and he and Clarence start off. "Wait," she says, "are you sure everything's okay?"

Clarence turns. "Nothing to worry about," he says. The look on her face—this nigger is speaking to *me*?!—gives him a chuckle.

They check Hooky's flop and Bert Vogelmann's house. They come up empty both places.

Denny takes the lead again in the office at Cass Technical High School. "We're looking for a student, Janice Malinowski," he says. "Is she in school today?"

Clarence is reminded that Denny might be different from the others, but he's still a white cop, assuming he's in charge.

The woman shuffles through a pile of attendance cards on her counter. "Let me check attendance."

She gets to the end of the attendance cards. "I don't see her marked absent. Her schedule's up in her counselor's office. Alfred Bracciano. He's in—"

"Any way you could call up for us, save us a trip? This is urgent."

She's not happy about it, but she makes the call. In another minute she puts down the phone. She checks the clock on the wall. "Right now she's in Algebra. Room 412. It's the last class of the day and it's going to be over in ten minutes. Better hurry if you want to catch her."

Clarence and Denny hotfoot it up the stairs. Clarence's metal plates and his age weigh him down; he waves Denny on and trudges up more slowly.

Clarence catches up to Denny, who has gotten lost looking for the room number. Just as they find it, the bell rings. In seconds students fill the hall, anxious to escape their prison.

One of the students rushing out of room 412 is a white girl with blonde bangs. She hugs her notebook and textbook to her chest.

Denny steps in front of her and moves her to the side.

Denny directs her to an empty classroom. He closes the door behind them.

"Remember me?" he says.

"Yeah."

"This is Detective Brown."

She gives Clarence a quick look but keeps her attention on Denny.

"We're looking for Charlotte," Denny says.

"So?"

"So where is she?"

"How should I know?"

"Don't screw us around," Clarence says. He's going to play the heavy. He looms over her. Glowers at her. She seems to shrink under his gaze. Not the first time he has played on white fears.

"I don't know," Janice says. "I'm telling you the truth."

Clarence says, "Then tell us where Bert Vogelmann is."

The name brings a slight narrowing of her eyes. It's her tell; she knows where both of them are, Clarence thinks.

She denies it.

Clarence says, "Janice Malinowski, I'm arresting you for obstruction of justice and harboring a fugitive."

"What!"

Clarence pulls out his cuffs. "Turn around."

When she doesn't move, Clarence says, "Turn around."

She looks at Denny. "Are you going to let him do this to me?"

"I'm not his boss," Denny says.

Clarence clicks the cuffs on her. He tightens them so they are too snug.

"Ow!"

Clarence is enjoying this.

"Why are you doing this to me? I haven't done anything!"

"But you know where Charlotte is," Denny says.

"If I tell you where they are, will you let me go?"

"Got no time to bargain," Clarence says. He takes her arm and pulls her to the classroom door.

"No, wait," she says. "I do know where they are. Charlotte and Bert."

Clarence makes a big show of not wanting to stop.

"She's at the Leonhardts'," Janice says.

"Where's that?" Clarence asks.

"I know the place," Denny tells Clarence. "It's a rooming house. I tailed a guy there one day. The FBI has it under surveillance."

Clarence says, "What for?"

"It's the center of a German spying operation. Charlotte and Bert Vogelmann are both there?"

Janice says, "Yes."

"Why?"

"They're laying low until they can leave."

"Leave town?"

"Yeah."

"Why?"

"Look, I really don't know," Janice says. "Please. I'm telling you the truth."

"You better be," Clarence says.

It's all he can do to keep from smiling at the look of fear on her face.

74

ELIZABETH WATERS

[Tuesday, June 24, 1941]

She gets her answering service messages when she gets back to her office in late afternoon. She sorts through them, separating the urgent from the informational messages—until she gets to Eva's and Denny's.

The answering service transcribed Eva's:

> *Eva Szabó called. She remembered something important. Please call her as soon as you can.*

She tries calling the nurses' station at the hospital, but the phone rings and rings.

She hangs up. Paces around her office for five minutes. Tries again.

This time she gets through.

"Hi," Elizabeth says, "I'm trying to get in touch with Eva Szabó."

"Oh," a nurse says, "she's gone out with her beau."

"Her what?"

"The young man who comes to visit her. He took her out yesterday, too. She came back all flushed and sunburned. She said it was because she was sitting outside, but I think it was because of her young man. He certainly does like her."

"Did she say where they were going, by any chance?"

"When patients leave, they have to sign out with their destination. Let me see if she remembered to."

Elizabeth hears her put the phone down. Footsteps and the turning of pages in a notebook.

Footsteps returning.

"No," the nurse says. "She must have forgotten to sign out. Sorry."

Then Denny's message, as transcribed by the answering service:

> *Meeting tonight about the defense worker housing project—disputes about where it goes because it's for Negroes. Pershing High School, Detroit, 8:45 pm. Thought you'd be interested.*

Oh, I am, she thinks.

I am.

75

DENNY RANKIN

[Tuesday, June 24, 1941]

On the way to Garland Street, Denny tells Clarence about his run-in with the FBI the last time he was there.

Clarence says, "So we can expect to see them again today?"

"I wouldn't be surprised."

When they get to the rooming house, no cars are on the street. No watchers anywhere either detective could see, up or down the block.

"Guess the G-men are taking a break," Denny says.

A spare, stern woman answers their knock. Mid-50s, large wire-rimmed glasses. She gives the two detectives on her porch the once-over. "Yah?"

Denny identifies them. They flash their badges. "Emma Leonhardt?"

"Yah?"

"May we come in?"

"For what reason?" Heavy German accent.

Before Denny can respond, a man appears behind her in the hall. Tall, military haircut, ramrod straight. Denny expects him to click his heels.

"Carl John Heinz Leonhardt?" Denny asks.

The man says, "I don't have to tell you. What is this about?"

"These men are policemen," the woman says. "They want to come in."

"I'm looking for a young woman named Charlotte Wheaton and a man named Bert Vogelmann," Denny says. "Are they here?"

"There is no one here by either of those names," the tall guy says. "Goodbye."

He pulls his wife away from the door so he can close it.

Denny reaches a hand out to keep the door open.

"Charlotte Wheaton is a minor child," Denny says. "If you're harboring her, I will arrest you on a charge of unlawful imprisonment of a minor. That's a federal felony. Vogelmann is a fugitive. I will also arrest you for harboring a fugitive from justice."

The man and woman have a brief argument in German.

Finally, the woman opens the door. "Come. She's upstairs."

"You may not enter this house," the man cries. "I know my rights as an American citizen."

"Those rights you and your Nazi pals are trying to overthrow?" Denny says.

Mrs. Leonhardt elbows her husband out of the way and steps aside for them to enter.

Her husband shouts, "I'm calling my attorney."

"Knock yourself out." To Leonhardt's wife, Denny says, "Where?"

"Two A, second floor."

Denny leads the way up. Raps at the door. He hears rustling inside, like the scurrying of mice. He tries the doorknob. It won't turn.

He rears back and shoulders in the door.

Behind him, Mrs. Leonhardt says, "Hey!"

Charlotte Wheaton and Wanda Mueller sit together on the unmade bed.

The room is small, with space enough only for the twin bed, a makeshift sleeping pallet on the floor, and a dresser with a basin for water. Clarence looks around, points a thumb out the door. Denny nods; he's going to check the rest of the house.

"What are you doing here?" he asks Wanda.

"Hiding out from my family," she says.

"Is this where you brought her the other day?" Denny asks Charlotte.

She nods. "Did you follow us? You said you wouldn't."

"I didn't. Do you know what this place is? It's filled with Nazi spies and collaborators."

"We know," Charlotte says.

"And you're okay with that?"

She gives a defiant nod. He says, "I can't let you stay here."

"You can't make me go back."

"And I refuse to go home," Wanda says.

"Where's Bert Vogelmann?"

The two young women share a look. Denny gets a chill down his back from the intense silent communication that flows between them.

To Charlotte, Wanda says, "We have to tell him."

Denny says, "Tell me what? What's he up to?"

"Never mind," Charlotte says. "We'll tell you where he went if you don't give us up."

"I'm almost twenty," Wanda says. "Charlotte can stay with me."

"She's not your legal guardian," Denny says.

"Then we won't tell you where Bert is," Charlotte says.

"Fine," Denny says. "I'm arresting you both for obstructing police and abetting a fugitive."

"What fugitive?" Charlotte says.

"Bertrand Vogelmann. He's wanted for Burglary-Forced Entry, Statutory Rape, and Kidnapping."

"That's all bullshit!"

"Then help me find him and prove it's bullshit. Especially if he's going to get in even more trouble."

Wanda says, "Charlotte, you have to."

Charlotte stays mum.

Denny says, "Wanda, where is he?"

She pipes up, "He went to shoot my brother."

"Where?"

"He's supposed to meet Heinz at a meeting at some high school in Detroit."

"Pershing?"

"Yeah," Charlotte says. "That's the one."

76

EVA SZABÓ

[Tuesday, June 24, 1941]

Several hundred people fill the Pershing High School auditorium on the east side of Detroit. Negroes sit on one side of the center aisle. On the other side are more numerous and more rancorous whites.

Hal Perlman parks Eva in her wheelchair in the rear of the auditorium, out of traffic lanes. He has hung his camera bag on the back of her wheelchair; she sits with his tripod across her lap. He begins wandering the theatre, taking photographs.

The people who run the meeting are members of the Conant Gardens Community Association. On the way to the school, Hal gave Eva the background. Conant Gardens is a middle-class Negro section. The United State Housing Authority had authorized housing units for Negro defense workers to be built between Conant Gardens and an all-white Polish community, St. Louis the King Parish.

Neither the Negroes nor the whites want the housing project built. The Negroes fear their home values would decline so near to what they believe will be temporary housing that would draw pool-halls, bars, crime, and prostitution, which would make it even harder to obtain home loans. The whites are concerned about the housing project because they do not want Negroes living so close to them under any circumstances.

Hal told her it was going to be an interesting meeting.

She thinks that's probably an understatement.

The shouting begins as soon as the Conant Gardens Community Association calls the meeting to order. One white man after another stands and shouts out their objections to the project. The men who run the meeting ask the crowd to behave civilly. Sitting behind a table on the stage framed by a proscenium arch, they ask for people to wait to be called on.

Nobody obeys.

One white man stands up and shouts he's a real estate agent and owns a thousand homes in the area and he says the value of the property, and the ability of the homeowners to get FHA loans, will take a nose dive with colored people living so close.

When a priest stands up, the whites quiet down. People seem to recognize him and let him speak.

A murmur goes through the crowd: "Father—it's Father—"

He starts to talk, calmly and apparently reasonably.

"I am Father Constantine Dzink," he says, "pastor of the St. Louis the King Parish Church. We're here this evening because the United States Housing Authority and the Detroit Housing Commission want to build a low-cost housing project near Fenelon and Nevada Streets. This project will be for use by colored people. I am convinced that project would mean utter ruin for many who have mortgaged their home to the FHA."

An angry murmur goes through the white crowd.

Father Dzink raises his hands for silence.

"In addition," he continues, "I have spent many sleepless nights since the endorsement of this project . . . most particularly worried for the safety of our many white girls, since no colored presently live nearby."

Now the Negro section gets restive.

"Finally," Father Dzink says over their protests, "this project would ruin the neighborhood, which could be built into a fine residential area instead of a project guaranteed to promote race riots in the foreseeable future. Make no mistake: It's the Jew and the colored behind this, not the friends and neighbors gathered here tonight."

Dzink sits down to applause.

This brings an angry chorus from the Negroes. The whites meet it with more shouting.

A tall white man stands. "Keep our neighborhood white!" he

cries above the din. "Which means no niggers allowed!"

To Eva's horror, she recognizes the man. It is Mutt. From her nightmares.

The man who tortured her until she gave them what they wanted . . . the name of the person who hired Eva to be a union spy at the Rouge plant. It was the question she had finally remembered from her dream, and the reason she had called Elizabeth earlier today.

At first she resisted them, but when they persisted in hurting her, to her everlasting shame she gave up Elizabeth's name.

She had wanted to confess to Elizabeth . . . she, Eva, betrayed the woman who was trying so hard to help her.

She sees Mutt because he's tall. From where she's sitting, she can't see above the seated crowd to know if his partner Jeff is with him.

I can't stay here, she tells herself.

Now that she knows Mutt is here, she has to escape.

She wheels herself out from the rear corner where Hal has stashed her.

With difficulty she negotiates the heavy swinging doors to the outer hallway. She halts beside the school trophy case in the hall and catches her breath.

All the while keeping an eye on the auditorium doors.

77

CLARENCE BROWN

[Tuesday, June 24, 1941]

All along the streets leading to Pershing High School, Clarence sees posters nailed to light poles:

There will be a meeting of all residents of the Conant area Tuesday, June 24, 8:45, Pershing High School.
We are meeting to further the protest on the proposed location of homes for defense workers near Atkinson School.
Time is vital and we must act at once if we are to protect our home investments.
Come out Tuesday and be on time.

The school is massive, three stories covering a city block with an ell-shaped projection on either side. Signs point Clarence and Denny toward the auditorium inside the building. It is a huge theatre holding several hundred people, Negro and white. The races are on opposite sides of the seating area, separated by a center aisle.

Yelling and name-calling have already begun.

Denny gives Clarence photos of Heinz Mueller and Bertrand Franz Vogelmann. Clarence goes down one side aisle to the front of the house. Denny takes the other side aisle.

They work their way down the aisles, scanning the crowd in the white section for either Heinz or Bertrand.

They walk back up to the rear of the auditorium.

Clarence attracts the white crowd's hostility like a magnet. He hears all the names: nigger, spook, jigaboo, spade, smoke. They scream at him to go back to Africa.

Clarence lets it all roll off his back. It's not easy to do with furious white faces popping up like jacks-in-the-box as he goes up the aisle. He keeps his face impassive and focuses on finding either of the two men in the photographs Denny gave him.

He and Denny reconnect at the rear of the auditorium. "Did you see Heinz?" Denny asks.

"No. Let's switch aisles and do one more walk-through."

Clarence takes the aisle Denny first went down, and Denny takes his. A whole new set of abuse comes his way.

Still no sign of the two men.

Clarence and Denny meet up again at the back. "I still don't see them," Clarence says. "Let's go outside. If they're not here yet, maybe we can spot them as they come."

They go through the lobby lined with trophy cases. Outside, traces of lilac-hued light remain in the sky at nine o'clock. The air is cooling after another hot day; it feels good to be out, away from the angry atmosphere in the auditorium.

There are two entrances to the building. Denny says, "I'll take this entrance. How about you take the one over there? Whichever way Heinz comes, in or out, we'll get him."

Clarence agrees. He stands inside the doorway. He can still hear muffled shouting from the auditorium.

The high school is on Ryan Road, near the Conant Gardens community. Clarence sees a car pull to the curb on Ryan near the school. A figure gets out and fast-walks toward the high school.

Clarence consults the photo Denny gave him and sees this is Heinz Mueller, heading for the entrance where Clarence waits.

Another man, tall, in a short-sleeved khaki work shirt and a French sailor's beret, steps out from behind a corner of the building near where Denny Rankin stands.

Bertrand Vogelmann.

He rushes out pointing the long thin barrel of a handgun at Heinz.

Before Clarence or Denny can react, Bert Vogelmann fires.

Heinz goes down.

78

ELIZABETH WATERS

[Tuesday, June 24, 1941]

The behavior of the whites in the auditorium is shameful. They stand and shout racial slurs at the Negroes.

She sees two men walking down the side aisles, scanning the crowd. Denny Rankin and Clarence Brown. They're looking for someone.

They switch aisles and make the long walk down the auditorium aisles and back again.

Clarence absorbs all the racial hatred flung at him with steady grace.

Elizabeth sees a photographer flitting around, taking photographs of the speakers and the crowd. She recognizes him as the young man who was chased out of the National Workers League meeting.

At one point, a priest stands and holds his arms up for quiet. He is evidently known to most of the crowd of whites, as they shush as soon as he stands. He identifies himself as the Reverend Constantine Dzink, pastor of the St. Louis the King Parish Church.

She can't make out much of his remarks, but she does hear him say the Jews and coloreds are joining to break up their neighborhood.

Nothing says Christian fellowship like a nice hearty dose of old-world racism and anti-Semitism.

She listens for a few more minutes, then rises to leave the auditorium. What she hears from the whites in the crowd makes her feel dirty and ashamed of being a white woman in Detroit.

She goes out to the lobby.

She doesn't see the short, thick man standing off to the side at the front of the auditorium, watching her leave the theatre. Then following her up the aisle.

79

DENNY RANKIN

[Tuesday, June 24, 1941]

Heinz cries out.

Vogelmann's gunshot hits Heinz in the belly and doubles him over on the sidewalk.

Denny bursts out the door of his entrance. "Bert!"

He rushes at Vogelmann.

Out of the corner of his eye, Denny sees Clarence spill out of the entrance to the doorway where he waits. Awkward in his armor, he makes his way toward Heinz.

Vogelmann turns his gun on Denny. Fires. The shots go wide. Denny hears them chink off the brick on the brick wall behind him.

Denny runs toward Vogelmann. He goes low and knocks Vogelmann off his feet.

Denny is back up at once and jumps on top of the other man. Vogelmann thrashes. He tries to raise his gun hand.

Denny registers Vogelmann holding a Walther P38.

That sweet little weapon.

Denny leans his knee on the gun and shoves his .38 into Vogelmann's face.

"Drop it or you're dead," Denny breathes.

80

EVA SZABÓ

[Tuesday, June 24, 1941]

Elizabeth Waters hurries out of the auditorium. She rushes by Eva sitting in the hall. Elizabeth doesn't see her as she makes for the exit door.

A man follows Elizabeth.

It's Jeff. Pointing a gun at her.

"Elizabeth," Eva cries, *"look out!"*

Eva darts forward in her wheelchair and with all her strength swings Hal's tripod at Jeff's head.

It knocks Jeff to the ground. Jeff's gun goes off and shatters the glass door leading outside.

Jeff recovers quickly and turns the gun on Eva but Elizabeth yells, "Hey!" to draw his fire. She dives out the empty doorway.

Jeff struggles to his feet and fires off another round at Elizabeth.

81

CLARENCE BROWN

[Tuesday, June 24, 1941]

"*Elizabeth—look out!*"

Where did that voice come from?

Clarence is half-way to Heinz lying on the sidewalk when he hears the woman's shout from inside the school.

It's followed by a gunshot and the crash of glass shattering.

Then another gunshot and a pounding on his back as though he has been hit with a baseball bat on his metal plates.

It takes the wind out of him and sends him to his knees.

He turns toward where the shots are coming from, inside the school.

He pulls his .45s. Scopes out the situation in a half-second. Sees Elizabeth Waters dashing away from the school and a short stout white man shooting at her.

Clarence aims at the short man.

Fires.

82

ELIZABETH WATERS

[Tuesday, June 24, 1941]

"*Elizabeth—look out!*"

Elizabeth barely hears it over the unruly yelling in the auditorium behind her. But she clocks it as Eva's voice.

She turns. Sees a man—Jeff, Carmine Sant'angelo, she realizes—coming at her, holding a gun. She sees Eva Szabó rolling her wheelchair toward him. Sees Eva clock him with something long and thin.

Sees him turn and point his gun at Eva.

She makes an instantaneous calculation: Carmine is after Elizabeth, not Eva. Elizabeth yells, "Hey!" and jumps through the school entrance door to draw his fire.

She makes it outside. From inside the foyer Carmine shoots at her. He steps through the empty doorframe. He fires again.

Elizabeth stops, hits the ground. Grabs her .22 from her purse.

Before she can get a shot off at Jeff, she hears a tremendous BANG!

Carmine grabs his belly and falls backward through the doorframe.

She spins to see Clarence on his knees, holding his smoking gun.

Elizabeth runs to check Carmine.

He's alive. He wails like a baby.

Elizabeth kicks his gun away and runs inside to Eva. "Are you okay?"

Eva is sobbing.

Elizabeth puts her arms around the young woman. "It's alright, honey. It's alright."

Eva sobs and shakes her head. "This is my fault."

"No, it isn't. None of this is."

"It is. I remembered something else about what happened. They kept asking me who I worked for—over and over again. And I didn't tell them."

"It's okay."

"But then I did," Eva gets out. "They hurt me so bad, Elizabeth. I told them it was you who hired me to spy on the factory. Just to make them stop hurting me."

Mutt and Jeff tortured Eva until she told them who hired them. And then they started coming after *Elizabeth*? That's why Jeff shot at her.

"I'm so sorry!" Eva says.

"Oh no no no," Elizabeth says. "I'm the one who put you in the middle of this. None of this is because of you."

Elizabeth wraps Eva in her arms and holds her while the younger woman weeps.

83

DENNY RANKIN

[Tuesday, June 24, 1941]

Three men are down. Heinz Mueller, Bert Vogelmann, and a short guy Denny guesses is the one Elizabeth calls Jeff. Nobody's dead.

Clarence secures the three injured men and checks on the two women. Denny calls it in on his car radio. The people inside the school auditorium are too involved with their own race-fueled hatred to know what's going on outside.

Just as well. This would have inflamed the anger of both sides.

Police sleds show up. Then more police. Then the ambulances.

Ambulances take away the wounded before the meeting breaks up. Denny, Clarence, Elizabeth, and Eva watch them drive away.

"Everybody okay?" Clarence says.

Denny and Elizabeth say they are. In her wheelchair, Eva seems calm, though her face is red and puffy as if she has been crying. Elizabeth stands beside her with a hand on Eva's shoulder.

To Eva, Denny says, "You alright?"

Eva nods.

"She saved my life," Elizabeth says. "If you hadn't clocked Jeff with that tripod, I'd be a goner."

Eva shrugs away the compliment. "I did it without even thinking."

"You're a tough one," Denny says. Eva dips her head in

acknowledgement.

Denny says, "I better get back to the station and start to process all this." To Clarence, he says, "Why don't you come with me and we'll interview Vogelmann together."

Clarence agrees.

Denny turns to Elizabeth. "When we're finished, want to meet up for a drink?"

"It'll be too late for me. Raincheck?"

"I'll hold you to it."

"I'll expect you to."

84

EVA SZABÓ

[Tuesday, June 24, 1941]

After the community meeting finally breaks up, Hal Perlman helps her into his car. He stows the heavy wheelchair in the back seat.

He slides into the driver's seat. Eva and Elizabeth have filled him in on what happened while he was taking his photos. They explained the shootings. They told him about seeing Mutt and Jeff, the men who put Eva in the hospital. About the exchange of gunfire and Jeff getting shot. About Mutt escaping in the confusion.

About Eva saving Elizabeth's life by skulling Jeff with Hal's tripod.

Hal was completely unaware of what was going on outside. He was concentrating on the battle inside the school.

Eva has herself under control now. She surprised herself with her presence of mind. She broke down when she was telling Elizabeth about what she remembered from her ordeal in the meat locker, but now she is composed.

"Do you want to stop and get something before we go back to the hospital?" Hal asks.

"I'm not hungry," she says. "But I don't want to go back. Not yet anyway."

"I know just the place."

Belle Isle, in the middle of the Detroit River between Detroit and Windsor. He stops at the side of a deserted road on the far east side of the island. They sit in his car facing the dark waters of the river rolling past.

"Are you cool enough?" he says. The windows are all rolled down. A slight breeze brings the smell of water into the car.

"I am."

"It must have been awful. All the shooting around you."

"It was. And to know I was the cause."

He reaches over to take her hand. His hand is large, soft, warm. "Don't say that. You said Elizabeth told you it isn't your fault."

"I know. But she was just saying it to make me stop crying."

"Then it worked."

He gets a smile out of her.

"Look," he says, "even trained spies crack under torture. You're only human. Give yourself a break."

"I wish I could."

"Well, we'll have to work on that, won't we?"

We.

The language of coupledom.

It moves her greatly.

She slides across the bench seat to get next to him. The move pinches her ribs, which are still tender.

"I'm not sure I'd be as calm as you are," he says.

They exchange a long look. His eyes shine in the darkness.

"Kiss me," she says.

He does.

85

CLARENCE BROWN

[Tuesday, June 24, 1941]

When they get to Denny's station, Clarence calls Bessie to let her know he'll be late. To his surprise Malone answers.

"Malone," Clarence says, "didn't expect to hear your voice. Is Miss Brown okay?"

"She's fine. She was getting kind of sleepy, so I helped her into bed."

"I'm not going to be home till later. Are you planning on staying with her?"

"I can."

"I'd be obliged if you would." Clarence knows Bessie can stay by herself, but he's glad to have Malone home.

"Thank you, Malone."

"Happy to help, Mr. Clarence."

Denny and Clarence do the interview with Bert Vogelmann. The ambulance technicians examined him at the high school and pronounced him fit to be released. He wasn't shot, just roughed up when Denny barreled into him.

Vogelmann slumps at the interview table with his arms folded like a million mooks before him. Clarence notices the tattoo of an anchor on his forearm.

"We've been looking for you for a while, Bert," Denny says.
Vogelmann stays silent.

"What's your relationship with Charlotte Wheaton?"

"What's that got to do with anything?"

"Answer the question."

"We're engaged."

"You know how old she is?"

"So?"

"Ever hear of the Mann Act? It makes it a federal crime to transport a girl across state lines for any immoral purpose."

"We're in love, me and her. We're going to blow town and get married. What's immoral about that?"

"Where were you going?"

"I got a shipboard buddy in Cincinnati. We were going down there."

"What were you waiting for? Why didn't you just leave?"

"I had to take care of some business first."

"What kind of business?"

"It was personal."

"With Heinz Mueller?"

Vogelmann nods.

"What kind of business, Bert?"

"About what he did to me. And his sister."

"Which was what?"

"He set me up," Vogelmann says. "And he's been raping her. For years."

Denny remembers the locks on the doors to their bedrooms at the Mueller house.

He also remembers Prentiss Mueller telling him Wanda has serious mental problems with a bizarre fantasy life.

Denny says, "How do you know this rape actually happened?"

"Wanda and Charlotte are friends. Wanda told her what he does to her. Charlotte told me. Heinz told me, too."

"Heinz told you he's been molesting his sister?"

"He's got this crazy idea he's in love with her, and she's in love with him. That's why he stole the money—he was going to run away with her."

"Stole what money?"

"He stole eight grand from his old man."

Denny says, "Heinz stole his father's money?"

"Yeah. Bet you thought it was me."

"I did."

"Everybody does. Because Heinz set me up for it. He told everybody I took it. He made it look like a break-in. But it was him all along."

"And what about Thaddeus Ostrowski? Where does he fit in?"

"Heinz told his father I stole the dough," Vogelmann says. "Mueller told Ostrowski to get the money back from me any way he could. Ostrowski knew we all hung around the Woodmont."

"You and your Nazi pals."

"Yeah. He waited there for me to show up. Except by the time I showed, he was too sauced. Couldn't do nothing."

"Not too sauced to have a gun fight with you in the street. You know you plugged an innocent bystander," Denny says. "Edgar Vanarian, the dishwasher at the Mayflower Café."

Vogelmann says, "I was just trying to protect myself. That Polack was shooting at me. What was I supposed to do? I was sorry about the other guy. That was a mistake."

"How does Ostrowski know you?"

"We're both in the National Workers League."

"You met Prentiss Mueller there, too?"

"Yeah."

"And Charlotte?"

"She used to come with her old man."

"You're talking about Phil Wheaton?"

"Yeah."

Denny and Clarence share a look. Phil Wheaton again.

Denny says, "Detective Brown, you have some questions?"

Clarence says, "Tell me about the baby."

"What baby?"

"The baby I found in Black Bottom a few months ago. Stone cold dead. The one you left there."

"I never left any baby," Vogelmann says.

"I have a witness who said a man fitting your description left the child at a tenement on Beaubien in Black Bottom."

"I don't care what you got. It wasn't me."

Clarence watches him. Vogelmann can't meet Clarence's eye. Clarence says, "But you know what baby I'm talking about." A statement, not a question.

Vogelmann shrugs.

Clarence says, "Whose baby was it?"

"Wanda's," Vogelmann says.

"Wanda Mueller?" Denny asks.

"Yeah."

"Wanda was telling the truth," Denny says. "She did have a baby."

"Yeah."

"Who's the father?"

"Heinz."

"Charlotte told you this, too?"

"Yeah."

"Tell us what happened," Clarence says.

"Wanda went into labor," Vogelmann says, "and Mueller called this doctor. He's part of the group."

Denny says, "Fred Thomas."

Vogelmann says, "Yeah. Mueller called him to come and deliver the baby. But the baby only lived for a little while."

Clarence says, "Whose idea was it to get rid of the body?"

"Thomas's."

"And who actually left with the baby?"

"One of the cops in the Workers League. Guy named Clendening."

Clarence and Denny share another look. "Another name that keeps popping up," Clarence says.

Outside the sweat room, Clarence asks, "What are you charging him with?"

"Attempted murder of Heinz Mueller," Denny says. "Involuntary manslaughter of Edgar Vanarian. If he's telling the truth, he's off the hook for the death of the baby and the Mueller robbery. Big if about the robbery, though."

"You know this doctor?"

"I do. He's a straight-up Nazi. Sounds like you solved your dead baby mystery. Clendening left him where you found him."

"I still have to find out what happened to him," Clarence says. "And then I have my own plans for Clendening."

"Franklin," Denny says.

"What?"

"Franklin. That's what Wanda told me she named the baby before they snatched him away. After the president."

Bessie is still asleep when Clarence gets home. Malone Coleman snores on the sofa in the living room.

Clarence closes the apartment door softly. The metal plates clank when he lifts them over his head. You saved my life again tonight, boys, he tells them.

The noise wakes Malone. "Hey."

"Sorry," Clarence says. "I was trying to be quiet."

"It's okay."

"How you doing?"

Malone sits up. Wipes the sleep from his eyes.

"Good to see you here," Clarence says.

Malone says nothing.

"You're welcome to stay. Long as you want."

"Thanks."

"I appreciate your taking care of Miss Brown for me."

"We have a good time."

"She's the best person I know."

Clarence sits in his chair. It feels like the first time he's had the chance to relax in a week.

"Did you get dinner?" he asks Malone.

"I ate when I got Miss Brown's dinner ready. You hungry?"

Clarence shakes his head. He has no appetite even though he hasn't eaten since earlier yesterday. "Everything okay?"

Malone takes a few moments, as though to brace himself for what he's about to say.

"Mr. Clarence, that boy got shot Sunday at the grocery store?"

Ernest, the boy who Darron Cummings shot when he went to take revenge on the grocer who turned him in.

"Yeah," Clarence says. "What about him?"

"I knew him. Him and me, we run together."

"Know who did it?"

"Boy named Darron Cummings." After a moment, Malone says, "I know him, too."

"Then you know he's gone, right?"

Malone nods.

In a few moments, Malone says, "I know where he stay."

"I need to find him."

"Yes sir. I know."

Clarence gives Malone some time. Then he says, "Where is he, Malone?"

When Malone doesn't reply, Clarence says, "Ernest was just standing there. He's wasn't about to hurt anyone, just trying to bring in money for his family. And now he's dead because of Darron."

Malone thinks about it some more. He says, "Hiding out on St. Antoine. Used to be a barber shop there? Empty now."

"That's where he is?"

Malone nods.

"You're a good man," Clarence says.

Malone shrugs away the compliment. He doesn't know quite how to take it. Probably hasn't gotten much praise in his life.

Clarence says, "Let's talk more about it in the morning. Not going to do anything about it tonight. Meantime I'll get you a pillow and blanket, make you comfortable."

86

ELIZABETH WATERS

[Wednesday, June 25, 1941]

A s it turned out, she could have met Denny for a late drink after all. She had a sleepless night.

Too many frayed nerve endings, too many Old Fashioneds before bed to try and tame those nerves, too many thoughts rambling around in her head.

She got a few hours' sleep just as the park outside her window started to brighten with the day's sunrise.

She takes her time in the morning. She treats herself to a long shower. She makes a breakfast of fried eggs and toast, more than she usually has.

She's not anxious to go back out on the streets after what happened the day before.

Only her stubbornness gets her out the door of her apartment. She hates being intimidated.

Still, she makes sure to lock the outside door to her office when she gets in.

She calls the building's answering service to get her messages. She's been giving her work cases short shrift, and her clients are annoyed about it.

One of the clients who's most upset is the owner of People's Outfitting Co., a department store downtown. He suspects one of his employees is stealing from him and he wants Elizabeth to find out who. She's already met him after hours and he gave her a list of employees. First she wants to go over his books to make sure he is, in fact, being robbed. She knows a forensic accountant in the Barlum Tower; she wants to bring him to the store so he can go over the records.

Elizabeth calls the accountant to find out when he's free. Then she calls the store owner back to set up a time.

He won't take her call. He instructs his secretary to tell Elizabeth he couldn't wait for her; he hired another detective agency to move ahead with the project much faster than she was doing.

He wants Elizabeth to return the retainer he paid her.

She thanks the secretary for the information. Elizabeth says she will deduct from the retainer the time she's already put into the job, and send a check for the rest.

She calls the accountant back. Tells him the job isn't going to happen.

Not a good way to start the day.

She turns her attention to the next case she's behind on: a divorce.

When she started her business, she refused to do divorce work. The image of the sleazeball private eye peeping on cheating husbands turned her stomach. She quickly realized a job means a paycheck, and she began taking divorce work out of necessity.

The latest job is for a woman who believes her husband, a biology professor at Wayne University, is having an affair with one of his students. She wants Elizabeth to bug their bedroom to catch the cheaters in the act.

Elizabeth told the woman if they were in fact having an affair, they were probably going to a hotel to do the deed. But she was convinced they were meeting at her house because she said she smelled another woman's perfume in the bed.

Elizabeth doesn't set up bugs. She contracts with another investigator who specializes in bugging. She calls him to set up a time to plant them.

She hangs up and hears a knock on the outer office door.

She slips the .22 from her handbag and goes out to see who's there.

All she sees is a sheet of paper slipped under the door, and the shadow of a figure moving away.

The paper is folded in half. She opens it.

And almost falls over.

"Holy shit."

It's from Ben Rubin. A ghost from her past.

Hello Elizabeth,

I came by earlier this morning but you weren't in. Apparently, you're not in now, either. So I'm just leaving you this note.

I'm on my way to report to Fort Custer in Battle Creek. I joined up. I think war's inevitable, and I wanted to get in early and do my bit.

I was hoping we could grab a cup of coffee and maybe catch up. But I'm going to be late for my train, so I have to get going.

Sorry I missed you.

Be well,

Ben

She unlocks the office door and throws it open. The corridor is empty and silent. She calls: "Ben?"

Nothing.

He's gone, before she had a chance to say hello. Or tell him to take care of himself.

She relocks the door and goes back to her inner office. Stows the .22 in her purse. Sits down behind the desk. Rereads the note.

She remembers him telling her his older brother died a hero in the Great War. Is that the destiny he has in mind for himself? Except for the part about dying?

She realizes the visit saddens her . . . not simply because she missed him, and not from any lingering affection she might still have for him. Whatever she might have felt faded away a long time ago. Rather, what she feels is a stab of mourning for the lost possibility he represented.

He's a reminder of a different time in her life, when different choices stretched out before her. They were choices she made for good or bad—like the decision not to keep in touch with him— choices she then has to live with.

And now he's come into and gone out of her life. Again.

Like the Groucho Marx line. Hello, I must be going.

Into who knew what horrors when the war comes?

She shivers, imagining the danger he will put himself in.

Her phone rings. She picks it up before the answering service gets to it.

A man's voice. "Miss Waters?"

"Speaking. Who's calling?"

"Special Agent Douglas Duhamel, FBI. Returning your call. What can I do for you?"

It takes her a moment to get her thoughts together.

She says, "I called at the suggestion of Detective Denny Rankin."

"Detective Rankin and I are acquainted."

"I have information about subversive activity in the city."

"I'm all ears."

She tells him about Garland Alderman and Parker Sage and their plans to disrupt the Negro defense worker housing project. And the meeting she went to at the high school last night.

"How did you happen to be there, Miss Waters?"

"I'm a private investigator. I've been probing fifth column activity around the city. I heard about the meeting and wanted to see for myself what's going on."

"What else have you found?"

She fills him on all the names and places she knows about, grateful to think about something else besides Ben Rubin.

87

DENNY RANKIN

[Thursday, June 26, 1941]

A message awaits him at the precinct house in the morning: Seymour Traub, one of the owners of Traub Bros. & Co. Jewelry.

Please call back.

At first Denny thinks it's going to be about the jewelry store robbery he was working on when Dietrich pulled him off and put him on the Mueller break-in.

He readies himself for Sy's complaint about the lack of progress.

It turns out to be about a completely different matter.

Heinz Mueller is out of surgery at Detroit Receiving. Vogelmann's Walther did a lot of damage.

Denny finds Prentiss Mueller sitting in the Intensive Care Unit waiting room with his wife, the Countess von Whatchamacallit. It's a small, plain area with an artificial plant on a table in the corner.

Mueller stands by the door, smoking. He gives Denny the fisheye. "Do I have you to thank for my son's condition?" Mueller demands.

"Thank Bert Vogelmann."

"You're lying."

"I saw him do it. He's in the lockup at the precinct."

Before Mueller can reply, Phil Wheaton comes around the corner.

He carries a tray with three steaming mugs.

He stops short when he sees Denny. "Who's in the lockup?"

"Bert Vogelmann," Denny says. "What are you now, Phil, their coffee boy?"

Phil sets the tray down on the table with the plant. Says, "What are you doing here?"

"I could ask the same of you."

"Come with me."

He steers Denny out of the room and down the hall.

"Why is Vogelmann locked up? I closed the Mueller break-in. It wasn't him."

"Damn right," Denny says. "It wasn't the rummy you tagged for it, either. It was Heinz Mueller."

Phil stares at Denny.

"I talked to Sy Traub this morning," Denny says. "He's a jeweler. Heinz tried to hock his mother's jewelry at Sy's store."

"How did he know it was Heinz?"

"Sy described him to a tee. Right down to the fascist duds, which the Jewish jeweler took particular note of. Heinz stole the money and blamed Vogelmann."

"Why would he do that? If he wanted money from his father, he could have just asked for it."

"He had a fantasy about running away with his sister. Who, by the way, he's been fucking for years. You know these people—you're part of their Nazi cabal—did you ever wonder why Wanda's such a mess?"

"Prentiss said it was mental problems."

"Yeah, mental problems from being abused by her brother and doped up to the eyeballs by Fred Thomas. Heinz told his father Vogelmann stole the money and jewelry to put the onus on him. Then Prentiss sent out Ted Ostrowski—another cop who's a Nazi sympathizer—to get it all back. Being the fuck-up he is, Ostrowski screwed it up and Vogelmann wound up killing a civilian.

"But you know all that, right? It's the reason you framed Herbert Anderson. Vogelmann's part of your group of Nazis—if we got him to talk, it would all be over for you. When Ostrowski screwed up, you wanted to keep Vogelmann out of the picture. So you fingered your fall guy. And surprise, it was Heinz all along."

"You don't understand," Phil says.

"You're goddamn right I don't. What happened to Wanda's baby?"

"I don't know what you're talking about."

"Don't bullshit me. Why did her dead baby wind up in Black Bottom?"

"Thomas wanted to use the baby to stoke up racial trouble. Show the world what this country is really like."

"How did you get involved?"

"Fred Thomas wanted somebody to set this up. He knows Charles Spare. Spare was once Duncan McCrea's investigator in the Black Legion Trial in the thirties."

Duncan McCrea, former Wayne County prosecutor currently convicted in the graft trials.

"I've known Spare since the Black Legion investigation in the thirties," Phil says. "I used to be assigned to the Wayne County Prosecutor's office. Spare knows I was part of the graft but wasn't indicted. He reached out to me and said if I didn't do what Thomas wanted, he'd give me up to Judge Ferguson."

The one-man grand jury judge investigating the graft conspiracy.

"I came up with the scheme," Phil continues. "I knew Clendening from the National Workers League. I know he runs a string of whores. I convinced him to drop the baby off in some shithole in Black Bottom, then get one of his whores to lie that some coons kidnapped her baby. Then she was supposed to disappear back under a rock.

"Clendening was supposed to get an 'anonymous tip-off,'" Phil says, "and find the body. But Clarence Brown found him first, before Clendening could arrange to get a prostie to say he was hers. That juiced our plan."

And Clarence Brown couldn't let the matter rest.

Any more than Denny could let the Mueller house break-in be pinned on an innocent rummy from the Cass Corridor.

"You went after the Jews with all the anti-Semitic flyers around town," Denny says, "and you went after the Negroes with the dead baby plot and the Hamtramck riot . . . all part of your Nazi propaganda to keep us all at each other's throats until the country was all white, Protestant, and working for the success of Germany."

"Don't be so naïve." Wheaton points toward the surgical waiting room. "These people are patriots. *I'm* a patriot. Roosevelt's taking us head-first into a war the people of this country don't want and we're the only thing standing in his way—people like me and the Muellers."

"Is that why you were supposed to take over Mueller's break-in? Because you'd keep it quiet? Pin it on a schnook like Herbert Anderson and keep the real thief under wraps?"

"Anderson's a nobody. There's bigger things involved here. Democracy's done, Denny. It's over. The only thing that can save us now is a strong leader. A Christian nationalist to return this country to its roots."

"And you're doing everything you can to make that happen."

"You bet your life we are."

Then Phil says, "What are you going to do about this, Denny? Are you going to make trouble?"

"I'm going to do my job—if that's what you mean by trouble. Mueller can't get off. He's an accessory to manslaughter for the dishwasher Vogelmann killed, and the attempted murder of Bert Vogelmann."

"You're going to take him in?"

"You bet I am. I'm also going to nail Heinz for robbery and the rape of his sister. Assuming he makes it out of the hospital."

"What about me?"

"I told you. I'm going to do my job."

Denny turns to leave.

Phil grabs his arm. "What does that mean? You can't charge me with anything."

"Is that so? How about we start with false arrest and conspiracy to file a false police report and go from there. We'll work out way up to treason."

Denny pulls his arm away.

Keeps walking.

Behind him, Phil says, "Don't do this. Don't do this or it's going to come back and bite you in the ass. Believe me."

"It's not my ass you should be worried about."

88

EVA SZABÓ

[Thursday, June 26, 1941]

When Eva gets out of the hospital, she moves back in with her stepmother. Josef moves out immediately.

Eva says, "Can't you ask Josef to stay a little longer? I just got out of the hospital. I can't take care of you the way I used to."

Ágnes sits at the table in their kitchen, staring glumly at the bowl of tomato soup in front of her. She shows Eva two fingers and the back of her hand and pushes the bowl away. Soup slops on the checkered oilcloth.

"Come on," Eva says with a sigh. She helps her stepmother to her feet. Eva doesn't have to use a wheelchair to get around the small house, but she does need a cane.

It's not easy managing both Ágnes and the cane but Eva gets Ágnes upstairs and into bed. She will work on bathing the old woman in the morning.

She gets ready for bed herself.

The doorbell rings downstairs, followed by insistent knocking.

She throws on a robe and hobbles back down.

Vincent Németh's at the door.

Josef's friend who thinks Eva is his girlfriend.

Exactly who she doesn't want to see.

Still, she knows how persistent he will be if she doesn't answer. He'll stand knocking for hours.

She opens the door and lets him in.

He says, "Hey. I saw Josef at Kovac's. He said you were home. Glad you got sprung?"

"Of course."

"Getting around okay?"

"Yeah, good. Vincent, it's late and I'm—"

"I hope this makes you see factories are dangerous places for a girl like you."

"What do you mean, a girl like me?"

"You know . . ."

"No, I don't. Tell me."

"Who's trying to be a 'spy.'"

"What are you talking about?"

"Hey, I know all about what you tried to pull at Ford's."

"What did I try to pull?"

"Going undercover? The whole Mata Hari thing?"

"How do you know about that?"

"Oh, right, it's supposed to be a secret. I forgot."

"No, I'm serious. How do you know? I haven't told anybody."

"Maybe not. But you told your diary plenty."

"You read my journal?"

"No. But Josef did."

"When?"

"Before you went in the hospital."

"Josef read my journal and told you what I was doing at Ford's?"

"He sure did."

"And you kept it to yourself, I hope?"

"Forget it. Water under the bridge."

"No, did you tell anybody?"

"Forget I said anything."

"Who did you tell!"

"Just this buddy of mine, works there."

"Who?"

"You don't know him."

"Where does he work?"

"Jesus, what's with the third degree?"

"Where does he work?"

"The Service Department."

The floor dips and buckles. She has to hold onto the doorframe.

"What did you tell him?"

"I told him the truth. You were lying about why you were there. You were trying to sniff out anti-union dirty business for somebody."

"Oh, Vincent. Do you know what you did? Do you know what you did? That's why they beat me up and left me for dead. They were trying to find out who I was working for! Why would you do that?!"

She is screaming now. "Why would you do that to me?!"

"So what, it's aces for you to lie to me? And see other guys, on top of that? Oh, I heard all about that kike you spend time with. Josef told me plenty. And I can't tell the truth about you? Grow up."

She holds her head in her hands. She feels like she's going to throw up.

Instead, she says, "Get out." Very quietly at first.

"Aw, look," he says, "I just wanted to do what was right for you. The factory, it's no—"

"Get out," she says again. Not as quiet this time. "Get out. Get out! GET OUT OF MY SIGHT!"

She pushes him out the door and slams it in his face.

That's it.

That's how Mutt and Jeff knew she wasn't simply a receptionist at the hospital.

They didn't figure it out—how could they, those two dopes? And it wasn't Anton and his pals. It was Vincent's buddy at the Service Department who spread the word.

That's how they knew what to ask while they were torturing her.

It was the journal her stepbrother read and then told Vincent about.

She limps to the kitchen sink. She leans over it and dry heaves until she has no more strength left.

89

CLARENCE BROWN

[Friday, June 27, 1941]

Malone told him Darron is hiding out in a vacant barber shop on St. Antoine.

Clarence takes Francis Pitts with him, along with a pair of bluesuits.

Malone also said Darron's boys bring him food and whatever else he asks for. Most likely they're dropping off the take from suckers buying reefer and illegal hooch. All the activity goes through the back door.

Clarence didn't ask Malone how he knew all this. Better not to probe and drive the boy away again.

Now the four policemen sit in Clarence's unmarked down the alley from the shop.

Francis says, "How are we going to get him out of there with all those knuckleheads going in and out?"

"We're going to wait our turn," Clarence says.

He watches the store for a while. Notices once Darron gets a delivery, the delivery crew stays in the store for a few minutes, then leaves. Between twenty minutes and a half hour, the next crew comes.

They wait.

A quartet of young men comes up to the boarded-up rear of the store. One of them carries a brown paper shopping bag.

"Wonder what's in the bag," Francis says.

After a few minutes, they watch the four young men leave Darron's hideaway without the bag they brought in. When the four turn down Eliot Street, Clarence says, "Let's go."

The cops spill out of the unmarked. Clarence and Francis carry shotguns. The uniformed police have their sidearms out.

With Clarence in the lead, they shoulder through the back door, guns up and ready to blast away.

Clarence sees Darron Cummings stretched out on the bare wooden floor. On the nod, completely oblivious to the four police standing around him. His eyes are closed, his mouth gaping and drooling.

Clarence indicates the two uniforms should search the building.

"Now we know what was in the paper bag," Clarence says.

Denny Rankin said Dr. Fred William Thomas lives on Audubon in East English Village. The east side of Detroit. Clarence and Francis go to pick him up. Clarence could bring a variety of charges against him, but for now he just wants to get Thomas on improper disposal of a body.

Then they'll get fancy.

They pull up in front of Thomas's house. It's a modest Tudor of brick, stucco, and wood. Clarence doesn't know what he was expecting for a German spy, but it wasn't this plain American home.

They climb the two front steps onto the porch. Ring the bell.

A white woman comes to the door. She conspicuously locks the screen door when she sees two Negro men standing there.

They both show their badges. "We're looking for Dr. Frederick William Thomas," Clarence says.

"He's not here."

"Do you know where we can find him?"

"No idea," she says. Clarence knows she's lying; she won't tell them because they are Negroes or they are cops. Take your pick.

"Does he have an office, ma'am?"

"I don't know."

"Are you Mrs. Thomas?"

"I might be."

"And you don't know if your husband has an office?" Clarence gives her a sly smile, tips his fedora. "We'll find it. Thank you for your time, ma'am."

She slams the door. Clarence and Francis share an amused look.

They get back in Clarence's car and drive a block. A black Ford cuts in front of them. Clarence has to stand on the brake to avoid a collision.

Two white men get out of the car. Gray suits, white shirts, fedoras.

One man goes up to Clarence's window. Motions Clarence to roll it down.

He shows Clarence an FBI ID. "Special Agent Douglas Duhamel." He motions to the other man, standing outside Francis's side window—"Special Agent Carmichael."

Carmichael holds up his ID.

"You are?" Duhamel says.

"Detective Clarence Brown, Detroit PD. This is Detective Francis Pitts. If you'll let us get our badges out, I'll show you."

"Just you," Duhamel says.

Clarence eases his badge out of his coat pocket. Hands it to Duhamel, who examines it.

"What's your business with Dr. Thomas?" Duhamel says.

"I'm coming to arrest him."

"On what charge?"

"Unlawful disposal of a body."

"Excuse me?"

"It's a long story."

The agent hands Clarence's badge back to him. "I have one word for you, detective. Don't."

Now it's Clarence's turn to say, "Excuse me?"

"The FBI has an ongoing investigation into Dr. Thomas, and I'm ordering you to drop your own inquiry. Ours takes precedence."

"I don't take orders from you," Clarence says.

"That so? Why don't you call John Hays and discuss it with him?"

"Why are you looking at this guy?"

"I'm not at liberty to say. All I can tell you is, your involvement with him stops now. I don't want to see you anywhere near him. Got it?"

"I got it fine."

Clarence parks at the Hunt Street Station.

"Where you going now, big man?" Francis says.

"One more thing to do today. Then I'm finished," Clarence says.

"For the day?"

"Forever."

"You know you don't mean that."

Clarence looks up at the three-story building, red brick on top, pale limestone blocks on the first story. His work home since 1927.

"No," he says, "I probably don't."

He wishes he did.

"No," Francis says. "We had a good day. We took Darron Cummings off the street. And if the G-men blocked us, well, there's lots of other bad guys to catch out there. Now you go get you a good night's sleep and you'll be back tomorrow, good as new."

"Hope you're right."

"You know I am. This thing you got to do, need me to come with you?"

Clarence shakes his head. "This one's all mine."

"Okay, then. I'll see you tomorrow. Alright?"

"Alright."

Francis takes off. Inside the station, Clarence stops at the service desk. Monaghan, the duty officer, gives him the eye.

Clarence says, "You got something for me?"

Monaghan hands him an envelope. Clarence opens it, sees what's inside.

Two warrants. Both are signed by Junior Lieutenant William Wilson of the Detroit PD.

Clarence says, "Where is he?"

"Try the canteen."

The canteen is in the basement. As usual, Roger Clendening sits laughing with a half-dozen of his white cronies at the front of the room. A few Negro officers sit towards the back.

Clarence has avoided Clendening out of concern for what he might do to the corrupt white detective if he ran into him. Now Clarence is calm and clear-headed.

The conversation stops as Clarence approaches the table.

Clendening smirks, says, "Look what the cat dragged in."

Clarence pulls out the envelope Monaghan gave him. Removes

one of the papers.

"Roger Clendening," Clarence says, "I have a warrant for your arrest for assaulting a police officer in the execution of his duty, battery upon an individual, and conspiracy to file a false police report."

Clarence smiles. "That's just for starters."

"Let me see that," Clendening says.

He snatches it out of Clarence's hand and looks it over.

Clarence says, "Stand up."

Clendening looks around at the others at the table, then up at Clarence. "This your idea of a joke?"

"I said stand up." Clarence hauls Clendening to his feet. Turns him around and cuffs his hands together behind his back. Clarence glares at the other police around the table, daring them to say anything.

They sit rooted to their chairs.

"How come nobody's laughing now?" Clarence says.

He drags Clendening away to be booked.

Clarence stands silently as Dr. Cavanaugh, director of the Receiving Hospital morgue, reads the search warrant signed by Junior Lieutenant Wilson. Cavanaugh gives Clarences a frown, then leads him to a ledger.

Cavanaugh pages through the record book. Sees what he's looking for. Goes over to a file cabinet and finger-walks through the folders in one of the drawers. Signals that he's satisfied with a small grunt. Takes the folder out and opens it on his desk.

"This is the child," Cavanaugh says. A black and white photograph is stapled to the inside of the folder. It's a picture of the child Clarence found in the tenement in Black Bottom. The blanket he was wrapped in is gone, replaced by a white sheet under the child's body. The folder is labeled "Baby Boy Doe."

Clarence asks, "Where is he?"

"Gone," Cavanaugh says. "If the bodies are unclaimed after sixty days, they're sent to a local funeral home for disposal."

"Does it say where he went to?"

Cavanaugh checks the file. Says, "Hmm."

"What?"

"It doesn't say where the remains were sent."

"Is it possible they're still here?"

"They shouldn't be," Cavanaugh says. "But . . ."

He leads Clarence to the crypt. A room lined on all four sides with white-tiled drawers. Cavanaugh checks the folder in his hand, then pulls open one of the drawers.

Inside are the remains of the child Clarence has been looking for. Franklin, Denny said his mother named him.

At long last we meet again, Franklin, Clarence thinks. I told you I wouldn't forget you.

"Well," Cavanaugh says. "I guess we're behind. We'll have to get the remains sent out to the funeral home we use."

"Which one is it?"

Cavanaugh mentions a name Clarence is not familiar with. "Can you send him someplace else?"

"As long as they're on our approved list of funeral homes. Where do you want him to go?"

"Kennedy Funeral Parlor."

The funeral home run by the husband of Rosie Kennedy. His old love.

"Isn't that the colored funeral home?" Cavanaugh asks.

"Yeah. Is it on your list?"

"Well, yeah. But . . . Sure you want to send him there? This was a white infant."

"I'm sure."

"Mind if I ask why? Just it being a colored funeral parlor and all."

"Because I know this child will finally get the respect he deserves there," Clarence says. He'll call Rosie and make sure her husband gives Franklin the dignity he missed in his abbreviated life.

"If you say so," Cavanaugh says. "I'll start the arrangements."

"One more thing—the baby's name is Franklin Mueller."

Sidney Washington stands behind the register at his market.

Clarence says, "Darron Cummings is in custody."

"Thank you, Jesus."

Jesus had nothing to do with it, Clarence thinks. He says, "He won't be out for a while. Darron, that is. Not Jesus."

The grocer shakes Clarence's hand. "I can't tell you how grateful I am."

"Happy to help."

"What can I get you, my friend? Anything. You name it."

"Bessie gave me a list of groceries. We're starting up our Saturday afternoons in the rec room again. Got to stock up for the kids."

"She must be feeling better?"

"She is."

"Wonderful. I don't know what we'd do without you, Mr. Clarence. That's the truth. I hope you never retire."

90

ELIZABETH WATERS

[Sunday, June 29, 1941]

Eva doesn't have much—just her clothes, her bed, the dresser from the house, the nightstand, her journal, a few books.

Hal helps her. He borrows a truck from a friend, and along with the friend he has her moved into Elizabeth's in no time.

Eva tells Elizabeth her stepmother didn't even say goodbye. After Eva told Ágnes she was moving out so she should ask Josef to move back in, Ágnes had nothing to say to Eva.

"It was a relief, to be honest," Eva tells Elizabeth. "Not to have to look at her sour face every day and have to guess what awful things she was thinking about me."

Elizabeth says, "It sounds like she'll be happier with your step-brother, from what you've told me."

"Josef is 'her' child, after all. I'm just the poor stepdaughter."

"And she's the evil stepmother," Hal says. "Just like in a Hungarian fairy tale."

"Not just Hungarian," Elizabeth says. "Evil stepparents are universal."

As she well knows.

With her cane, Eva stumps into her new bedroom in Elizabeth's apartment in Palmer Park. It used to be Elizabeth's office, but with her large space in the Barlum Tower she doesn't use it anymore.

When Elizabeth visited Eva, she saw how unhappy Eva was

living with her stepmother. Elizabeth suggested moving in with her.

"I have to tell you this first," Eva said. "I found out how Mutt and Jeff knew about me. My stepbrother read my journals and told his friend Vincent, who told a buddy in the Service Department I was a spy. Then when I told them who I was working for, they went after you."

She couldn't look Elizabeth in the eye.

Elizabeth said, "Don't worry about it."

"I wanted to get this out before you said yes to my moving in."

"It doesn't make a bit of difference. The answer to the question of your moving in is still yes."

Elizabeth likes Eva's new assertiveness with her stepmother. Elizabeth is glad she followed her instincts about her; Eva's going to make a fine investigator.

When the time is right, Elizabeth will talk with her about going to college and then to law school. Elizabeth has decided law school is in her own future, just as Maurice Sugar recommended. She sees the same for Eva.

For now, Ben Rubin's note had made an impression on her, short as it was. She wants to join the war effort, too. Because Denny Rankin is right: war is inevitable.

Now she hears laughter from Eva's room. It's good to hear her laugh, Elizabeth thinks. Good to see her smile. She's earned the right.

The resilience of youth.

Eva and Hal come into the living room. "We're going out to get something to eat," Eva says. "Would you like to come?"

"No thanks," Elizabeth says. "I have work to finish first. Bon appetite, you two."

She hears their happy voices fading away down the hall outside her apartment.

She goes to the picture window overlooking the park.

She thinks again about the time she stood here watching Ben Rubin lurking in the park over ten years ago. He was drifting through the trees across from her building; he was worried about her. She had been picked up in a sweep of Communists in the days following the Ford Hunger March; she spent a few days in jail until Ben got Maurice Sugar to get her out. They kept switching her from one precinct house lockup to another so no one could find her. Looping, they called it then.

She thinks about the brief time she spent with Ben.

From there her thoughts wind around to Denny Rankin.

For all the attraction she feels toward him, she really doesn't want to get involved. For one thing, he's police, and she's often on the opposite side in her cases.

For another thing, he doesn't seem like the most stable man in the world.

And for yet another thing, she can't bear the thought of being in a relationship again. She's better on her own. Which may change, but for now when he calls for a drink she'll have it, but that'll be it.

Besides, she knows it won't be long before the country is engulfed in a storm such as the world has never known. A fling with a policeman will be the last thing on her mind.

She wants to keep things simple.

As though the decision closes a circuit, the phone rings.

Eerily, it's Denny.

Calling to collect on that raincheck.

"You promised," he reminds her.

They meet at the Kow Kow Inn, the Chinese place in Palmer Park near her apartment.

She first came here with Ben Rubin years ago. The owner, Madame Chen, remembers her because she's been back many times since then.

"Thanks for meeting me," Denny says. "You worried me, with that long pause after I asked you. Felt like you were trying to think of a way to get out of it."

"If you want to know the truth, I was."

Watching him, she remembers their long conversation after the Hamtramck riot. How it had changed her image of him.

"You don't look so good," she says.

He tells her about arresting Phil Wheaton and Prentiss Mueller.

She says, "Will there be consequences for arresting another cop?"

"I can pretty much count on it."

Madame Chen brings their drinks. She gives Elizabeth a wink.

Elizabeth and Denny clink glasses. "To a short war," she says.

"Dream on."

"You don't think so?"

He shrugs. "What do I know?"

"What will you do when it comes?"

"Good question. At my age, they might take me, but I'll be more use where I am. Assuming they don't cashier me or toss me in jail. You?"

"I read in the paper Edith Nourse Rogers introduced a bill in Congress to create the Women's Army Auxiliary Corps. If Roosevelt signs it, I'm going to join. If he doesn't sign it, or I'm too old for it, I'll find another way to help."

"What about your business?"

"I'll let Eva carry on with it."

"Does she have the experience?"

"She'll learn. I'll introduce her to attorneys in my building. They'll be crazy about her."

"Sounds good."

"Yeah. Then after . . ." She sighs. "'After the war' is too nebulous. Too far in the future. It presumes we'll all be alive and kicking after whatever the war brings. First we'll have to fight it."

"And win it. Which is by no means assured."

"We'll be fighting two wars against fascism. One overseas and one here."

"And in the war over here," he says, "the combatants won't be wearing different uniforms."

They decide to supplement their drinks with an order of egg rolls. That turns into sharing a beef chow mein and another drink.

Then more conversation.

She tells him about her call with Special Agent Duhamel.

"He seemed like a good guy," Denny says. "He might not be able to prevent anything. If the whites do riot, he'll know who caused it, thanks to you."

Madame Chen comes over to tell them she's closing soon.

Elizabeth can tell Denny doesn't want to end this.

Neither does she.

So much for her earlier decision.

"I'd ask you up to my place," she says, "except Eva's staying with me."

"No worries. I have another idea."

She stands in the entranceway to the Tropics, the bar next to the Wolverine Hotel.

The joint jumps. A combo on stage at the Native Village is playing their hearts out. She recognizes the tune: "Frenisi."

The dance floor is jammed with men and women making laughable attempts at the samba.

Elizabeth takes in the dancers and the cheesy décor. The musicians. The smoke from cigarettes and cigars wafting lazily in the air.

"No," she says.

"Not for you?"

She shakes her head. "Not for anybody. Where's your room?"

"In the hotel next door."

"Lead on."

"Apologies for the mess," he says, even though the single room is too small to be messy. He takes a shirt off the bed and hangs it in the closet.

"I like what you've done with the place," Elizabeth teases about the barren cell.

"You wouldn't believe what the decorator charged."

There's no chair in the room. They sit on the bed beside each other.

It happens gradually, then suddenly.

They lean together, then kiss, then undress each other slowly, taking their time. Then they make love as though the room were on fire and they have to get this done before they need to flee.

Afterwards they lie in each other's arms. Denny is panting so hard she's afraid he's going to have a heart attack.

"It's been a long time," he says.

"For me, too. I thought this part of my life was over."

"No," he says. "You have too much to offer."

She traces his lips with her fingers.

"That's a bullshit line," she says. "You know that, don't you?"
He gives a small snort of amusement.
"Still," he says, "it's nice to hear, no?"
She has to agree.
When was the last time anyone said something like that to her?
She can't remember.
He cups her cheek. Drinks in her eyes, nose, mouth.
"I wasn't planning on seeing you again," she says.
"I know."
She sighs. It's not a sigh of contentment or ease, but an expression of perplexity about this situation she's put herself in. So much for simplicity.
She closes her eyes.
He lays soft kisses on her eyelids.
"What made you change your mind?" he asks.
"I'm not sure," she says. Eyes still closed. "A combination of things."
"I'm glad you did, whatever the reasons."
She is silent.
He says, "Here's the part where you say, 'I am, too.'"
Now she opens her eyes and gives him a thin, ironic smile. "That remains to be seen."

91

DENNY RANKIN

[Monday, June 30 — Wednesday, July 2, 1941]

In the morning she's gone when he wakes up. All that's left of their night together is the smell of her hair on his pillow, her body on the sheets.

And what he remembers.

He showers, shaves, dresses.

He's feeling better than he's felt in a while.

Not that that's saying a lot . . .

The feeling lasts until he walks in on a celebration in the squad room.

Captain Dwight Dietrich stands up front, beside Phil Wheaton.

The last time Denny saw Phil, he was in a detention cell. Prentiss Mueller was in the cell next to him. Denny wanted to speak with Dietrich before filing charges; charging another officer, even one like Wheaton, was not to be done lightly.

He called Dietrich, but when he never heard from his captain Denny took it on himself to go ahead and file charges on Wheaton and Mueller.

Now Denny sees Phil standing beside Dietrich with a shit-eating grin on his puss.

"As I was saying before Detective Sergeant Rankin decided to join us," Dietrich says to muted laughter, "I'm very happy to announce our friend and colleague, Phil Wheaton, will assume command of the Robbery Squad at the Twelfth Precinct. To go along with his new assignment, he'll bring a new rank. I present to you Detective Inspector Philip Wheaton."

General applause from the room. Whistles.

Denny leans over to Burner Buntzen standing next to him. He asks, "Is this a joke?"

"Nope. Couldn't happen to a better man."

Well, yes, Denny thinks, it actually could. I arrested his Nazi ass.

"Drinks are on Phil after shift at the Anchor Bar," Dietrich shouts over the clapping. "Now get to work, you bunch of degenerates."

Dietrich shakes Phil's hand and starts for the door. Denny intercepts him like a shot.

Denny says, "Can I talk to you?"

"I'm late for a meeting," Dietrich says.

"I'll walk with you."

Denny follows Dietrich down the stairs. "What just happened?"

"I thought it was fairly obvious."

"I left Wheaton in a cell. I called you about charges. I never heard back. Now you're giving him a promotion?"

"I came into the station to talk with you. You were already gone. I read your preliminary report and went to talk with Phil."

"About what, the wisdom of arresting him? Gee, I wonder what he said?"

"I don't like your tone. I thought the charges were bogus so I had them dismissed."

"And then gave him a promotion and a transfer so he wouldn't feel bad about the whole thing?"

They reach the bottom of the stairs. Dietrich goes straight out the door to where his driver opens the door for him.

He pauses before getting inside the car. "I told you, Denny, do well and you'd get the promotion and the assignment. So what did you do? You fucked it up. Phil didn't. He closed the case. What did you expect to happen?"

"Did you see who he fingered for it? An old rummy who couldn't find his ass with a road map."

"I reviewed his charge sheet. It sounded solid to me."

"I suppose Prentiss Mueller's also on the street."

"As a matter of fact, he is. I didn't see just cause or sufficient evidence to charge him."

"I don't believe this."

"Don't push it, Denny."

"Or what?"

Dietrich leans in to Denny. He's close enough for Denny to smell his Listerine. "You know what this was? A test."

"For what?"

"To see if you're one of us. Me, Phil, Roger Clendening. It was a test. And you fucking failed."

"Testing to see if I was corrupt enough to be promoted?"

Dietrich gives him a sneer. "To see if we could trust you. You proved we can't. You don't like how things are turning out, that's too damn bad."

"You're part of it, too," Denny says. "Which group are you in? The Christian Front? The National Workers League, with Wheaton and Mueller? The Silver Legion? Or maybe just the traditional Klan? If you think—"

"One more word—one more word, Denny, and you'll earn yourself an insubordination charge. Then *you'll* be the one in front of the Trial Board."

Dietrich steps into his car. The driver shoots away into traffic.

Leaving Denny Rankin standing in front of his station.

Thinking: One more word?

Seriously?

Oh, captain, I got lots more words.

And I'm going to use them all.

*   *   *

Two days later, he sits in an office filled with dark, heavy oak—the door to the office, the desk, the chairs, the shelves lined with law books. Even the lamp on the desk is dark oak.

The man behind the desk has the look of a country lawyer, with a full head of white hair over a pale broad forehead. Steel-rimmed glasses. Clean-shaven. Double-breasted suit buttoned all the way up.

His calm, steady look takes in Denny sitting on the other side of his desk.

Beside him a stenographer sits poised in front of a bulky stenograph machine on a platform.

All the times I've been in court, Denny thinks, and I still don't

417

have the first idea how that machine works.

The man behind the desk says, "I have to ask you once again, detective. Are you certain you don't want an attorney present?"

"Yes your honor," Denny says. "I'm certain."

"All right, then." He nods to the stenographer. As soon as the judge starts speaking, the steno's fingers pump the huge rectangular keys. "I am Circuit Court Judge Homer S. Ferguson conducting this interview on Wednesday, July 2, 1941. The time is 9:30 a.m. Please state your name for the record."

"Detective Sergeant Dennis Rankin, badge number 4969."

"You're here of your own volition?"

"I am."

"And you've refused a lawyer."

"I have."

"Alright. Go ahead with your statement."

Denny reads from a sheet of paper.

"While serving as a detective in the Detroit Police Department in 1935, I accompanied Samuel Block on numerous occasions when he picked up illegal collections of money intended for Wayne County Prosecutor Duncan C. McCrea. These were funds provided from brothels, policy books, and owners of slot machines to overlook or otherwise fail to investigate or raid illicit activities. I provided protection for Samuel Block. For this I received a percentage of the money he collected.

"I am also aware at least two of my colleagues in the Department, Captain Dwight Dietrich and Detective Sergeant Philip Wheaton, also conspired in the collection of money or other illegal activity in furtherance of the corruption conspiracy then rampant in the Wayne County Prosecutor's Office and the Detroit Police Department.

"Furthermore, I have evidence that Detective Roger Clendening collaborated in a scheme to file a false police report with the aim of provoking racial discord, and that Detective Sergeant Wheaton filed a false police report in furtherance of a fifth column conspiracy.

"I am here today," Denny continues, "in the hope of clearing my conscience and furthering Your Honor's efforts to eradicate corruption in the Detroit Police Department.

"I am prepared to face the consequences of my actions, however serious Your Honor deems those consequences to be."

92

ELIZABETH WATERS

[Wednesday, July 2, 1941]

She testifies in the hearing for a soldier who came home from a night of drinking and started an argument with his wife because he claimed another man, her lover, was hiding in the next room.

The soldier claimed that other man shot at him, and he returned fire, striking his wife. Elizabeth's testimony proves the other man was nowhere near the house when this happened. The soldier shot his wife because he thought she was being unfaithful to him.

Afterwards, she waits for Denny in the courthouse lobby. "Well?"

"Well is a deep subject," he says.

"It must have gone okay if you're in the mood to joke."

"Will you wait for me until I get out of prison?"

"Depends how long you're in for."

"It may be until I'm an old man."

"No chance."

"Will you visit me?"

"Forget it, jailbird."

They give each other their tired, seen-it-all smiles.

"Seriously," she says, "what's it look like?"

"Hard to say. I did the crime, I'll do the time if I have to. Meanwhile, it's off my chest."

"Feel better now?"

"I do."

"How about we get some lunch while you're still a free man?"

"Ever been to Tipton's?"

"What's that?"

"A luncheonette in Black Bottom. If we hurry, we can make the lunch special."

"Which is?"

"A hot hamburger sandwich and mashed potatoes."

"Just the ticket," she says.

"I have an in with the waitress there."

They walk out of the court building together.

93

CLARENCE BROWN

[Saturday, July 12, 1941]

Laughter. Shouts. Demands for his attention.
The ceiling in Clarence's basement is low, so the sounds are magnified. In the background, almost drowned out, Duke Ellington on the radio. "It Don't Mean a Thing (If It Ain't Got that Swing)." An essential part of educating these children.

Bessie sits with a few of the girls, who show her their dolls. The dolls are hand-made out of old socks and the sleeves of shirts sewn together by mammas and grandmas. Bessie oohs and aahs and asks questions as if the dolls were real children with names and families.

Clarence helped her down the stairs. Now she's having as much fun as she ever did.

More, even, because she doesn't have to run around serving the food and cleaning up. Now Clarence does it.

Clarence, with his helper Malone. Because here comes Malone down the steps with a pan of fried chicken. Bessie made her special recipe this morning. After the kids polish off the chicken, Malone will go up and get a tub of ice cream and bowls and the kids from the neighborhood will dig into their dessert.

The greasy aroma of fried chicken fills the basement. Clarence stands and watches. A few kids play doubles in ping-pong (the low ceiling adds another flat surface the ball can careen off of). The rowdier young boys run around playing tag, and the older boys, the hep young teens, sit by themselves guzzling Coca-Cola and bragging about the things young men brag about, mainly girls.

A few of the newer parents in the neighborhood who aren't sure if Clarence is a pervert stand off to the side. They look on, amazed.

Clarence comes next to Bessie. "Been a while," he says.

"Yes it has. Good to hear all this hubbub again."

"Doing okay?"

"Doing fine."

They watch Malone dishing out the fried chicken.

"Your helper seems like he's having fun," she says.

"Yeah."

"Surprised?"

"A bit. When his friend got killed at the grocery store, I guess he decided he didn't want to be part of that life after all. Not yet, anyway," he adds.

No sense in getting too hopeful.

They both have their eye on Malone. Then they share a look. Clarence knows they are both thinking about their son DeMarco.

"He's not going to replace him, you know," Bessie says.

Clarence nods agreement. "Never." Then he says, "But it's nice to have another chance."

Bessie pats his hand. "The boy's his own self. Don't forget it. He's not going to fill the space DeMarco left."

"You're right. As always."

Across the room, Malone pretends to drop a chicken leg off the serving pan. The little kids laugh and laugh.

Malone does, too.

It's a high, joyful sound.

94

FROM EVA PERLMAN'S JOURNAL

September 30, 1954

*T*he habit of a lifetime, impossible to stop. Still the last thing I do at night. Every day, no matter what does or doesn't happen. Three shelves of notebooks filled since I began.
Sometimes I take them down at random and read through them.
And remember.
By the end of 1941, war came, as we knew it would.
It was longer and nastier than we expected, and when it was over we had yet another up-close look at the bottomless barbarism of the human race.
Elizabeth was able to join the Women's Auxiliary Army Corp, as she wanted. The upper age limit was 50, and she was younger than that so she joined. She became an officer (of course) and ran a motor pool in England. She loved being in the fight against fascism.
Or should I say the overseas fight against fascism. As we saw, fascism was alive and well in our own country, and our own city. I'm still not sure we beat it over here.
In February of 1942, the Negroes who wanted to live in the Sojourner Truth homes—that's what the defense worker housing project was named, after the activist against slavery—tried to move in. They were stopped by a violent mob of a thousand whites who wanted to keep them out. The KKK burned a cross. Neighbors put up signs saying, "Help the white people keep

this district white."

The governor mobilized state troops and between them and the police, the families got to move in after all, but not until the end of April. Elizabeth told me the same people who caused trouble at the meeting we went to at Pershing High School led the battle against housing for Negro defense workers. Because she told the FBI about them, the FBI was able to arrest them after the riot.

I kept Elizabeth's detective agency going while she was overseas. Much of the work turned out to be cheating spouses on leave from the service, but a good portion of my time had me helping root out espionage in Detroit industries. I did whatever I had to do.

Hal Perlman was drafted and became a photographer for the Army Air Corps and the Office of War Information.

When he knew he was going to be drafted, we got married. After he went overseas, I found out I was pregnant.

I lost the baby early on.

In a way it was just as well, because I went to college during the war and it would have been hard to run a business, go to my classes at Wayne University, and take care of a baby by myself.

My stepbrother Josef was drafted, and decided to make the army his career so he never came back to Detroit, not even for his mother's funeral in 1943. I never hear from him. I don't even know if he's alive.

After the war, Hal stayed in Europe to document the concentration camps. He showed me his photos. Even now when I look at them, I lose a piece of my heart at the loss, and the unbelievable—but all too real—cruelty and hatred.

After the war, Elizabeth used the GI Bill to go to law school. Once I finished college, I started law school, too.

Now we're both lawyers. We formed a law firm together: Waters, Perlman and Associates.

We specialize in civil rights litigation.

In Detroit, we're always busy.

Clarence and Bessie are still going strong. Rumors have been flying around that the city will tear down Black Bottom and Paradise Valley in the name of "urban renewal"—which the residents there have started calling "Negro Removal"—so they moved with Malone into a house in northwest Detroit. With Malone's help, Clarence still runs his baseball league for kids. He even lets girls into the league now. Bessie is still active in her church work and her ankle is fully healed. Clarence's health isn't too *good—he developed diabetes—and he's been talking about retiring.*

After the war Hal became a free-lance photographer. He sells his photographs to all the top magazines. His photos even wind up in museums. The Detroit Institute of Arts even has a few.

We tried to have another baby, Hal and I, but every time I got pregnant, I lost the child. We've learned to enjoy the life we have with each other.

Denny Rankin didn't go to jail for what he did during the graft scandal, but the Police Trial Board busted him back to patrolman. By the time Elizabeth came home from the war, Denny was divorced from his wife. Elizabeth and Denny found each other again, and eventually decided to marry. They adopted two children, two cute little sisters. Denny left the police force to join our law firm as an investigator.

Elizabeth seems content.

And she deserves to be. When I think of how far I've come from the mousy young immigrant with no prospects beyond toiling away in a grocery store in a dusty corner of the city, I can't quite believe it.

I have her to thank for it all.

I'll always be grateful.

DONALD LEVIN

Extras

Cast of Characters

Author's Note

About the Author

Also by Donald Levin

Cast of Characters

GARLAND L. ALDERMAN, Real-life National Secretary of the National Workers League.

HERBERT HENRY ANDERSON, Detective Phil Wheaton's fall guy.

ALFRED BRACCIANO, counselor at Cass Technical High School.

BESSIE BROWN, Clarence Brown's wife.

CLARENCE BROWN, Detroit Police Department detective.

JOHN BUGAS, real-life Special Agent in Charge of the Detroit FBI office.

CHARLES W. CHILL, real-life secretary of the central committee of the German-American Societies in Michigan.

ROGER CLENDENING, Detroit Police Department detective.

MALONE COLEMAN, troubled young man from Clarence Brown's neighborhood.

MARY COLEMAN, Malone Coleman's aunt.

FATHER CHARLES COUGHLIN, real-life radio priest from Detroit.

ELMER "HOOKY" CONROY, pinsetter at Play-Mor Recreation.

DARRON CUMMINGS, armed robber.

NADINE DENTON, head nurse, Ford River Rouge plant hospital first aid clinic.

DWIGHT DIETRICH, captain in the Detroit Police Department.

THEODORE DONAY, real-life owner of the German-American Europe Import Company and Nazi sympathizer.

DOUGLAS DUHAMEL, Special Agent in the Detroit FBI office.

FATHER CONSTANTINE DZINK, real-life pastor at St. Louis the King Parish Church.

FRANK ENNIS, Ford Motor employee and union activist.

TOM GLOVER, city editor at the *Detroit News*.

FRITZ HEILER, real-life German Consul in Detroit.

LARRY HOPKINS, Denny Rankin's son by Lulu Hopkins.

LULU HOPKINS, Denny Rankin's former lover and mother of Larry.

JOSEF HORVATH, Eva Szabó's stepbrother.

ROSA KENNEDY, formerly Madame Rosita, a brothel-keeper.

BOGDAN KOWALCZYK, Ford Motor employee.

CARL JOHN HEINZ LEONHARDT, real-life Nazi sympathizer and husband of Emma.

EMMA ELISE LEONHARDT, real-life Nazi sympathizer.

ANTON LUEDKE, Ford Motor employee.

JANICE MALINOWSKI, student at Cass Technical High School and friend of Charlotte Wheaton.

DAVE MARSHALL, Detroit Police Department detective indicted in the graft scandal.

SONNY MCGHEE, Clarence Brown's neighbor and Ford Motor employee.

KEVIN MCNAMARA, Ford Motor employee.

TITUS MORAN, leader of the Detroit branch of the Christian Front.

FRIEDA MUELLER, (AKA THE COUNTESS FRIEDA VON SCHONBURG-GLAUCHAU), Prentiss Mueller's wife

HEINZ MUELLER, Prentiss and Frieda Mueller's son.

PRENTISS MUELLER, Ford Motor chemist and Nazi sympathizer.

WANDA MUELLER, Prentiss and Frieda Mueller's daughter.

BRIAN MURRAY, graphic artist in the Ford Motor Company advertising department.

VINCENT NÉMETH, friend of Eva Szabó's stepbrother Josef Horvath.

FRANCINE OSTROWSKI, Thaddeus Ostrowski's wife.

THADDEUS OSTROWSKI, Detroit Police Department patrolman.

HAROLD (HAL) PERLMAN, free-lance photographer.

FRANCIS PITTS, Detroit Police Department detective.

CURTIS PIXLEY, Lincoln Park Police Department detective sergeant.

DENNIS (DENNY) RANKIN, Detroit Police Department detective sergeant, Robbery Division.

HAZEL RANKIN, Denny Rankin's estranged wife.

EUGENE RUMSON, patrol officer with the Dearborn Police Department.

PARKER SAGE, real-life treasurer of the National Workers League.

CARMINE SANT'ANGELO, member of the Ford Motor Service Department.

ARAM SARKASIAN, chief of service at the United Artists Theatre.

JOHN SCHREIBER, real-life German-American Bund leader in Detroit

CAL SEIDENSTICKER, Detroit Police Department detective.

EDDY SINGLETON, Ford Motor employee.

MICKEY SMITH, member of the Ford Motor Service Department.

CHARLES E. SPARE, real-life head of the Michigan KKK.

MAX STEPHAN, real-life owner of the German Restaurant and Nazi sympathizer.

ÁGNES SZABÓ, Eva Szabó's stepmother.

EVA SZABÓ, Elizabeth Water's employee.

LUCILLE TAGGART, (AKA BELLE BAXTER), a prostitute.

RUDOLPH TENEROWICZ, Representative from Michigan's 1st congressional district to the Seventy-Seventh United States Congress.

DR. FRED W. THOMAS, real-life physician and Nazi spy.

EDGAR VANARIAN, dishwasher at the Mayflower Café.

BERTRAND FRANZ VOGELMANN, Nazi sympathizer.

SIDNEY WASHINGTON, grocer in Black Bottom.

ELIZABETH WATERS, private investigator.

SOL WEINTRAUB, owner of the Rexall drug store in Paradise Valley.

HERMAN WEISKOPF, assistant Wayne County coroner.

CHARLOTTE WHEATON, Phil and Lena Wheaton's daughter.

LENA WHEATON, Phil Wheaton's wife.

PHIL WHEATON, Detroit Police Department detective, Robbery Division.

WILLIAM WILSON, assistant supervisor of the segregated Detroit Police Department squad handling Negro cases.

AUTHOR'S NOTE

This is a work of fiction. Even so, in these pages I have tried to remain true to the City of Detroit's historical, political, and economic past in the years leading up to Pearl Harbor and the nation's entry into World War II.

All of the organizations mentioned in Chapter 45 and throughout the book are actual groups that were active at the time. With one exception, all of the incidences that Clarence Johnson and Denny Rankin investigate (including the house break-in in Chapter 3, the drunken policeman's shooting in Chapter 12, and the Hamtramck racial violence described in Chapters 57 through 67) are actual events and crimes that took place in Detroit during the time-frame of the novel; I changed participants, locations, timing, and contexts to suit my narrative purposes. (The invented crime is the body that Clarence discovers in Chapter 2, together with all of the incidents connected to that discovery.)

In my efforts to portray as accurately as possible the real-life events described in the book—most especially the Ford walkout of 1941, the racial tensions in the city, the conflicts over the Sojourner Truth Housing Project, day-to-day life on the streets of Detroit, and the presence of pro-Axis collaborators active at the time—I consulted a number of works that I would like to acknowledge here:

Steve Babson et al, *Working Detroit*; Arnie Bernstein, *Swastika Nation: Fritz Kuhn and the Rise and Fall of the German-American Bund*; Albert E. Kahn, *High Treason: The Plot Against the People*; Michael Sayers and Albert E. Kahn, *Sabotage: The Secret War Against America*; Thomas J. Sugrue, *The Origins of the Urban Crisis: Race and Inequality in Postwar Detroit*; Gerald Van Dusen, *Detroit's*

Sojourner Truth Housing Riot of 1942: Prelude to the Race Riot of 1943; Donald Warren, *Radio Priest: Charles Coughlin, the Father of Hate Radio*; and Kevin D. Williamson, *What Doomed Detroit*.

In addition, I consulted the following resources: The Henry Ford Museum and its Digital Resources, The Detroit Historical Society, and The Walter P. Reuther Library, Archives of Labor and Urban Affairs, Wayne State University.

I consulted the following newspaper archives: The *Detroit Evening Times*, the *Detroit Free Press*, the *Detroit News*, and the *Detroit Tribune*.

I am indebted to historian Thomas Klug, Ph.D., for his help with Detroit history, and for reading an early draft of this book.

All mistakes, errors, and inaccuracies are my own.

Warm thanks to Virginia Lark Moyer and Harlan Moyer for their editorial expertise; to Lisa Allen for reading an early version; and to Jerry van Rossum, Paul Burns, and Peter Werbe for their support and encouragement.

Thanks to Gary Van Gorp for suggesting the idea of a sequel to *Savage City*.

My great thanks go to Joe Montgomery for his design of the cover.

As always, my deepest appreciation goes to my wife, Suzanne Allen, my first and best reader, whose love and support continue to sustain me.

About the Author

Donald Levin is an award-winning fiction writer and poet. He is the author of *Savage City*, a historical novel set in 1932 Detroit (the precursor to *The Arsenal of Deceit*); seven Martin Preuss mystery novels; and *The House of Grins* (Sewickley Press, 1992), a novel; two books of poetry, *In Praise of Old Photographs* (Little Poem Press, 2005) and *New Year's Tangerine* (Pudding House Press, 2007); *The Exile* (Poison Toe Press, 2020), a dystopian novella; and co-author of *Postcards from the Future: A Triptych on Humanity's End* (Whistlebox Press and Quitt and Quinn Publishers, 2019). He lives in Ferndale, Michigan.

To learn more about Donald and his works, visit his website, www.donaldlevin.com, and follow him on Twitter @donald_levin and Instagram at donald_levin_author.

If you enjoyed this book, please post a review on Goodreads, Amazon, or your favorite book review site.

ALSO BY DONALD LEVIN

Savage City

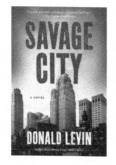

Detroit, 1932. The fates of four people converge during a violent week of labor unrest in the bleakest year of the Great Depression. Against the backdrop of the bloody Ford Hunger March, events hurl these four in the center of a political storm that will change them—and their city—forever.

The Martin Preuss Mystery Series

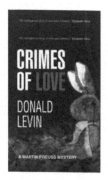

One cold November night, police detective Martin Preuss joins a frantic search for a seven-year-old girl with epilepsy who has disappeared from the streets of his suburban Detroit community. Probing deep into the anguished lives of all those who came into contact with the missing girl, Preuss must summon all his skills and resources to solve the many crimes of love he uncovers.

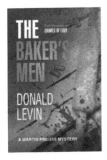

Easter, 2009. Ferndale Police detective Martin Preuss is spending a quiet evening with his son Toby when he's called out to investigate an after-hours shooting at a bakery in his suburban Detroit community. Struggling with the dizzying uncertainties of the case and hindered by the treachery of his own colleagues who scheme against him, Preuss is drawn into a whirlwind of greed, violence, and revenge spanning generations.

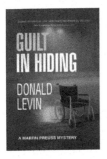

Preuss is called out to search for a van that has disappeared along with the woman who was driving and her passenger, a handicapped young man. Working through layer upon layer of secrets, Preuss exposes a multitude of contemporary crimes with roots in the twentieth century's darkest period.

When a friend asks newly retired detective Martin Preuss to look for a boy who disappeared forty years ago, the former investigator gradually becomes consumed with finding the forgotten child. Preuss revisits the countercultural fervor of Detroit in the 1970s—and plunges into hidden worlds of guilty secrets and dark crimes that won't stay buried.

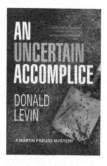

Twenty years have passed since Raymond Douglas went to prison for the kidnapping and murder of a local businessman's wife. Now Douglas's daughter has hired private investigator Martin Preuss to track down a previously-unknown accomplice to the crime—who may or may not even exist.

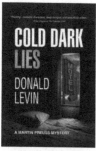

A young man takes a walk on the wild side and ends up clinging to life in a suburban Detroit motel. When private investigator Martin Preuss searches for the reason, he plunges into the young man's dark world of secrets and lies.

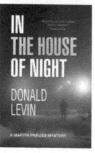

When the police investigation in the murder of a retired professor stalls, friends of the dead man plead with PI Martin Preuss to learn what happened. The twisting tale leads him across Detroit into a treacherous world of long-buried family secrets . . . where the painful relations between parents and children meet the deadly gathering storm of domestic terrorism.